That Da

Alexandra Campbell is the author of three other novels, *The Daisy Chain, The Ex-Girlfriend* and *The Office Party*, all published by Penguin, as well as two books on interiors, co-written with Liz Bauwens, *Spaces for Living* and *Country in the City*. She lives in South London with her husband, David, and twins, Freddie and Rosalind.

That Dangerous Age

ALEXANDRA CAMPBELL

PENGUIN BOOKS

PENGUIN BOOKS

Published by the Penguin Group
Penguin Books Ltd, 80 Strand, London WC2R ORL, England
Penguin Putnam Inc., 375 Hudson Street, New York, New York 10014, USA
Penguin Books Australia Ltd, 250 Camberwell Road,
Camberwell, Victoria 3124, Australia
Penguin Books Canada Ltd, 10 Alcorn Avenue, Toronto, Ontario, Canada M4V 3B2
Penguin Books India (P) Ltd, 11 Community Centre,
Panchsheel Park, New Delhi – 110 017, India
Penguin Books (NZ) Ltd, Cnr Rosedale and Airborne Roads,
Albany, Auckland, New Zealand
Penguin Books (South Africa) (Pty) Ltd, 24 Sturdee Avenue,
Rosebank 2196, South Africa

Penguin Books Ltd, Registered Offices: 80 Strand, London WC2R ORL, England

www.penguin.com

First published 2002
1

All the characters in this book are entirely fictitious and any resemblance
to anyone real is entirely coincidental, but Sh! in Hoxton exists, as does
the website www.blissbox.com. They are both great fun.

Set in 11.75 on 14pt Monotype Garamond
Printed in England by Clays Ltd, St Ives plc

To David, for the good bits

I

I slept with that man once.

The thought flashed up in Lucy's brain as she braked. He'd appeared from nowhere at the end of her car bonnet, shocking her memory into a sudden, graphic revelation. Lucy had forgotten that she had ever been that person. The one who spent ill-judged nights with men she hardly knew.

His eyes popped at her over the slapping windscreen wipers, and he mouthed something – perhaps 'Careless cow' or even 'Sorry'.

One-night stands belonged to a long time ago, thought Lucy, watching him vanish as suddenly as he'd appeared. It was a wet night, full of sodden people in dark clothing hurling themselves in front of her car. Lucy worried about them, her hands tightening around the steering wheel, because Lucy was now a responsible person. A nurturer. A partner. A grown-up. A nice girl.

A nice woman, she supposed she would have to call herself now, except that it sounded so dismal. Nice girls might be found in unexpected places, such as seedy nightclubs or backpackers' bars. Nice women were not discovered anywhere exciting, because no one would be looking for them there. They belonged in the background, oiling the wheels, serving the tea, chairing the meeting, sharing the school run, doing their stint at the home-baked cakes stall for charity . . .

And that wasn't Lucy. OK, she had chaired the PTA and miscellaneous committees, but you couldn't count those. Not really. And she did a school run, but children had to get to school somehow. But she'd never baked a cake – not since hash brownies in 1975, when a non-smoking flatmate had wanted to get stoned. They'd been rather a success, she mused. Hm. This year, she'd been allocated the Guess the Weight of the Cake stall at the village Christmas fair (or Fayre, as the *Bramsea Bugle* insisted on calling it). Might the addition of marijuana confuse even the most experienced cake-weight guesser?

No, Lucy was not going to call herself a nice woman.

Lights twinkled and spangled everywhere, like thousands of Christmas trees, but failed to illuminate any of the invisible hurrying shapes until they were almost under her wheels. They kept on coming, from so many different directions, transforming Ipswich, where Lucy had been buying her Christmas presents, into a boiling cauldron of frenzied shoppers.

As she drove out of the city, intermittent patches of light from Suffolk villages glittered ahead in the rain, then disappeared behind the car. She changed the radio frequency on an impulse. Away from two sensible, balanced voices discussing the refugee issue to a thudding, repetitive beat. She recognized the music, it had drifted or thumped out from her sons' bedrooms often enough, but never before had it conjured up for her the dark, smoky, illicit world of men and women hunting for each other. Lucy did lots of things – chaired meetings, diagnosed cancer, heart disease or the reasons for flatulence, ironed shirts (badly), belonged to a reading group, sang in an amateur choir, bought organic food, helped Tom with his homework, tested Nico when he revised for exams, drove them both to and from endless activities and got pleasantly pissed on Saturday evenings, and often she did more than one of them at once – but she didn't dance. Or get dressed in the evening wondering who she was going to attract. Now her only experience of one-night stands was referring her patients to the Sexually Transmitted Diseases clinic in Lowestoft or Ipswich. She hoped that the man she'd nearly run over, whoever he was, hadn't come to live anywhere near. She didn't want to be asking him questions about his prostate at some point in the future.

She put her foot on the accelerator and belted out the words in an impromptu flying karaoke session. She was almost relieved, fifty minutes later, to arrive back in Bramsea and sanity.

Bramsea, once a Georgian village and now a sprawling seaside town, had grown up as a trading post for local cod and mackerel. It had escaped development because its inhabitants had been poor for centuries. Now its picturesque heart, known as the Old Town, was preserved in aspic, relying on the twenty-first-century pillars of telecommunications and tourism for its livelihood. The only concrete to be seen was the thin strip keeping the sea at bay, but even that was disguised as a promenade, garlanded with gaily painted beach huts. These, once considered humble amenities, and then risible, like music-hall jokes, now changed hands for astonishing sums. Celebrities drank champagne in them, while, beyond, a single ice-cream stall sold ices that tasted of sweet shaving foam. Generations of children had relished their bland stickiness while their parents reassured each other that Bramsea would never change. Yet the sea quietly eroded the clifftops, and the new housing estates and out-of-town 'business centres' expanded around its rim like a puddle of rust in the rain.

After Ned and Lucy had lived in Bramsea for a couple of years, they'd managed to buy a run-down Victorian boarding house facing the common and, over its rough, flat grass, the sea. The street had been shabby and genteel, its Victorian and Georgian houses owned mainly by little old ladies padding out their meagre pensions by taking in lodgers. Now smart young professionals and second-home owners parked big, shiny cars outside the houses, which had gradually, one by one, changed back from bedsits and bed-and-breakfasts. Friends from the London days came to stay with the Dickinsons and told Lucy how much they envied her – an interesting job, two gorgeous boys, Ned, and, instead of pollution, mugging and traffic, the cobbled streets and sea breezes of Bramsea.

'You're so lucky,' they'd sigh, as they packed up their cars to queue on the A12 for their return. 'You've got it all.'

And Lucy tried not to sound smug when she agreed. After twenty years of living and working in Bramsea, she still felt lucky.

Ned's key turned in the lock as she juggled chopping an onion for a simple pasta sauce with queries from Tom about homework. She looked at the clock. Eight-ish. Late, but not too late (although too late for Tom still to be doing homework, she thought, with a stab of bad-mother-itis). As Tom threw himself into his father's arms, her heart twisted with love. The best thing about Ned was that he made her laugh. Not with the frenzied, gag-a-minute humour of a man desperate to be liked, but with the odd wry remark that made her smile at her own ridiculousness or the occasional sharp observation that showed he had been listening after all. Best of all, though, he seemed to enjoy her jokes. She always knew how to make him smile. When she wasn't too tired.

Tonight he looked grey. His battered-looking face wasn't conventionally good-looking – when she'd first met him, she'd thought he was almost ugly, like an avenging Old Testament angel, his strong, male features and broken nose crudely contrasting with the long, blond, rock-star hair all the boys flaunted in those days. But, even now, with the hair shorter, thinner, faded to beige, and always slightly awry, as if

5

he'd been blown in by the wind, he was her Knight on a White Charger, who had swept her away from the stale atmosphere of parties and clubs. He made her feel safe, and she loved him.

As Tom scuttled upstairs, Ned kissed her, dropping his bag on the floor.

She dodged away from his lips. 'Don't just leave that there.'

He looked at the floor, littered with several pairs of football boots and a pile of carrier bags. 'Why not?'

'Because it's untidy. Soon we won't be able to get in the door.'

'Oh.' Ned didn't often notice untidiness. It was like finding the butter in the fridge. It just wasn't there when he looked at it. But occasionally he did recognize mess, and demanded to know what it was doing there.

This was one of the times when the realization dawned on him. 'It looks like a tip round here. What are these doing in the hall?' he demanded. 'Boys! Boys!' His shout was rough.

Lucy's optimism drained away. She hated her role as the household's Clean and Tidy Fairy. 'They said they'd clean them and put everything away later.'

Ned put an arm round her. 'Sorry. Didn't mean to bark. But those boys must learn somehow. They can't go on just leaving everything for you.'

But they could, Lucy knew.

That night she pulled the duvet over her ears. Ned

flung an arm over her, and kissed her ear. 'Night, darling.'

She pretended to be almost asleep and grunted something.

But he didn't move away, and, a few seconds later, she could feel him stroking her breast and tucking himself around her back as if they were two interlocking spoons. As she felt the tip of an erection pressing against her thigh, Lucy thought desperately of sleep. It was just there, drawing her down and away into the ultimate in peaceful, soft comfort, and the fingers gently teasing her nipple were an irritation, tugging her back.

Suddenly awake, she snapped in exasperation, 'For God's sake.'

Ned withdrew his hand, and turned away. 'Sorry.'

Lucy clutched her head in despair. She was thoroughly awake now and feeling guilty. 'I didn't mean it. Really.'

'That's OK.' Ned sounded understanding. 'I know I ought to apply in writing, three weeks in advance. Planning permission for the erection of a stiffened structure adjacent to my wife. So that it can be passed by the proper authorities as being of the correct proportions and elevation.' He kissed the back of her neck.

Lucy didn't feel like laughing. 'Not really. Just not now.'

'I know.' He caressed her back, and Lucy tensed, hoping that this wasn't a renewed attempt. But it

7

wasn't, or didn't seem to be, although she didn't want even to think about enjoying his touch in case it turned into one. 'You're just tired,' he told her. 'Go to sleep.'

In a few moments she could hear his breathing even out, while she lay awake, rigid with hatred at herself.

He doesn't seem to have minded, she told herself. He never minds. That's what's so nice about him.

But it took her a long time to get to sleep, and the following morning she felt tireder than ever.

The tiredness followed her around all the next day, like her own personal raincloud. Everything lasted longer and seemed flatter than usual. Getting Tom and Nico off to school, then the surgery, with its trail of identical symptoms, claiming to be pre-Christmas flu, which usually turned out to be a mixture of bad colds and hangovers, and finally the delay while the washing machine repair man failed to turn up.

She fumed. It was both Nico's and Tom's school carol service at 6 p.m., when the junior and senior schools merged in a sea of boys. Lucy did not have time to sit on the big, shabby, comfortable sofa that had been passed down from Ned's parents, looking at her stripped floorboards and white walls. On her left shoulder, an invisible monkey chattered, pointing out that the latter needed re-painting soon. Would there be enough money left over after Christmas? If they were careful? Another invisible monkey on her right shoulder argued the merits of re-upholstering the sofa over the re-painting, while anxious thoughts about a patient whose tests seemed suspicious and about what Tom's next school should be also bobbed up and down between them, interfering with her efforts to get on with the reading group's current novel. It was about Japanese stokers before the war, and had copious lyrical descriptions – which had been highly praised – of men chewing, spitting and swallowing. Not a great deal else, apart from the odd grunt, had happened in three hundred pages and she'd already decided to skip to the end, hoping that there wasn't a major catastrophe buried in the pages of detail which would find her out. She flicked through the pages, and marked a chapter that she might be able to comment on, just to seem as if she'd actually read the middle of it. With any luck everyone else would be bluffing too. Oh, come on, she muttered generically to the Japanese stokers and the electrical repair man. Come *on*.

The man arrived, charged an amount which would have made her London friends gasp in envy again, and disappeared, promising to return one day with a spare part.

But she was late for the service. She edged her car into too small a space, almost bumping the one behind, out of which another latecomer emerged. The doors had just been closed by the School Secretary, a forbidding woman who treated parents as if they were unwanted intruders at the best of times.

'We can't go in now,' Lucy whispered. Suddenly she

could have cried with exhaustion. 'It'll be the solo verse of "Once in Royal David's City" and we can't interrupt that.'

The other woman, with great dark eyes and a tousled caramel-blonde bob, was wearing jeans and a leather jacket, a combination that no other mother in Bramsea would have considered appropriate for the school carol service. She stamped her feet and blew on her hands. 'It's fucking freezing.' She had a low, husky voice. 'Look, why don't we nip across the road to that wine bar, have a couple of drinks, then sneak in at the end and pretend we've been there all along?'

Anxiety – that familiar vertiginous, edgy feeling – washed over Lucy. Going to the end-of-term carol service was something that parents had to do. It came with the territory, the dull bit of parenthood that included sewing name tapes on endless pairs of socks, delivering two children to opposite ends of town at the same time to their various friends, and remembering which days everyone had to take what pieces of kit where.

But a drink, a seat and some warmth would be very welcome. She agreed.

'I'm Grace Morgan.' The stranger extended a hand.

'I know. I've seen you at school.' Lucy felt it soft and icy in her grasp. So she was meeting the exciting, exotic Grace Morgan at last. A glimmer of interest penetrated her tiredness. Unlike the other distracted, harassed or worried mothers at school, Grace Morgan glowed with good fortune. Everything about her was blonde. She reminded you of honey, champagne, butter-yellow suede and creamy, sunlit stone. She was tall and wiry, with spiky heels and tight trousers, making other mothers beside her look small and stodgy, their outlines blurred in layers of murky greys, blues and black.

Sitting in the wine bar, Grace suggested cocktails. 'They're back in fashion.'

Fashion? Lucy had forgotten about fashion. Once she'd been the first to wear her skirts shorter or longer, or tighter or looser. Now it wasn't relevant to her life. She nodded, relieved to have someone else take a decision for her, however tiny.

Two Pink Panthers arrived at the table, garishly decorated.

'To us.' Grace had raised a glass. 'Us escaping mothers.'

Lucy smiled and took a swig. A fiery sensation slipped down her throat and set her heart on fire. Suddenly she didn't feel so tired and cold any more. 'Mm. Not bad.'

They swapped details. Grace was married to Richard, a venture capitalist, who travelled constantly on business, and they had a son called Luke who, at ten, was in the same class as Lucy's Tom. Grace had been a fashion adviser-cum-personal shopper in a big London department store until Richard started a branch of the company in Norwich, so she'd just started up her own business from home, advising women on what to wear. 'I help people change their lives,' Grace said lightly, and Lucy replied, only joking, of course, that she could do with some of that.

Grace unwound a soft, brilliantly shimmering blue velvet scarf from her neck and deftly arranged it around Lucy's neck, her fingers brushing against Lucy's cheek as she twisted the fabric into exactly the right position. 'Start with this. It's just the right shade to make your eyes even bluer. You've got the most amazing eyes.' She leant back and studied Lucy, who blushed. 'It suits you much more than me – why not borrow it?'

Lucy was embarrassed. Suppose she left it somewhere? And she had so many things – a husband, children, plants, guinea pigs, hamsters and committees – to look after that even a scarf seemed an extra responsibility, but Grace insisted. 'Give it back any time. Look, there's a mirror behind you – see what that colour does for you.'

And Lucy, warmed and exhilarated by the Pink Panthers, saw a new and sparkling person reflected in the glass, one that was faintly familiar from long ago. Her eyes glowed an almost turquoise blue and her cheeks were touched with colour from the alcohol. The way Grace had shaped the scarf made her dark hair frame her face in a softer, more rounded way. Instead of flyaway and bushy (the English madwoman look, Lucy always called it to herself), it seemed full and bouncing. She looked . . . well . . . she had to admit it, if only to herself . . . pretty. She'd forgotten she could look like that. It stirred up uneasy memories.

When she told Grace that she was married to Ned, a paediatric surgeon, that as well as Tom she had Nico, who was just doing his A levels, and that she was a GP, it seemed as if Grace looked at her hungrily. 'So people come and talk to you about their problems, do they? Or is it all sore throats and piles?'

Everything, Lucy replied, wondering if something particular was worrying her. Surely not. Grace, with her expensive car and extensive wardrobe, did not seem the sort of person to have problems.

'It must be tough, doing that all day,' observed Grace. 'How do you cope with having to tell people that they've got something very wrong with them?'

Lucy shrugged. 'Most of my patients are what we call the "worried well" round here. But sometimes when I get someone's tests back, I realize I've got information that will change their lives for ever. Those are the bad days.'

'I admire you.'

'It's just a job, honestly. There's nothing heroic about it.' But Lucy was warmed inside, because – and not that she minded in the least – it was usually Ned's job, saving babies and children with his surgery, that people talked about. 'What's the hardest thing about your work?'

Grace looked surprised, as if no one had ever asked her that. With a small, reflective laugh, she rattled the ice round her drink. 'People come to me saying that they want to look different, but they don't really. So if

I do manage to make them look more glamorous, or prettier, or younger, they panic. Or their husbands, partners and families are furious. I had one Norfolk farmer turn up on the doorstep with a shotgun last year, demanding to know what I'd done to his wife. She'd been with a group of Wives in Mixed Farming who'd come to me because they felt stuck in a rut.'

Lucy smiled. 'Surely some of them want to change?'

'Mm.' Grace's deep brown eyes studied her. 'Occasionally, I find someone who does. And that's when the trouble starts.'

Lucy paused. She wondered what Grace did then, but didn't feel she knew her well enough to ask. Did she offer follow-up counselling? Or keep Do-It-Yourself Divorce leaflets next to the make-up charts? There was something about Grace that made her want to find out more.

'I'd never have expected you to be late for the carol service,' Grace queried. 'You always seem so in charge at school.'

Lucy was flattered, but wanted Grace to know that she wasn't quite the pillar of society that she seemed, so she explained about being tired, and how it had stemmed from the man she'd nearly run over the day before.

'I realized I'd had a one-night stand with him. A long time ago. In my early twenties. He was called Miles, or Giles, or something like that.'

'Was he any good?'

'No,' she rummaged through her memory and came

14

up with a verdict. 'It was a bit of a mistake. Basically rather boring. In bed and out of it.' Being with Grace suddenly reminded her of being single, all those years ago, when Lucy and her friends had dissected men and their actions with the ruthlessness of pathologists on a murder case. Since the curtain of marriage had descended twenty years earlier, she'd lost the knack of discussing such things.

'Not an enema man, then?' Grace sounded so sexually experienced. Even half a lifetime as a GP hadn't quite inoculated Lucy from mild shock.

'I don't do enemas,' Lucy told her. 'I see too much of that end of people at work to want to have anything to do with it in my spare time. And I don't do corporal punishment either. Or bondage.'

'You are dull,' teased Grace. 'I mean, what do you do? Just missionary position?' Grace flicked her hair away from her face and ordered another round. 'We can get one more in before the end of the service. We can see the doors open from here.'

They discussed the latest film showing in Bramsea and discovered they'd both been bored stiff by it, after which they found out that they both adored Christmas, in spite of the work.

When the church doors opened, about fifteen minutes later, there was so much that Lucy still wanted to talk about. Nico was at the door with another prefect, holding the collection plates.

Grace seized her arm and steered her across the road. 'Just tell Nico to keep his mouth shut. If you don't want Tom to get upset that you weren't there. Lord knows why it's so important to them, but it seems to be.' She introduced herself to Nico with a smile that etched itself deeply into the honey skin, crinkling to the corners of her eyes. 'I've been leading your mum astray,' she said. 'It was just a quick drink. But as far as Tom's concerned, we were at the carol service, OK?' She laid a hand on Nico's arm, and he blushed. Then he grinned.

'Cool.'

'This is Mrs Morgan,' added Lucy.

'Grace,' corrected Grace. 'Mrs Morgan is my mother-in-law, who is as mad as a hatter. Unfortunately.'

Nico and Grace shook hands, and Lucy's heart warmed at the old-fashioned courtesy. Perhaps she and Ned hadn't done too bad a job on him after all.

As they slid into the back of the church, waiting to beam at the younger children as they filed past in neat pairs, Grace hissed into Lucy's ear, 'He's gorgeous, your elder son. I bet the girls have a hard time.'

Lucy had no idea. Girls and boys appeared at their door, in twos and threes, with their peachy young skin, long legs and sharp elbows, with studs stapled through their tongues or their bare, flat stomachs. They trooped up to Nico's room, and clattered back down again. It was impossible to tell what any of them did up there, except for sporadic group raids on the refrigerator. Nico would stand by it, door open, and ask 'if anyone was hungry'. A week's shopping would disappear in a matter of minutes. Otherwise they all seemed surprisingly demure and hard-working, and often surprised her by saying 'please' and 'thank you' and occasionally even helping her. This well-mannered, if secretive, adolescence offered no clues as to what was really going on in Nico's head or his life.

'How did he come to be Nico?' Grace was still watching him, holding the plate out to parents with apparently perfect manners. 'It sounds foreign.'

Lucy grimaced. 'He was christened Nicholas. Sensible, English Nicholas. We called him Nicky. Then he wanted to be Nick. Now it's Nico. It's incredibly difficult to remember. I feel as if my little Nicky was another person from another age.'

Grace's face registered amusement. 'I suppose that's growing up.'

The following day, feeling furtive, Lucy checked the practice records to see if Grace was one of their patients. It wasn't strictly correct, but Lucy knew she'd never tell anyone anything she might find in there. She'd woken up with an image of Grace's face in her mind, and was sure that there was something she'd wanted to talk about behind the jokes and the cool façade. But she didn't know if she was relieved or disappointed to find that none of the Morgans were registered. They must be with the other practice.

That evening she asked Tom if he liked Luke Morgan.

17

There was a short pause. 'He's all right,' replied Tom, finishing his third yoghurt.

'Would you like to have him round to tea on Saturday?' Lucy wanted an excuse to see Grace again.

Tom considered it for a few moments. 'OK.'

She whipped a few plates into the dishwasher, knowing that over the next few weeks of Christmas a layer of mugs, discarded food and plates would spring up continually, apparently out of nowhere, covering every surface like a rash. Telling boys to put plates in dishwashers was the triumph of hope over experience, as Johnson might have said. There seemed to be a hollow tube linking their ears, through which any such instructions travelled, shimmering out into the ether on the other side. In the sink floated a football shirt, which had turned a patchy shade of muddy grey in spite of the claims made by several manufacturers about whiteness. Lucy sighed. How had she turned into a person to whom stain removal was a burning issue? She thought of the previous night in the wine bar, and resolved to call Grace that evening.

But the phone rang before she'd wrung out the shirt, and as soon as she heard the voice, Lucy was conscious of a leap of pleasure. Grace had rung her first. She said that she knew how busy everyone was near Christmas but, with Richard away, she wondered if Lucy had a free evening to come to dinner?

'Just us.'

Between the Residents' Association Christmas party in the local hall, the surgery's cheese and wine party, the trip out into the countryside to fetch her father for Christmas and a charity Christmas party for the Old People's Home that she'd always allowed herself to get involved in, Lucy managed to find a space. 'Though I'll have to drop Nico off at a party near you, and pick him up afterwards.'

'Doesn't Nico drive himself?' asked Grace.

Lucy shuddered. His driving test was in February, and, if he passed, she knew that she would hardly be able to sleep for visions of him lying like a broken doll in a ditch somewhere. 'Don't,' she begged. 'Just don't even think about it. Sex and drugs are nothing to worry about compared to when they start to drive.'

When she put the phone down, she felt less tired. The boys' tea, involving industrial quantities of food and an endless round of clearing up, usually finished her off for the day, but when she'd eventually cleared the table of crumbs, cleaned out the guinea pigs' and hamsters' cages (why couldn't the bloody things die, it was years since either boy had shown any interest in them) and put out the usual half-dozen bottles for recycling, she felt invigorated.

It was almost as if she'd been invited out on a date.

2

On the night of her dinner with Grace, Lucy drove out to the edge of town, where the Georgian town streets gave way to Victorian terraces and villas, then 1960s and 1970s bungalows, and, finally, the 1990s 'executive' estates with their double garages and copious dormer windows. Part of the anticipation was the thrill – oh, that thrills these days were so innocent – of being able to see inside the Morgans' house. Originally a big suburban Victorian red-brick villa, it had been turned into a children's home, and successive local authorities had tagged on ugly extensions that stacked up around it like matchboxes, making it too small for an institution, too big for a private house and too ugly for a hotel. After the home closed, it had languished on the market for over three years. But eventually local gossip reported that a couple from London had bought it, and were 'throwing money at it like there's no tomorrow'. And when it was clear that all the horrid modern extensions were being demolished and a smaller red-brick one rebuilt at the back, in the style of the original house, 'well, some people have money to burn'. Lucy had followed the stories with fascination, only recently connecting them with the large dark eyes and self-contained air of the woman who always stood alone in the crowded reception area at school, eyed by the other mothers. Sometimes she looked like a gypsy – she'd carried off the petticoat, cardigan and flip-flops fashion better than anyone else could have – and at others there was more than a dash of the corporate wife about her linen suits. Once she'd worn something like a man's jacket, and occasionally there was a whiff of trashy goddess style, with leather trousers and tight, spangly tops.

'Well, I know it's probably just a question of wanting to be fashionable,' Josephine Saunders, the school grumbler, had said once to Lucy, following the perfect proportions of Grace's departing backside as it wiggled out of the school door, 'but I've found a style that's me, and I stick to it.' Lucy had agreed, but vaguely and without any enthusiasm. Grace reminded her of the days when getting dressed meant asking yourself who you wanted to be tonight. It had been fun to try out different versions of yourself, and then to toss the latest variation back into the wardrobe or onto a pile on the floor at the end of the evening. When had the look settled into something that might as well have been a uniform? Like Josie Saunders, Lucy Dickinson, mother, wife and doctor, had found a style that stuck.

When Grace opened the door, Lucy was surprised by how light and modern the Victorian house seemed. It was a blonde house, like Grace, all pale wood, cool blues, honey tones and soft greys. Grace herself was wearing black leggings and sloppy joe, but on her feet were a pair of scarlet mules, high-heeled and feathered. The effect was bird-of-paradise slobs out.

Lucy followed Grace into a large, long kitchen, with a weathered refectory table stretching out towards a huge black Aga, and a massive French armoire converted to hold modern equipment. Two cavernous, battered leather armchairs beckoned beside a roaring fire. The smell of wood smoke mingled with garlic and wine.

'Take a pew,' Grace indicated the chairs. 'Although I warn you, once you're down, you won't be able to get up in a hurry. I ought to re-upholster them really, but I love that feeling that they've been in a gentleman's club for centuries. Imagine how many old buffers must have dreamed or dozed or died in them.'

The chair swallowed Lucy up, and she realized that not only was she not able to get up, but she had no desire to do so.

'Do you like champagne?' Grace called from a larder room beside the Aga. 'Not everyone does, I know. There's white wine, red wine, vodka –' she rootled around inside '– some filthy treacly stuff we got at the bottle stall at the Christmas fair . . .'

'I think we donated that,' admitted Lucy. 'If it's a Finnish liqueur. Someone gave us a couple of bottles once and we had to get rid of it somehow. It tastes like drain cleaner. Anyway I absolutely love champagne. When I get it, which is hardly ever.'

Lucy looked round while Grace was pouring. Most

22

of the pictures were framed children's drawings. It must be almost all the artwork that Luke had ever produced. In their house, the boys brought pictures home at the end of term, which dutifully spent a few weeks floating around inconveniently, after which they were ditched.

Grace followed her gaze. 'I like keeping Luke's stuff around. He's growing up so fast.' She sounded wistful, and Lucy wondered why she'd never had more children. Perhaps that was what Grace wanted to talk about. A late baby.

Grace handed Lucy a glass and sat down. 'Do you think cosmetic surgery *works*?' She had a way of making every question sound monumentally important.

Lucy was taken aback. 'What do you mean, "works"? I mean, if you want to look a bit less tired, or to improve the shape of your nose, or to smooth out the odd line, yes, it works. But if you want it to get your husband back or to find a better job, no, it doesn't. Not usually, anyway.'

'Oh.' Grace sounded discouraged. 'Oh, well. Would you have it?'

'God, no.'

'Liposuction?'

'I don't think it would even dent my massive haunches.'

Grace flicked an expert eye across Lucy, but the chair had been designed to envelop the majestic posteriors of Edwardian men and revealed nothing.

'Rubbish. And what about a vaginal nip-and-tuck?'

'What?' Lucy nearly choked on her drink. 'Why on earth would anyone want one? Except for strictly medical reasons?'

'It's the latest In operation. The New Facelift is a Front-Bottom-Lift, apparently. Something to do with the growth in popularity of oral sex.'

Lucy sniggered. She couldn't help it. Even after a lifetime of being hardened to the bizarre nature of other people's private lives. 'No, no, and absolutely no. I keep that part of myself to myself.'

Oops.

But Grace was laughing too much to notice. 'We must talk about something else apart from sex. Or you'll think I have a one-track mind. What are you reading at the moment?'

Lucy told her about the Japanese stokers and their chewing.

'You are clever.' Grace sounded sincere. 'Do you think it's a parable for something?'

'Sex, probably.'

They both spluttered again, like schoolgirls. This was ridiculous, but it was the first time for a long while that someone had wanted to know about her, Lucy thought, rather than about Tom, Nico or Ned, or the progress of something through a committee or what their blood tests meant. It was exhilarating, and warming, to be appreciated.

And it had been too long since she'd talked like this. She'd become sealed up behind her public persona. The doctor, the mother, the chairwoman, the wife, the good neighbour. Party-going, man-hunting, giggling Lucy seemed to have vanished completely. Until now, Lucy hadn't missed her.

In a desperate attempt to avoid the subject of sex, they talked – snuffling with suppressed giggles – about the traffic instead. Lucy, reminded of the breathalyser, switched from champagne to water. Next time she saw Grace she'd leave the car behind. Grace said that she was terrified of the way pedestrians hovered at the lights, then dashed across just as they turned red.

'Perhaps it adds excitement to their lives,' suggested Lucy.

'A sort of domestic version of running the bulls at Pamplona, d'you think? Maybe.' Grace was suddenly serious for a moment. 'Perhaps I should try it out.'

'Bored?' Lucy asked, her professional antennae quivering. She still thought that something was bothering Grace, and that she needed to talk. She was sure that something darker lay behind the jokes and gaiety. But perhaps it was only ennui.

Grace's voice was casual. 'Everything's fine. Great, I suppose. I'm working for myself at last, Luke's settled into school really well and the house is more or less finished. Up to a point. We keep having to have the builders back from time to time, of course, but I don't mind that.'

'And Richard?' Lucy spotted the omission.

'Oh, I know I'm so lucky to have Richard. My mother was thrilled when we got married. And I adore him,' she added, in a tone that made 'adore' sound tarnished to Lucy's practised ears. 'I really do. But I worry about him, too. He works so hard all the time.' She sounded so matter-of-fact that Lucy nearly missed what she said next. 'But, Lucy, we don't do it any more. Ever. It's been eight years.'

As Lucy struggled to sit up in the welcoming embrace of the armchair, she tried to classify what Grace had told her, and to think of an appropriate reply. 'Have you tried talking to him about it?'

'He won't discuss it,' said Grace, standing up and walking over to the big mirror over the fireplace, flicking her caramel hair behind her ears. 'I don't look bad, do I?' she asked Lucy. 'I'm forty-five, you know.'

'Younger than me,' said Lucy. 'I'm forty-nine. But I don't think that it's necessarily about looks or age,' she added, having recently had several women who were plainer, older or fatter than either Grace or herself reporting to the surgery with venereal diseases or unexpected pregnancies. She'd read – in some medical magazine – that sexually transmitted diseases were increasing faster in the over-fifties than in any other category. She remembered sighing. Couldn't sex just be abolished after you'd had your two-point-four children?

'Well, maybe not,' said Grace. 'But I wish I knew what it *was* all about. I always think it's worry about this deal, or that deal, and then I thought it was the fuss of the move, and then if only the house was straight . . . there's always some way of avoiding even talking about it.' She picked the bottle out of its chiller and topped up their glasses again. 'The trouble is,' she curled back down into her chair again with her glass and stared into it, 'I want a fuck. I desperately, desperately want a fuck.'

There was a silence, until Grace re-filled her glass with a laugh. Lucy waved the bottle away, and topped up her water. 'And,' Grace looked Lucy in the eye, 'I love my husband, I couldn't possibly imagine not being married to him, so I don't know what the hell to do about it.'

Lucy collected Nico from his friend's house at midnight, parking round the corner and waiting at a pre-arranged spot because he didn't want to be seen being picked up by his mother. As she sat in the dark, cold car, giving Nico another five minutes, then ten, before deciding whether to blow his cool by ringing the doorbell and demanding that he leave, she thought about Grace. She'd been shocked by that word. Fuck. And yet even well-brought-up children wrote it in the dust on their parents' cars. Tom, only the other day, had said it while she was testing his grammar.

'Give me examples of verbs and adverbs,' Lucy had demanded.

'What about "fuck off"?' had been his reply. Lucy had crisply replied that 'off' wasn't an adverb. It was a preposition. She wasn't sure whether she was right, but at least it had stopped him showing off, which was what she suspected he'd been doing.

Even Ned often used the word when he tripped over clutter in the house.

No, what was so shocking was hearing 'fuck' used properly. Hearing it with meaning. Grace wasn't talking about love or romance. She wanted sex.

But why wasn't she getting it? Perhaps Richard was having an affair. It would explain his long absences and his lack of interest in his wife.

Tiredness suddenly overwhelmed her, as if she'd been coshed on the head with something heavy and hard. Damn Nico. As she began to get out of the car and prepared to run the gauntlet of disapproval, he appeared, and slid into the passenger seat with a grunt.

'You're late,' she grumbled. 'It's twelve fifteen. I'm tired. I've been up since six. I've got to do early surgery tomorrow. I –' She realized he was gazing out of the window, taking no notice of this litany of complaints. Oh well. If she went on, he'd just say that she didn't have to pick him up, secure in the knowledge that no Bramsea mother would allow their teenage children to walk two miles across the fields in the depths of December, particularly as the route home ran through Bramsea All Saints (jokingly referred to by Ned as Bramsea All Sinners), where a run-down estate welcomed middle-class youths as a useful source of mobile telephones and illicit cash. Although crime levels were amongst the lowest in Britain, rumours of knives and robberies floated around these estates, and no one wanted to take the risk. There was no question of a bus, of course. Not anywhere near midnight. She switched tack.

'Good party?'

He grunted again.

'Was there anyone I know there?' She remembered taking him to parties when he was little, and staying to drink tea with the other parents.

'No.' Nico laid his head back on the headrest, and dropped off to sleep.

Lucy returned to her own thoughts. If she talked to Grace about her own problems with Ned, she knew that her friend would envy her. She'd say that she was lucky to have him. And she was. He didn't seem to care whether any part of her, from her brows to her breasts to her bottom, drooped below the ideal. He wouldn't have noticed whether what she was wearing was in fashion. He just wanted her.

Rather more often than Lucy wanted him. She must try. She must try harder, she thought, her eyes straining into the darkness of the side streets, as she drove the car towards the safety of Bramsea's Christmas lights and the main road. Or one of these days Ned would meet a Grace, and everything would fall apart. Lucy felt, suddenly, very frightened, as if a dark abyss had briefly opened up ahead and then disappeared again, leaving her lost and wondering if she'd dreamed it.

3

Lucy's dinner with Grace had lifted her out of what she now recognized as having been a small grey patch. The evening had glowed and sparkled, while life the day before had seemed dull and dragged down. She wanted to see her again.

So Lucy rang her the following day, to thank her for supper and to suggest that she and Luke come round some time over Christmas.

'Richard'll be back.' There was an excited warmth in Grace's voice. 'He rang late last night after you'd gone to say that he'd completed the latest deal early and was going to take a few more days off over Christmas. He's so exhausted. Honestly, he works so hard, I can't tell you.'

Lucy suspected that something must have gone wrong with the girlfriend and, as a result, Richard had found himself with unexpected spare time on his hands. And she wondered if Grace regretted last night's outburst.

'Bring him along too. Just kitchen supper.' She wasn't sure she was going to like this Richard, but she could hardly avoid extending the invitation.

Grace sounded enthusiastic. It took a while to arrange the date, as they both grappled with the complexities of their diaries, which, rather than being filled with fun and Christmas parties, seemed to be clogged with commitments like dentists' appointments in inconveniently distant towns ('we won't be back till late that evening so there probably isn't time'), events that had to be attended for work reasons or local beanos at the church hall. The only date Lucy could do was 23 December.

'Damn,' said Grace. 'I've got my mother-in-law to stay by then.'

'Bring her along. I've got my father. They can be company for each other.'

'I'm afraid Marjorie's pretty much lost her marbles. Not that she ever had many to start with. She just burbles on, although she's got all the right social gestures. She smiles, gesticulates and nods her head. It's like watching a film in a language you don't understand. It drives Luke mad. We have to drive two hours to get her from her flat, then two hours back, and he just can't stand hearing her repeat the same things over and over again.'

Lucy laughed. 'She'll be perfect for Dad, then. He comes from the generation that never listened to anything women said, anyway. We all talk rubbish, according to him, so he won't notice.'

'Well, if you're sure.'

Lucy was sure. She wanted her first meeting with Richard to be as chaotic as possible. Otherwise she felt that he'd be able to read the truth in her eyes – 'I know you don't make love to your wife' would be written all over her face, along with a faint air of accusation.

'And drop Luke off here before the journey, if you like,' she added. 'No sense in giving him half a day in a car when he could be downloading pornography off the Internet with Tom.'

'Really? That would make the most amazing difference if you truly don't mind. And is there a time when you need to get rid of Tom? Why not drop him here when you get your father? And have some lunch at the same time.'

By the time they'd rung off, various arrangements for Luke and Tom to be exchanged between the Morgan and Dickinson homes had been set into place so that Grace and Lucy could get things done. Lucy felt a sense of relief as she put down the phone. Having lived in Bramsea for so long, she'd had several of these interdependent childcare relationships with friends, which had started when Nico was born, but recently friends had begun to shift away, moving, divorcing or sending their children to different schools. It made Lucy uneasy, as if she was going to be left behind somehow. Although she could sometimes rely on Nico to keep an eye on his younger brother, he was inclined to be grumpy about it. In some ways, she needed a new friend as much as Grace seemed to.

The twenty-second of December arrived, satisfyingly cold and frosty. As Lucy drove out of town with the electronic burbling of Tom's Gameboy echoing faintly from the back seat, the world spread out around her like a sepia pen-and-ink drawing. A thin wash of icy frost outlined the brown of the bare trees and fields, and the sun, low in the sky, shone into her eyes. She'd done morning surgery, and, after a succession of almost uniform colds, flu and 'stress' symptoms, was setting out on the familiar winding journey that would take her to her father, who would be irritated to leave his vegetables. Owen Fraser, a fiercely independent eighty-two-year-old, had been enraged the year before to have his driving licence revoked because he could hardly see. Lucy had dragged him away from the hospital, while he'd shouted about 'people who come over here and stick their noses in where they're not wanted', suggesting that the ophthalmologist should 'sugar back to his own country if he couldn't get a simple thing like a chap's ability to drive right'. 'I was driving when you were sitting in front of a mud hut playing with a stick,' had been another of his barbs. Lucy had bundled him out, muttering, 'So sorry, frightfully sorry, dreadfully sorry,' to a succession of patient faces who had seen it all before, as he'd roared, 'Why should you be sorry?' and 'I'll give them sorry.'

Ever since then he had sniped at Lucy's driving every time she went to fetch him.

But between the endless drip of noses in the surgery and Owen's cantankerous complaints, Grace had suggested she stop off for a quick salad when she dropped Tom round to play with Luke.

'Drink?' Grace waved a bottle of white wine at her.

Lucy shook her head regretfully. 'Driving.' The bottle looked crisp and alluring. 'Well, one can't hurt,' she conceded. There seemed to be something about Grace, she thought, which always led her astray.

Grace poured her a glass. 'How's your day been?'

Lucy told her. Grace listened with sympathy. 'You are amazing. I don't know how you manage,' she said. 'Well, I've had a heavenly time. The builders are back. Bliss!'

Lucy was disconcerted. 'Bliss?' Builders, in her experience, were usually considered hell.

'One of them is absolutely divine,' explained Grace. 'And I wouldn't push the other one out of bed either. I have to say, the sight of those forearms does do me good.'

Lucy wondered if she could prescribe builders' forearms to some of her patients. After all, drugs don't do the decorating for you as well.

'The thing is,' Grace clattered around the kitchen pulling food and dishes out of cupboards, 'at our age, there aren't any decent men to flirt with any more. They've all got eyebrows with tentacles waving out of them or awful dry-skin conditions that look like facial fungus. I mean it's all very well saying that men like younger women, of course they do. But what no one ever seems to admit is that we like younger men too.'

'Do we?' Lucy had never given younger men much of a thought, but felt something distant and strange stirring deep inside her. For the second time in less than a week, she felt nostalgic for those days before

AIDS, herpes and marriage. When you could go to a party and wake up with your face in an ashtray and a complete stranger on the pillow.

'Speaking personally,' giggled Grace. 'Still, I have a plan.' She expertly twirled a salad in a huge wooden bowl and took up the conversation from the other night as if Lucy had never gone home in the meantime. 'A secret weapon. Lingerie.'

'Lingerie?' Lucy did not have lingerie. She had underwear. It was stretchy – sometimes to the point of bagginess – and ranged in colour from greyish-white to greenish-grey because there was never time to separate the whites from the coloureds in the wash.

'I was reading a piece by this psychologist.' Grace whipped out a couple of big white plates and set them out on the table, dispatching the boys to the television room with a heated-up pizza. 'I wanted to chat to you alone about it all, and you can't talk about bras in front of them.'

Lucy thought it was unlikely that Tom would have listened. He only noticed girls and their accoutrements if they got between him and the television set.

'Bras?' she echoed, wondering if morning surgery had leached all the intelligence out of her.

'Bras. You see, this man who's terribly, terribly well known although I can't quite remember his name . . .' Grace started thumbing through a pile of magazines, and gave up. 'Anyway, he said that men are very simple creatures and designed to respond to very basic stimuli. So what you need is a bra that pushes everything very high up and pointy – that's natural selection ensuring that they choose someone young and fertile – and then you get it in lace and silk, and make sure either that it shows through something transparent or that you wear something low so that a bit peeks out of the top. And it works every time. Apparently.'

This did sound basic to Lucy's ears. Very elementary. It was obviously time for a proper discussion about Grace's problem.

'I think encouraging Richard to talk would probably be much more effective in the long run,' she pointed out. 'I mean, hasn't he given any clue why he doesn't want to? And when did it all begin? Or, rather, end?'

'I can't remember when it became a problem.' Grace sighed. 'We've known each other for ever.' She looked embarrassed. 'Don't tell anyone this, but he was the first man I ever slept with.'

Lucy was surprised.

'My parents were absolutely determined to keep me virginal. I thought that if you slept with a man, you had to marry him. And Richard was a bit older than me, and about a zillion times more sophisticated. We went out together for five years, although we kept splitting up. He used to say that he needed his space, and all that. My mother was awfully worried, because she really believed that if I didn't stick with Richard I'd become a complete tart, and she believed that a woman without a husband – however unfaithful – was absolutely lost. I think he thought that too, so eventually he asked me to marry him. Very lucky, really, because I couldn't imagine being without him.'

It didn't quite add up to a reason to marry someone in Lucy's opinion, but she kept silent. 'Was . . . sex . . . OK between you then?'

Grace screwed up her face. 'I don't think the first time is ever the best, is it?'

'Mine certainly wasn't,' agreed Lucy, suppressing the memory.

After that we were engaged for years, and then he broke it off. He said I was too young. I was twenty-four by that time, and my mother was appalled. I was absolutely heartbroken. I couldn't believe it.

'Anyway, I went out with a few men, but they weren't Richard. I even – please don't tell him, I couldn't bear for him to know – went to bed with two of them. Then he suddenly came back – about three years later – and said he'd made the most terrible mistake, and would I forgive him? He said he thought we ought to live together, just to make sure, and, of course, I said yes. I mean, I was twenty-seven by then, so time was getting on. As he pointed out.

'He had very strong ideas about how we should live – we had a loft apartment before they were fashionable, with space and light and fabulous views over the Thames, and we had friends we met in restaurants, and his and hers soft-top sports cars. He's so good at making friends.'

'And you . . . had sex?' queried Lucy. What was the right terminology? 'Made love' sounded too intimate.

Leg over, beast with the two backs, end away . . . all too jokey.

'Oh, yes,' conceded Grace. 'At that point, we definitely didn't have a sexual problem. Or certainly not one that I can remember looking back on it. I mean, every now and then, he'd get really fed up with me, and say it just wasn't working, and I'd be terrified that he was about to leave, but it wasn't about sex, I don't think.'

Lucy wondered if perhaps Richard's libido had merely dropped with age. He was now in his fifties. But she was still betting on there being a girlfriend around somewhere. 'So when did it all go wrong?'

Grace twisted her wedding ring. 'I know this sounds silly, but the first time I can remember worrying about it was on our honeymoon. We flew to the Caribbean where we stayed in a huge room on stilts with a massive bed and a giant fan, and a huge great fridge full of champagne. All you could hear was the soft whisper of the sea outside the window, and all you could see were endless creamy sands, with hardly anyone else about – except for room service, of course.' She looked wistful.

'The first night we got in at 2 a.m., so I didn't expect anything. The second night he claimed to be jet-lagged. The third night he was drunk. And so on. And the days weren't much better. He always found someone to chat to in the bar. Or invited other couples to join us for lunch. Organized all-day outings to neighbouring islands.'

'Did you say anything? Ask him about how he felt?'

Grace looked ashamed. 'I was frightened to. I mean, if you can't be blissfully happy on your honeymoon, what hope is there for you?

'And then it took ages for me to get pregnant, which reduced our sex life to a series of charts and tests. All the spontaneity went out the window. Sex to order. No pleasure at all. Then, when I finally had Luke, I thought everything would go back to normal again.'

'But . . . ?'

'I remember thinking that once I was slim again, it would all be all right.' Grace poured herself some more wine. 'Then there was a big deal he had to work on. And so on.'

'But have you tried to talk about it since?' Surely Grace must want some answers, thought Lucy. Surely every fibre of her being must be screaming why, why, why?

Grace shook her head. 'I've tried to, once or twice, but he's either treated it as a joke or snapped. Told me not to put pressure on him, or that I'm being absurd. But I'm not, am I?'

Lucy put her hand on Grace's. 'No. You're not.'

'He reacted so badly that I decided that perhaps the best thing to do was to ignore everything and pretend it was all OK. If I try to get him to talk about it, he accuses me of . . .' Grace turned away, but not before Lucy could see her eyes glisten. She opened a cupboard door, ostensibly to get out a jar of chutney to go with the cold meat. 'Look, this is home-made. By me.' She brushed her cheek so quickly that Lucy couldn't tell if it had been a tear or not. 'Well, being obsessed with sex. But I did so desperately want another child. So, so much.' She looked Lucy directly in the eye. 'I expect it's too late, now, though.'

'Almost definitely.' Lucy had seen too many women in the surgery with problems conceiving at thirty-six to give anyone of forty-five any hope. Although it could happen, as one of the health visitors was always telling women. The ones whose lives would be utterly destroyed by a baby were almost guaranteed to get pregnant at any age.

'I don't think you ever give up wanting another baby, do you? No matter how many you have?' Grace sounded wistful.

'Mm,' said Lucy, who didn't feel that way at all. But she did feel a spasm of anger at Richard Morgan, who left his wife alone so often while denying her the children who would have kept her company.

'Still,' Grace sounded more cheerful. 'Perhaps Richard didn't want another. Perhaps he doesn't want sex in case I get pregnant. If that's what it is. Perhaps the menopause will be a good thing? Don't you think? He might not be so worried about it all?'

Lucy wouldn't have put money on it. 'Do you get on in other ways?'

She pondered it for a moment. 'Yes. Of course. Anyway.' Grace played with her food. She ate very little, Lucy noticed, and her wrists were as thin as matchsticks. 'Will you help me with my lingerie plan?'

'Me?' The only attempt that Lucy had ever made – some twenty years earlier – to encase her breasts in lace and silk had been met with polite incredulity by the overly made-up women with cigarettes hanging out of their mouths who then wielded the tape measures in department stores. 'We don't do those in your size, dear,' one had explained, steering her towards a cantilevered piece of engineering in sensible cotton, marked 36E. Lucy had felt such a freak that she'd never dared go back again, and had stuck to Marks & Spencer, knowing that she was almost certainly one of the estimated sixty per cent of women in the UK who were wearing the wrong size bra. She had read, occasionally, that 36E, although generous, might not now be considered far off normal and that silk and lace had recently been designed in huge, capacious, billowing cups for misshapen women like her, but she didn't want to risk it.

'I just wondered,' Grace pleaded, 'if you wouldn't mind having Luke again tomorrow morning so that I could go into Norwich.'

Lucy sagged with relief. Literally, she reflected, hauling a slipped bra strap up from about her elbow. It was about time she bought a new one, but nothing would have persuaded her to do so in the company of someone who was so clearly a perfect 34B. 'Of course. You don't have to ask.'

'The other burning decision of the day –' Grace began to pull paint charts and wallpaper samples out of a pile '– is the decoration of the spare room. Tell me what you think. I've always had a hankering for *toile de jouy* in pink or blue, but do you think that would be a bit much?'

'I've always loved *toile de jouy*,' said Lucy. 'It reminds me of a little old French hotel we stayed in once, with a tiny bedroom and a huge double bed, and the smallest bathroom imaginable, which had a pull-out bidet.'

'France?' Grace's eyes lit up. 'I love France. Shall we go one day, just you and me? To get away from our humdrum existence.'

Lucy told Grace that her existence was anything but humdrum, and Grace laughed. 'We could go somewhere, though, couldn't we? It would be such fun.'

It would be, if Lucy ever had the time to do it. She felt a pang of regret. Perhaps she'd make time.

After a pleasurable hour spent poring over swatches of wallpaper and furnishing fabrics, Grace returned to her worries about lingerie.

'What do you think? Really and truly?' She sounded as if Lucy's opinion was the only one that mattered. 'What colour would be sexiest? On me?'

Lucy tried to believe that the right colour bra would sort out all Grace's problems.

There was a knock at the kitchen door, and Grace brightened at the sight of one of the builders. 'Sean. Have a cup of tea. Or a drink.'

Sean was in his mid-twenties, surprisingly bronzed

for East Anglia in the middle of winter, and was wearing battered jeans hanging fashionably low down off his hips, and a skimpy vest with cutaway shoulders. Tiny pinpricks of sweat trickled down between his shoulder blades. Lucy restrained herself from asking him if he wasn't too cold or suggesting he put on a jumper. She hadn't turned into her mother yet. His forearms, indeed, were muscular and covered in a faint dusting of blond hair. They had a sheen and a tautness to them that had disappeared from Ned's skin some years earlier. It was difficult to take your eyes off such sculptural perfection, thought Lucy, once Grace had pointed it out.

'That spare room wardrobe's a real weight,' he told Grace. He wanted to know exactly where she wanted it once the room was painted. 'Because I'm not moving it twice.'

Grace flushed. 'No, no, of course not. Do be careful of your back . . .'

Sean looked dismissive of people who worried about backs. He really was raw caveman, thought Lucy.

'Tea?' squeaked Grace.

'I'll have a cup later, if that's OK.' His eyes lingered fractionally on Grace's long elegant legs in their dark tights.

They watched his departing back, with its tightly packed shoulder muscles moving like pistons. 'Do you think,' asked Lucy, 'that young men like that deliberately wear as few clothes as possible to show off their bodies? A bit like everyone thinks girls do when they wear short skirts or crop tops?'

'It's a thought,' conceded Grace. 'And if I went to court for raping him do you think the judge would let me off because he'd brought it on himself by dressing provocatively?'

'Grace,' warned Lucy. 'Don't go there. Just don't.'

Grace giggled. 'I know. I know. But a girl can dream. Or fantasize. Until a couple of years ago, I never fantasized. Now I can sit here in the kitchen asking Sean if he'd like PG Tips or Earl Grey and think about what it would be like to shag him senseless against the worktop and then just walk away.'

Lucy was curious. 'When did that start happening?' It sounded fun.

Grace thought. 'About eighteen months ago, I was walking past a building site, and thinking that when I was twenty-something they all used to more or less down tools and shout things like, "Cheer up, it might never happen, love" and things like that . . .'

Lucy nodded. It had always been a long, mildly terrifying exercise in embarrassment and humiliation. She remembered her cheeks burning, going patchy and hot under the mocking gaze of half a dozen burly men. Occasionally one would try to be friendly – possibly authentically – but the idea of responding was too scary and she'd hurried on, with cries of 'Stuck-up cow' following her. She never wanted to go back to those days again. There were some bonuses to getting older.

44

'Anyway,' Grace continued. 'I think one of them might have looked up briefly, and maybe gone on looking slightly longer than he would have done if I'd been a nun but otherwise I was pretty invisible. You know, middle-aged . . .'

'Comfortable . . .' added Lucy.

'That's right,' agreed Grace. 'So I was able to look at them for a change. I can do that now. And I suddenly realized that one of them was stunning. It was a hot day and he'd taken his top off, and he had this tight bum in jeans and a back that was just the most beautiful thing I'd ever seen. Since then, I've realized how heavenly looking at men can be.'

'Be careful that it doesn't go any further than that. Not unless you want to tear your life apart,' warned Lucy.

Grace shrugged. 'Well, if your own husband doesn't find you attractive, you're hardly likely to pull a builder, are you?'

'Grace! You look great.'

'Hardly. Well put together, perhaps, but not sexy. Don't worry . . .' Grace put a hand on her friend's arm. 'I've got used to it. I look good in clothes, rather better than out of them. I can only assume that I'm just not . . . well, never mind. So I enjoy a bit of ogling to cheer me up. Someone once told me that as you get older you get more male hormones so women start behaving more like men. What do you think?'

Lucy thought about it. Ever since Nico had been

born, nearly eighteen years ago, she had been sur-
rounded by men. She loved them, adored them and
looked after them. She did not look *at* them. Ned's
bum, she remembered, had been small and tight once,
but now resembled a loaf of bread from behind. But,
then, so did hers.

'Hormones are very complicated.' She looked at
her watch. 'You can't be that black and white about
them. I ought to be off. Will Sean be safe here alone
with you?'

Grace grimaced. 'The boys can chaperone him.
Anyway, I might think about it. I might talk about it.
But I can't imagine actually doing anything about
it. Not in a million years.'

'Mm.' Lucy thought about the consequences of
infidelity that inevitably finished up in the surgery,
each sad little story trailing a comet's tail of human
misery. 'The trouble is that, occasionally, people do.
And that's when it gets dangerous.'

'Well, you don't need to worry about me. Mrs
Respectable, that's my name, not Mrs Robinson. Now
let's have a decision about the lace bras before you
go.'

It took Lucy an hour to shoe-horn a grumbling Owen
into the car. He insisted on checking the house three
times before leaving it, and had then fussed over the
way she backed out of the drive. 'It's not that I mind
it being done badly,' he muttered, twitching his long
thin legs in the cramped front passenger seat with

difficulty. 'It's just astonishing finding it done at all. George Bernard Shaw. On women drivers.'

'It was dogs dancing on their hind legs, Dad, and you taught me to drive. And I don't think it was Shaw.'

'Well, who was it then, clever clogs?'

Lucy admitted that she didn't know, and tried to tune him out while she wondered whether Grace's pressure on Richard to have another baby when he was reluctant had made him withdraw. She could understand that one. Perhaps it had been the fertility treatment which their sex life had never recovered from. But her money was still on the mistress kept far enough away from the family home to prevent her turning up on the doorstep but close enough for a man who travelled regularly on business to travel rather further than strictly necessary.

As she forced herself to concentrate on negotiating the Suffolk lanes, her thoughts drifted to buying something high and pointy in lace and silk. Perhaps she should. It might be fun. Something almost stirred in her, until she remembered that trying to haul the 36E cantaloupes even up to ninety degrees in the past had left her with a shelf-like bosom on which occasional small crumbs of food were liable to land. Still, perhaps today's technological advances might give her twin slopes, down which these could ski to the safety of the napkin on her lap.

She shook her head. This was absurd. There was no point wearing anything that might inflame Ned's interest any further.

4

The following day was the twenty-third, when Grace and Richard were due round for supper. Lucy woke up with that fluttery feeling of tension that reminded her of taking a new boyfriend to meet her parents. She couldn't decide whether she wanted Ned to like Grace, or whether, especially considering the potentially dangerous implications of too much liking in that direction, it would be better if their friendship remained mainly a woman-to-woman affair. And, as for Richard, well . . . she was curious. And it would be interesting to see what Ned thought about him and the situation. On the other hand, she didn't want Ned thinking about black lace bras and women who wanted a fuck.

She ought to do something about that side of things. But she had a full list at the surgery first, so she pushed it to the back of her mind until her last patient of the day.

'I can't seem to fancy it, doctor,' said the large middle-aged woman perched uncomfortably on a chair beside Lucy's desk. She had iron-grey hair and a face like a currant bun, and her words echoed Lucy's own thoughts so exactly that Lucy was aware of giving a slight jump. 'You know . . .' she dropped her voice. 'It.'

She clearly didn't want to say the word 'sex', so Lucy filled it in for her.

The woman nodded, her chins wobbling like jellies at the thought. 'But he's very insistent. I do it some-times just to keep him quiet, but it turns my stomach, it really does. And he's said he's off if I don't do something about it.' She took out a tissue and blew her nose. 'I love him. I don't know what I'll do without him.' She put the tissue away. 'He says he loves me. He says I'm the only woman for him, but that a man needs . . . well . . . you know.'

Lucy did know. 'I think,' she said, as gently as possible, 'that this is really a problem you need to deal with together. It's not a question of your fault or his. I'm going to refer you to counselling.' She scribbled a name on a piece of paper, and paused for a moment while it stared up at her. Philip Gray. 'Now call here, and ask your husband to attend the session with you. Well, maybe you could go to the first few sessions alone if that would make you feel better, but I do recommend talking to him about it and seeing this through together.'

The woman nodded. 'I thought there might be some books or something. I don't like the thought of talking to strangers about . . .' Even at this stage of the conversation, the word 'sex' was still beyond her.

'It won't be as bad as you think, I promise. Good luck.'

As the door closed behind the woman's back view, which suggested several ferrets fighting in a sack, she tried to imagine herself discussing some kind of therapy with Ned. They were both doctors. Surely they were beyond all that? And, anyway, Ned didn't seem too unhappy about the situation. He grumbled, occasionally, but, as far as she could tell by the jokes amongst their married friends, this was all too common a situation. He'd hardly got to the point of threatening to leave. He might not even have noticed that they had a problem. No, it was probably better not to raise the subject unless he did.

As she made a note in the file, she noticed her patient's birth date at the top of the page. She was fifty-nine. So the problems weren't just going to go away. It was no good expecting time to sort out everything between Ned and herself.

Before she closed the file on the patient, Lucy wondered, idly, if there'd been some kind of abuse or violence in the background that might have made her wary of men. Well, that would be for the counsellor to find out. But she might use this patient as an excuse to ring Phil.

Phil Gray was a Cognitive Behavioural Therapist who was attached to the practice one day a week and spent the rest of the time working from a picturesque little cottage in a quiet village some miles away. He'd been something in the City for nearly twenty years, working long hours and coining huge bonuses, until, at the age of forty-two, he'd suddenly decided to re-train and 'put something back into society'. His wife, facing a significant drop in income, had promptly left him to marry another merchant banker and he'd moved up to the area, where several local divorcees had fallen on his now-single neck. But, seven years later, Phil had stayed single – and a subject of much local speculation. He often popped in to chat to Lucy when he was at the surgery.

'Phil?'

'Lucy.' He always sounded pleased to hear from her. She explained about the patient.

'There are some books you might like to recommend in cases like these. Particularly if someone's reluctant to come for counselling in person. Do you want to have a look at a few?'

The thought of borrowing books on sex from Phil was alluring. She and Ned, of course, couldn't possibly consult him – you could hardly discuss anything like that with someone who sat opposite you in meetings – and the next qualified therapist worked a good thirty miles further away. But perhaps it might be worth her having an informal chat with him, though . . . She could pretend she was talking about a patient who refused to come for counselling in person.

Mm. She drifted off for a few moments, looking out of the window at a leafless tree without really seeing it.

'Phil' she wrote in her diary for the Tuesday between Christmas and New Year, with a sense of anticipation.

By the time she got home she felt fuzzy with tiredness. Not quite all there. Owen and Nico had theoretically been in charge of Tom and Luke all day, and, as a result, the house looked ransacked. There were crisp packets all over the sofa, a half-played board game and some empty tins of Coke on the table, and layers of cushions, plates, books, magazines, balls and shoes over every possible surface. Tomato ketchup was smeared over one of the worktops and, as she walked across the kitchen, she was aware of her feet sticking to something tacky that had been spilt over the floor. Drawers and cupboard doors drooped open, and Christmas decorations were festooned over everything, there was a wobbly tree piled high with glittering clutter, and dozens of Christmas cards balancing on window ledges and side tables.

Lucy let out a roar, and three sheepish boys slithered down the stairs, agreeing to 'clear up'. Lucy supposed, as she lay in the bath, that she really ought to have an au pair again. She'd hoped that working three-and-a-half days a week would be the perfect compromise, leaving her enough time to run the home without having anyone else living there. It was like having another child around and potentially fraught with difficulties now that Nico was older. Visions of sobbing Brigittes, anorexic Anjas and sexually predatory Kirstens wearing crop tops or revealing nightwear at the breakfast table drifted through her mind.

Sex. It all came down to sex in the end. Was she worried about the Kirstens, Anjas and Brigittes because of Nico, or was it really about Ned and her?

And yet she knew that this was completely unfair to Ned, who had never, to her knowledge, so much as looked at any of their au pairs unless she asked his professional opinion on their anorexia, bulimia or flu.

Well, she didn't have time to think about it now. There was a major mopping-up operation to go on and supper to get before the Morgans arrived at 8 p.m. She was just about to dash downstairs when she caught sight of herself in the mirror.

If Grace was coming, she'd better put on some make-up. Her pallid, crumpled face looked so undressed next to Grace's carefully enhanced dark lashes and berry-coloured mouth. She ferreted about in her washbag to find a hardened lipstick, some dusty grey eyeshadow and a mascara that glopped a series of dark, sticky clumps onto her lashes. It was still an improvement. She looked less like a white rabbit and more like a woman.

'This place is a mess,' said Owen, emerging from the basement with a screwdriver, when she got down-stairs to the kitchen. 'An absolute disgrace.'

'If you don't like it,' Lucy had had enough, 'you can clear it up yourself. Really, Dad, don't you have the faintest idea about keeping an eye on the boys? What did you do when I was young?'

'I had nothing to do with you when you were young,' said Owen in tones of pride. 'Your mother did it all. Now there was a fine woman.'

'Well, men have domestic responsibilities, too, now.' She gave the floor a hasty mop-down before peeling the potatoes. 'Times have changed.'

'Not for the better,' replied Owen, heading upstairs. 'For anyone. You look absolutely exhausted. Working and then all this. I don't know. It isn't right.'

'Where are you going, Dad?'

He sighed. 'Fixing the handle to the bathroom door. That husband of yours hasn't the first idea about these things. He ought to have a proper toolkit.'

Lucy couldn't be bothered to explain that some people were good with toolkits and others with dangerously ill children in intensive care units and the two skills weren't necessarily interchangeable. It was a relief to have the handle to the bathroom door mended, anyway, and while he was about it, there were a few other jobs that needed seeing to.

At ten to eight, Ned got back from the hospital, his slightly battered face ashen with tiredness. He was one of those men who always looked as if he'd just got out of bed. He'd actually been asleep in the hospital canteen when she first saw him, sprawled over two chairs in a leather jacket, looking more like a motor-cycle messenger than a junior doctor.

'Who's that?' Lucy had been intrigued by the way he was able to sleep, like a cat, with all the noise and bustle and clattering around him.

'Ned Dickinson. He can sleep anywhere.' There had been a note of proprietorial disapproval in the nurse's tone.

Interesting, Lucy had thought. 'Doesn't he worry about snoring in front of people?'

'He doesn't care about anything very much,' the nurse had said, regretfully. 'He's so laid-back he's almost horizontal.'

Lucy had been stabbed by a sudden desire to make him care.

He'd opened his eyes and seen her. 'Who are you?'

'I'm Lucy.'

'Bed?' he'd enquired. There had been an easy gentleness about the way he said the word, as if he was comfortable with his own body, and would be tender with hers. Although a proper date would have been nice first. Not to mention a conversation. She'd wanted to find out why two nurses and a female doctor were hovering near him with such interest.

'In your dreams.' She'd stalked off, knowing that he was watching her.

He'd sought her out a few days later, and apologized.

'You're not in the operating theatre now,' she'd told him. 'One-word commands like "scalpel", "forceps" and "bed" won't have us all leaping at your every command.'

He had raised his eyebrows in acknowledgement. 'What would have you leaping at my command? Perhaps you could tell me over dinner?' He'd looked at his watch. 'Or rather, as I'm on call, a bacon butty in the canteen?'

She had hesitated, knowing that as they were both working such long hours, unless they snatched time when they could, they'd never get to know each other. 'A bacon butty would do nicely.'

'I like a cheap date,' he'd grinned.

'We're going Dutch,' she had informed him. 'If you want a date, it'll have to be dinner. And you'll have to ask properly.' She wasn't usually so confident, but somehow she had had faith in him. She'd known she could be herself.

When they'd each piled up their individual trays with carbohydrate to get them through the night, they hadn't been able to stop talking, the only ones left in the half-lit cafeteria. His bleep, miraculously silent, had gone at 3 a.m. He had looked at his watch in amazement. 'I've never had this long without being bleeped.' He had shaken it. 'Perhaps it's faulty.'

'Oh, no. We could have had three hours' sleep,' she'd pointed out. Sleep, in those junior houseman days, had been more precious than anything.

'Three hours of you is much better.' He had kissed her cheek. 'Same time tomorrow? Bleep me when you're free.'

She had liked the fact that he trusted her to contact him. He wasn't going to play games, or leave her waiting for phone calls.

Six weeks later they were living together.

Having recently finished a brief, irritating affair with

someone called Tony, who'd flipped if she put down a cup of coffee without using a coaster first, she had liked his casual attitude. And, although Ned had been one of those men who was rarely without a girlfriend – she'd caught him just after the end of an affair – he had generally been monogamous, which was a huge relief after her time with Tony's predecessor, Robert, who never came back from a party without at least three new phone numbers secreted about his person. And he had a steady, if demanding, job, which was an improvement on Nigel, Robert's forerunner – oh, all right, overlapper, if there is such a word – who had lived on social security and was so stoned all the time that he liked to say that if he died and was cremated, all the birds would fall out of the trees from the fumes.

And over the twenty years, he had remained relaxed, monogamous and in a steady job. There had been no nasty surprises.

He threw his coat over the banisters. 'Sorry. Operation overran. Complications.' He still spoke in short-hand when he was exceptionally tired.

Lucy's heart turned over. 'Bad?' All Ned's patients were children, and some of them were very sick indeed. Sometimes he came home white with defeat, and told her about the terrible news he'd had to break to parents who could usually scarcely believe what they were hearing.

He squeezed her shoulder before kissing her. 'Think we managed it. With luck. A sweet little girl with a heart condition. Just a bit more complicated than we'd realized. Still, as long as –' He looked up as a head of dark curls followed Tom's unruly mop out of the sitting room and upstairs with a drum roll of pounding feet. 'Who was that?'

'Luke Morgan. He's been here for the day while Grace was shopping. As company for Tom.'

Ned frowned. 'Shopping? He's been here quite a bit lately, hasn't he? I hope your new friend, Grace, isn't using you.'

A spurt of irritation flashed through Lucy. Men never understood. 'No.' She kept her voice deliberately calm. 'I don't think Grace is a user. She's had Tom over twice when I needed some help, and I feel she's one of those people I could call on any time. Here.' She opened a bottle of red wine and poured them both a glass. 'Have one of these.'

'Good. I just worry about you, that's all.' Ned took a gulp, put the glass down and put his arms around his wife. 'It's good to be home.'

Lucy leant into his warm, comforting body with its faint tang of the operating theatre and familiar smell of man, and tried to resist the sudden temptation to cry. He felt broad and safe and solid. The reassuring roughness of his coat brushed against her cheek as he gently turned her chin up for a kiss, but as soon as she felt the tip of his tongue between her lips, she curled away, like a snail retreating into its shell.

'They'll be here in a minute.' She drew away and stirred the potatoes.

If Ned knew that boiling potatoes didn't need stirring, he didn't reveal it. 'Of course. Give me two minutes for a wash, and I'll lay the table.'

Damn, she thought. Damn, damn, damn. Why does sex have to ruin a simple, affectionate cuddle?

By the time the doorbell rang, at twenty-five past eight, everything was done – although Ned had had a series of calls about the little girl with the heart condition, and Lucy'd had to put everything out on the table herself. But at least the crisis was over at the hospital and she was sitting down at the big round table in the bay window, listening to the distant, comforting roar of the sea over the common, and on her second glass of wine. Too much, she thought wearily, she mustn't drink too much or she'd have a hangover. It was so dull, always thinking about tomorrow.

Grace was first in the door, wearing leather trousers and a simple shirt in soft, honey-coloured silk. It was a beautifully understated, tactile combination. She'd left the top few buttons of the shirt casually undone, and wore a plain gold chain with a tiny diamond nestling in the hollow at the base of her neck.

'I chose black,' murmured Grace into Lucy's ear, with her low, confiding laugh. 'Do you think that's terribly wicked?'

Lucy suppressed a giggle, because Ned was watching them, suddenly alerted, like a hunting dog, by what appeared to be an exchange of feminine secrets.

Grace leant forward slightly towards Ned as she put out a hand to shake. The honey silk shimmered, revealing occasional flashes of black lace against the curve of a freckled breast. Lucy thought Grace did look sexy.

Judging from the blank, slightly pop-eyed expressions on Nico's and Owen's faces, they obviously thought so too. Grace leant forward again as she met each of them, kissing Nico because she was the sort of person who kissed everyone she'd met before, however briefly.

Once Owen and Nico had stopped goggling at Grace, their eyes swivelled round to Lucy and they both looked at her with the kind of bemused alarm that made her wonder if she was wearing her knickers on her head or had accidentally left her skirt off. Then she realized that they were probably both wondering what was different about her. As none of the men in the household ever seemed to care what she looked like, she'd completely stopped wearing make-up except for Ned's annual departmental ball. Putting on mascara was tantamount to announcing that you were about to run off with the milkman.

Nico went off to get Grace a drink without remembering to ask anyone else if they wanted one, and Lucy, after rounding up everyone else's orders, came face to face with Richard Morgan.

She'd expected someone puffed up with wealth and

with his own importance. Very smooth – probably even quite good-looking – with success embroidered all over his handmade shirts.

This Richard Morgan was smiling, hand outstretched. 'It's such a treat to be invited out,' he said. 'I spend all my life going to stuffy functions, and we hardly know anyone up here yet.'

He had a pleasant, open – yet outstandingly ordinary – face. A complexion that was ruddy enough to spell golf and beer, but not the ruby-terracotta shade that spoke of alcoholism or a lifetime outside. Not sex on legs, obviously, but then most men these days weren't. And Grace clearly wanted him. You'd have thought he'd have been grateful.

'This is my mother, Marjorie,' he added, guiding an elderly lady towards them. 'Aren't the decorations lovely?' He raised his voice to her, as if talking to a deaf child.

Condescending? Or kind to a confused old lady? Lucy hovered between the two conclusions. He passed her on to Owen, and almost immediately turned to Ned again, with a remark about house prices along the Bramsea seafront. 'This was obviously a very good buy. You must have got it for a song if you've been here over fifteen years. These streets have really come up in the past few years.'

Ned looked surprised. He never thought much about house prices, and anyway the Morgans' house was so much bigger, smarter and, being in Bramsea St Mary, in a more exclusive part of town. Once again,

Lucy wondered. A chance for Richard to point out his own relative wealth and knowledge of the property market? Or a genuine attempt to put the Dickinsons at their ease?

She came to the conclusion that she was the one at fault. She had been so determined to dislike Richard that she could hardly judge him properly. She must stop trying to turn round everything he said, looking for something to criticize about it. He was making an effort, and that said a lot about anybody.

'I do love your decorations,' said Marjorie, looking round the room and directing her comments at Grace.

'They're not my decorations,' said Grace, raising the volume of her voice while carefully keeping it kind. 'They're Lucy's. It's Lucy's house, you know. We're going back to our house later.'

'Lovely decorations,' sparkled Marjorie again, nodding and smiling at everyone, as she fussed about settling herself on a chair next to Owen, who'd intercepted Nico to talk about gardening before he could get Grace's drink.

'The thing about vegetable gardens –' Owen leant forward to direct his words at Marjorie as well, and Nico took the opportunity to slip away '– is that you have to do the groundwork. No wonder they grow these spindly things today. They don't know the meaning of double-digging.' He rumbled on while Ned distributed glasses of wine.

'So,' she heard him say to Grace, 'I gather you've been leading my wife astray.'

Grace giggled. 'I hope you don't mind.'

Ned grinned. 'Why not? You're only middle-aged once.'

'*Brief Encounter*.' Grace recognized the quote. 'My favourite film. I cried and cried and cried.'

'Did you?' Ned was surprised. 'I think she loved the nice, sensible, safe husband, after all, and went on to have a long, happy life and lots of adoring grandchildren.'

'That's because you're not a romantic,' challenged Grace.

'On the contrary, it's because I *am* a romantic,' he contested.

Lucy, keeping half an ear on this conversation, decided to intervene. Ned sometimes loved to wind people up. 'Don't let my husband bully you, Grace.'

'Bully? Chance'd be a fine thing,' joked Ned putting an arm round Lucy, and Grace obliged him by giggling again. 'This wife of mine, she runs me like a train, you know.'

'Yes, you're always late, and in urgent need of repairs.' Lucy suppressed a moment of irritation at the childish feeling that Ned and Grace might gang up on her.

'There's something really lovely about Christmas, and all its decorations, don't you think?' asked Marjorie, with the sprightly air of someone delivering a new and fascinating insight. She twinkled at Owen, and raised a glass to him.

'I make my own compost, you know,' he added.

'It's all in the compost, that's what you have to realize. That's how I've got to eighty-two without a single illness. Eating home-grown vegetables, grown with the right compost.'

'Eighty-two?' replied Marjorie with a sudden, disconcerting flash of sanity. 'You don't look eighty-two. You look very young to me.' She nodded and smiled again.

'Bloody woman's after me,' rumbled Owen in an audible undertone to Lucy. 'They can't resist a spare man, can they? They're after one's back collar stud as soon as look at one.'

'Sh.' Lucy nudged her father. 'Don't be rude.'

'Nonsense,' said Owen in a carrying voice. 'She won't understand. She's completely loopy. Makes no sense at all. None of you women make any sense.'

Lucy sighed. 'Dad.'

'All right, all right, I know when I'm out of line.'

'I like your decorations,' said Marjorie to Nico, who was dutifully circulating with a bottle.

She beamed vacantly around, and Owen, who, whatever he said, liked to have an audience, turned to her again. 'I start work on the garden in January, you know. Just because the ground's hard, it doesn't mean there aren't chores. That's where so many people go wrong . . .'

On the whole, thought Lucy, it was all no worse than lots of conversations at parties. There was no real need for topics to intersect in any way, she supposed, unless the people speaking really wanted them to, and both Marjorie and Owen were perfectly happy to have someone to talk at.

'What a nice little boy,' said Marjorie of Luke, as he helped himself to some crisps in a bowl beside her. She looked at Lucy. 'Is he yours?'

'No.' Grace raised her voice slightly. 'He's your grandson, remember? Luke?'

Marjorie gave a high social laugh, as if to imply that she'd been making a joke. 'Of course, Luke. Of course.'

She fumbled in her bag and gave him a two-pence piece. 'There you are. I know boys like to have a bit of money. Now don't spend it all on sweets.'

Lucy saw Richard fix Luke with a stare, and Luke dutifully thanked his grandmother with every appearance of pleasure.

'The decorations are lovely,' she heard Marjorie tinkle, in the tones of a socialite entering a room for the first time. 'Simply lovely.'

Grace had told her that sometimes Marjorie repeated the same phrase over and over again, twenty or thirty times in an hour. She wondered how Grace managed to keep her temper.

'Never mind the decorations, for heaven's sake,' grumbled Owen. 'Listen to what I'm saying. You women never listen.'

On her left, she could hear Richard quizzing Ned on what he did, asking him if he knew various friends of his. They were all senior to him, and one, whom Richard described as 'an excellent golfer, really a first-class chap' was Ned's direct boss. Richard was older than they were, Lucy remembered.

'I've been involved with fund-raising for your lot,' he said. 'I feel it's important to do a bit of charity work. Give a bit back to society, you know. We've installed those new machines for the special care babies. They should make your job a lot easier.' He chuckled. 'The great thing about them is . . .'

Ned was treated to a five-minute discourse on how a machine that he used every day worked, but he just smiled. He was too kind and laid-back to challenge Richard, thought Lucy, although she could hear him getting several points wrong. She'd better step in to rescue them before he made a complete fool of himself. He was trying a bit too hard, she thought, but you couldn't hold that against him.

'Ned, do you want to start serving everyone? It's just buffet-style, but we'd better get the children and the oldies sorted first.'

Ned squeezed her shoulder in acknowledgement of the rescue, and her heart warmed as he dropped a kiss on her forehead. 'OK, babe. Hm. Looks good.' Still with his arm round her, he turned to Grace. 'Lucy's chicken curry is the best you'll get this side of India.'

Grace looked at Ned hungrily.

Once everyone had gathered up their plates from the buffet and found somewhere to perch, she came to sit on the arm of Lucy's chair.

'I think it's so lovely when men praise their other halves in public.'

Lucy suppressed surprise. She'd never thought about it.

'And I love your house,' Grace continued.

'Oh, er . . .' Lucy looked around as if she'd never seen it before. It had taken them years of stripping, sanding, polishing and painting to reclaim the bones of the house from under the boarding-house fire doors, cheap woodchip wallpaper and smoke-stained varnish. They'd done it themselves where they could, but even so, there hadn't been much left over for decorating – the big, light rooms had white walls, stripped wooden floors and were filled with Ned's parents' furniture, which was not always what she would have chosen. But it had the comforting air of home, and, for parties, filled with people, lots of candles, a big vase of white lilies on the mantelpiece and a log fire, it made her feel happy.

'You look great. I haven't seen you wearing make-up before.'

'Oh.' Lucy blushed. 'I just thought I would. I've rather lost the habit though, except for a splash of lipstick.' Sometimes she thought Grace praised things a little too much – surely everything couldn't always be wonderful. Still, it was so much more life-enhancing than the constant drip-drip-drip of complaint from someone like Josie Saunders.

'You'd look good in eyeliner,' mused Grace.

'Funnily enough, I wore eyeliner every day of my life until . . .' Lucy thought. 'Well, until Nico was born, I suppose. Then everything became such a fiddle, and when I tried it again, years later, I'd lost the knack. I looked like an extra from *Zulu*.'

'Mm. It's all a question of technique.' Grace assessed her. 'Look, I start my New Year New You sessions on the tenth of January when the schools are back. What if you and I have a practice session beforehand, and I could try out my spiel on you, and you could try out a few new looks?'

Lucy felt that she could hardly refuse, although the thought of being coerced into altering a wardrobe packed with loose-fitting black or navy clothes with elasticated waists was truly horrifying. 'Um. Er. Well, if you're sure . . .'

It wasn't until she was stacking a few plates in the dishwasher that she got the chance to talk to Richard. He appeared in the kitchen doorway.

'Do you mind if I smoke?'

She was disconcerted. 'Oh, of course not.' He seemed to be a model of consideration to others so far. He stood just outside the door, so that she was aware of him, and of the plume of smoke curling up from his fingers.

'You don't have to do that outside, you know. We don't smoke ourselves, but we don't mind the odd fag. We're not obsessive about it.'

This was her chance to find out more about him.

Out of the corner of her eye, she'd been monitoring him all evening, and had noticed him talking to Owen about gardening, murmuring something knowledgeable about the organic debate as she edged past with a bottle, and then she'd overheard him advising Nico on what A levels the world of industry and commerce looked for these days. He'd even bent over to Tom to talk about how cricket and football had changed in schools since his day (not a lot, by the sound of it). Far from being the stuffed shirt she'd expected, he seemed genuinely interested in everybody.

'So what made you move up to this part of the world after the excitement of London?'

'I was born here.'

'Oh, where?' This surprised her.

'At the cottage hospital.'

'As it was then,' she filled in, helpfully. 'It's a minor treatment unit, now. You'd have had to be born in one of the big town hospitals now.'

The conversation faltered to a complete stop at this point. She tried to think of something else to say, but all she could summon up in her mind was 'Why don't you make love to your wife?', which was obviously out of the question. The thought blanked out any other, until she eventually came up with, 'It's been so nice getting to know Grace. She's great fun.'

He nodded, and stubbed out the cigarette, grinding it into the ground with his shoe and then kicking it into the darkness. 'I travel a lot, and she's on her own rather too much. So she's enjoyed meeting you too.'

This was progress. It might actually turn into a proper conversation. Lucy wondered if there was any button she could press to reveal the real Richard. She studied him as she tidied up around him, prodding him to say more about why he'd come back to this part of the world. He managed to tell her that he'd always intended to return. The chance to set up an office in Norwich had been a dream come true, but he knew it had been hard for Grace to leave her friends and her life in London.

She'd expected a suit – an expensive, beautifully tailored one with an exclusive silk tie – but he was wearing an open-necked shirt and pullover. She'd expected him to fill the room with his confidence, but he seemed polite and even slightly reserved. She suspected him of being a little dull. Perhaps Ned could get more out of him. She resolved to discuss it all with him. Just as long as talking about Richard and Grace's sex lives didn't lead on to having to say what they each thought about their own sex life.

Hm. That way danger lies. So perhaps better not to mention it.

She indicated the door. 'Shall we join them all again?'

Nico, with his shock of bright blond hair, baggy jeans and sweater, came in as she left the room, to find another bottle. 'We've run out of red.' As she saw Richard glance up at him, another reason for Grace's problem occurred to her, with a jolt.

Perhaps Richard was bi-sexual. There was no mistress tucked away in a sleepy Norfolk village, but there could be a young man, with long, strong limbs and a sullen resignation to Richard's regular return to his wife.

But he didn't seem in the slightest bit interested in Nico.

Really, he seemed to be a nice, ordinary man who loved his wife and family. Too ordinary, if anything. Perhaps Grace was neurotic. She heard Ned's familiar shout of laughter in the other room, followed by an echoing ripple of amusement from everyone else. Some story of his that she'd already heard twenty times, probably.

5

Christmas passed in a welter of trailing present wrappers, a queasy-making mixture of alcohol, cold remedies and an endless succession of meals, padded out by unnecessary festive snacks that lingered on plates everywhere, uneaten even in a house populated by normally starving adolescents. Christmas cake languished on the sideboard like an icon from a former culture, along with all the other detritus of the festive season – empty boxes, undelivered presents and things, like ugly vases or garish place mats, which had no obvious place in life and were ultimately destined for the next school raffle.

It was a relief to get back to the surgery on Tuesday and Wednesday, particularly as few people seemed to bother to get ill between Christmas and New Year.

At lunchtime, Phil tapped on her door, came in and sat calmly on the chair beside her desk, laying a pack of sandwiches on her desk. Phil did everything calmly. Lucy sometimes suspected, from odd things he'd let slip, that his wife had actually divorced him not so much for changing career but for remaining utterly and completely unmoved in the face of flooding washing machines, failed GCSEs and towed-away cars. Nothing seemed to faze him, which made

72

him a perfect colleague. But, although it would be bliss to have more calmness around, perhaps being married to that kind of impassive stoicism might have been infuriating on occasion.

'My treat.' He indicated the sandwiches.

'Thanks.' She looked at him. You could tell he came from London because his dark hair was shaven-short, belonging more to Soho than Bramsea. He was wearing his usual clean, pressed jeans and a charcoal lambswool sweater, and there was a stubbly shadow across his chin. He was spiky all over, with the short hair and the dark, streaked stubble almost fusing into each other, but Lucy instinctively knew that if you were to stroke it, it would feel surprisingly soft, just as if you talked to Phil, the cool exterior occasionally revealed a glimpse of a man who could be unexpectedly warm. How did he keep it exactly that length, Lucy wondered. Was there the shaving equivalent of a lawn-mower that could be set to shear a few millimetres above the skin? And could she ask him? Phil gave the impression of a man who guarded his secrets warily; although, if you asked him something, he usually, after a certain amount of thought, gave a full and satisfying answer. But Lucy was constantly aware of a line drawn between them – or perhaps it was a line drawn between Phil and the rest of the world – and she was careful not to step over it and intrude.

'What are you looking at?'

She smiled. 'You. I was trying to imagine you in a

City suit. I've never seen you in anything but jeans.'

'I didn't like suits.' He flashed her a quick grin. 'So I left.'

Lucy took a bite of the sandwich and felt her headache diminish. 'Just what I needed. Tom was sick twice in the night, then the cat upchucked her breakfast on the carpet. I could write a bestseller called *Everything You Ever Wanted to Know About Sick But Were Afraid to Ask*.'

Phil smiled in acknowledgement. Lucy was always conscious of the difference between his controlled, organized single life and her mad scurry through a pile of toppling laundry, her crates of supermarket shopping and endlessly juggled appointments. She hadn't seen Phil's cottage, but according to the local divorcees it was 'amazing'. Very modern, apparently, with a huge, sexy sofa in porridgy colours and out-standing modern art acquired during his days in the City. There were no pets and just two twenty-some-thing children who occasionally appeared but who scarcely counted in the day-to-day scheme of things. So far no woman had managed to hang on in there very long, but no one knew whether Phil got bored first or whether they found something awry beneath the perfection. His relationships always seemed to end amiably to the extent that it was very difficult to tell whether a girlfriend was past or current.

'So. Patients with sexual problems.' Phil's voice was as even and understated as the rest of him. Sometimes Lucy just longed to bottle it, and unstopper a whiff when Ned was roaring at the boys about leaving their kit about. Just to remind herself that there was a life on the other side.

Lucy told him, carefully disguised, about Grace.

'Mm,' said Phil. 'Forties. That's the peak time for affairs for women.'

'Really?' Lucy couldn't think where they all got their energy from. She tried to imagine fitting in an affair between dishing out the fish fingers and counting the games socks. How did people manage it?

'And men's libido starts going down.'

'Does it?' Lucy wished she didn't sound like an echo. Ned's libido appeared unchanged as far as she could see.

'Although not always,' added Phil with another grin, and she suspected he was talking about himself. 'But if you've got a heavy smoker or a drinker, or a diabetic, or someone who is stressed, on anti-depressants or with high blood pressure, well . . . loss of interest in sex and impotence is always a possibility. Not to mention all the more serious diseases, such as cirrhosis or AIDS.'

'I suppose so.' Lucy, who theoretically knew all this, realized she'd got so hooked on the mistress – or master – theory that she hadn't been thinking like a doctor. 'God, I hope he hasn't got anything like that. I'm sure his . . . er . . . wife would have mentioned any medication.'

They munched companionably on sandwiches, although she was aware of taking smaller, more careful bites and discarding half of it in the waste-paper basket. There was something about Phil that made her want to suck in her stomach.

'He may just not fancy her any more, of course,' Phil suggested.

'I think she's very attractive. For a forty-something.' Lucy wondered if it was only she herself who thought that Grace actually looked beautiful. Perhaps men were only interested in twenty-three-year-olds.

'I like forty-something,' said Phil. 'Nice and uncomplicated.'

'Phil!' She blushed.

'I'm just saying –' he rolled up his sandwich paper and threw it across the room, hitting the bin with perfect accuracy '– that from a personal point of view, speaking as a man not a counsellor, women are very sorted by then. They're not trying to have your babies and they've got their own money and their own lives to lead. They're quite powerful.' He looked at her. 'I find that attractive.'

'Oh.' Lucy felt anything but powerful; but then, she was a happily married woman. She thought of the different women she'd seen around town with Phil. Powerful. Maybe.

'Anyway, I digress. This isn't helping your patient. Sorry about that.'

'Don't you ever want to get married again?' She hadn't intended to be so personal, but she did question whether his immaculate life might not be a bit sterile.

There was a pause, and she wondered if she'd

stepped over that invisible line that marked out his privacy.

But he replied quite easily. 'In principle, I do. I mean there are a lot of reasons why it's better to have someone else alongside you in life. And I see people with good marriages like you and Ned, and I feel quite envious. But when you split from someone you discover a different part of yourself and that makes it complicated. I don't know if that part would survive in a marriage, even a good one. And now I've found it, it would be difficult to let it go.'

Lucy thought she knew what he meant. She thought about the easy comradeship between her and Ned, the comfortable Saturday nights in front of the video, the shared jokes and the 'family hugs' when Tom, still a cuddly little boy at heart, drew them both together so that he was sandwiched between them. They'd all lean into each other's warmth and draw strength from it. But Phil, with his grown-up children, had passed through that stage of life, and unless he wanted to start it again with someone much younger, he had a different set of parameters now.

'Anyway, back to the patients,' murmured Lucy with difficulty. 'That woman I had in here the other day is worried about hating sex with her husband. It must be something to do with their relationship, don't you think? Or some kind of early trauma?' She held her breath, not meaning to.

Phil looked thoughtful. 'We're still pretty much in the dark ages as far as understanding female sexuality is concerned. It's like male impotence around thirty years ago when all they had to deal with it were a few psychological tactics. Fine for some, but hopelessly inadequate overall. But since then it's been the focus of most research, which equals more understanding and more cures. Like Viagra, and penis implants. And all that. But women . . .' He looked outside at the grey skies. 'No one knows much about women. There've been studies showing that fifty or sixty per cent of women have problems with sexual response or difficulty in achieving orgasm. But quite a lot of them say they still enjoy sex, which is baffling for us men.'

'Oh, it's the old lie-back-and-think-of-England principle. Except we're probably thinking of Ibiza or France or somewhere exotic these days. Anything to keep the old man happy.'

She swallowed, wondering how much she'd revealed. She didn't want to be disloyal to Ned.

'Anyway,' his voice was gentle, 'it's not something people initially ring me up or come in about.'

She shrugged. 'Me neither. They don't like admitting it, I suppose, even these days. The odd patient starts off coming in for back ache or depression or something, and then over a number of sessions, the subject of sex suddenly pops up. They usually think they're not doing it enough.' She wanted to go on talking to Phil about it all indefinitely, but she didn't want to talk about herself. Well, she did.

They studied each other. He smiled. 'That's exactly it. It doesn't seem to matter what patients come to me for in the first place – anxiety, phobias, depression, anything – we get to about session three, and then it all comes out. Everybody in the world thinks they're not doing it as much as everyone else, and that worries them. From people who have to have it at least once a night to those who just about manage once a year. They all think everyone else is doing it more, enjoying it more, and is better at it.

'Anyway, your patient.' He pushed over a couple of books. 'Have a flick through these and see if you think they're suitable as recommendations.'

'Oh, yes. Of course.' Lucy wanted to make a joke. Get everything back onto an easier, less personal, track. She caught a glimpse of a diagram on the first few pages. 'I see it's one of those books that starts by telling you how to inspect your own vagina. They used to have seminars on that in the 1970s apparently. Does it do any good, or is it just a load of self-indulgent twaddle?'

'It can be quite helpful, apparently,' said Phil. 'Not that, as a mere male, I've tried it myself. I think some women are slightly afraid that that part of themselves is ugly, and that inhibits them with men.'

They exchanged, with a sudden twinge of shocking desire on Lucy's part, a look of complicity. They seemed to have stopped talking like professionals, and almost begun to talk like lovers. She remembered the days of the Mileses and the Gileses, when you actually talked about sex. Usually just before or after doing it.

'Oh, well, let's see how poor old Mrs Thing gets on with it.' She laughed. 'Although how anyone who can't even say the word "sex" is going to manage to inspect herself with her legs akimbo and a mirror, I can't imagine.'

Phil's face cracked in a smile, and she thought he was going to get up and go, but he cocked his head at her. 'And you? How are you?'

'What do you mean?'

'I just wondered if there was anything on your mind. Sometimes recently, I've thought you seemed a bit down.'

Lucy suddenly wanted to wrap her arms around him and rest her head against his chest. Just to feel some simple, gentle strength from someone who didn't need her to collect some dry-cleaning or cook a meal in return. He would know, she thought, he'd know about women's bodies and why they don't work sometimes, and she felt that sudden, unfamiliar warmth inside her deepen to an ache at the thought of his hands caressing her. But she forced her attention back to sitting opposite each other on two swivel chairs.

'I think it's just domesticity getting me down. There're the boys, and Ned, and Dad lives miles away and needs ferrying to his hospital appointments for his eyes . . . Oh, and I don't know. I love what I do, and I love all of them, but sometimes I think, Is this it?'

He grimaced. 'I know what you mean. That's what

I felt about being in the City. That's why I came up here and changed everything.'

'But I don't want to change anything. I've got everything I ever wanted. Really. I'm fine.' She couldn't quite identify the source of the itch herself.

'Well, I'm here if ever you want to chat. Sometimes all this —' he indicated the surgery '— gets a bit much, I know. Just come and dump on me any time you like.'

Lucy could feel colour rising up her neck. 'And you, too, Phil,' she forced herself to say, feeling embarrassed at the thought he might think she was coming on to him. 'Just drop in any time. You must find things, er, a bit much, too, sometimes.'

He stood up and grinned, leaning forward to kiss her on both cheeks, and she could feel his face briefly rasp against hers. That was very Soho, too, she thought. When colleagues said goodbye in Bramsea, they hovered uneasily between a handshake and a kiss and usually settled for bobbing around and blushing but doing neither.

Or had it been an excuse to come close? She could feel the texture of his cheeks for several moments afterwards, reliving it in her mind. Perhaps he had really wanted to kiss her.

'I'll see you then.' She flicked through the books, and wondered if she ought to pass them on to Ned. Tell him that if he put away *Yachting Monthly* and *Paediatrics Today* and read about her body instead, she might be more enthusiastic in a certain department.

She had a brief vision of him coaching the boys at football. He and they would go on perfecting a goal, a pass or a kick for hour after hour in complete father–son symmetry. The thought of that kind of intensity being turned onto summoning up a response from her body was more than she could face. And he was so obliging that if she suggested he read books about sex, he'd read books about sex, however bemused he was by the request. What if she just wasn't sexy any more? Perhaps she was simply past it.

On the other hand, talking to Phil about it, however indirectly, had definitely stirred something up, although she suspected that the pecks on the cheek hadn't been anything more than his usual sophisticated way of saying goodbye. Feeling much happier, she pressed the buzzer for the next patient.

The following day the subject of change came up again. What was it about everyone at the moment?

It was her day off, and she was spending it with Grace, going through Grace's New Year New You programme.

'Now.' Grace stepped back and folded her arms. 'What do you want to achieve?'

'Achieve?' The thought of achievement made Lucy feel tired.

'What do you want out of this transformation? People usually have a goal in mind when they come to these sessions.' Grace sounded briskly professional.

Lucy was too polite to say that she was here because

she'd been railroaded into it. 'Well, I . . .' She looked around for inspiration.

'What do you want to change?'

'Nothing.' The much-loved faces of Nico and Tom swam into her vision. She had no desire to trek the Himalayas or start her own company or do all those other things that she read about women doing.

'Come on.' Grace was smiling. 'This is me. Grace Morgan. You can't fool me. The first thing you told me was that you wanted to change your life. Or some of it.'

'Did I? I can't remember.' She couldn't, she really couldn't. The evening in the wine bar was bathed in a retrospective glow of friendship and discovery.

'You're being very difficult,' Grace teased. 'Now just pick something, anything, that you'd like to do differently or sort out about yourself. Out of the blue. Even if it isn't very important. It could be anything from looking good at a cousin's wedding to wanting to wear nail varnish.'

Lucy rummaged in her mind for an event she wanted to look good for. The following Tuesday, when Phil Gray was due in the surgery again, was a possibility, but she suppressed the thought

Grace drew up a chair and sat down next to Lucy. 'Shall I tell you something?'

Lucy knew that this would be a bad idea even before she nodded.

'You're very pretty.'

Lucy opened her mouth.

83

'Don't get me wrong,' warned Grace, 'but you're hiding behind all those swathes of black clothes and that hair . . .' She got up again and picked up Lucy's fuzzy, charcoal hair, gathering it up in her hands and shaping it, her eyes meeting Lucy's in the mirror. 'See. It's too long, it makes your face seem down. It needs shape. And colour.'

This was true. It was now at the dull iron-grey end of the spectrum. Lucy flushed.

'But,' Grace repeated, 'you are very pretty, you know. Richard said so, too, after he met you.'

This was embarrassing.

'But we can't do the hair today, so let's start on the make-up. And the clothes. We'll go down to London for the hair.'

Being looked at again felt strange. It had been so long, and there had been so many changes. She'd never laid claim to 'beautiful', but had assumed that the time for 'pretty' or 'attractive' had gone. She'd refused to mourn them. She'd envisaged only goals like 'well-dressed' or 'well-preserved' or 'smart' lay ahead and they seemed so unutterably dull that it was hardly worth aspiring to them.

'I know I'm being tough,' said Grace. 'But you need it. Or you're just going to go to waste.'

'I've got a patient,' said Lucy suddenly. 'She looks like an ageing prizefighter and her husband wants to make love to her. And she doesn't want to. She really can't face it. Do you think that part of her problem is that she feels bad about the way she looks?'

Grace sat down again, and took her hand. 'I think feeling bad about how you look really doesn't help,' she said, gently.

Holding another woman's hand made Lucy uneasy so she left her hand in Grace's soft one for as long as seemed polite and then carefully withdrew it, as if she needed it to push a bit of hair behind her ears.

She hoped Grace didn't think she was talking about herself. Sometimes she found the intimacy that Grace generated almost overpowering.

'But, also,' Grace added in warning, 'perhaps she doesn't love the husband any more.'

'She says she does. Or, at least, she needs him.'

'It's not the same thing,' said Grace quietly. 'Is it?'

'No,' admitted Lucy. She desperately needed to change the subject. 'Did the black lace work?' As soon as she asked, she realized that this was a terrible point in the conversation to ask that question.

Grace efficiently pulled out some make-up brushes and frowned over a succession of bottles of foundation. 'This one looks about right.' As she rubbed a small patch of the creamy substance onto Lucy's skin, she added, 'No. I'm afraid it didn't. We went out a lot over Christmas, and both Luke and Marjorie needed attention. So we didn't get much time on our own, and when we did he was really tired. I've never seen him so whacked, so I didn't bring it up.'

The doctor in Lucy wondered about that. Was it normal for a healthy fifty-something man to be exhausted all the time? She resolved to keep an ear open for any other symptoms and perhaps even suggest he get a blood test. Particularly, and her heart went cold for her friend, if her theory about a man rather than a mistress being at the root of Richard's absences was correct.

'Richard wasn't at all how I expected him to be,' she said, suddenly. 'I thought he was . . .' Now she'd dropped herself in it. She still hadn't worked out what she thought about him. '. . . nice,' she concluded. At least that was true. He was a bit pompous, but he wasn't the domineering, successful businessman she'd feared.

'He's very popular at the golf club,' said Grace. She rubbed another strip of foundation on Lucy's jaw and turned her chin towards the light. 'Hm. That's better. We have a good life together. Just not . . . in that way. Still, I suppose it's better than being married to a tiger in bed who's constantly running off with other women or can't keep a job down.'

Lucy wasn't sure that that was necessarily the complete range of options open to Grace, but decided not to say anything. Talking to someone about her husband was as dangerous as walking over hot coals.

'Well, anyway!' Grace sounded determined to be cheerful. 'My new year's resolution is to forget about sex.' She began stroking foundation over her friend's cheeks with neat, practised movements.

She stood back. 'The secret to your life is eyeliner.'

Lucy laughed. 'That simple?'

'That simple.' Grace took a tiny enamelled box out

of a toolbox stacked with make-up. 'I'm going to give you your face back. Then you'll be able to tackle anything. And I'll feel confident enough to tackle five women from a reading group in Bramsea St Mary who have decided they need a New Them.'

6

A cottonwool mist seeped in from the sea the following day, muffling the fragile cream and white
houses in cool, damp air. It was a day for ghosts,
thought Lucy, sniffing the salty chill on her way to the
surgery. She hoped it would burn off by the time she
had to drive Owen home. He'd been with them for
almost a fortnight, which was about four days too
long for everyone concerned, and he'd been twitchy
with impatience to get back to his greenhouse once
he'd fixed all the odd jobs around the house.

Lucy was wearing eyeliner, the way Grace had
showed her, and every time she caught sight of herself
in the mirror, she saw more life and definition in her
face than she'd seen for years.

'You're looking well,' said Polly, the receptionist at
the surgery. 'Is that a new sweater?' And one of the
older partners, Michael, who usually more or less
ignored her, walked through the surgery while she
was checking her lists with Polly, stopped, and simply
stared. She felt like telling him to close his mouth.
Eventually he stopped goggling, and said good
morning, with more warmth than usual.

'Morning, Michael.' She tried not to laugh.

By twelve o'clock, surgery was over, and the sun

shone cold and bright. She even felt a tingle of anticipation at the thought of driving away and winding
through the small, apparently deserted villages.

'There.' Owen slammed the car door with relish,
as Lucy revved up the engine. 'Now that should keep
even you two going for a bit.' He began to list the
door handles he'd screwed back on, the curls of lino
that he'd stuck down and all the odd bits and pieces
around the house that had been falling apart until he
came along.

'Thanks, Dad.' Lucy felt weary with the effort of
all the gratitude expected. But it did help. Neither she
nor Ned had the time or patience to fiddle around
with toolboxes.

'Oh, I know you're busy,' his voice softened. 'Just
glad to be of help.'

Lucy was touched. 'Well, you are a great help. And
it's been lovely having you.' She could say this with
conviction now that the end was in sight.

'You've done a good job on those boys.'

'Have I?' Lucy was surprised. It was rare for Owen
to compliment her on anything. He must be growing
soft.

'Nicky got a girlfriend yet?'

'Nico,' she replied, automatically. 'It's Nico,
remember?'

Owen grunted in disapproval. 'Well, has he?'

'I don't know. There seem to be a lot of girls
around.' She knew the sub-text of this conversation.
Owen never stopped worrying about whether one of

his grandsons was going to grow up a 'pansy' and had been deeply worried by a leather thong with a silver bead on it that Nico wore round his neck, not to mention the hours he spent in the shower, emerging in great gusts of Lynx aftershave. 'Honestly, Dad, Nico will find his own way. Whatever it is. There's no stigma any more.'

'Hmph.'

They drove in silence for most of the winding miles, but when they got to Owen's cottage he seemed reluctant to let her go.

'Have a cup of tea.' He fussed around in the kitchen, opening cupboard doors and shutting them again without taking anything out.

'Really, Dad, I should be off.' She looked at her watch. 'I hate driving round those roads in the dark.'

'Five minutes won't hurt.' He sounded gruff. 'Anyway I want to talk to you.'

What on earth about? Lucy was irritated but forced herself to sit quietly on the sofa while he made the tea, painstakingly pouring milk into a little jug and putting two biscuits on a plate. Just get on with it, she wanted to scream.

Finally, he settled down.

'My dear.' He never called her this. 'I've got bowel cancer.'

Lucy talked about such things every day in the surgery but was unprepared for the wave of panic that swept through her. 'Thank God you've come to me in time.' She put a hand on his arm. 'The treatments these days are wonderful. It'll hardly be more than . . . than . . . than . . .' She flailed around for some trivial treatment and couldn't think of one. 'We'll get you through it.'

He shook his head. 'Bit late for that, my dear. It's quite far advanced. They're talking months. Maybe years, but not many. I'm dying.'

'No!' It was a cry of pure pain. Lucy couldn't believe it. Medical miracles could happen. Every time she'd left Owen in the past few years, she'd always said goodbye as tenderly as she could, and had driven away thinking that it might be the last time she ever saw him. She had expected him to keel over in the middle of his cabbages, or fall asleep in his favourite chair. Because that was the way he wanted to go, and Owen, in a sense, was still the all-powerful father of her childhood. If Owen said he wanted to have a quick, fatal heart attack in the potting shed, well, she had the utmost faith that that was what he would do. In her own mind a part of him was still omnipotent. The thought that he might not be shook her to the core.

'Why didn't you mention it to me earlier?'

He snorted. She knew why. There was no way 'Daddy' was going to talk to his darling daughter, even if she was a forty-nine-year-old doctor, about 'down there'. She was astonished to feel her hands shaking, but made an effort to pull herself together and ask the right questions about symptoms, treatments and experts. It wasn't the same when you were talking to a member of your own family, she thought. But she had to stay calm, for his sake. She mustn't break down. It would only make him feel worse.

'Do you need me to take you to hospital appointments?' Selfishly, her heart sank. Her days were so tightly packed anyway. She began to mentally run her eye down her diary to see what she could get rid of. Everything seemed essential.

'People round here can do that. The Brightmans have offered. And Mavis Fletcher. Most of the time, anyway.' She knew how much he hated being dependent on people. Until he'd lost his licence he'd been the one to offer lifts.

Aware of tears stinging her eyes, Lucy kissed him goodbye. 'Will you be all right here on your own?'

Owen harrumphed. 'Don't be silly. Been alone a long time. Didn't want to spoil Christmas, you see.'

She squeezed his arm, and forced herself to smile and wave as she drove off. He stood at the door until she could no longer see him in the car mirror.

The journey home turned unexpectedly into a crazy fairground ride. Lucy missed a turning, did a three-point turn to get back onto the road and reversed the car into a lamp-post, got distracted and went up on the verge at least twice (luckily no one was around), carved up a juggernaut at a roundabout, and, finally, as she realized that her hands were shaking, she parked in a lay-by, and laid her head on the steering wheel, images of Owen running through her mind. Running to greet him at the door when she was five, jumping up into his great strong arms and being whirled round, laughing. The endlessly sunny days of a walking holiday in Scotland when she was ten, trudging across the heather after his tall, confident figure as the smell of pine cones sharpened the air. His face, full of pride and love, when she stood at the door of the church about to marry Ned. The way he patiently played chess, and even Warhammer, with Tom, quietly on the little boy's wavelength in a way that no one else in the house had time to be.

And finally the handle he'd mended on the bathroom door, and the other jobs he'd worked his way through. He might be an infuriating old man at times, but he was still so very much her father. And soon he would be gone, and she would never be a daughter to anyone again.

She wasn't sure how long it took her to realize that she couldn't sit in a lay-by in the dark indefinitely. She had to carry on.

As she drove back past the dark fields and into town, she passed the high wall of Grace's house, and saw lights blazing over the top of it. On an impulse she drew into the semi-circular gravel drive, and parked.

Grace's face lit up when she answered the door. This instant response was one of the things that Lucy liked best about her – the way her voice brightened on the telephone when she called, and the look of real pleasure that would cross her face when she first saw Lucy. 'Hey! You look as if you need a drink.'

'Is Richard here?' She didn't want to intrude, or to make polite, pointless conversation with Richard.

Grace merely rolled her eyes in exasperation, and led her through the welcoming kitchen to grab a bottle of white wine.

'Come and tell me all about it.'

Lucy got as far as gasping a few muddled words as she sank into the welcoming embrace of the battered leather chair. 'I know I'm being silly. He is eighty-two.' And she drew her knees up to her bowed chin and began to cry.

Later she was to wonder what had happened to her homing instinct, and how it had become so damaged that she had headed for the lights of Grace's house rather than back to Randall Road, where Ned's broad shoulders were waiting.

7

After Lucy had given Grace a muddled account of her father's illness and how she felt about it, Grace touched her gently on the arm. 'But that's not all, is it? There's definitely been something worrying you for a while.'

Tears and alcohol, and the suddenness of Grace's question, broke down all Lucy's defences. 'I just don't like sex any more. I can't feel anything. It's like being completely numb from the waist downwards. And for a while, I just managed to go on doing it, but now when Ned wants to –' and she put her head on her arm again and sobbed some more.

Grace waited quietly, not judging, or trying to comfort her. She just let it all come pouring out.

'So when do you think it all started?'

Lucy shrugged. It seemed like a problem that had been with her for ever, although she knew it hadn't.

'OK. Let's go back to the beginning. When can you last remember sexual pleasure?'

'Sexual pleasure?' To Lucy this sounded as if it was a contradiction in terms, and she gulped down her wine. 'I did once have quite a strong sex drive. I thought. I mean, I can remember a whole weekend once . . .' She suppressed the memory. She'd never talked about her past to Ned, and had got into the habit of pretending it had never happened. 'I can't remember exactly when it stopped being enjoyable. I mean, at the beginning, it was all so muddled up with having a boyfriend . . .'

'And where the relationship was going,' agreed Grace. 'I remember that.'

Lucy nodded. 'And what he expected, and whether it was right to sleep with him or not, and, once you'd decided that, whether you were *doing* it right.'

'And what he'd think of your body.'

'Well *you* wouldn't have had to worry about that. I had cellulite from the age of nineteen.'

'But at least you had tits. At least, I presume you did.' Lucy and Grace both looked at Lucy's comfortable shape and then at Grace's angular torso, and laughed.

'Tits were just another thing to worry about. Did they pass the pencil test?' Lucy remembered the mortification of being told that breasts were supposed to be perky enough for someone – some spotty boy, she thought – to be able to place a pencil beneath them without it staying in place. 'I could have wedged a whole pencil case under mine quite comfortably, which meant they were too droopy.' She sniffed and blew her nose. 'I failed the pencil test.'

Grace poured them both another glass. 'Well, it's not like A levels, or anything. It doesn't get you into university.'

Lucy smiled weakly. 'It might. You never know.

And even if the tits were fine, then you'd have to worry about whether he'd ring again afterwards . . .'

'And then there was the biological clock, and should you be doing it to have babies?' Grace sighed. 'I never really believed that you could leave it too late, but we did. For two children, that is.'

'And then you had to worry about whether you were a tease for not sleeping with a man and a slag if you did. Although I don't think anyone ever dared put it in those terms,' Lucy added. 'But I often felt it lurking like a hidden agenda. It seemed terribly unfair, you weren't supposed to sleep with too many men, but you *were* supposed to sleep with whoever you were going out with at the time, *and* you ought to be brilliant in bed. Without apparently having had much practice.

'I remember reading glossy magazines from about the age of twelve, and from then on, they were like my bibles,' she continued. 'And they told me everything I needed to know about sex. I thought I was an expert. But it was all about it being a performance, like this is what you need to know to be good in bed. Not about what you really feel. It's only recently that I've thought about what I would actually like to do, as opposed to what I ought to do. And I feel cheated, because it might be too late.'

'I don't think I knew anything,' said Grace. 'My mother told me – didn't all our mothers tell us – that if you sleep with a man, he won't respect you, and that if you wanted to get married then you had to save it for Mr Right. I didn't exactly save it, but I felt I had to keep men at arm's length. As if they were dangerous.' Grace, judging by the photographs around the house, had been one of those glamorous ice queens, thought Lucy, those beautifully, fashionably dressed girls with an air of 'don't touch me' sealing her in a world of her own. She'd probably frightened off a lot of men. Richard obviously had a great deal of confidence in himself.

'Mm.' Lucy picked at a hangnail on her thumb and began to chew it. Then she giggled. 'I do remember one bloke telling me I was terrible in the sack. And I remember another telling me he'd slept with a woman who had amazing internal muscles that she could ripple. It made it all a bit like being the worst at rounders again. I always felt that I was just terribly boring and inexpert in bed.'

Grace, who did not have hangnails, eyed Lucy's thumb with disapproval. 'It wasn't your fault. Haven't you heard the saying, "There are no frigid women, only clumsy men"?'

'Well, it's not easy for them either.' Lucy liked to see everyone's point of view, although that occasionally made it difficult to determine her own. 'I mean, as a woman you can get by with wiggling your hips and moaning, but men actually have to do something. Anything that goes wrong with them is all too obvious. They have to have a hard-on, for a start.'

'Mm,' said Grace. 'They do.' Lucy saw her eyes flicker to the wedding photograph on the mantelpiece of herself and Richard. It was in an ornate silver heart-shaped frame, and showed a conventional happy couple, she with clouds of white muslin around her face and a tumbling bouquet of roses in her hand, and he flashing a soppy smile like a labrador. They looked untouched by time, as if they'd been newly minted for the day.

'Any luck?'

Grace shook her head. 'Either I really do forget about sex – and it isn't easy, I can tell you – or it's going to have to be affairs, I'm afraid. Or an affair, anyway.'

'I'd lend you Ned,' said Lucy, feeling worried. 'Except that I think it'd be a total disaster. I'd mind so terribly, you see.' It was the nearest she wanted to come to saying 'hands off'.

Grace laughed. 'That's sweet of you, but I don't do marriage-wrecking. I'm just looking for a little light diversion. What I need is a landscape gardener.'

'A gardener?'

'All my friends in London have affairs with their landscape gardeners. They're so strong because of lugging wheelbarrows and slabs of York stone around, and there's something terribly sexy about all those shoots and fronds springing forth under their hands. And, of course, they're around during the day when husbands are at work.'

'I don't think they have landscape gardeners in Bramsea. Just horny-handed sons of the soil, aged about eighty-five. They'd be very good at dealing with infestations of warble fly, but I don't think they'd be up to anything more demanding.'

'It wasn't horny hands I was thinking of,' replied Grace, with a glint in her eye. 'Aren't there any male masseurs? Personal trainers? Bodyguards, even?'

Lucy shook her head. 'No gigolos either. The entire concept of a service industry, as it is known in Wandsworth, Putney and Fulham, has yet to arrive up here.'

Grace sighed. 'I shall have to hope for a nice window cleaner, I suppose. I presume the inhabitants of Bramsea do have their windows cleaned?'

'You don't even want to find out.' Lucy shuddered.

'Well, never mind. Let's get back to you. Have you seen any professionals?'

'Hardly,' Lucy said. 'Not in my position.'

'No, well, perhaps not. What about self-help books?'

Lucy was aware of having to articulate just slightly more carefully in order to sound sober. 'I've read a few. They seem rather male.'

Grace raised an eyebrow.

'Well –' Lucy tried to formulate something very, very important, but it eluded her. What was it? She had another sip of wine. Oh, yes. 'Well, they concentrate on different positions. Press this button, rev her up and pow! I mean, if you don't want to do it in the most comfortable position, you'd hardly want to do it in a more uncomfortable one, would you?'

'Er. No. But you used to enjoy it? Have orgasms?'

'Oh, God, yes. Masses. You sort of had to, really, didn't you? It was all part of the performance, I suppose. Unless you were into faking it, and I'd feel so silly. All that gasping. No good at lying, me. What about you?'

'Things were good between us, you know.' She sounded as if she was trying to convince herself. 'Before we had Luke, I suppose. Unless, of course, he was going through one of his "I'm not ready to be tied down" phases. As for orgasms. When things were good between me and Richard, I could have two sometimes.' Grace looked wistful.

Lucy spluttered into her drink. 'Two! No wonder you like sex. I've never met anyone who had two before.' She thought for a bit, or tried to stop a series of unconnected ideas from bouncing off the ceiling, which came to much the same thing in her state of mind. 'Actually, no one's ever told me how many orgasms they have. Perhaps everyone has two and I'm a freak.'

They looked at each other. 'I'm sure you're not.' Grace sounded uncertain and almost frightened. 'It's more likely to be me.'

'Unless we're both normal.' Lucy cheered up. 'Anyway, orgasms. I did have them. Ages ago. I think you can learn them, really, like squash. Something you can get good at, if you try, even if it doesn't come naturally at first. I was never any good at squash, either. Maybe I ought to train myself back into orgasms again. When Nico's finished his A levels and the choir's rehearsals for *Carmina Burana* are over. And when the reading group suggests a book that's a little less meaty than *The Poisonwood Bible.*'

'Can't you think about sex as fun?' suggested Grace. 'More fun, for example, than doing the washing-up. That's what it ought to be, now, because all those pressures have gone. All the original reasons – finding a partner, having a baby – well, we've done all that. Society doesn't expect anything of us, sexually. In fact,' there was a trace of bitterness in her voice, 'society doesn't really expect us to have sex at all.'

Lucy thought that was a bit hard. 'Yes, it does. Look at all those "Forty and Fabulous" features in *Hello!* and *OK!*. TV presenters in black basques. And all the other forty-somethings that do the Oscars with backless dresses. I'm sure sex is allowed at our age now. It never used to be, of course.' She began to theorize in a mildly drunk fashion. 'Any woman who did it was branded a witch or desperate. Perhaps the Government or the Church was secretly worried that if men kept bonking not-very-fertile forty and fifty-somethings, then the human race would die out, so sexy mature women had to be demonized.'

'Mm.' Grace thought about it. 'It's different in Europe, though. The Latin countries want to keep their young girls pure until marriage, so if young men are expected to get any practice in – and I think they are supposed to know what goes where by the time they go up the aisle – it has to be with older, married women. It sounds an excellent system.'

They giggled. 'And all we white Anglo-Saxon Protestants have got as a role model is sad, sexually frustrated Mrs Robinson,' mused Lucy. 'Forced back into her pantry with her cupcakes for wanting a bit of fun.'

'I think this age is enormously liberating, sexually.' Grace sounded so brave and unafraid. 'It's now only a question of whether you want it or not. That's why I say I just want a fuck.'

'Be careful, Grace.' Lucy tried to make her brain feel less hazy. Thoughts were weaving in and out in a random fashion. 'Believe me. I see it in the surgery all the time. There's no such thing as safe sex. And by that, I mean the whole mess your life gets into.'

Grace didn't want to hear. 'I think,' she said, dreamily, 'that this must be how men feel. Young men. The ones who just want to get their end away. I don't want to wreck my life. I don't even want to change it. I don't want to divorce Richard, or anything. I just want a bit of excitement.'

Lucy sighed. She could see that Grace didn't need much more of this before she did something that would change things for ever. But if Grace was behaving dangerously, then so was she. Ned, easy-going, essentially faithful, affectionate Ned, was still a man, and if he didn't get what he wanted, he, like Grace, was going to start looking for it elsewhere. She would have to have more sex, and not think about whether she liked it or not. She could probably manage once a fortnight, just by gritting her teeth and getting it over with. And that would probably be enough to satisfy him. He didn't need to notice.

'Might it be the menopause giving me more testosterone?' asked Grace, clearly still wedded to her theory of women-as-men. 'Doesn't that mean a higher sex drive? More male hormones meaning a more male attitude? I mean, sometimes, you know, I even fancy women. And that never used to happen.'

Lucy was startled. Did this explain Grace's sudden desire to be friends?

But there was nothing about the way Grace was sprawled elegantly across the other armchair that indicated any desire for physical closeness. 'For God's sake, Grace. I've told you. Hormones are complicated things. You do have more male hormones now than you did in your twenties, but I really, really wouldn't want to say that's the reason why you want to fuck your builder and walk away without having any sort of relationship.'

'But it might be?' teased Grace. 'Just possibly?'

'Don't count on it.' Knowing that she'd have a terrible hangover in the morning, but deciding it was worth it, Lucy topped up her glass again. 'Anyway, I don't believe that you do want sex without any of the emotional stuff. If that was the case, you might as well use a vibrator. I'm sure you could get sex from somewhere, but I don't think it would satisfy you. And if Richard found out, which he definitely would in Bramsea . . .'

'If he was ever in Bramsea . . .' interjected Grace.

'He'd find out. Sooner or later. I mean there's nowhere to have an affair round here.'

Grace leant forward with interest. 'Now that really

is what I've always wondered about infidelity. Where do people actually do it? I mean, you can hardly disport yourself in your own house, with your children about to come back from school, and your mother-in-law and the cleaning woman, and neighbours who see which car is in the drive, not to mention your husband who comes back unexpectedly sometimes. And isn't it a bit yucky – not to mention hideously expensive – to go to a hotel? And how would you start an affair? I mean, you can't ask a married woman out, so what do these landscape gardeners do? Suggest that you come and look at their beds of delphiniums?'

Lucy shrugged. 'Well, there are four hotels and fifteen guest houses in Bramsea, an extremely posh hotel in Bramsea St Mary and a doss house in Bramsea All Saints, and I can't imagine anyone checking into any of them for a few hours in the afternoon. Not without it being talked about in every pub by the evening.'

'What do your patients say?'

'Well, the affairs are usually only mentioned in the context of the sexually transmitted disease or the unwanted pregnancy they generate,' she paused to allow this to sink in, 'so I can't exactly ask where they had it off. Can I?'

'Well, I wish you would. And report back to me. I mean, cars are just too uncomfortable at our age, and anyway, even if you parked in the most rural spot, some chap would turn up in a tractor . . .'

'Or you'd get ramblers or twitchers. With their

binoculars. And groups of primary school children on Nature Discovery Trails.'

'I think the world was less crowded in Lady Chatterley's day,' mused Grace. 'They had summer houses and follies and gardener's cottages. And they still got caught.'

'What I can't understand is how people get from flirting to doing it.' Lucy was thinking of Phil. The space between his chair and hers when they chatted in her surgery was less than a couple of feet, but it might as well have been a chasm. There was no way a decent man – and Phil was nothing if not decent – was going to lean across it and say that he found her attractive. If he did. Or kiss her on the basis of a bit of flirting that he might, or might not, have noticed. The thought stirred something deep down inside her. She felt warm and relaxed, thinking of Phil kissing her, and his hands gently touching her.

She wrenched herself back to the conversation. 'When we were younger and single, it was all so much more clear-cut. You knew if you were out on a date, so you knew if someone fancied you. It was more a question of when either of you would make the move rather than if.'

'I just can't imagine that move from standing there formally in your clothes a few feet away from someone to being in their arms,' said Grace. 'It seems such an incredibly big jump. I think you'd need to be cooped up with someone and unable to get away. Marooned together in a mountain hut, and cuddling up to each other for warmth, or something?' She looked puzzled. 'It does all seem rather contrived and unlikely. I mean, one just wonders how you'd get to the mountain hut in the first place. It's a bit difficult to visualize.'

'How do people in offices manage it?' asked Lucy. 'Isn't that where most affairs happen?'

'The disabled lavatories.' Grace spoke with authority. 'They're unisex and there's masses of space. There was a couple in the office where Richard last worked, who used to go there every lunchtime, but, of course, it got caught on the security cameras, so everybody knew about it. Even so, I still don't see how you get around to it. Do you suppose people have conversations about never having seen the inside of the disabled lavatory, and then the other one saying they'd love to show it to them some day, and then they pencil it in their diaries?'

Lucy couldn't help giggling. 'Well, the only disabled lavatory I've got access to is in front of seating for about twenty patients. It would cause a great stir if I went in there with Phil Gray, however we staggered our entrances and exits.'

'Who's Phil Gray?'

'Phil Gray is just about the only man in Bramsea you could possibly have an affair with,' said Lucy, with a huge sense of regret welling up inside her. But if she was going to hang on to Ned, she couldn't be selfish about Phil. And he was so calm and nice that he'd look after Grace and give her back her faith in herself without hurting her. 'He's got a cottage. All by himself.'

Grace looked interested. 'Attractive?'

Lucy couldn't help smiling. 'In an unconventional way. He's not good-looking or anything, but...' Describing Phil was beyond her in her befuddled state.

Grace raised her eyebrows. 'Are you sure I wouldn't be treading on toes here?'

'Absolutely not,' Lucy reassured her, hiccuping again. 'As you know, I have no sexual feelings left.'

'Hm. But tell me more.'

'Well.' How could you define Phil? She concentrated on the kind of facts that would be required for a 'Wanted' poster. Height. That sort of thing. The image of Phil wavered in her mind's eye and almost disappeared. 'He's got very intense eyes, that's what you mainly remember about him, although I'm not quite sure if they're blue or green. Quite a shock with the dark hair, anyway. The rest of him is sort of average. Slim. Tall. Lanky-tall. Nice-ish. I'm no good at this.' She sighed. 'Supposing he went missing and I was the only person who could put out a description of him? He'd stay lost for ever. Oh, I know. Very short hair. Conscious design decision rather than just balding. Bristly. You want to run your hand over it.'

'Sophisticated,' agreed Grace. 'Much the best way to go these days.'

'About our age. And he's got designer stubble. Darker than the hair. And only a tiny bit peppery-and-salty.'

'Yum,' said Grace. 'You do seem to have very good

recollection of parts of him. That reminds me, we had a wonderful Australian au pair before we left London who told me that the fashion now is for designer stubble pubic hair. Now that's the sort of thing I presumably need to know if I'm going to have an affair.'

Lucy was temporarily flummoxed. 'Well, it's not a fashion that's arrived up here if what I see in the surgery is anything to go by. And wouldn't it be a bit like making love on sandpaper?'

They looked at each other, and Lucy suppressed a giggle.

'Still, I suppose it's easier than shaving it into a heart shape like everyone did in the 1990s,' added Grace.

'They did?' Lucy felt she must have missed the 1990s in that case. In fact, she had. Nico, and then Tom, had been effective distractions from the dizzy concentric circles of hair fashion, pubic or otherwise.

'Richard likes me to keep it properly pruned, but he says he doesn't mind about the shape.'

That was big of him.

'I mean sometimes I wonder if it's things like that that are putting him off. Perhaps I'm not careful enough.'

Lucy was lost for words. Any such demands from Ned would have been the equivalent of an Intercity 125 train driver complaining about Railtrack's maintenance of the hedgerows around a tunnel mouth as the train roared into it. And it was difficult to reconcile the image that she'd seen of Richard as a very ordinary, loving, if rather asexual, husband with the despot who had views on bikini-line stubble that Grace liked to portray. Again she wondered if Grace was just a bit too neurotic.

'Anyway,' she was struck by a pang of conscience. 'Even in an affair, I'm sure that what you feel about him and what he feels about you is more important than how you shave your pubic hair.'

'You are sweet,' said Grace, absent-mindedly. 'So high-minded. But, we digress. Phil. How do I get to meet him?'

'Well, I'd like to have him to dinner.' Somewhere in the recesses of her addled brain, Lucy summoned up enough common sense to hope that she wasn't making a huge mistake. 'So I'll invite him, and you can see what you think.'

'What I think . . .' Grace stretched out her bare toes and luxuriated. 'I think that you fancy the socks – or maybe I should say, the pants – off Mr Phil Gray. And I think dinner would be a very good idea, because you can ogle him, and I can flirt with him, and you can go and work off all those feelings he stirs up on your heavenly husband, and I can angle for an invitation to his lonely little cottage. And we'll both be happy.'

'Do you know what?' Lucy suddenly felt that Grace was the dearest, cleverest and most sensitive friend she'd ever had. 'That'sh a smashing idea. Just smashing.' And she flopped, with an inelegant thud, onto the arm of the chair, into sleep.

Grace later told Lucy that she'd phoned Ned, who had been worried about where his wife was. He'd chortled with relief, and had said, 'Getting rat-arsed is probably just what she needs after all the work of Christmas. Don't worry, I'll come over and shift the corpse.'

'Ned is such a lovely man, you know,' Grace told Lucy enviously when they next spoke.

'I do know.' The guilt washed over her and she pushed thoughts of Phil away. Ned was lovely.

8

Lucy woke up, not only with a crashing hangover, but with the realization that something she had tried to prepare herself for was, indeed, finally happening. That a disaster she'd rehearsed in her own mind, over and over again, to lessen its pain, had arrived. Today was a day that had once been perpetually in the future, and was now, incontrovertibly, here at last. It hurt just as much as if she'd never been through all the mental preparation. Her father was going to die, and the news was as fresh and as painful as if she'd never thought about it before.

She felt frightened, and sick, but the sick was probably just the alcohol. She turned her head to see Ned looking at her, his face crumpled and yellowing with the night's rest. He looked old, suddenly. She probably did, too.

'Feeling rough?'

She winced. 'Did Grace tell you?'

He hesitated. 'Yes. Is that OK?'

She nodded.

He put an arm out and she rolled into it, smelling the acrid scent of sleep. Ned's shoulder was soft under her head, and she wondered when that had happened. He'd always felt so firm, like a block of carved wood.

He now seemed fleshy and vulnerable. Everything she'd taken for granted seemed to be shifting. 'Ned?'

'Mm?' His arm tightened around her.

'Nothing.'

'Silly.' But he kissed her forehead, and drew his other arm around her, rocking her gently. 'You'll want to spend some time with him.'

'I haven't got any time.' She spoke into his chest.

'We'll find you some.'

It was all very well for him to say that, but she knew that it couldn't be magicked out of nowhere. It would be the end of reading novels about Japanese stokers, and she'd have to pull out of the choir. All the things she enjoyed.

But she hugged him tightly, in the hope that she could recapture the days when she'd thought he could do anything, and as she did so, she thought, this is the only man I'm ever going to sleep with again. It seemed an incredible thought.

That is what marriage is, she told herself. Not having sex with anyone else, ever again.

Once upon a time, there were always possibilities. She'd grown up to be told that she had a right to sexual satisfaction. That she could do with her body what she wanted. She hadn't made use of that freedom. Now it had gone for ever. She wished she'd appreciated the opportunities for what they were at the time. Diversions. Pleasure. Never serious. This was serious. Lying in bed, thinking about the death of someone you loved.

She didn't care about the lost diversions. Did she?

He stroked her cheek. 'Are you OK?'

Ah. Sex. Not now. She could spot it coming. She turned over and pushed her back against him, half affectionately.

'Of course, you're not.' He answered his own question. 'I'm sorry, baby. Is there anything I can do?'

She was torn between saying, 'Yes, the laundry' and 'Whisk me away, now, for a few days of passion in Paris.' But they couldn't do a few days in Paris. They had jobs – responsible ones – that required lots of forward planning before time off. The boys needed looking after. Even the goddam guinea pigs and hamsters needed feeding. The infrastructure they supported was so complex that the effort of replacing themselves in it for long enough to get away would in itself be a major exercise. There could be no spontaneity.

No. Running away, which is what she wanted to do, was childish.

And you can't be childish when your father is dying.

Was it worth sharing all that with Ned? Did he sometimes want to run away as well?

She studied his dear, irritating, familiar face as he looked down on her. 'I wish –' she began.

'Shit! Is that the time? Bugger. Operation this morning.' He began to hop round the room, pulling on his trousers, odd socks, his tie awry . . . No wonder he missed out on promotion. He looked like a medical student who'd been left out in the rain, and had come in all crumpled.

'Sorry, darling, what did you wish?'

'Nothing. I can't remember.' She felt angry.

'Tell me this evening.'

She swung over the side of the bed with a sigh, and looked at her watch. Would Grace be up yet? In the school holidays, the mad dash up to eight fifteen and school leaving time became a sluggish amble. Tom switched on the television at 7.15 a.m. and stayed there, blank-eyed, until about ten o'clock, while Nico remained an immobile lump in a darkened room until about midday. Bad mother, she reminded herself. Bad mother. Good mothers would have them doing something improving, like tennis or chess.

In the silence of the bedroom, she began to regret pushing Ned away. If you had love, if you actually had it there in front of you, not remote like Grace and her virtually telephonic relationship with Richard, you should never take it for granted because you never know when it might get whisked away from you.

She rolled back into the bed again, and turned her face into the pillow, feeling too sad to be able to cry. She'd better get up and cope. That's what she was good at. Ring Owen and make some proper plans for helping him. Find out what he really needed.

Owen was tetchy and independent. No, he didn't want her to take him to any hospital appointments. He'd already told her that. She had quite enough to do as it was. He wasn't sure about coming to Sunday lunch. It seemed rather a long way.

'We'll come to you, Dad.' Why did he have to make himself so deliberately unlovable? He'd always been like this at times of emotion – prickly and gruff. Her heart sank at the thought of trying to steer him to some kind of peace, at the daunting prospect of telling him she loved him. When Sarah, her mother, had died suddenly of a bewilderingly early heart attack at the age of forty-eight, everyone had said that that had been the worst of it. The not being able to say goodbye, or to tell her how much she was loved. But when it came down to it, would she and Owen be capable of those sorts of conversations?

She was better at practical help. 'If we come to you, I'll bring the food.'

'It's a lot of trouble for you,' he grumbled.

'I *want* to take trouble.' Even now, he was still trying to be her father, all-powerful and in charge – the one who did things for her, not the other way around. He didn't want to betray any weakness. The realization pierced her with sadness. 'Tom would enjoy coming out to the country,' she added, to persuade him, knowing that Nico had passed the age for family Sunday lunches unless he really didn't have anything better to do.

She unwound the coils of the telephone cord as Owen grumbled away, suddenly realizing that in a few years' time, there'd be no family. Nico would have gone. Tom would be almost adult. And Owen would be dead. There would just be Ned. The two of them.

Owen reluctantly conceded that it would be all right for them to come. 'But don't bring any vegetables. I can't abide those tasteless supermarket thingies.'

Now all that remained would be to persuade Tom and, if possible, Nico, that for the next few months, Owen would need to see more of them. The one good thing was that she knew she could rely on Ned. He wasn't the kind of husband who would protest at having to spend most of his precious Sunday driving to and from his ill father-in-law. Ned was always generous, and deserved just as much love back. Ned definitely deserved more than she was giving him at the moment.

Meantime, she needed to get Nico at least semi-conscious and remind him that he was in charge of Tom for the morning.

She strode into his bedroom and ripped the curtains open. There was a grunt of protest. She sat down on the side of his bed, and put a hand on the lump of bedding. 'I need to tell you something.'

A bloodshot face, pocked with one or two raw adolescent spots and the faintest trace of stubble, appeared over the edge of the duvet. He'd been so beautiful and blond just a few years ago. Like a cherub.

She told him about Owen.

He shot up. 'Shit, Mum. Is Grandad going to die?'

'Don't swear,' she said, automatically. 'I'm sorry.'

He glared at her as if it was all her fault, pulled the

bedding back over his head again, and turned his back on her with a grunt.

'Nico?' She shook the duvet. 'Nico, please.'

'Leave me alone.' His voice was muffled. With sleep, irritation, grief, or all three. She never knew these days. Nico might as well be on another planet. Should she stay and insist they talk it through? She looked at her watch.

'I'm not going to tell Tom that Grandad's dying, just that he's ill. OK? But you're old enough to know the whole truth.' Was that true? Was he, in some ways, just as much of a child inside as Tom was.

The duvet rustled and a red eye appeared over it. 'So you're going to lie to him?'

'Well, no, not exactly . . .' She trailed off. Perhaps there wasn't a right way or a right time to tell anyone these things. Surely there was some middle way between brutal honesty and lying? She floundered. 'I mean, ultimately, obviously . . . but for now I'd be grateful if –'

'If I just lie when Tom asks, as he will ask, if Grandad's going to die? Fine.' The last word was delivered in a derisive snort. 'You've always said it's important that children aren't brought up in a house full of secrets. You *said* that you always urge your patients to be completely straightforward about these things with their children.' The duvet twitched over his head again, muffling the words, 'It's all do as I say, not do as I do around here, as usual,' to the extent that she wasn't sure whether he'd said them.

Bad mother again. Useless, hopeless mother. She would have been impressed with the length and coherence of this conversation – particularly before breakfast – if she hadn't already noticed that Nico could summon up the loquaciousness of a prosecuting barrister if he had a point to make about the deficiencies of her and Ned as parents. Well, at least it proved he could talk.

It was hard to tell whether his reaction was just the raw selfishness of youth, or whether he was more upset than she'd expected. She'd thought that because he had his own life and his own friends, kept secretively to himself, that he wouldn't really care deeply about what happened in the family. That he'd just accept it, as a 'bummer', and move on. But perhaps she'd been wrong. It was probably better to let him come to terms with it on his own. She closed the door softly, feeling that she'd failed him somehow.

At least she had Grace. Grace would make her laugh. Grace offered one thing that no one else could. Fun. A chance to relax.

9

Grace didn't let her down. Lucy looked out of her window at 7.30 a.m. several weeks later to see the mist curling away to promise a crisp March day. Tiny crystals of snow dotted along the Victorian terraced roofs of the Old Town and windscreens of the cars parked along the street. The tops of dustbins looked as if they'd been dusted with icing sugar. Not proper snow, then. Just a hint. A warning from the weather about travel.

'Are you really off to London with Grace just for the day?' Ned made it sound as if she was planning a trip to the South Pole.

'Of course.' She opened the bathroom door to head off any more questioning.

'You haven't really told me what you're going to do there.'

'Haven't I? It's not a mystery . . .' And she turned the shower on, full blast, and stepped into it. Aargh. The water was still cold. With any luck, he'd forget about it by the time she got out. She had an extra quick shower, because she had to get the boys up and breakfasted before Grace arrived.

Tom refused to wake up, and she eventually had to drag him out of bed, pulling his pyjamas off and forcing his school clothes on, almost deafened by his howls of rage. It was like wrestling with a piece of farm machinery. Nico, who was now too old for such indignities, was more difficult, but eventually agreed to surface from a mound of bedclothes. Nico was going to take Tom to school on the bus, and Grace had persuaded her cleaner to pick up both Luke and Tom from school afterwards and give them tea. So the day would be theirs, once she got everyone out of the house.

Lucy hadn't had a whole day to herself for longer than she could remember. 'Come on, Tom! Please! Just get on with it!' There was no answer. 'Tom! For Christ's sake!'

He stumbled downstairs and put his arms round her, burying his head in her sweater. 'I love you,' he mumbled. 'I love you lots and lots and lots.'

'Oh, Tom. I love you, too.' And she rubbed his sleepy head, kissing it and feeling guilty. Just when you felt most infuriated by children, they could wrong-foot you by turning back into the babies you'd cherished. She shouldn't be shouting at them just because she wanted to go to London.

She still hadn't quite decided whether what she was going to do there was really a bit silly. But she felt a sense of excitement, as if she and Grace were sneaking off to have an affair.

Eventually the door closed on satchels, games kit and grumpy boyish faces, and opened on Grace, shivering like a saluki in her leather jacket and a black scarf spangled with gold glitter. 'Jesus! I'd have worn thermals if I'd known it was going to be like this! You'd never think it was March.'

When they were finally settled opposite each other as the train rattled out of the station and across the curving, frosty landscape, Grace pulled out a thermos. 'Real coffee.' The whiteness of the wintery sun was harsh on her face, making it look sallow, but then she smiled and the tissue-paper folds highlighted her angular cheekbones and dark laughing eyes.

'So,' said Lucy. 'We're off to the smoke in search of satisfaction.'

'Titillation.'

'Excitement.'

'Provocation.'

'Definitely provocation.'

They smiled at each other.

'And a decent haircut for you, at last,' added Grace.

Lucy raised her eyebrows. 'We do have hairdressers in East Anglia, you know. There's no need to be quite so snobby about it.'

I'm sure you do, but I haven't found the good ones yet. Someone told me there was a brilliant girl in Ipswich, but I don't know her name. And, obviously, neither do you.' She beamed at Lucy to diminish the insult. 'A good haircut is the best investment a girl can make. Economize on anything else in the world, but never hair.'

'I used to have smart haircuts. They just got lost somewhere along the way.'

The sun had bleached the fields of almost all colour, but far away, near a brown fringe of mud, Lucy saw a tiny horse lift its nose, sniff the air, and break into a gallop, wheeling round the muddy grass, and then stopping again just as abruptly, as if it had suddenly wanted to test its freedom, and then decided it was too much bother.

'And this . . . Sh! . . . place . . . we're going to . . .' Lucy hesitated, 'isn't going to be full of sleazy old men in dirty macs?'

'Apparently not. Men are only allowed in with a responsible woman.'

'Hm.' Lucy took a sip of coffee. 'As you know, I'm very responsible. But just run it past me one more time.'

'I love the smell of London,' said Grace, as they waited for the Tube. 'A sort of dirty metal scent. It smells of money changing hands, and people rushing everywhere in cars and trains, and machines that never stop. You've always got the feeling that anything could happen.'

As they settled themselves in a half-empty carriage, Lucy prodded Grace. 'Look,' she whispered. Grace followed her gaze. A magazine lay discarded on the seat opposite, with the word 'SEX' clearly emblazoned across the cover. Lucy had discovered, quite early on, that, in the world of work, it was a huge advantage to be able to read upside down as it gave you an opportunity to glean interesting details from other people's desks. After squinting a bit, she could see what it was about. 'It's a contact magazine,' she murmured. 'Men looking for women. Women looking for men. People looking for other people.'

Grace paled slightly. 'Scary. Imagine meeting a complete stranger with that in mind. I mean, it could be anyone on this Tube.'

They looked around. There was a tramp smelling of urine, a tired-looking young girl drooping over a novel and an old man muttering to himself.

'Of course, it's not the rush hour,' Grace added. 'You'd see a bit more talent then.'

The doors slid open and a smartly dressed man in his forties stepped on, looking up and down the carriage. His suit was clearly tailor-made, his briefcase and shoes shone with privilege, and a touch of grey distinguished a mullet cut as his hair flopped over a well-chiselled, if slightly weatherbeaten, face. His tie was pure silk, and a cashmere coat was neatly folded over his arm.

Grace and Lucy raised their eyebrows at each other. 'Not bad,' hissed Lucy. 'Don't you think?'

'Mm.' Grace nudged her to be quiet.

The man spied the magazine, picked it up as he sat down and tossed it onto the seat beside him in disgust. Grace and Lucy hid smiles. 'I think he's shocked,' murmured Lucy, raising a newspaper so they could talk about him without him noticing.

'Mm,' whispered Grace, eyeing his signet ring as

he, in turn, shook out a copy of *The Times*. 'Probably married to a Camilla, and does his PA on the side. Both missionary position.'

They all got up to get out at Oxford Circus. Out of the corner of her eye, Lucy saw the man look around hastily, drop his briefcase over the contact magazine, and scoop them both up together. When she turned to look at the seat it was empty.

'Of course, what we should have done,' said Grace later, 'was tap him on the shoulder and say, "Excuse me, that was my magazine." I wonder how he'd have got out of that one.'

'It looks like Camilla and the PA weren't quite enough for him, after all,' said Lucy, visualizing him circling a name, and turning up to a meeting in an anonymous hotel, while his wife entertained her girlfriends in Surrey. Perhaps no one is ever satisfied and everyone is just waiting for a chance to cheat to drop into their laps like a stray magazine.

By the time they rang the Sh! doorbell in Hoxton, Lucy's hair had been cut into a bouncy bob, and the colour had been subtly sharpened up. 'God, talk about taking ten years off in one afternoon,' pronounced Grace.

Lucy felt good. She'd caught a man's eye at Old Street underground station, and he had quickly looked away. She'd forgotten what it was like to be looked at.

When Grace had suggested that they should visit a sex shop, she'd been appalled at first, thinking of dark, menacing places selling red crotchless satin knickers, manacles and penis-shaped ice cubes.

'But this was started by women for women,' Grace had explained. 'After all, it might have something that would help one of us. You did say that if all I wanted was a fuck without any emotional ties, then I might as well try a vibrator.'

'Isn't it a place for lesbians?'

Grace hadn't thought so. 'Well, not necessarily. It seems cheerfully heterosexual to me. Their website is bracingly jolly-hockey-sticks. Rather Famous Five Start a Sex Shop in tone. 'It's how Enid Blyton or Angela Brazil would have written about needing a sexual lubricant – or "lubes" as they call them – if that sort of thing had been required in the dorm at midnight. It makes me feel positively normal.'

'Couldn't we just buy from the website then?' Privately, Lucy had realized that 'lubes' would undoubtedly be a help in her particular situation, and, as a doctor, she should have thought of that before.

'We could,' Grace had agreed, 'but apparently the most . . . er . . . stimulating things – according to an article I read in *Cosmopolitan* – are some extraordinary vibrators that looked, as far as I could see from the photograph, like carrots bred too close to a nuclear reactor. They're sort of twisted, with several extras sprouting around the root. And they rotate. I couldn't really face getting one through the post unless I knew what it was going to do.'

'Rotate?' Lucy'd winced. In and out was bad

enough. 'Well, that's certainly something new to worry about.'

So they'd got here. Lucy wondered if anything ever again would make her feel turned on and, if so, what that would be like with Grace beside her. Could she honestly buy a sex toy, knowing that her friend knew? Could she buy a sex toy in public, full stop, as if it were just a packet of soap powder?

The shop seemed to be full of middle-aged, earnest-looking *Guardian* readers murmuring interestedly over items such as inflatable bondage chairs and kits for moulding your own breasts in chocolate. These were offered in a choice of cup sizes from A to D. So as not to waste chocolate, presumably.

She and Grace found themselves looking at a shelf full of rubbery-looking dildos. 'It says here,' whispered Grace, 'that if you don't know what size and shape you want you should try out a few vegetables first.'

The shapes of the dildos did remind Lucy of carrots, parsnips and cucumbers. Something for everybody. 'If I don't want sex with my husband,' she muttered back, 'I'm hardly likely to want it with my vegetable basket. And what are those?'

'Harnesses. For the dildos.'

Grace handed her a piece of literature that explained that one in three of these were bought by heterosexual couples so that women could penetrate men anally.

'That's definitely a step too far, even for me.'

*

127

So far, Lucy felt nothing more than mild curiosity. 'Look,' she tugged Grace's sleeve. 'The vibrating nuclear carrots. Apparently they're called "rabbits" because the two prongs at the front look like rabbit ears.'

They examined them, pressing buttons. The rabbit squirmed and shuddered, and tried to wriggle out of Lucy's hand. 'I can't turn it off.'

'Perhaps it turns off when you put it down.'

Lucy put it back on the shelf, and it juddered purposefully off on its own steam, wiggling and inching crazily along and threatening to dislodge everything else in sight. 'Suppose that happened at home? You'd have it whirring and heaving under the bedclothes until it ran out of batteries. It would terrify your cat.'

'Terrify my husband, more like,' giggled Grace.

The assistant rescued them, and showed them the stop button. Lucy heaved a sigh of relief as the rabbit was returned to its box, alongside all the other rabbits.

'What do you think these are?' asked Grace, of two small gold balls in a box. They were about the size of large marbles.

'They're the original Chinese balls,' explained the assistant. 'You put them up you and jiggle about.' She swayed her hips from side to side, helpfully. 'You can't walk around with them, of course, or they'd drop out. We do have some larger ones that stay in, if you're interested.'

'Possibly,' said Lucy, wondering if she could face asking, 'Up where?' There seemed to be so many possibilities.

Two stocky women in Canadian lumberjack shirts, jeans and Doc Martens paid for a frilly basque and a string of anal beads.

'I don't think we should leave without buying something,' said Grace. 'On principle.'

Lucy caught sight of a prettily wrapped pale blue basket, like a small present of delicious soaps and aromatherapy oils. She picked it up, and read the label. Anal Gift Set. She could see the word 'Probe' through the cellophane. That could give someone a fright if it turned up under the Christmas tree.

Grace headed off to the basques. 'There's no point in these unless you have tits,' she observed. 'But I'm very tempted.'

The least revealing way of dealing with the necessity to buy something was to pretend that they were just buying the cheapest thing as a joke, and Lucy noticed that without saying anything to each other, they both bought cock rings. These were small rings of some flexible material with different knobbles attached to them. 'They're only £4,' said Lucy.

'Well, we can't leave without buying something,' repeated Grace. 'Have we got the same one?'

When they got home, Lucy collected Tom from Grace's house, and, as she unlocked the front door, the telephone began to ring. She rushed for it, dumping her bags in the corridor. It was a call from Owen, pretending to be 'absolutely fine, in tip-top condition'. Sinking onto the chair for a long chat, Lucy knew that he always called on Fridays and that he never called at any other time unless he really needed to. Something was obviously wrong. Tension gripped her insides, in short, sharp bursts.

She looked up ten minutes later to see Tom rifling through the bags for his trainers and pulling out the cock ring, which was packaged on a card depicting a blonde with over-inflated breasts. He looked puzzled. 'What's this?' He began reading. 'Gives her . . .'

'Hang on a sec, Dad.' She whipped it out of Tom's hand. 'Something medical. I get given all these free samples in case they're useful for my patients. So that I prescribe them and the drug company gets to earn money. But I've no idea what they are until I read the literature,' she improvised. 'It's probably something to stop people snoring.'

'Oh, OK.' Tom let the matter drop, but she could see him looking confused. 'Your hair's different,' he said, accusingly.

She tried to wave him away to concentrate on Owen.

'I liked it better before,' he pronounced.

As her father cranked up towards admitting that he felt 'a little low', she followed the line Tom had been reading out loud on the cock-ring pack. 'Gives her the clitoral attention she craves.'

Well, thank God it hadn't been Nico looking for

his trainers. Presumably he knew what a clitoris was by now.

The thunder of two pairs of large boots down the stairs drowned out Owen's next remark, and Nico, followed by an identikit friend (could it be Martin, or even Lawrence?) crashed into the hall.

'Bye, Mum.'

'Sorry, Dad . . .' She put her hand over the receiver again. 'Where are you both going?'

But they'd gone, out of the door, virtually arm in arm. Hm. There was something very feminine about either Martin or Lawrence. Like Nico, they did seem very interested in their appearance. Much more than Ned had ever been.

Perhaps Nico was gay after all, she thought. He never seemed to be alone with a girl up there.

'Are you listening to me?' demanded Owen.

Ned got home in time for them to eat stir-fried fridge leftovers together. He didn't notice her hair.

'I went to a sex shop with Grace today,' announced Lucy, still buoyed up with the sight of her transformed face in the mirror.

'Good grief!' Ned stopped chewing and looked baffled. 'Do you think Grace is a lesbian?'

Ned was *so* irritating these days. He just didn't see. 'No,' she snapped. 'But Richard's not boffing her, so she thought she might try a vibrator.' She secretly hoped he'd ask why she'd gone too. And then prayed he wouldn't.

It didn't seem to occur to him. He just raised his eyebrows. 'Phew. Wonder why not? Is it something he's taking?'

'Well, she'd know about that, wouldn't she? I mean, he'd hardly be on anti-depressants without her knowing.'

Ned shrugged. 'People do all sorts of things without telling their wives.'

'Like take mistresses, I thought.'

'Hm. Not sure. Don't think so.'

Lucy did think so, still. But she couldn't resist getting the conversation back to 'us'. 'Anyway, I bought a cock ring.'

Ned looked horrified. 'Why?'

Lucy spread her hands. 'Well, it was the cheapest thing in the shop and it seemed a bit silly to come away without anything.' Weasel, she told herself. Weasel. So she added, 'You know ... er ... to improve sensations.'

Ned looked utterly blank.

'Experimentation?' She tried again. 'Fun? A bit of variety in the humdrum of married life? I mean, we're not dead yet.'

'I don't see what's wrong with the way we always do it,' asserted Ned.

But I do, she screamed silently.

'What is it, anyway?' asked Ned. 'Can I see it?'

'It's called a Clit Bumper,' she read out the label on the back of the package.

'Sounds like that padded thing that Nico had when he was a baby.'

'That's a cot bumper, you daft twerp.' She handed it over.

He indicated the busty blonde. 'She looks a bit of all right.' He lingered over the image for a few moments and shook the packaging to see if the lurid image moved. 'What's she wearing?'

Lucy thought she might scream.

He handed it back. 'Well,' he declared, 'you're not catching me with that round my willy. It might cut off the circulation. And you wouldn't like that. Ha, ha.'

Lucy tried to conceal her irritation. 'I'm sure that it wouldn't be for sale if it gave men gangrene.'

'Nonsense. People just wouldn't own up to it.'

'Well!' Lucy picked up their plates, feeling obscurely rejected. 'I'm sure that if there was a plague of gangrenous willies around the country, we'd read about it in the *BMJ*.'

Ned gave a shout of laughter, and slapped her on the bottom. 'That's why I love you. You've always got an answer.'

Lucy almost threw the plates in the dishwasher and shut it with a bang.

'Anyway,' Ned got up cheerfully. 'All this talk of sex . . . am I in luck tonight?'

Mindful of her resolution, Lucy supposed so. But she couldn't help thinking that if someone Phil was involved with had presented him with a clit bumper, he'd have suggested that they talk about it.

The thought of his interested face and his calm, matter-of-fact voice, tinged with affection, stirred a warm, liquid ache deep down inside her. As Ned went into the bathroom to clean his teeth, she reflected that Phil was probably uninhibited enough to kiss her clitoris before bumping it with anything. As she drifted off into a dream, she began to stroke herself between her legs with mounting pleasure. Phil would part her legs and gently explore her until she could bear it no longer.

Ned strode back in sawing his teeth with dental floss, which he threw in the waste-paper basket. Picking up a pair of clippers, he began to cut his toenails, flicking the hard, yellowing shards across the bed.

He hadn't noticed what she was doing with her right hand, so she slid it away and sat up. 'Ned! For Christ's sake. Are you in training for the Least Sexy Man of The Year Competition?'

His face split into a broad grin. 'That's marriage for you, babe.' He snapped the clippers shut. 'Now, about this rumpy-pumpy we're going to have . . .'

Lucy lay back with exasperation. 'Just get on with it, then. I've got an early surgery tomorrow morning.'

Ned thought that was very funny.

As she tried to get to sleep, Lucy felt a sudden, hot stab of anger at Ned. Surely, if he loved her, he'd want to find out why she couldn't respond. It was as if he hadn't even noticed.

10

Lucy took ages to blow-dry her hair and get her eyeliner right the following Tuesday morning after Ned had left for the hospital, trying on clothes and discarding them in a mounting pile on the bedroom chair. Tom and Nico, left to themselves, consumed almost an entire packet of cereal and two litres of milk, leaving a damp, milky trail of soggy crumbs across the PVC tablecloth. Usually she'd have been down there in the thick of it, fighting a losing battle against the onslaught of breakfast's debris. Today she accepted that this was no longer a battle she could win. The milk could stay there, in an almost invisible pool against the pattern of the tablecloth, until it turned Ned's newspaper soggy that evening. If you mopped up one puddle, she reflected, others merely sprang up to replace it. Not bothering with breakfast herself, she took a black coffee upstairs.

A suit? Smart and flattering, but way too formal. They didn't do suits at the surgery.

Jeans? She tentatively shoe-horned her smallest pair on, and was thrilled to discover that they did up. Just. She'd stopped nibbling biscuits since she met Grace, and the result was beginning to show. She sighed. Even her smallest jeans still covered an enormous amount of territory, and Phil might not be into that tribal big-bottomed African fertility symbol look. All the divorcees she'd seen him with had been long and slender, or neat and petite. Modiglianis rather than Renoirs or Rembrandts.

She reminded herself that this was not about Phil. It was about self-esteem. If a smaller pair of jeans made her feel good – even sexy – she should wear them. On the other hand, sitting in them all day was likely to put her back out. She sat down experimentally on the pile of clothes and felt a twinge around the base of her spine. The jeans came off.

A safe pair of black trousers was probably the best option, and then she could concentrate on the top. Her jumpers divided into those which flattered her colouring but made her boobs look enormous, and black polo necks which made her look like an off-duty traffic warden but marginally thinner.

Lucy decided to go for the boob-revealers, although what they revealed often proved to be something of a responsibility. It was almost impossible to find a bra that fitted, so she was always hoicking straps up and round, and everything seemed to get in the way somehow – she sometimes felt as if the two cantaloupes pushed themselves forward to enter a room ahead of her. Occasionally – although much less often these days – men addressed her chest rather than her face.

But. This is me, she told herself. I'm old enough to enjoy my body, even the imperfect bits. You're never going to look like a ballerina, Lucy Dickinson, so make the most of what you've got.

And Phil's opinion is neither here nor there, she added to herself, and spent the rest of the morning in a fever of anticipation every time someone knocked on the door. It was always another patient.

Where had this obsession suddenly come from? Phil had been just a friend until a few weeks ago when they'd talked about the patient whose problems so closely mirrored Lucy's own. She sighed and pressed the buzzer. 'Kylie Smith to Room 2, please.'

Kylie was tiny, frightened and pregnant. Not quite fourteen, according to her patient records. Kylie herself was in no state to tell anyone anything, not even her age. She sobbed like the little girl she still was.

Lucy got up, knelt down beside her and hugged her. Her shoulders seemed more fragile and bony than ten-year-old Tom's. 'There, there.' It seemed so inept.

Eventually she managed to worm the story out of her. She'd had sex – in a school music practice room that had been left unlocked – with a fifteen-year-old boy in a class two years ahead of her. 'I thought it would make him like me,' she gulped. 'But he told all his friends I was a slag, and never spoke to me again. Now everybody in the school knows I did it.' She began to cry again. 'My mum will kill me. I didn't think you could get pregnant the first time.'

That old chestnut. Lucy couldn't believe that, with the amount this child had heard about sex in her short life – willing sex, unwilling sex, heterosexual sex, homosexual sex, sex to sell products, sex to shock and sex for the sake of it, from practically every television programme, advertisement, magazine and film she'd ever seen – she still didn't know the basic facts. All she knew, foggily, was that it could be a route to being loved. She just didn't understand enough about it to read the right signposts.

'It hurt,' added Kylie. 'It still hurts. You know. Down there.'

She could probably have talked about fellatio more confidently than about her own vagina. And blast it. Maybe she'd caught something too. Lucy felt a sense of despair.

'You could have an abortion,' she suggested gently. 'You really aren't old enough to bring up a child.'

Kylie looked shocked. 'But that'd be murder. Murdering a baby.'

Abortions were deeply out of fashion, Lucy knew. Not only were these poor kids under pressure from every angle to have sex earlier and earlier, but they were expected to live with the consequences. Morality hadn't disappeared, it had just shifted, but it was no easier on girls like Kylie.

By the time she'd contacted social services, set up a support network for her, and tried to put the idea gently into Kylie's mind that she could consider an abortion, she'd forgotten about Phil.

He tapped softly and came in to find her with her head in her hands.

'Sorry. Teenage pregnancy.' She told him about Kylie.

He sighed. 'Some of these kids just haven't got a chance, have they? Especially the girls. Sandwich?'

She took it. It was her favourite – avocado from the organic shop. But it tasted like cottonwool. She tried swallowing it, and had to take a sip of water to get it down.

'Are you OK?'

'Absolutely fine.'

'You look great.'

She remembered the eyeliner and the hair. They'd worked. 'Thanks.' Did Phil fancy her? It was impossible to tell. Did men fancy women in their forties? Phil had said he did. But did anyone find her – Lucy – sexy? After twenty years in the purdah of marriage and children, she had less idea than she'd had when she was fifteen. Sometimes, recently, she'd felt strong and attractive and vibrant. At others, she was embarrassed to even think that Phil – or anyone else – might be drawn to her. Sharing a sandwich with a colleague was scarcely a date, and if it had been a date, he wouldn't have offered it. And she wouldn't have accepted.

She could always ask Ned if she was still attractive. He'd always be honest, and she knew he'd say, loyally, that she was still attractive to him, no matter what, but she couldn't quite face the riders that might come with the words. Things like 'well, you're obviously not exactly young any more'.

She pushed the thoughts away. Attractiveness was no longer an issue. Except for Grace. She remembered Grace's plan.

'Ned and I were wondering if you'd like to come to dinner,' she ventured.

His face lit up. 'Love to. I'm away the week after next, though.'

Phil had a lovely life, thought Lucy. 'Where to?'

'Petra,' he replied. 'The rose red city half as old as time. I've never seen it, and I thought I should.'

'Lucky you. What about the week after you come back?'

They agreed on the Wednesday.

'Is there anyone you'd like to bring?' Lucy held her breath. Not that it mattered, of course, as she couldn't possibly actually have an affair with Phil, no matter what sort of fantasies she had, and if Grace did, it wouldn't be a relationship. It would be something that existed in a vacuum, on a separate planet to either Grace's or Phil's daily life.

He shrugged. 'I can, if you like. But there's no one special.'

'Well, I'm not bothered about equal numbers. Just come as you are. We've got another couple coming who are fairly new here – Richard and Grace Morgan – and I thought it'd be nice if they met some locals.' She added this so that Phil wouldn't think she was setting him up with Grace when she appeared alone.

'Fine.' He leant forward. 'That's pretty.' He lightly touched her throat, where a silver heart that Ned had bought her for her birthday five years ago nestled in the hollow of her neck. If her neck still had a hollow. She hadn't looked recently.

When he was this close, she longed to stroke his designer stubble to see what it felt like.

'Is that the time?' He looked at his watch. 'Next patient almost due . . .

'By the way,' he added, as he left the room. 'I like the new hair. It suits you.'

Lucy smiled to herself, feeling warm and happy, as she reached for the phone to call Grace. 'It's me.'

'Hello, you.' Grace always knew her voice.

'I've been talking to the gorgeous Phil.' She could only call him the gorgeous Phil to Grace. 'Can you make three weeks on Wednesday?'

Grace could, if she could bring Richard too. 'It's the only night he's around that week. After all, I'm not seriously going to have an affair with your friend, Phil. I'm just going to look, like a dieter in a sweet shop.'

'Or a size 16 in a designer clothes shop.'

Grace never had any trouble in designer clothes shops, and her amusement drifted lightly down the phone. Suddenly Lucy realized that she was sick of black and voluminous. It was time to dress up as someone else. 'Grace?'

'Mm?'

'Will you come shopping with me? I want to feel different.'

'I'd love to come shopping with you,' said Grace,

sounding as if she meant it. 'It would be a heavenly change from trundling round Ipswich colour-coordinating the Lady Mayoress of Bramsea, which is how I spent yesterday. But I don't suppose this has anything to do with the gorgeous Phil, does it?'

'I just feel that all this baggy black I wear is like going around under a burka.'

'Ah. You're waking up,' commented Grace. 'That's what I make my money on. Women spend ten years choosing clothes that won't show sick stains, or buying things because the label says "machine washable", and then, suddenly, they come in thinking about embroidered cardigans and visible cleavage. I knew it when we had that first drink during the carol service. Ready to break out, that's what I thought about you.'

'Honestly,' protested Lucy, 'I just haven't bought any new clothes for ages. I've simply forgotten what suits me.'

'Hmph,' giggled Grace. 'That's what they all say. But I have to warn you, it can be a dangerous age. First stop new cardigan, last stop new husband.'

'Absolutely not.' Lucy laughed. 'Ned is not only washable but irreplaceable. He's a one-size-fits-all, so I'll never grow out of him.'

'I should think not,' asserted Grace. 'He's adorable.' And she put the phone down, leaving Lucy turning the word over and over in her mind.

Adorable as in sweet, harmless, slightly tasteless, cuddly toy? Or adorable as in 'I'd adore to rip your clothes off and ravish you the minute your wife is out of the room'?

She considered the possibilities with interest, rather than concern.

11

When, during surgery the following day, she read the name Sean Williams on the list, it never occurred to her to remember Grace's builder.

But the door opened just as a slant of sunlight lit the room, and Lucy had a brief impression of the arrival of a young god.

He swaggered in. Literally. He was, she thought, proud of his body, and completely at home with it. Unlike the women she saw.

He sat down on the chair, dwarfing it, and placed the large, strong hands at the ends of bronzed, sinewy forearms, on his knees.

'What seems to be the matter?' Lucy thought her voice sounded more squeaky than usual.

'It's me belly.' The strong, but surprisingly well-manicured hand indicated what was almost definitely the nearest Lucy would ever be to a perfect six-pack washboard stomach. She had an irresistible desire to see it. She had to concentrate extremely hard to focus on the symptoms he reeled off. It sounded like diverticulitis.

'Yes, well,' she fiddled with her notes. 'Just take off your clothes and jump up on the couch so that I can examine you.'

He swished the privacy curtain closed behind him, and then popped his head out again. She couldn't help wondering if the spiky blond hair was dyed, or whether he had Viking blood. 'Everything?'

She nodded, feeling guilty. She could quite easily have examined him by asking him to pull up the shirt and open his trousers. Although, on reflection, any mention of that particular area of trouser might have been something of a distraction. Aargh. Stop it. You're a doctor. She swallowed and breathed deeply. 'To your underwear,' she added, almost in a whisper. The complete tackle might be a bit much, however used to people's bits she was.

As she carefully pressed around his stomach area, he watched her face.

'I know,' he exclaimed. 'You're that Grace's friend.'

She nodded. 'Are you still working there?'

'Not often. More's the pity. She's real posh totty, she is.'

Lucy tried not to raise her eyebrows, and told him to breathe in, then exhale slowly, and considered prodding him particularly hard in a painful bit to take his mind off Grace.

It didn't stop him talking. 'We get all sorts, you know, us builders. You always know when a woman's interested because she offers you cups of tea.'

Lucy was stung. She'd always offered all workmen cups of tea, even if they'd been one-eyed, hunch-backed geriatrics. 'I expect she was just being friendly.'

'Friendly,' grinned Sean. 'I know friendly. But you

know you're really in luck if you get offered a bacon sandwich. Don't ask me why, but once that bacon starts sizzling, they come up very close with their top buttons undone. Or suggest that there's a bit of touching up in the bedroom that needs doing.'

Lucy asked him if it hurt there. She pressed gently down. 'And here?' His skin was smooth and firm, and her hands ran across it as if over a piece of sculpture.

'Your friend, though,' he sighed. 'Bit of a handful, if you ask me.'

Lucy raised her eyebrows. She hadn't.

'I stay out of trouble myself,' he added, leaving Lucy pondering how he managed this considering the number of bacon sandwiches he clearly ate with other people's wives. Why was Grace so much more trouble than any other woman whose wardrobe he'd had to shift? She wished she could ask him.

'Still,' he brightened. 'If ever she fancies a bit – of bacon, that is – you tell her my sandwiches are the best in town.'

Lucy could hardly keep a straight face. 'I think Grace is very happily married,' she said, demurely. 'That's all. You can get dressed now.'

Sean rolled off the examination table in one fluid movement, and landed with a spring and a shout of laughter. 'You're the doctor,' he said, 'I'm sure you know best.'

Sean had clearly sensed the attraction that Grace felt for him, and knowing that, Lucy wondered why he hadn't made a move. Perhaps he had so many women crawling over him that he didn't need to.

'Yes,' he buttoned up the shirt, 'definitely posh totty, she is.' He shook his head. 'I don't know how that husband of hers does it.'

Does what? Attract a woman like Grace? Or could even the builders see that he wasn't exactly doing it? It was difficult to concentrate on his possible diverticulitis as she wrote out a prescription and gave him a few instructions.

As the weeks went on, Lucy found herself consciously scraping her butter thinner, peeling fewer potatoes, clearing away the remains of the boys' biscuits without shovelling a few in her mouth, and walking past the Pringles in the supermarket in order to pile the trolley up with crisps that were good enough for hungry boys but could scarcely be described as tempting.

'What's happening to me?' she asked her thinner face in the mirror, as Ned and the boys grew more indistinct and only Grace seemed as vibrant a part of her life as ever. She found herself abstracted when Tom wanted her to practise spellings with him. She'd always had to coax him before.

The night before the dinner party, when Tom was asleep, Nico was out and Ned was working late, she tried on the new clothes she'd bought with Grace – a clingy red cashmere number with a delicious line of beading around it ('It doesn't make me look too fat, does it?' she'd whispered nervously to Grace) and a black skirt that revealed more leg than she was comfortable with.

'You've got good legs,' Grace had assessed her dispassionately. 'You ought to show them off more.'

'No one's seen my legs for years,' Lucy had muttered. 'Except Ned.' And you couldn't count a quick scuttle from the bathroom to the shelter of the duvet cover.

'What does he say about them?'

Lucy had gazed at Grace incredulously. Ned remark on her legs? Or any other part of her?

'What does Richard say?' had been all she could think of as a reply.

'Oh, Richard likes me wearing short skirts. As long as they're not too short. He hates me looking tarty.'

Hm, Lucy had thought. So he had an opinion then. And he still looked at his wife properly, unlike most men at this stage of marriage.

'You don't look tarty.'

Grace had shrugged. 'Sometimes he makes me go up and change. But he's right. I know. He just doesn't want me to look like mutton dressed as lamb. So he's thinking of me.'

Lucy had tried to work out why she found this so distasteful, and tried re-arranging it in her head to fit in with what she saw in the pleasant, courteous man, who always offered her a drink and showed her the latest gadget he'd bought with an almost endearing innocence. 'What do you think?' he'd asked, flashing a remote control at his new wide-screen TV, as if her opinion really mattered to him. 'You don't think these things are too hideously big, do you?'

And he always seemed relieved when she reassured him that, no, she thought it was fine, and she knew Ned would love something like that one day . . . 'We'll have to save up,' she'd add.

She'd distracted Grace from the conversation by discussing shoes, while she worried about Richard. Suppose there was some dark, terrible secret about his sexual orientation? Did he have anyone he could talk to? And was there anything she, Lucy, could do? As a doctor or as a friend? And why did Grace, who seemed so confident, shrink away from discussing things with him?

Grace had advised high heels. Lucy had listed the ankle, knee and hip disorders she suffered from or would suffer from if her heel was higher than a few millimetres. Grace told her not to be so boring.

Back to Tuesday evening. She decided to fling caution to the wind and forget about alcohol-free days (usually Mondays and Tuesdays). She poured herself a glass of red wine, jumping guiltily at the soft pop of the cork, and tried on the clothes, turning the radio on deafeningly loud in order to dance with her reflection in the window glass.

Until the phone rang.

Lucy felt her stomach, her slightly hungry stomach, contract in a lurch. Perhaps it was Phil cancelling. Perhaps she just wasn't used to being hungry, she reminded herself, answering in a tentative voice.

'Lucy?' She instantly recognized the quavering voice as her father's.

'Dad.' How could she be so selfish as to think about . . . well, she wasn't going to admit to thinking about Phil, so she amended her thoughts . . . shopping with Grace, when her father was so ill?

He didn't want to trouble her, but . . .

'It's no trouble, really.'

'I feel very guilty asking you, but . . .'

'Honestly.' She felt irritation rise up in her throat. Why was loving people so difficult?

Eventually he revealed that Mavis Fletcher had her grandchildren to stay, and that the other people in the village, for various reasons, weren't able to take him to his next appointment at the doctor's.

'Of course I'll come, Dad. You only have to ask.' Lucy spent the next ten minutes reassuring him that she could swap her surgery that afternoon with one of the other doctors (not Michael – he regarded any request by a woman for cover as typical of the kind of 'special pleading' that working women today were always expecting). 'Anyway,' she concluded, 'it's about time I talked to your specialist. I need to know what's happening and how I can help. And, at some point, if you can't manage alone' – her heart sank at this point – 'you'll probably have to come and live here.' They'd have to convert the living room into a bedroom while he was ill, and live in the family room and kitchen. It could be done. Or perhaps they could squeeze a bed into the study and clear out years and years of books and files . . .

Her mind was racing ahead, planning, as he rang off with the words, 'I'm not leaving my vegetables. I'm dying in my own home.'

No, he'd want to be at home. Of course, he would. Which would mean she'd have to divide herself between Bramsea and her father, just over an hour away in the countryside. The boys and work during the day, she supposed, and the nights with Dad. Ned would have to hold the fort at home.

It really was time he learned how to use the washing machine. She couldn't bear the thought of driving endlessly from one pile of washing to the next.

The phone rang again, while she was still sitting in the relative darkness, staring at it as if it offered her the answer to her problems. She jumped.

'Yes?'

'It's Grace. Are you all right?'

'Me? Fine. Yes. Do I sound funny?'

'A bit. Have you had supper, or am I disturbing it?'

Lucy tried to remember supper. 'Oh. That. I don't think I'll bother tonight.'

'I hope you're not buying a ticket for that long-running play, Woman Gets Thin And Finds Happiness. Because everyone who's been there knows it's a very disappointing performance. In spite of rave reviews throughout the ages.'

'I eat masses. Anyway, if I'm interested in anything it's Woman Gets Thin And Finds Outfit That She Can Wear. It's like money. Being thin doesn't make you happy but at least you can enjoy your misery dressed in something nice.'

'Hm.' Grace managed to inject a note of caution into a very short syllable. 'As long as it's not Woman Gets Thin And Finds Trouble.'

Lucy felt a shock of excitement shoot through her. 'Do you think I'm really still capable of trouble? That sort of trouble?'

'Oh, darling,' said Grace, in her jokey, society voice. 'I think the only way you and I are going to stay out of trouble is to have an affair with each other.'

They both laughed, but Lucy felt something lurch inside her. She recognized it as a feeling she hadn't had in years. It was somewhere between joy and unease.

They exchanged a few childcare arrangements. Grace wanted cover for next Tuesday afternoon, but suggested taking Tom tomorrow so that Lucy had time to cook and dress. Normally Lucy would have shrugged the offer off, declaring herself capable of swapping one black top for another while making a vast vat of pasta, but suddenly neither seemed good enough.

'Where does this Phil live?' asked Grace. 'Does he have to drive in from far away?'

'Not far in country terms. About three-quarters of an hour. Over by . . .' She visualized Phil's village on the map and suddenly realized that it was just off the road she took to Owen's house. 'Well, quite close to my father's place, in fact,' she concluded, with that fizzy feeling she'd felt earlier returning under her breastbone.

'And how is your father?' asked Grace.

'Determined not to need me,' replied Lucy. 'But he does. I'm going to have to base myself there more and more over the next six months.'

Grace refrained from pointing out the obvious. 'Let me know if there's anything I can do. Honestly. I can do shopping for you, or have Tom any time. Nico, even. They're great boys.'

As Lucy put down the phone, she could feel her eyes filling with tears. They were great boys. And what was going on in her head seemed like infidelity to them, not just to Ned. Even though, of course, nothing was going to happen. She put the cork in the wine bottle and went upstairs for an early night, looking in on Tom's angelic sleeping face as she passed his room. His cheeks were so soft, she thought, as she kissed him. Finer than silk. He stirred and opened his eyes. 'Love you, Mummy.'

'Love you, Tommy. Now, sh.' She pulled the duvet up over his chin, and tried to get to sleep early herself. The wine, on an empty stomach, disturbed her dreams and she struggled to embrace an image of Grace, naked in bed beside her, her long, thin, boyish legs and arms contrasting with large, brown, puckered nipples.

She felt a hand touching her. 'Are you all right?'

It was Ned, back from the hospital, hearing her moan in the dream. He drew her towards him and she rolled into his arms, feeling, for the first time since she could remember, a surge of desire. 'Mm. I'm fine.'

'Time for a quickie?'

Lucy's instinct was to pull away, instantly, with an excuse, but she thought again. The word 'quick' had a certain appeal. Not too long, in other words. And she might as well make the most of feeling sexy.

But as Ned moved through his tried-and-tested routine, the dark, slightly reckless feelings of warmth and craving ebbed away, and as his final shudder subsided, she kissed him with affection and dropped into a sound sleep, with the satisfaction of having done her duty for the next week or so. 'That's sorted, then, for a bit,' drifted through her mind, along with a minor niggle about the erotic dream.

But the most outrageous people pop up in erotic dreams, and it doesn't seem to mean anything, she comforted herself.

12

'Remind me about this party tonight.' Ned kissed the back of Lucy's neck after he walked in the door. 'The who and why.' He looked at his watch. 'And when.'

'When is the most important. Half an hour from now.' Lucy was irritated by the brief touch. She checked the seasoning on a slow-cooked lamb shanks casserole with that over-stretched feeling she remembered from childhood, when something important, such as a holiday, or Christmas Day, had seemed endlessly far away for too long, and had then suddenly appeared when she was too tired to enjoy it. The idea of Grace and Phil having an affair seemed daft, a stupid idea conjured up on a drunken evening. It was embarrassing, her feet ached in her new, pointy scarlet shoes and she felt like a lumpen, over-dressed doll in her new clothes.

'So who's coming?' repeated Ned, stealing an olive from the dishes laid out for the first course. Lucy tapped his hand in reproof.

'Just Phil, Grace and Richard. That's all. Look, if you can't be helpful, stay out of the kitchen.'

He peered into the pan. 'Six lamb shanks. Who's the last one for?'

Lucy shrugged. 'No one really. I just thought Phil might bring someone, but he's not.'

'Nico can join us, if he wants to.'

'Nico?' Lucy was taken aback.

'Why not? It's about time the boy was exposed to some civilized company. And he can damn well do the washing-up afterwards. NICO!' he roared, without even bothering to move to the bottom of the stairs. Lucy jumped at the suddenness of the noise. The faint chunker-chunker-chunker of music drifted down from Nico's room on the second floor.

'He's hardly likely to want to come. He can't stand the sight of us at the moment.' Lucy was disconcerted. If Nico was there, she wouldn't feel able to flirt with Phil; but, then again, flirting with Phil wasn't the point of this anyway.

Ned bounded up the stairs two at a time to rootle Nico out of his den, returning with the news that Nico would love to join them.

Love to? Was this Nico speaking? Almost definitely not. Lucy shook her head in amazement and laid another place at the table.

Grace and Richard were the first to arrive. Grace, in a cloud of delicately expensive scent, bringing a bunch of white hyacinths tied up with a piece of silver-wired ribbon, while Richard pressed a bottle of fine burgundy into Ned's hand.

'That looks like a good one,' approved Ned.

Nico hovered to take their coats. He'd obviously been given a talking-to about behaving properly from his father. Ned was so much better with him than she was at the moment. Everything she did or said just seemed hopelessly wrong.

Tom trailed downstairs in his bare feet and pyjamas to see what the commotion was about, pink from the bath and with the tips of his hair damp. He exuded delicious childishness. 'Where's Luke?' he demanded.

'Tucked up in bed,' smiled Grace. 'Where you should be.'

Tom grimaced. 'At half-past eight? I bet he isn't. I bet he's watching the match.' And he scampered upstairs before anyone could tell him that watching it to the end wasn't allowed on school days.

Lucy saw Grace look fondly after his retreating back. 'They're such good friends. Luke adores Tom.'

'They're so easy at that age,' she warned Grace. 'Just you wait till you get one of those.' She indicated the tall figure of Nico, who was opening a bottle of wine in the kitchen at the end of the corridor. She still hadn't managed to 'talk' to him properly about Owen. He brushed her off with a grunt every time she tried to find out what he really felt. Perhaps any discussion about feelings was just too excruciatingly embarrassing.

'But Nico is heavenly,' said Grace. 'And all those gorgeous friends of his, too. Doesn't it cheer you up having lots of lovely young men lounging around the house? I simply can't wait.'

'No,' said Lucy, rather more sharply than she'd intended. 'It wears me down, to be honest. For anyone without a training in army catering, it's extremely tiring.'

Richard was chatting easily to Ned. Men, she had long ago decided, didn't really care a great deal about who they were friends with. They fitted in with the pack. If they were canoeing, all their best mates were in the canoe club. If they were drinkers, they hung out with drunks. And if they were married, they just got on with their wives' friends' husbands. Anything for an easy life.

When the doorbell rang again, her stomach flipped over. Was there lipstick on her teeth? Was the new cardigan too exposing? Did it make her look fat? She wanted to run upstairs and change into the black burnous look again.

Ned let Phil in, and there were introductions all round.

'You look great,' said Phil, kissing her on the cheek. 'I like the red.'

'Yes,' demanded Ned, noticing what she was wearing for the first time this evening. 'What is all this about? You're all dressed up.'

'No, I'm not.' She glared at him. Husbands were so embarrassing. 'Just sick of black, that's all.' The three men looked at her, consideringly, and she decided, with a leap of her heart, that the clothes Grace had helped her choose were fun, after all. 'It is spring,' she pointed out.

'It's well past spring,' said Phil. 'Not that you'd notice it with all this rain.'

Phew. Conversations about the weather. Where would we be without them? She began to gabble, and Phil just went on looking at her, with an expression of affectionate amusement on his face, as if she was fragile, and slightly loopy.

'How was Petra?' she asked.

'Stunning.' He wasn't exactly tanned, just healthier and more alive-looking than the rest of the winter-white faces around him. 'It's just amazing to see a city built into rock.'

'I think I've seen it on an Indiana Jones film,' said Lucy, feeling she ought to say something, but not being able to summon up anything culturally meaningful.

Ned and Richard went back to talking about private funding for health projects, and Richard explained what was working best and why in the current climate. Ned nodded, smiling, but Lucy could see that his mind was drifting, which was presumably what he did in departmental meetings about finance, and was possibly another of the reasons why he was not regarded as suitable for promotion. Grace merely stood there, looking beautiful in a leopardskin top and a gold silk skirt, smiling politely, but not engaging with anyone.

'Well,' she concluded, remembering that the point of this evening, bizarrely, was for Grace to meet Phil. 'I must sort things out in the kitchen.' They both asked, simultaneously, if she wanted any help, and she brushed them off, feeling like a dog breeder leaving two mating dogs to themselves without any great hopes of anything happening. Grace, who never stopped talking about sex and flirted with builders, seemed struck dumb when faced with a real man she might have an affair with.

Having opened the bottles of wine, Nico didn't reappear until the meal was served, obviously preferring to watch the match with his brother.

'United's winning,' he offered, when Lucy called him downstairs. It was the first time he'd voluntarily addressed her beyond 'Where's my football shirt?' since she'd told him that Owen was going to die.

She tried to remember what team he supported, and, in her panic about the vegetables, failed. 'Is that good?' was the best she could muster, but she was determined to keep the channels of communication open somehow.

Nico grunted.

Oh dear, wrong again. And the broccoli was a bit soft, but never mind. You could overdo the 'crunchy' aspect of veg. She began trying to light the candles, but, in her hurry, the match blew out. Phil appeared beside her and took the matchbox away. 'Here. I'll do that.'

Lucy pushed her hair out of her eyes. 'Thanks. Sorry. I keep trying to do six million things at once, so I do them all badly.'

'Nonsense,' he said, appearing to mean it. 'You're an excellent doctor and, from the delicious smells that keep wafting past, you're obviously a brilliant cook, and I'm sure Nico here can testify to your being a very good mother.'

Nico laughed, surprisingly normally. 'She does all right.'

Lucy nearly fell over with shock. When he was ten, he'd told her she was the best mummy in the world – quite often – but for the past few years any acknowledgement of a relationship between them, let alone any sign of affection, appeared to be too mortifying for him even to consider. Perhaps Ned was right and 'civilized company' was what he needed. She sat Grace between Phil and Nico, and herself between Phil and Richard. This left Ned sitting between Nico and Richard.

Richard seemed more relaxed than usual. Perhaps he was getting used to them. He asked her and Phil several questions about the practice.

'Lucy's the most popular doctor,' said Phil, almost with pride, and Lucy blushed.

'Don't be silly.'

'I'm not being silly. No one can stand that Gardner man . . .'

'He *is* awful,' interjected Lucy.

'And Eric's sweet, but a bit doddery. I don't think anyone wants to consult him about anything more complicated than athlete's foot. And Andrew is so hesitant and young-looking that no one takes him seriously . . .'

'But he's actually a brilliant doctor, I hope the patients start to realize that soon.'

Lucy could feel Richard looking from her to Phil, and back again, as they prattled on with surgery gossip, finishing each other's sentences and laughing at each other's jokes.

'Well,' he said. 'It sounds a very lively practice. Perhaps we should change. Grace! Darling!'

Grace, who was imitating a client of hers who claimed to want a make-over, but refused to try anything remotely different, jumped slightly. 'Yes?'

'Are we registered with the best GPs in Bramsea? Oughtn't we to be with Lucy's practice?'

'We didn't know Lucy when we registered.' Grace sounded wary.

'Yes, yes.' He sounded impatient. 'The point is, did you choose the best?' He turned to Phil and Lucy. 'After all, it's not what you know in this world, it's who you know. Everybody's aware of that.'

'Honestly, I'm sure the other practice is just as good as we are. We share night and weekend duties with them, and there've never been any complaints. And, of course, if Grace ever wanted an informal second opinion, she could always talk to me.' Lucy worried that Richard was going to make Grace get up that moment and find a Best Buy list for GP practices.

He looked mollified. 'Very kind of you. After all, your health is too important to take any chances with it. Especially with a young child.'

Lucy told herself that his heart seemed to be in the

right place, even if he had an odd way of showing it.

Over the main course, the topic of holidays came up. Nobody had arranged any.

'Why don't you all join us at the villa this year?' suggested Richard.

Grace's face lit up. 'Oh, yes, do. It would be such fun.'

'The villa?' enquired Ned.

'Grace and Richard have a villa in the south of France, near Agen,' explained Lucy, suddenly remembering that Grace had told her that it was Richard's brother's house, but that he lent it to them regularly.

'My brother has it for most of August,' said Richard. 'But we're going down for the last week of July and the first week of August. You must come.'

Lucy looked at Ned, and a brief message of acceptance passed between them. She couldn't think of anything better than to go on holiday with Grace, but she wasn't sure how everyone else would feel. Tom, perfectly happy, presumably. But what about Ned and Richard? And could they leave Owen for two weeks? What if he got worse, suddenly?

And Nico? The impossibility of going on a holiday that would suit them all washed over her. 'There won't be anyone of Nico's age,' she remembered.

'He can bring a friend. There's plenty of room. We can sleep ten. And there's a hayloft that's been roughly converted to be perfect for teenagers.' Richard turned a surprisingly charming smile on Nico, who blinked in surprise. 'You can be independent there and play music as loudly as you like.'

'There's a swimming pool, and a tennis court, and the local town has got several good restaurants,' added Grace. Lucy got the feeling that both Richard and Grace, for different reasons, needed them to be there. She remembered Grace saying that Richard always contrived not to be alone with her on holiday.

'Well, we'd love to,' agreed Ned. 'Nico?'

Nico nodded. 'Cool.'

'That's settled then.' Grace looked happy. 'And you, Phil, you'll come too, won't you?'

Phil looked taken aback at being invited on holiday by a couple he'd only just met. 'Well, it's very kind of you . . .' he prevaricated.

'You could bring a friend,' added Grace.

'I . . . er . . . well . . .'

Grace pressed his arm, and fluttered her eyes flirtatiously at him. 'Do come. It'll be such fun.' She was revving up the flirtatiousness, but not very convincingly. Perhaps she was nervous with Richard there.

Phil's smile seemed to spread over his whole face. 'Look, in principle, I'd love to, but I don't know what my plans are. Though if you really mean it, I'll let you know as soon as possible.'

'I'll phone you,' said Grace, taking a microscopic beaded notebook out of a tiny sequinned bag, and writing down his number. 'Where do you live?' And she leant forward on her hand and fixed him with what Lucy thought of as her 'listening' look.

Richard didn't seem to have noticed, and got up to help Lucy take the plates back to the sink, in order to dive out into the garden and have a surreptitious cigarette.

Lucy grappled with the cream whisk, until Phil appeared at her elbow. 'Shall I do that?'

'Oh, thanks.' She could see Grace over his shoulder. She was now leaning towards Ned and Nico, who were laughing at something she'd said. Seeing them silhouetted in the candlelight, she suddenly saw, for the first time in years, how one had led to the other. Nico was taller than Ned, so although he had a similar broad build, he seemed less bulky, and his hair was blonder and slightly floppier – it was falling over his face now until he ran his hand through it, pushing it back. But their profiles echoed each other, and they had the same easy smile, directed like two mirror images at Grace. Everyone must think their boy is beautiful, thought Lucy, but Nico really is. I'm sure of it.

When she took the bowls in, Grace's head was almost touching Ned's as she arranged a pattern of matchsticks on the table to explain something. Her delicate French-manicured hands sketched out something to do with the villa in France. The low neckline of the leopardskin top dipped, revealing two soft smooth curves. Lucy wished she had a cleavage like that, instead of the cantaloupes. Well, more like giant marshmallows really. Or a pair of large feather pillows stuffed into too small a pillowcase.

Phil appeared with two more bowls. 'Where do you want these?'

'Oh.' She blushed. Staring at another woman's cleavage could get you misunderstood, and she knew, from the things he said, that he noticed things like that. 'There and there. Thanks.' Flustered, she sat down, and saw Grace pretend to read first Ned's palm, then Nico's. They both seemed to be enjoying themselves. Lucy's heart ached for the affectionate, rumbustious little boy that Nico had been. She missed him terribly. Perhaps a holiday all together, with friends like Grace and Richard, would prove to be the turning point for him; Grace treated him like an adult, and he responded like one. If only she could be so relaxed, but then Grace didn't have to do his laundry or provide massive plates of food for him three times a day or make him tidy his room. As she so often said, 'I don't *want* to nag you,' to which Nico would either shrug or say, 'Well, don't then.' And that was pretty much it between them.

Richard returned from the garden and began to talk to Phil about investment.

'I keep my hand in,' said Phil. 'On the Internet.'

'You can lose a packet like that,' commented Richard.

'Mm.' Phil sounded doubtful. 'You have to be careful.' It was clear, from his tone, that he was.

Lucy listened to them both, trying to pick up clues about what made Richard tick. He talked about 'his' company, she noticed, although she knew, from the way Grace had explained it, that he didn't own it, and had merely been employed to start the East Anglian branch. But perhaps that's just the way men were in his field. They had to talk big to be taken seriously.

'What do you think of Richard?' she asked Ned, after everyone had gone, and she could still feel the soft roughness of Phil's face against hers as he'd given her a social kiss goodnight. They'd stood close together, as if in an old-fashioned waltz, in the hallway as everyone said goodbye. Lucy had been aware of the space his body occupied, while she'd kissed everyone else goodbye in a general fumble of coats and laughter.

She made herself think of Richard again. 'I mean, would you really be happy to go on holiday with them?' She crossed her fingers. Two weeks of Grace would be enormous fun, she knew, particularly with Phil thrown in, but what would Ned think of it?

Ned filled a bowl with washing-up liquid and hot water in order to wash the best glasses. Nico could do the rest. 'Richard? Nice enough bloke. Bit pompous. Nothing wrong with that. Plenty of it around by our age. But there's no chemistry between them, though, don't you think?'

Lucy was taken aback. She hadn't expected Ned to be so perceptive. 'What do you mean?'

'They don't talk to each other.'

'We don't talk to each other in public.'

'Yes, we do. We talk to each other in public the same way as we do in private.'

'What, "Pass the butter" and "Can you pick Tom up today"?'

Ned grinned. 'That sort of thing.'

Lucy was drunk enough to be rash. 'Perhaps we should be talking about more important things?' She wanted to recall the words as soon as she'd said them.

'What, like the state of the nation, or the state of us?'

'Well,' she dried the last glass vigorously. 'Us. I suppose. We never talk.'

'What do you want to say?' He didn't seem worried.

'I don't know,' she weaselled out, then remembered the effect it had had on her when Phil had lightly touched her arm with his hand to emphasize a point. She'd felt like Grace had with the builder, Sean. She'd wanted to fuck him. Desperately. Passionately. She had felt intensely, vibrantly sexual in a way that she never did when Ned began his sex-by-numbers patrol of her body. She had hardly been able to think of anything else, and when Richard had asked her if she knew the area around Agen, she'd mumbled something stupid.

And now Phil had gone, and if she didn't do something to assuage the fire he'd started, she thought she might go mad. As Grace had predicted, she was ready to transfer some of that heat into the dying embers of her sexual relationship with Ned.

'We could talk about sex,' she offered.

Ned looked up. 'Nico.' He threw him the apron and the washing-up liquid as he came in from the

168

other room. 'Your ma's tired. We're going to bed. Do what you can and we'll finish the rest. And then go straight to bed. It's school tomorrow.'

Nico rolled his eyes, but set about doing the washing-up without any signs of resentment. If that had been me, thought Lucy, there'd have been ten minutes of arguing.

'Now what's brought this on?' Upstairs in the bedroom, he unbuttoned his shirt, revealing a smattering of grey in his chest hair.

Lucy turned her head away. The evidence of Ned's ageing reminded her that her own body was crossed with dimpling, spidery veins, the occasional bright white scar and the shiny snail-track lines of stretch marks. She pulled the duvet up to her chin. 'Let's turn the light out.'

Ned turned the light out, and she thought they were both drunk enough to let the matter drop. It would be easier just to sleep.

'What kind of sex?' He propped himself up on his elbow to face her, and she could see him silhouetted in the narrow strip of light from the street lamp outside.

'Different sex, I suppose. We always do the same thing. We could experiment.'

He laughed. 'Every time I experiment, you say, "Ouch" or "What are you doing?" or "Get off, that tickles." So I gave up doing anything different years ago.' He didn't sound resentful.

'Do I?' Now he mentioned it, she recognized that there was a certain amount of truth in the accusation.

'Well, that was years ago.' When I had aching breasts and sore nipples, or hadn't slept all night because a child had been sick, she thought. 'It's different, now. We should . . .' She trailed off. What on earth should they do? She'd got completely out of the habit of seeing Ned as a sexual being.

'If you tell me what you want me to do, I'll do it,' he said, agreeably.

Lucy felt like screaming that that wasn't the point. 'I don't know. We could . . . explore each other's bodies, or something. Like they do in books.'

'If we found anything we hadn't seen before in the twenty-odd years we've been together,' Ned pointed out, 'it's probably something that ought not to be there, and should be taken to a doctor.'

Lucy giggled. She was being absurd and unreasonable, she knew. 'Well, I am a doctor, and so are you.'

'Well, where shall I start?' Ned was still being so utterly sensible that she felt like hitting him.

'Oh, I don't know.' She gave up.

Instead of reaching for her left breast, he started on her right. It was a change of sorts.

Later, relieved that it was all over, but warm at the thought of having done it without actually hating it, she curled up in his arms and asked him if he thought Grace was attractive to men.

'Mm?' He sounded drowsy. 'Grace?' He was silent so long that she thought he'd slipped off to sleep. 'Yes. She is. Very.'

13

A few days later, Lucy flicked, fascinated, through *Becoming Orgasmic* and several other sex books, as she ate her sandwich, although she was startled by one book's suggestion: 'Why not masturbate in public?' Lucy could think of a number of reasons why not, but then she lived in Bramsea. The author, she noted from the blurb, divided her time between London, New York and Sydney. Perhaps it was different there.

Really, it would be so much better to go for a bracing walk along the seafront – the turquoise May skies concealed a breeze with an exhilarating bite of chill in it – or go home and stuff some washing into the ever-hungry mouth of the washing machine. But *Becoming Orgasmic* hypnotized her. You'd think a sexually experienced forty-something woman, who's had two children and been married for twenty years, would pretty much know it all, she thought in wonder.

She remembered being obsessed with books on sexual technique as an adolescent, along with her best friend at school, Sue. Even at the age of fourteen they had understood the words perfectly well, and could have drawn the diagrams blindfold, but it had all been fundamentally utterly meaningless to them both. They'd never admitted it to each other, but none of it had made much sense. Perhaps that's why the Kylies of this world could watch endless soaps where girls get pregnant 'doing it once', and are still astonished to find themselves in absolutely the same situation. She and Sue had ploughed through every sex manual they could find – in fact, she remembered being in Smith's once, in Norwich (in their school uniforms), and shouting to Sue, 'Look, I've found *Sex Manners for Advanced Lovers*.' Sue had hastily left the shop so as not to be seen with her. 'You're so embarrassing, Lucy, you really are,' she'd said later, whisking *Sex Manners for Advanced Lovers* out of her hands. It was the last sex book they'd read together, possibly because neither had wished to reveal to the other that she hadn't understood a word of it. Sue had found another 'best friend', and Lucy had buried herself in O levels.

Since then she hadn't bothered with sex books. So why was she so wrapped up in this one? 'Most women have a definite preference as to how they like their breasts to be touched,' she read.

They do? It had never occurred to her to express a preference. Or that there might be a choice about the matter. It was an exciting thought. Her nipples tingled. She could express a preference. But how? There were the kneaders, the twiddlers and the jigglers, basically; and men who could do all three, which could be rather tiring. Ned was a kneader. Hm. Phil, she suspected, drifting off into one of the now ubiquitous Phil dreams, perhaps he would know exactly how she liked to be touched without her having to express a preference.

On the other hand, she thought, summoning up her logical self, rather than the dreamy side of her nature that seemed to be so dominant at the moment, that wasn't, perhaps, fair. On Ned or anyone else. She wouldn't expect either Ned or Phil to know what she wanted in a restaurant (although men in the 1940s and 1950s did apparently order for women without consulting them, according to Owen; 'Women can't be trusted to know their own minds,' he'd harrumphed), so she could hardly expect them to know how she liked her breasts touched. Particularly as she hadn't given the matter much thought herself.

Perhaps today's confident young women – the ones who discussed pubic hairstyles as openly as the hair on their head – gave crisp, clear directions. 'No, not like that. Roll it between your fingers as if you were rolling a joint.' Perhaps she and Grace belonged to as much of a lost generation in these matters as the women who'd sat, smiling politely, as they were ordered Brown Windsor Soup and Roast Beef, when they were secretly longing for Consommé and Fried Dover Sole.

She looked at her watch. Shit. Should have started surgery ten minutes ago. Reluctantly consigning her fantasies of Phil and what he could do to her breasts to the back burner, she remembered the statistic about men in their teens and twenties thinking about sex every six minutes. Were there any statistics saying that women in their forties thought about sex every six seconds? Almost definitely not. Stop it, Lucy. Direct these fantasies towards your husband.

She pressed the buzzer, but was still dreaming when a sturdy blonde girl appeared. 'Oh. Ah. Imogen . . . er . . . Jones.' Lucy shuffled papers on her desk to find the notes. 'Yes. Now, what I can do for you?'

'I'd like a referral to a cosmetic surgeon.' There was a certain amount of defiance in Imogen's attitude, as if she expected Lucy to refuse her. 'I know it'll be private, of course,' she added, as Lucy opened her mouth.

'I want a breast reduction.'

A spasm of pain virtually shot through Lucy's breasts, newly sensitive as they were to the possibilities of preferences, and she almost had to refrain from shielding them with her hands. 'I see. Why?'

'Well, I would have thought that was obvious.' The girl sounded shirty, as if Lucy was being deliberately obtuse. Lucy studied her. She seemed well rounded rather than top heavy. 'I'm sick to death of having big ones. My back aches. I get shouted at by men the whole time, and I can't wear halter tops or bikinis. Or practically anything fashionable.'

'None of us are happy with our breasts,' commented Lucy, thinking of the burden that the cantaloupes had been to her over the years. 'Coming to terms with your body is part of growing up. Nobody is perfect.'

Imogen looked irritated at the cliché. 'If you don't

give me a referral, I'll have to use the advertisements in magazines, and everyone says that's where you get the butchers. Nothing you say is going to change my mind.'

Lucy felt like snapping that she didn't like blackmail. 'Well, it is better to go to your GP because there are incompetent surgeons and disreputable clinics out there. And all surgery carries a risk, sometimes quite a considerable one.' She leant forward. 'I'm not refusing you, but I wanted to feel sure you've really thought about it.' She didn't know why she wasn't just writing out the name of the perfectly good cosmetic surgeon and sending the girl on her way.

'I'm prepared to take any risks.' Imogen was beginning to sound sullen.

'Have you got a boyfriend?'

'What's that got to do with it?'

'Nothing,' conceded Lucy. 'But I'd feel happier if I knew this was entirely your decision, and not something that you're being pressurized to do by somebody else.'

'I make my own decisions. He likes my breasts as they are. But he says he'll back me up if I want to have smaller ones.'

That sounded OK. Anyway, it was rare for men to press for a reduction. 'What about your family life?' Lucy persevered. 'Is everything stable there at the moment?'

'Look, what is this?' Imogen sounded weary. 'I'm just here for a pretty bog-standard cosmetic surgery referral, not for psychotherapy. I'm sure they'll give me counselling there, anyway, if that's what you're worrying about.'

Lucy was sure that some kind of self-hatred or personal distress lay beneath the desire for this operation. If, after all, women could express a preference as to how they liked their breasts touched, it followed that this could be a source of pleasure. And here was a girl opting for an operation that would almost definitely reduce that element in her life. She was intending, deliberately, to remove part of her sexual response in order to look better. Lucy couldn't work out why she found that so distressing suddenly. She'd referred women before without worrying about it.

'Did you know,' she asked, abruptly, 'that the sensitivity of your nipples will probably be reduced considerably by the operation? That that will probably lessen your sexual response? And that ultimately you may have some trouble breast-feeding?'

'Good,' said Imogen, brutally. 'I can't bear the way they go straight for my tits. I feel fingered. Like something on a shelf in a supermarket. Men. They're just obsessed. The less I can feel, the better. I'll be well out of it. And, as for breast-feeding, well, it'll just have to have a bottle. If I ever have one of the little bastards, which I hope I don't.'

Looking at this girl, Lucy couldn't help feeling that behind all those breezy articles on pubic hairstyles and sexual technique hid a generation that was just as unawakened as hers had been.

Lucy gave up, and scribbled out a name. 'Here you are. But do think about it.'

As Imogen got up to go, she looked directly at Lucy's breasts. 'I'm surprised you haven't had it done yourself.'

It was rare for a patient to see a doctor as a person. They usually came in completely obsessed with their own problems. So Lucy was too astonished to speak for a moment.

'That's because I know more than you do about what surgery can do,' she said, her voice sharper than it should have been. 'I've never wanted to mutilate myself.'

Imogen flushed. 'They said you were more sympathetic than that Dr Gardner,' she spat. 'But I won't be coming back to you again.'

Lucy suppressed the word 'good' and pressed the buzzer for the next patient with a shaking hand. She usually tried to remain absolutely impersonal about the people who came into her surgery. She hadn't done anything wrong, but, deep down, she knew she'd been unprofessional in the way she'd let Imogen get to her. Still, it was nothing to what Michael Gardner would have been like if she had gone to him. He'd have shouted in derision and told her that she was a very silly girl.

She should be more sympathetic to women who wanted a choice. She knew she should be. She just didn't think this was about choice. It was about someone looking for answers but asking the wrong questions.

Never mind. She'd done her best. With the uneasy feeling that she hadn't, she composed her face to look sympathetic and suitably encouraging for the next patient.

In the end, to get the time off to take Owen to the hospital, she'd had to swap a surgery with Michael after all, because the other two partners both had cast-iron reasons why they couldn't. Michael had grumbled. 'You women. If it's not one thing, it's another. The minute your children can get from A to B on their own, you're rushing into hospitals with your parents. Or neighbours,' he added, sounding as if it was sheer self-indulgence on Lucy's part. Lucy had found herself apologizing profusely, and telling him how good it was of him, but, as she finally accelerated out of town, going a little too fast because she'd got snagged by a last-minute phone call, she found herself seething. 'Bloody, bloody man.'

The road curved back and forward on itself so often that it was impossible to go fast comfortably, and the rhythmic twists and turns eventually soothed her into an almost hypnotic state. The fields and villages were waking up to spring, in impossibly girlie shades of lime green, sky blue and hyacinth pink, as the first leaves, pale and acidic, appeared on trees, and cascades of fragile cherry blossom carpeted lawns and pavements like a sudden fall of snow. This time of the year was so frivolous, she thought, thinking of Grace's bedroom, with its piles of jewel-coloured shoes, the beaded and sequinned handbags hanging on the walls next to strappy silk dresses in shades of lilac, peony and daffodil white, and an effusion of beads, bangles and ropes twisted around two candle sconces on a mirror. Spring was like Grace's bedroom – wantonly colourful for the sake of it. Everywhere you looked there was something else to delight – a drift of honey-scented blossom or a tiny, pretty scent bottle, which Grace would unstopper the way most people used shampoo. 'Here, have a splash,' she'd say, and the scent of flowers would fill the air.

Even Owen's rigorous gardening style had been unable to subdue the frivolity of the time of year, she thought, as she swung into the parking space in front of his cottage. Strictly a functional gardener, he regarded flowers as self-indulgent, and was so little interested in the aesthetic side of gardening that he suppressed weeds with rolls of old carpet, and marshalled military rows of sprouts into the central, most visible and, therefore, the sunniest spot. But the fruit trees, in clouds of white like 1950s debutantes in their first ball dresses, protested that prettiness was just as valuable in this world as vitamins, and self-seeded bluebells carpeted themselves at their base.

Once Owen had settled himself crossly in the passenger seat, her optimistic mood evaporated. She prayed that they weren't going to be too delayed at the hospital. She had to be back by six to pick Tom up from football practice, Nico needed dropping off at the school theatre at half-past seven and col-

179

lecting at nine, and the result of all these tightly interwoven logistics was that Owen would have to spend the night with them, and she'd have to get up at six the following morning to drive him back. Ned, in theory, could have helped with some of it, but if something unexpected happened at the hospital it was such an effort to re-organize her plans that it was easier just to leave him out of it.

The newly decorated reception area at the hospital promised a punctuality that failed to materialize. An hour and a half after their appointment was due, when a nurse had promised that there were 'only two patients ahead of your father', she rang Grace in desperation over collecting Tom.

'Of course. You should have asked me earlier. I said any time,' said Grace.

'I didn't want you to have to drive all the way over.'

'I never mind. Shall I keep him for the night?'

As she rang off, it occurred to Lucy that, on a practical, day-to-day basis, it would be easier to be married to Grace than to Ned.

Carefully suppressed fear filled the peach-tinted lobby. Two elderly men, alike enough to be brothers, sat side by side, one holding a notepad and pencil. A tired-looking woman sat beside a twenty-years-younger version of herself, who was heavily pregnant and trying to control a toddler, and another woman sat alone, not reading anything, staring at her hands in blank-eyed terror.

'I've just heard it's come back,' she said to a nurse.

'They told me I was clear, but it's come back.' The nurse smiled and murmured, squeezing her arm in reassurance, but Lucy sensed that the rest of the room didn't want to hear. They had enough of their own problems to deal with. Owen read a biography of an obscure general, hardly even glancing at the clock, and refusing the plastic cup of water Lucy offered him. By the time they were called in to the specialist they were both almost too exhausted to care.

The consultant, who seemed absurdly young – perhaps consultants were like policemen and you knew you were getting older when they started to look like teenagers – was brisk and factual. They could have been talking about options for repairing or maintaining a car, not about preserving what remained of Owen's life.

'You're a sensible man,' said Owen eventually, to Lucy's surprise. He didn't rate doctors usually. 'Now what I want to know is exactly how long I've got. Whether I should be planting for autumn or not.'

The consultant looked disconcerted at having to measure Owen's life in horticultural terms. 'I don't know much about planting,' he admitted. 'But I do know that cancer is far less predictable than growing potatoes. I think we can confidently give you, say, six months or so. Anything after that is a bonus. But I could be wrong. Completely wrong. I've just seen someone I gave three months to live three years ago. So I'd keep planting if I were you.' He smiled in a rictus of encouragement, but Lucy could see he didn't mean it.

Lucy counted on her fingers. It was now May, then that would take them to November. Not long. She hadn't expected it to be that quick. She wanted to lean her head on someone's shoulder, and for them to tell her that everything would all be all right in the end. Once upon a time, long ago, and in the faraway land of childhood, that shoulder had been Owen's.

Owen acknowledged the death sentence with a brisk, soldierly nod. Lucy visualized his neat rows of beans and peas lying unpicked in overblown pods, the slugs eating his lettuces, and weeds choking the feathery tops of the carrots until they could hardly be seen. Once he was no longer strong enough to garden, nature would sweep over it in weeks, smothering years of careful work.

They went over symptoms he should watch for, explained the medicine he should be taking, and Owen resolutely denied feeling anything but 'perfectly all right'.

Lucy thought this stoicism might be a mask for denial. Whatever gets you through, I suppose, she thought, taking his arm as they went back to the gleaming foyer with cheerfully 'patient-centric' mission statements nailed to the wall, which grated against her awareness of the delays they'd endured.

'I've joined these EXIT jobbies,' he said, as they

left the hospital. 'The suicide people,' he added, in case she didn't understand.

'Dad.'

'No, listen to me. I won't involve you because . . . well, you know. But if I decide to go on my own terms, don't stop me.'

'I won't,' she promised, wondering what the 'EXIT jobbies' might entail. Locked garages with running car exhausts, she supposed. The air in the hospital car park was cool and clear. Everything around her seemed normal – the cars with their drivers hurrying home, the nodding daffodils and a young mother struggling along the pavement, with a baby in a sling, a toddler in a buggy and a four-year-old hanging onto her coat. It seemed a long way from the fume-filled garage of her imagination, with Owen preparing himself for death as if it was a night's sleep. She'd have to identify his body. Ned's reassuring face appeared in her mind. Ned would do it. Perhaps that wasn't fair on Ned, but she knew he'd insist. He'd never let her go through with anything frightening if he could take it off her shoulders. So why did she feel so far away from him at the moment?

'I've always thought that when it all got too much, the National Health would give you a nice injection and you'd just drift away,' Owen said. 'But I've seen that it doesn't happen that way.'

'We're not allowed.'

'Hmph. Don't tell me there aren't ways and means.'

'Look, if there's one thing that Ned and I can guarantee you, it's that we won't let you suffer unnecessarily. I'll make sure that you get everything to make you comfortable. There's no need to . . . you know.'

'Comfortable. Huh. They revive you in hospitals these days,' he snorted. 'If I'm slipping away, I don't want that. I can't think of anything worse, being revived. And for what? More pain? I don't think so.'

'I promise you,' said Lucy again. 'No one's going to revive you, unless you specifically ask for it.'

'How do I know that some young whippersnapper of a doctor won't do it, just because he doesn't want to be arrested for being a Dr Shipman?'

Lucy felt unequal to the scope of this conversation. 'Because he won't. Believe me.' She thought of adding that hospital budgets today meant that young whipper-snappers of doctors were hardly likely to concentrate on reviving eighty-two-year-old cancer patients with secondaries everywhere, but decided that this would be a brutal fact too far.

They were stuck in a queue of traffic leaving the city, and Lucy consulted her watch. They'd just be back in time to drop Nico off. If this traffic jam moved soon.

'They're tarting up the roundabout,' grumbled Owen as they eventually inched round what appeared to be three workmen planting a tree. 'That's all they do these days. Prettify roundabouts and smarten up reception areas while everything underneath falls apart. It's all style in this generation, no substance. I'm glad I won't be living much longer. Heaven help you when you get to this stage.'

Lucy blotted it out of her mind. She had reached a point in her life when she sometimes almost agreed with Owen's opinions. Perhaps it was called getting old. She concentrated, instead, on what she was going to wear next Tuesday, to the surgery. She thought that maybe her tummy was getting a bit less like a huge, wobbly blancmange

'What's that smell?' demanded Owen, when they got home.

Lucy sniffed. 'Nico's scented candles, I think.'

'Scented candles? Scented candles? The boy's a complete poof.'

'It's the fashion nowadays,' she explained wearily. 'One of my friend's sons burned down the whole of the top floor of their house with his scented candles.'

For a moment, Owen looked impressed, as if scented candles had gone up in his estimation for being able to wreak such destruction. Then he snorted. 'For girls mebbe, but boys? Never. Not unless they're pansies. I don't know. My grandson a pansy! I was in the army at his age, not messing about with scented thingies.'

Lucy decided not to point out that at his age, he, like Nico, had almost undoubtedly still been at school. 'Yes, well, times have changed. Nico! Time to go.'

Nico took far longer than necessary to come down the stairs. Lucy ached to sit down with a drink rather than be back in a car again.

14

The following day was Saturday. Normally Lucy didn't do surgery, except for once every two months, but this was the day she was due to pay Michael back. She sat in her sunny room, seeing a succession of undemanding headaches, sore throats, vomiting and a case of chicken pox. She flicked through details of the back-up Owen could expect – the terminal grant, the district nurse, even some psychological help. She smiled. He wouldn't have anything to do with things he described as 'namby-pamby'. The word 'psychology' had him snorting derisively. But it must be so lonely for him, handling all this without talking to anyone about how he felt. Surely he must feel frightened, or angry, or sad? All he ever said was, 'I'm fine.' He didn't want sympathy, or – heaven help anyone dishing it out – pity, but he must, surely, want some kind of love or comfort? He must miss Sarah very much now. Or did you forget after so many years?

Nothing ever turned out how you expected it to.

The clock inched slowly round to twelve, and she shut the surgery and drove to Grace's house to collect Tom and have a quick lunch.

*

'Thanks for dinner the other night.' Grace opened a bottle of white wine. 'And I thought Phil was lovely.'

Lucy was surprised. Grace had talked to Ned and Nico for most of the evening.

'Unfortunately, everyone else in Bramsea seems to think so, too,' added Grace. 'So I haven't a chance.'

'What do you mean?'

'I was talking to that Josephine woman at school – the one who keeps complaining about everything –'

'Josie Saunders, I know,' interrupted Lucy.

'– and she mentioned his name. I can't remember why, exactly. Anyway, she was singing his praises, and then another mother – not one I've met before – said, "Oh yes, Phil Gray, I adore him, he's so sensible." '

'Sensible? Have we got to the stage in our lives where "sensible" is the sexiest thing you can say about someone?' Lucy couldn't help laughing, although the thought that she was just one of a large number of women having fantasies about Phil was crushing. She had to stop. This morning, she'd had a whole conversation in her head with him as she walked to the surgery, and had probably been smiling and nodding to herself like a madwoman.

'You won't have an affair with him, will you?' asked Grace, anxiously.

Lucy was taken aback. 'No, of course not. Why do you ask?'

'Because Ned's so nice. He just doesn't deserve it.'

'I know.' Lucy sighed. 'Nice. Sensible. God, what

have we come to? Where are the bad boys that made our younger lives such a misery?'

Grace smiled. 'I should think that anyone involved with Phil would probably find that, nice and sensible as he is, he's pretty difficult to pin down. Josie says that he's had a succession of different girlfriends since he came to live here. So he's hardly likely to fancy me. Not at my age.'

'Why do you always put yourself down? They all fancy you – Ned, that builder Sean . . .' She stopped. She hadn't been sure whether it was a good idea to tell Grace what Sean had said, in case it triggered off a disastrous encounter, but Grace seemed to think so little of herself that it couldn't possibly hurt.

Grace laughed with delight at the story. Lucy left out the bit about Sean thinking she was trouble.

'How's your father?' Grace twirled a bowl of green leaves together, and added a few drops of something dark and sharp. The French windows out of the kitchen were open and they could see Luke and Tom playing football. They'd been doing it for hours, according to Grace.

'Trying to pretend he's fine. His face looks like cracked porcelain, and he moves terribly slowly. He's getting very short of breath, too.'

'And how are you? About it all, I mean.'

Lucy sighed again. 'Well, you know. A mix of things. Regret. Fear. It's scary, knowing that someone you love is going to die, even if he's had his three-score-and-ten. It still seems such a waste. He's got all his marbles, and his health is fantastic apart from this. He could have gone on in his garden for another five or ten years very happily, and seen Tom grow up. I know he'd have loved that. But you must have felt all that when your father died.'

'When my father died,' said Grace, with an elaborate pretence of sounding casual, 'it was the end of a dream. A dream of ever expecting to have a father. A proper one, that is. He didn't want me from the start and didn't want me at the end.'

'Oh, Grace, I'm sure he did. Perhaps he just wasn't very good at showing it.'

Grace shook her head, and clattered knives and forks down on the table more noisily than necessary. 'I was the afterthought of the family, and I just irritated him. My sister and eldest brother were already at university, and John, the youngest, was at boarding school, so they decided – or, rather, I suspect my mother decided – to have one last baby to mend their marriage. Or perhaps she just wanted to prove to his mistress that they were still sleeping together. I think it worked for a bit. Of course, by the time she left hospital with me in my Moses basket, he'd started splitting time between us and some other girl. So I was a complete failure from the beginning.'

Lucy's heart cramped with sympathy for Grace. 'Oh, no. Didn't you have any good times together?'

Grace took a deep breath. 'Do you mind if I tell you something I've never told anyone?'

Lucy shook her head. 'Go ahead. Remember, I'm bound to have heard worse.'

'It's really awful. You won't like me any more.'

'Don't be silly, Grace,' Lucy touched her shoulder lightly. 'I'll always like you. No matter what you've done.'

'Do you think it makes things better if you talk about them?' Grace sounded anxious. 'Because sometimes I think I've forgotten all about this, and then it pops up, just when I'm looking at myself in a shop mirror, or when I'm talking to someone – well, a man, I suppose – that I like, and I remember. I'm a bad person.'

Lucy shook her arm. 'There's no such thing as a "bad person", and even if there was, it wouldn't be you. Tell me. I can't promise that it'll help, but it might.'

Grace took a deep breath. 'My father. I always wanted his attention, but he'd brush me away. He'd open my report from school, grunt and throw it away. Even if it was good. He never came to sports day, or to school plays, or to parents' evenings. He left all that to Mum. If I brought any of my paintings home, he'd tell me not to clutter up the house with trash. I don't think he intended to be particularly cruel – he was just very remote and uninterested in me. I suppose he resented me because my presence had tied him to a household he'd wanted to leave.' Grace twiddled her hair furiously, and then began to slide her wedding ring up and down her finger. 'So it wasn't really his fault. It was mine.

'Because as I grew up I soon realized that what he did notice, and did like, was pretty women. From the age of about eleven, I used to see him look at me. Look properly, that is, not just as if I was in the way. So I tried extra hard to look good – lost my puppy fat, refused to wear my glasses and chose clothes that were deliberately fashionable or sexy, or just to make the most of what I had. Tops that clung to make the most of my tiny tits, stuffing my bra with socks, hitching my school skirt up by rolling the waistband over and over – all those tricks.'

Lucy nodded. She'd twisted her own waistband over often enough in the 1960s, although she'd never needed to stuff her bra with socks. She'd envied those who did, though.

'Anyway, one day, just before my fourteenth birthday, I was particularly pleased with something I'd bought – do you remember hot pants? And that awful shiny, clingy material they were made in? I'd bought a hot pants set in red, and I was trying it on, looking at myself in my parents' long pier glass in their bedroom, because it was the only long mirror in the house.'

Grace drifted off, with a smoky look in her eyes, but pulled herself together, back to the present, and Lucy could see that it was getting difficult for her to talk. 'He came in,' she said, eventually. 'I hadn't heard him at the front door. He sometimes didn't come home for days at a time. He used to spend whole nights with Her, and my mother never dared say anything about it in case he never came home again. My mother would have done anything to keep him. Literally anything. You were no one without a husband in those days.

'He was drunk, I think. At least he smelt of wine and cigarettes. He was standing at the bedroom door, looking at me looking at myself in the mirror. For the first time ever, he seemed really pleased to see me. He put his hand out, and called me "darling".' Grace swallowed. 'And when he drew me to him, I was so thrilled. To be held by my father, like all the other girls I used to see hugging their fathers when they came to fetch them at the end of term, well, it was my dream. But he put his hand on my breasts, and then began to push the horrible clingy material of the top up and began to touch and pinch my nipples . . . and then . . .' she sighed, 'he went further, and began to undo the hot pants. I didn't know what he was up to, or what it all meant. I really didn't – you must think I was so stupid – although technically I knew all about sex. I just couldn't quite believe that this was what it was. I almost thought – don't laugh – that he was just trying to help me adjust my clothes. I'm so stupid. He kept calling me "darling" and breathing very heavily.' Grace hunched herself into her shoulders and avoided Lucy's eye.

'Anyway, he'd just got his hand down my knickers and was touching me, and pressing my hand to his trousers . . . well, you can imagine . . . and we heard my mother at the front door. She called my name. He just pushed me away, called me a slut and walked out of the room.

'And he never looked at me again. No matter what I wore – and I'm ashamed to say that I went on dressing as provocatively as I could – he turned his head away when I came into the room. We had no connection ever again.'

Lucy could hear birdsong outside the window, and the soft, intermittent roar of distant cars, but otherwise the room seemed very quiet.

'The trouble is –' Grace's face seemed very hard '– that it was my fault. I sort of knew what I was doing when I dressed like that. And those things he did . . . well, I thought it was all right. I thought it was love. So I . . . liked it. That's what's so bad about me.'

Lucy put her hand over Grace's. 'I promise you that very young teenage girls have the right to wear what they like without being assaulted by any man, particularly their own fathers. He was an adult, and even if he was drunk, it was entirely his responsibility. And he knew it. That's why he could never face you again.'

Grace shook her head. 'I wish I could believe that. I wish I didn't think that I have some perverted, abnormal sex drive.'

'Is that what Richard says?'

Grace scratched furiously at her arm, almost as if to draw blood. 'Yes. If I try to talk to him about sex at all.' She looked frightened for a moment. 'But he doesn't know. Promise you won't tell him. It'll just confirm all his worst suspicions about me – that I'm an over-sexed tart.'

Lucy winced. 'You aren't,' she said, trying to convey her conviction and undo over thirty years of Grace's self-hatred. 'And I promise you you haven't got an abnormal sex drive. Your husband doesn't make love to you, ever, and lots of women would find that very difficult.'

'But not you.'

'I don't get the chance to find out,' said Lucy. 'I mean, if Ned stopped wanting it, I might well start thinking about what I'm missing. But Ned's so straight up-and-down he wants it every Saturday night and twice a week on holiday.' She couldn't help laughing. 'He's just the nicest, most normal man in the world. It's me that's odd.'

Grace managed a watery grin. 'So both of us are weirdos.'

'And if it's any help . . .' Lucy retrieved a long-suppressed memory from her childhood, 'it's always a shock suddenly finding out how frightening sex can be.'

'You, too?'

'Not anything on your scale. There was an old man in the park who used to get hold of little girls – well, usually ten- and eleven-year-olds, who were beginning to mature but were still small enough to catch hold of – and put his hand down their knickers and push his fingers into their vaginas. He caught me one day because he asked me if I had the time, and pretended not to hear me, so I showed him my watch. He grabbed my hand and pulled up my skirt. I couldn't imagine what he was doing at first, so I didn't resist. You get into the habit of being polite to grown-ups, however oddly they seem to be behaving. But when I felt his great fat finger between my legs, I bit him, and he swore, and I managed to wriggle out of his arms. I didn't tell anyone because I was embarrassed, and I didn't want the fuss. And I thought it was my fault for being so stupid.'

'How did you feel afterwards?'

Lucy thought back to running upstairs to her bedroom, slamming the door and locking it, as if he was still after her. She'd thrown herself down on her bed, and her teddies and dolls had seemed to mock her, as if they belonged securely in a world she was locked out of for ever. She'd felt as if her mind and body had somehow become dissociated from each other, but she couldn't quite sum up the sensation for Grace. 'I thought . . .' she said, eventually, 'that nothing would ever be the same again. As if I'd been marked or branded.'

'And was it?'

'I felt odd for about a week. Different. Dirty. But it wore off. And when he did it again to another girl who was a bit braver than me, about a year later, she told the police. They caught him and he went inside, and I just thought, oh, he's been doing it all these years, and none of us has ever told. We should have done.'

'Do you think that's why you don't enjoy sex now?'

'No,' sighed Lucy. 'I don't. I don't know enough about the psychology of it all, but although it was horrid, it didn't really impinge on my daily life. I wasn't betrayed by a close friend or a relative. And it only happened once. Bad things do happen. They don't have to leave you scarred for life. What you went through, because it was your father, and the repercussions lasted so long, was much worse.'

'Do you think it happens to every little girl? In some way? Or is it just us?'

Their eyes met, comfortable and conspiratorial. 'I wouldn't be surprised,' said Lucy. 'Perhaps it's just part of growing up. The beginning of learning to be careful.'

She thought she saw some of the shadows leave Grace's eyes.

'If you had an affair with Phil,' Grace asked, just before they called the boys in to eat, 'would you tell me?'

Lucy laughed. 'It's not going to happen. It's all a fantasy. But, yes, if I did, by some mad accident, I would tell you.'

Later, as she drove home with Tom in the back, she realized that she hadn't asked Grace if she'd tell Lucy about an affair if she was having one. Surely she would, though. They talked about everything.

15

Later on that week, Lucy crept into Nico's room and surreptitiously extracted a smeared plate from under a pile of cheesy clothes. It rattled with a few hardened baked beans and a discarded crust. Almost bent double in her efforts not to make a sound, she felt like a nun attending to the temple of some obscure misogynistic sect as she quietly sifted out two football shirts, three non-matching socks and a pair of trousers that might or might not need washing. One trouser leg flopped against a book left open on the edge of the bed. It crashed to the floor, and Nico, who had been hunched over his desk, deliberately ignoring her, turned a face of martyred outrage to her.

'Mum! For God's sake.' It was the exasperated expression of a great man, engaged on important work, who is constantly distracted by trivia.

Lucy tiptoed out, apologizing, grabbing a last pair of pants from the back of a chair as she passed. She shut the door with a sigh. Not a bad haul. She'd asked him to bring his washing down that morning, and he'd glared at her.

'I am revising, you know. Do you want me to pass my A levels, or are you more interested in whether I'm wearing clean underpants?' His voice was scathing.

Lucy, who'd just read a piece in the *Guardian* about parents being supportive during exams by not nagging about minor issues, such as tidy bedrooms, had backed down immediately, but she knew that it was only a matter of days, or even possibly hours, before he strode downstairs demanding to know why he never had any clean clothes. The baked bean offensive was the first of a series of cunning commando raids she'd planned on his bedroom.

Tom sat disconsolately on the stairs. 'Nico shouted at me.'

Lucy sat down beside him, and put her arm round him, relishing the feel of his chunky, confiding shoulders. He still wanted cuddles. Heaven knows what Nico did for comfort. She looked reflectively at the closed door.

'He's doing A levels, darling. Exams. They're very important. We've all got to be very nice to him and not get upset when he shouts.'

'That's not fair.' Tom was indignant.

'Life's not fair,' she replied automatically.

'Your life is perfectly fair,' he observed. 'It's mine that isn't. Grown-ups keep all the fairness to themselves.'

'I don't think so, Tom. Honestly. Look, come with me to Grandad's. I'm going to cook him some supper and then come back here. He'd love to see you.'

'It's an awfully long way.' Tom wriggled out of her embrace. 'I think I'll just stay here on the computer.'

She contemplated knocking on Nico's door and

telling him he was in charge of Tom until Ned came back, but decided she didn't quite dare. A note would have to do instead.

'I don't like it when you aren't there to kiss me goodnight,' said Tom, suddenly looking like a very lost little boy. 'It feels lonely.'

Her heart twisted, as she gave him a last hug. 'Sweetheart. Daddy'll be home soon.'

'He'd better be,' she muttered, as she accelerated away from the house.

Lucy was beginning to hate the car. She went over to Owen's two evenings a week, plus one lunchtime at weekends, to cook for him, take in some shopping and generally keep an eye on things. That was six hours a week, in good traffic. More in bad. Almost a whole working day.

But you can't think like that when someone is dying.

Owen didn't seem particularly pleased to see her.

'Oh. It's you.' He was in the front garden, with a hoe, and she could see that whereas last year he'd methodically jabbed and cut at weeds, expertly flicking them out from between the plants, this year he lifted the hoe as if it was an unwieldy iron girder, dropping it down inaccurately and pausing as if to summon up the energy to lift it again.

'Why don't I do that?' Lucy hated weeding.

'Nonsense. Don't be silly. You've no idea. Not the faintest clue.' He glared at her. 'Just a bit of a hot day, that's all.' He didn't look hot. He looked almost transparent.

She urged him to sit down and take a break.

'Don't you worry about me, Missy Clever Doctor.' He turned away, lifting the hoe painfully slowly and letting it fall with a thump. Lucy winced.

'I'll just clear things away in the kitchen, shall I, and sort out dinner?'

'If you must.'

Why did they all think she wanted to spend her life scraping at encrusted plates and sifting laundry? Although Owen had always been fastidious, and wasn't as bad as Nico, she could see the signs of his deterioration everywhere. There was something stinking in a cupboard, where he'd placed it accidentally instead of in the fridge. Every week there was another major job to be tackled, such as the pieces of food that had slipped down the side of the cooker, and which his failing eyesight hadn't detected.

Lucy loathed housework and had never been good at it.

When he eventually came in, and sat down with a sigh, she asked him whether fish pie would be OK for him.

'I couldn't eat,' he said. 'I couldn't possibly eat.'

A worm of fear wriggled in Lucy's stomach. Was this the beginning of the end? She continued to lay the table. She'd let him get his breath back, and just put the food in front of him.

He picked at it, but ate a reasonable amount in the end.

She thought he might be amused about Nico. Ned and Owen were the only two people in the world who felt exactly the way she did about the boys. In the past, she'd often teased him out of a bad temper by telling him something funny they'd done.

He didn't appear to be listening. 'You spoil the boy. It'll do him no good,' he said when she'd finished.

Did she? Although she knew that it was only his bad mood speaking, she felt a clutch of panic inside. Was she setting Nico up to think that the world was going to wait on him? Should she be making a stand? She remembered the *Guardian* article. No. Now was not the time to make stands.

'Any news?' She tried to change the subject.

'What sort of news might you be expecting?' He was touchy about references to his illness.

'Any sort of news. For example, how are you feeling?'

'As well as can be expected,' he barked. 'For God's sake, woman, I'm going to be dead this time next year, how do you think I'm feeling?'

Lucy was determined to persevere. To try to penetrate the wall of bad-tempered loneliness he'd erected.

'Angry? Frightened?' She felt foolish, but she didn't know how else to reach him.

He glared at her. 'Don't be absurd. You've been talking to those trick-cyclist chaps again. They have to justify their jobs somehow, so they invent problems for people to have. It's just a damned nuisance, that's all. I shall be glad when it's all over.'

She looked out of the window. It was still light, and she could see a huge splash of fluffy blue ceanothus blooming against the old brick wall of the garden, and drifts of ivory-pink blossom on the apple trees. The birds swooped and dived, busy, busy, busy with their plans for nests and babies, chattering excitedly across the skies as their predators, the cats from next door, lay snoozing on the stone flagstones in the last of the evening sun.

There was so much loveliness in just one casual glance out of the window, and he would be glad when it was all over.

'Dad.' She put a hand on his arm and he shook it off.

'Don't pretend it's not true. I'm dying. The sooner the better. Then you'll get my money.'

'I don't want your money, Dad. I want you.' She took their plates out, and washed up. There was no point in staying any longer. She'd either snap at him or cry, and neither would help.

She thought he looked slightly ashamed when she came out of the kitchen. 'I've tidied it all up in there. I'll be back on Thursday.'

He nodded in acknowledgement. 'You don't have to. I can manage.'

'I want to.' She suppressed a sigh.

She felt lost as she drove back beside the grassy green hedges, as if her personality was seeping away into everyone else's problems.

'Where am I in all this?' Lucy asked herself. 'Who am I?' When Nico's A levels were over, and Owen was . . . she pushed the thought away . . . then she could think about herself. When they were all gone, there would be time. Sadness welled up in her.

She suddenly saw a sign on the left which said 'Little Topping   2'.

Phil lived in Little Topping. Lucy turned the wheel, almost without being aware of it. She might as well check out the village. She and Ned often looked around pretty rural villages 'for their retirement'. In reality, Bramsea, with its pretty, shop-filled, pedestrianized streets, was far more practical.

She parked the car on Little Topping's village green, feeling uncomfortably like a stalker. Was she doing this to bump into Phil, and if, by some bizarre accident, she did, how on earth would she explain herself? There was nothing in Little Topping's Post Office, its only shop, to explain the detour.

She stared at the village green, an irregular triangle chopped off at one corner by a pond and fringed with a medley of brick or pink-painted cottages. Astonishing puffs of lilac wisteria frothed up a wall, and columns of star-shaped pink clematis wound their way round trees and hedges. A half-timbered pub sprouted hanging baskets with draping greenery. The startling blues and reds of summer had not yet arrived.

She knew she'd forgotten something. They needed eggs. So the detour hadn't been a waste of time after all. Feeling almost cheerful, she edged into the village shop, past piled-up bread and newspaper racks and down two narrow aisles of brightly packaged toppling produce. As she stretched up to reach the eggs, her handbag swung out and hit the only other shopper.

'Excuse me!' shrilled the woman. 'Do you mind!' It wasn't a question.

Lucy jumped. 'Oh, sorry. I didn't see you.'

The woman glared at her. 'I'll thank you to be more careful in future.'

The roughness of the stranger's tone made tears start in Lucy's eyes. She hadn't cried for Owen since the night at Grace's, and she hadn't wanted to. Crying was so bleak. It hurt.

Her throat ached at the strain of keeping the sob out of her voice as she paid for the eggs, aware of the resentment simmering from the woman behind her. As she closed the door, she thought she heard her say something about inconsiderate.

It wasn't fair. Lucy couldn't explain why the bile of a woman she'd never met before was so much more upsetting than either Nico's or Owen's behaviour, but she had to swallow back her distress.

'Hello? What are you doing here?'

It was Phil. Being found outside his house in tears really was, as Nico might have put it, so not cool.

She tried to smile. 'Hi. I, er . . .'

'Are you all right?' He put his hand on her shoulder in instinctive sympathy. 'What's wrong?'

If I start to cry, she'd told herself so many times

recently, I'll never stop. And she thought, now, that she never would.

She was grateful for the silence as he led her towards his front door. It gave her a chance to pull herself together.

He opened the door of a small cottage, and they walked into a huge space flooded with light. She blinked.

'I bought three cottages and knocked them together,' he explained. 'Which meant I could have all three ground floors as one big room, and take out the two bedrooms of the middle cottage for a double-height ceiling.' She could see the old beams of the roof above her, and he'd left all the fireplaces as islands in the middle of the space. The walls were white, with just one fiery scarlet painting dominating the biggest space.

'Heavens.' She sniffed, and blew her nose. It was so empty. This room said that Phil didn't need things. And that was only a short step to saying that Phil didn't need people. There was one huge, comfortable sofa in front of a wide-screen TV. There was a wall of books. And nothing else. No rugs, vases, knick-knacks. No cushions, invitations or letters left around. No curtains or blinds. She could see the garden and the fields beyond. It reminded her, in some ways, of the rooms of men she'd known in her twenties. There were those who kept a suitcase on the floor of a rented flat and lived out of it, without moving or changing any item of furniture, however inconvenient or hideous. They could throw their clothes back in, lock the case and walk out in less than half an hour. I don't really belong here, the suitcases had said. I won't hang around. Don't count on me to be there.

Ned's first flat, shared with two rugby mates, had been cluttered with things donated by doting aunts and mothers. Most of them were repulsive, but the boys had been too lazy or sentimental to get rid of the bulging sofas, wobbly standard lamps and dismal shades of burgundy and beige. But it had given him an air of permanence, of being grounded. Of having emotions.

Perhaps you could read too much into possessions, though. 'This place is amazing.'

He poured them two glasses of wine.

'What are you doing here?'

Lucy felt her eyes fill with tears again. 'I don't know.' At least that was honest.

'Were you coming to see me?'

She nodded, then shrugged. 'I don't know,' she repeated. 'I don't think you have a very dropping-in-ish sort of life, so I didn't like to . . .'

He smiled, with affection. 'This evening I'm not doing anything and it would be much nicer to talk to you. So tell me all about it.'

She told him.

'I expect you think I should stand up for myself. And I'm quite capable of it. But now's not the time. Owen's desperately ill – he's hardly responsible for what he's saying, and I really don't feel that I can turn on him and tell him not to be so vile or else. Or else what? I'm hardly going to stop visiting him, am I? And Nico is at a critical time. I'll tell him to behave decently once he's over the exams, but for the time being it's like living with a grizzly bear just out of hibernation.'

'I don't want to sound too pat, or too much like a psychotherapist, but Owen's not angry at you. He's just angry at the illness, and you're the only person close enough for him to take it out on.'

She nodded. 'I know. But it's still horrible. And I'm afraid to challenge him about it.'

'Why not?' He spoke gently, not accusing her.

It was a very good question. Why wasn't she prepared to sit down with Owen, and tell him that she loved him, that she would always be there for him, and that nothing he did would ever drive her away, but that she could not accept being spoken to like that?

'We've never really had intense conversations about our emotions in our family, I suppose. We don't go around hugging each other or saying that we love each other. My mother, Sarah, hated sulking or arguments, and she liked everything to be nice all the time. So I just can't face stirring everything up. Not now, when it's all so . . .' She thought for a while. 'So terrible,' she completed her sentence. 'No, no I didn't mean that. At least, it's not terrible, not the way other people have problems . . . I mean, he's eighty-two, it's not like a child dying.'

He put a hand on hers for a few seconds. It was the lightest of touches. 'You're allowed to find it terrible. Just because other people have tragedies, it doesn't diminish your grief.'

'I know, I know.' She brushed off his comfort. 'But, honestly, we should be expecting parents to die. By our age. Shouldn't we?'

'There's no should or shouldn't involved.'

'Yes, there is. I should be handling this better. I shouldn't be afraid of talking about serious things to him. I did try today, but as soon as he got cross I backed off. I just want to make it all happy again, and –' she stared down at her wine glass '– it seems easier if I'm bright and jolly about it.'

'What about Ned?'

For a moment, Lucy wondered if he realized that she'd gone numb as far as Ned was concerned. 'What do you mean?'

'Is Ned helping?'

'Oh, helping.' She thought for a few seconds. 'Well, he spends most of his time saving babies' lives, so I can't exactly ask for any more than he already does. But he does what he can.'

'Oh, dear,' said Phil. 'It's like that, is it?'

'Like what?' Lucy was defensive.

Phil didn't answer directly. 'When my wife's mother died – her father was killed when she was quite small, so her mother, like Owen, was the only one left – she left me. I didn't think anything had changed. I hadn't changed. I didn't see why a marriage that worked before her mother's death should collapse afterwards. It's one of the reasons why I became a therapist. I started looking for reasons – because I thought that if I could find the cause I could mend it. I never did find out. I wasn't cruel or unfeeling. I sorted out her mother's paperwork and helped arrange the funeral. I took her to Venice for the weekend afterwards, but it was like travelling with a ghost.'

Phil had never talked about his wife before, and Lucy'd always assumed that she'd been a spoilt, materialistic City girl who'd left because he'd changed his job and would be earning less.

'It couldn't have just been that.'

'No.' Phil's stubble was the colour of zinc, she thought. She wanted to touch it. 'I'd thought we were a good partnership. I earned – a lot – and she ran the house and brought up the children. It seemed fair.'

Lucy nodded. It was a bit old-fashioned perhaps, but not unfair. 'A clear division of labour, anyway. At least you knew where you were.'

'Fenella never quite knew where I was, unfortunately. Or, more importantly, where I would be. When she left, she said it had been like being a very well-off single parent. She went to everything alone – parents' evenings, school sports days, their first Nativity plays – everything. Because I was always doing a deal that was valued at, say, ten million pounds, and you can't ever say that a primary school Nativity play is worth screwing up that much money for.

'It even affected our social life. We'd be invited out to dinner, and I'd ring up in the morning and say I had to work all night again, and she'd ring the hostess. Some would tell her not to worry and to come on her own, but quite a few wouldn't want an extra woman at the table messing up their numbers, and would say, "Oh, what a shame. Another time, perhaps." Fenella said it was as if she had no value as herself.'

'But when you decided to give it all up and be a therapist, and take more control of your hours, surely she must have been relieved? Wasn't that what she'd wanted all along? Yet, didn't she go and marry another banker, instead of coming with you?'

Phil pushed his hand back across his forehead, as if to sweep away the thoughts. 'I'd broken so many promises by then, I don't suppose she believed me. Or perhaps she didn't know any other life. Sometimes I think I'd trapped her in a gilded cage. That she'd become unable to fly out. Whatever.

'And sometimes I think – when I can bear to – that perhaps she simply loved the man she met at the school parents' evening. Where, of course, I wasn't, and neither was his wife because she'd left him. Simon's a nice man, and not as driven as I was. He's near retirement. And he cherishes her.'

'Lucky Fenella.' Cherish. It wasn't a word you often heard these days, but it summed up a certain kind of love. Lucy wondered if Fenella luxuriated in being loved at last, if she appreciated the cherishing, or whether she occasionally stifled a yawn and turned away from Simon in bed, claiming a headache, thinking of how Phil's body had felt against hers instead. Had Fenella found her happy ending, or had she closed the door with regret? It was all so unlike the vague stories that circulated round Bramsea about his marriage that she suspected he rarely confided in anyone about it.

'And you think her mother's death brought everything in your marriage to a head?'

'I know it did. Maybe it released her from being a good daughter, and therefore also a dutiful wife. Perhaps she saw time slipping away from her. Or it may merely have been a coincidence.'

'But you don't think so.'

'Lucy.' His voice was like a caress. 'Ned loves you, you know. He's proud of you. I can see that in his eyes when he looks at you across a room.'

Lucy was embarrassed. 'Not really. I'm an awful wife to him. Not the sort of efficient, perfect wife men want.'

'You're just overloaded at the moment. Is there anything – anything at all – that you can get rid of or cut down on in all this?'

Lucy wanted to lean her head against his shoulder. She shook her head. 'No. Sometimes I just want to escape from it all. I can understand now why people have affairs. It would be something that was completely selfish and that would be heavenly. To be completely selfish.' For a moment, she allowed the memories of the old days to surface, when her problems could be solved by a party, by meeting a new man. It had all been about newness – something new to buy, a new man to take off the new dress, a new club or restaurant, a new friend, a new job . . . each promising a possible happy ending. She could remember the tangle of unfamiliar limbs, the excitement of the chase, the discoveries, the fascination with each other, the tantalizing expectation of more to follow. And, of course, the tears and the betrayals, the belief that the party would soon be over, but always wanting just one more dance. When Lucy met Ned, she'd turned her back on all that.

'Lucy.' The timbre of Phil's voice could have been a reproach, a warning, or some kind of declaration.

Had she just propositioned him? She jumped up, flushed. She'd said she wanted an affair. He must think that's why she'd come. 'I must go. I'm late. Tom will –' She was babbling again.

As she stood at the car door, fumbling endlessly for her keys and not quite getting them into the lock first time round, he put both hands on her shoulders and kissed her cheeks, quickly and firmly. Chastely, but as if he meant it. 'Come back when you're visiting your dad. Whenever you want to talk. Ring me first.'

It was a command.

'Yes. I'll ring you first,' she promised.

*

When she got home, Ned was in bed, reading a magazine. He looked up over his glasses.

'You're late.' It wasn't a reproof. It was hardly even curiosity.

'I dropped in on Phil Gray on my way home from Dad.' Lucy held her breath. Would he be suspicious or jealous? If there was any sign of it, she'd stop all this now.

He put the magazine down. 'How was he?'

'Fine.'

Ned grunted, took off the glasses, turned off his bedside light and rolled over. 'Night.'

She considered cuddling up to him, telling him about Owen and Nico, and asking for comfort. She knew his arms would be warm and protective, and that he would be on her side, without any blame or doubt. On the other hand, this might be construed as an invitation to sex, and she couldn't face it now. She felt too bruised, somehow.

So she slid into bed after doing her teeth, turned out the light and curled up into a ball, with her back to him.

'Night.'

She fell asleep instantly, and dreamed that she was back at a party in her single days, and that Ned was there, but she couldn't find him in the swirling fog of cigarette smoke. She looked for him desperately, but other men kept coming up to her. 'Come with me,' they'd say. 'Come with me.'

'I've got to find somebody. It's very important.'

She'd break away, feeling the terrible, treacherous flames of sexual attraction licking up from deep down inside even as the sense of loss threatened to engulf her.

'He'll be here later,' the faces said. 'He'll never know. I know a secret place.'

And when she could stand the craving, burning, desperate feelings no longer, she pulled one of the men to her, but the very moment that she felt complete, and as she sighed with satisfaction, she saw Ned standing there with a look of such utter disdain on his face that she cried out.

'They all said you'd never be faithful to me,' he said, turning away in disgust. 'I should have listened to them.'

Lucy woke up, swamped by a sense of complete desolation.

16

The following day stretched out in front of Lucy like a seaside postcard: a cobalt sky and a brightness in the air that carried the promise of heat. It was nearly the end of May, and the tourists and weekenders were beginning to fill the Old Town with their huge cars packed to the gunnels with bicycles, cool bags and surfboards. Their voices dominated the shops, as they called to each other: 'Gin, darling, have we got enough gin?' or 'Oh Lord, there's no balsamic vinegar; you really know you're in the boondocks now.' People who belonged somewhere just shopped, she thought, they didn't use it as a bonding experience with their partner or have to discuss every aspect of whether the rented cottage had a decent pepper grinder at maximum volume over the tops of the supermarket shelves. Surely they didn't all shout like this at home?

'It's half term next week,' grumbled Josie Saunders, who was one ahead of her in the queue at the checkout. 'The place will be full of children. An absolute nightmare.' As Josie had three herself, this seemed a little harsh.

'How's your friend, Grace?' she demanded aggressively, as if Grace was a person with particular difficulties.

'Fine,' said Lucy. 'Very well, actually.'

Josie sniffed. 'I always see her car outside your house.'

Lucy, who never noticed what people's cars were like – Grace's was low-slung and black, but she had no idea of the make or licence plate, and couldn't have betted on picking it out in a crowded car park – was amazed. 'Mm,' was all she could think of to say. 'It's a lovely day, don't you think?' she added, in case Josie thought she was being unfriendly.

'It's not going to last,' asserted Josie, gathering up each item as it went through the till and checking it carefully in case it had been damaged by the till girl, before putting it in a bag.

In fact, Grace and Lucy had bagged a day off together, ostensibly to plan the holiday. Tom and Luke were on an overnight school trip in London and Nico was involved in his own mysterious concerns. Richard was away.

'I never used to have so much time off before I met you,' Lucy told Grace, as she settled down at her long kitchen table and Grace threw open the doors to the garden. The delicate fragrance of early jasmine and the faded-lipstick scent of wisteria floated in on the crisp, bright air. 'You're obviously a very bad influence.' She wondered, for a moment, whether the extra self-indulgence of an occasional day to herself was what had triggered off this obsession with Phil. She'd been on the treadmill of meals, school, surgery,

217

meals, homework, meals, bed for so long that she'd forgotten the other pleasures of being alive. She hugged the memory of their evening together to her, although she was still slightly worried about whether she'd come on to him with the remark about the affair. Could she talk about it to Grace?

No. Just saying the words would make it all seem so much more real. Fantasies belong in your head.

They'd sorted out the choices between flying and driving and the dates and times of arrival.

'Is Nico bringing someone?'

Lucy rolled her eyes. 'If I ask him, he tells me to get off his case. Or to cool it. Or some other meaningless phrase to make me go away. It's A level madness, at the moment.'

Grace's beautifully manicured finger traced the spidery lines of the map to see exactly where they were going. 'It's here, you see. In the middle of nowhere.' She got up and opened the fridge door, pulling out a bottle.

'I've never known anyone drink so much champagne,' commented Lucy. 'And certainly not at eleven thirty in the morning.'

Grace smiled. 'Let's take it upstairs. I need your help.'

Lucy lounged on Grace and Richard's enormous bed. It was firm and soft at the same time, and Lucy felt her limbs sink into a state of blissful relaxation. 'Champagne in bed,' she said. 'So decadent.'

Grace began opening endless lengths of cupboard doors. 'There's something so depressing about last summer's clothes, don't you think? They smell of old suntan oil, and they're always worn out, however carefully you look after them. I suppose cottons and things just don't last.'

Lucy, who merely exchanged her black jumpers for thinner, lighter black tops as the temperature rose, looked at the sunshine streaming through the glass and felt happiness rise up inside her like one of the bubbles.

'Right. Trying-on, throwing-away session.' Grace threw a pile of coat-hangers on the bed, and pulled off her dress, revealing a greyhound body and small, delicate breasts in cream lace. Lucy studied her. What must it be like to be so perfect, with bones like a small bird?

'Tell me,' said Grace. 'Be perfectly honest. I really need to know which ones make me look like mutton dressed as lamb.' A rainbow of silks and cottons lay strewn across the bed, and Lucy blinked at the colours.

Grace embarked on a frenzy of trying on, with each outfit generating a moue of disgust. 'This makes me look fat.' She tore off one top after another. 'God, orange just isn't my colour. The cut of those trousers – really, I must have thighs like an elephant.' The discarded pile grew.

Lucy kept trying to interrupt. 'Honestly. That doesn't make you look ... that orange is ... your thighs are really, really thin ...' Grace ignored her, wrapped up in what increasingly appeared to be an orgy of self-hatred.

'This would suit you, though.' Grace brightened at the thought of making someone else look good. 'Why not try it on?'

Lucy flinched at the prospect of trying to squeeze herself into something of Grace's, the material straining as the buttons gaped apart by inches. 'It wouldn't fit.'

Grace assessed her. 'You've lost quite a lot of weight. And it's a very loose cut. Go on. It would be perfect for long, hot afternoons at the villa. There's a big wooden table under a vine-covered pergola, overlooking the swimming pool.'

'It sounds perfect.' Lucy was trying to undress without revealing too much bluish-white, wobbly flesh.

But Grace noticed everything. 'I don't know why you think you're so fat. You're just a normal, pretty woman.'

'A lump of lard,' muttered Lucy, embarrassed, slipping the linen shift over her head, and expecting to see it humiliatingly tight in the mirror. It wasn't, but standing beside Grace made her look like a huge white elephant, and she flinched and turned away.

'It suits you. Have it. I never wear it.' Grace discarded it without a second thought. She picked out a tiny suit. 'Do you think lime green is terribly dated? Or not?' And she resumed her frenzied search through the cupboards.

Eventually she sat down on the bed, despondent. 'It's no good. Everything has to go.'

Lucy put a hand on the pale-honey flesh of Grace's bare arm. It felt warm and smooth, like satin sheets that had just been slept on. 'Grace. It's all in your head. The clothes look great. You look beautiful. Don't do this to yourself.'

When Grace turned her head to look at her, Lucy could see pure terror in her eyes. 'I'm sorry. I know I sound selfish. It's just difficult . . . well, you don't know what it's like. You've always been pretty.'

'What?' Lucy was bewildered.

Grace began to pluck at the bedspread. 'You've always been pretty,' she repeated. 'I can see that. I'm not pretty. I just have to try terribly, terribly hard to look even passable.'

The doctor part of Lucy's brain began to tick underneath the anaesthetizing effects of the champagne, and gave Grace a label. Body Dysmorphic Disorder. Seeing yourself as ugly. It had been so carefully concealed behind the perfection that even she hadn't spotted it until now.

Grace seemed hell-bent on proving her own disfigurement. 'When I was a buck-toothed, bespectacled, overweight ten-year-old, I remember my father saying that it was a shame I hadn't got the looks of Gina, my elder sister. And my mother said, "Oh well, at least it means men like you won't fall in love with her, so she won't be so disappointed." '

'That was them,' Lucy struggled to get through to

her. 'They had their own problems. Major problems. You don't have to believe them, and carry that through your life. Maybe you didn't look like Shirley Temple at the age of ten, but who does? It doesn't matter. You look good now, better than most of the Shirley Temples in your class do thirty-five years on, I bet.'

Grace, she could see, was incapable of believing any of it. 'I'm sorry.' She spoke in a whisper. 'I'm just being spoilt. I should pull myself together. Try harder. Get thinner. Go to the gym more often.'

'Get thinner!' Lucy nearly shrieked. 'For God's sake. Anorexia, here you come. Look, if you're even beginning to think like that, you need serious help.'

Grace tried to smile. 'I promise not. I've been there, done that. In my teens. I sort of know where to stop. I think, anyway.'

'Grace. Listen to me. You are beautiful.' Lucy had never told a woman that before, but she was aware that it was no good coming from her. Unless Richard said it to her, practically every morning and evening, she would never, ever believe it. And then he'd have to follow it up by making love to her.

'Men don't find me attractive. I know that.' Grace flipped over onto her stomach, and rested on her elbows, her long, slender feet criss-crossing and uncrossing nervously at the ankles. Lucy's eyes swept down the slope of her back, past each knobble of her spine and into the gentle curve of her bottom where a cream lace thong clearly matched the bra. For someone who wasn't expecting to be undressed by anybody, Grace was very carefully coordinated. Lucy tried to imagine the effect of such an item on her own cellulite-pitted buttocks and failed. No, cream lace thongs were for a different breed of woman. She turned her attention back to trying to convince Grace she was attractive.

'Yes, they do. Look at Sean, the builder. You'd only have to say the word and he'd be bringing bacon sandwiches over . . . but don't, of course.'

Grace shrugged. 'Builders find every woman attractive. It's all that manual labour. Keeps the blood flowing to the willy.'

'My builders have never found me attractive.'

'I'm sure they did. And Ned does. That's the difference between you and me. Your husband wants you. It just shows. There's something wrong with me.'

Lucy didn't mean to say it. It just popped out. 'Ned finds you attractive, too. Very. He said so.'

'Really?' It was the first thing she'd said that seemed to get through to Grace. 'You're so sweet to say so.' And she leant across the few inches of bed that separated her from her friend and kissed Lucy on the cheek. 'Thank you so much. It's really made my day.'

Lucy could smell Grace's perfume. It was a rich mix of roses and amber.

There was a stillness between them. Lucy was very aware of the softness of the silk bra, the astonishing fullness of Grace's small breasts, and the hard point of the nipple at its tip as Grace propped herself up on one elbow. From times they'd been changing after swimming together, Lucy had coveted the lusciousness of Grace's large brown nipples rather than her own inadequate, small, rosy tips.

Grace sighed, and relaxed into the bed. 'I don't know. Why are we still worrying about men after all these years?'

Lucy shook her head. She, too, had thought you married Mr Nice and got on with it. That you closed the door on doubt and uncertainty in favour of sensible grown-up things like listening to radio programmes about politics and making your own shortcrust pastry.

'Still, perhaps I should stop thinking about men. Maybe the answer is women. Have you noticed?' Grace seemed to be speaking through a dream. 'I think women fancy women now. At our age. More than before.'

With a lurch inside her, Lucy recognized that there was some truth in this – why else would she know the shape of Grace's breasts almost as well as her own? – but she turned away, ostensibly to take another sip from her champagne glass, with the sense that they had reached an important junction in their relationship.

'I hadn't noticed, no,' she lied. The next step of the conversation was to say, 'Do you?' but Lucy couldn't make that move forward. Perhaps this feeling for Grace, or for other women, was at the heart of why she no longer wanted Ned. But that wouldn't explain Phil.

An affair with Grace would hardly be disloyalty to Ned. The thought was heady. She wasn't free as far as Phil was concerned, but she and Grace could have each other discreetly, as if taking nothing that belonged to anyone else.

'It would be so much easier,' Grace continued. 'We'd know what each other wanted. We wouldn't have to explain things.'

We? Was that 'we' the sisterhood in general, or was it Grace-and-Lucy? Lucy wasn't sure.

Lucy wondered what it would be like to slip the slender strap of Grace's bra down, or unhook it at the back, and see her breasts fall forward.

And she realized that she could think about this, that she could find this thought enticing, but that something very fundamental deep inside her would stop her doing it. Something would be missing.

Grace seemed very still, as if she was waiting.

With an effort, Lucy gathered her wits. 'But then, being so relentlessly heterosexual,' she tried to smile, 'I probably wouldn't notice. I expect a woman could flirt endlessly with me and I'd never even realize what was going on.' The last thing she wanted to do was to add to the pile of rejections that Grace had suffered. Or to assume that an advance had been made when it hadn't.

Grace laughed easily. 'I went to a party the other day, at Richard's boss's house' – aha, thought Lucy, so Richard has a boss; he's not the absolute king of the heap, the way he likes to make out – 'you know, when we were in London the other day, and I met a woman who told me, straight out, that she was bi-sexual.'

'And . . . ? Did she come on to you?' Lucy was fascinated. The moment had passed and they'd slipped back to their old relationship without a ruffle. Had something happened there between them? Or was it just the champagne and the hot day adding to Lucy's new obsession with sex?

'She gave me her card. She said we must do lunch. What do you think?'

'Did you like her?'

Grace shrugged. 'She seemed all right. I just wondered if she could be the answer to my problems.'

'Grace.' Lucy finally decided that she had to say this. 'You've got so much going for you. You're bright, funny, absolutely gorgeous-looking . . . but sometimes anyone can need a bit of outside help. I think you've got to that point now. Just to talk to someone who might be able to help you sort your thoughts out. Only then will you know whether you and Richard are . . .' She faltered. She'd been going to say 'likely to stay together', but she knew that would terrify her friend. 'Whether you're going to be able to sort all this out in a way that will work for both of you,' she concluded.

For a moment she thought Grace was going to cry. As if the idea of letting go of the burden she'd been carrying for so long was a relief. But she merely flashed her jokey smile. 'I suppose this means the delicious Phil?'

'There isn't anyone else good around here.'

'Which pretty much knocks the idea of having an affair with him on the head, I presume? He struck me as far too decent.'

'He is.' Lucy enjoyed talking about him. 'Not to mention a stickler for professional ethics. And, whatever you might think, an affair is the last thing you need, I'm afraid. Get your head straight first, and everything else will follow. I'm sure of that.' What she wasn't sure of was whether 'help', however expert, could repair the damage that Grace saw every time she looked in a mirror.

'And what about you, my friend? How are we going to sort you out?'

'Me?' Lucy felt that her problems were insignificant beside Grace's self-loathing and insecurity. 'I'm fine.'

'Of course, you are,' Grace laughed. 'Of course you are.'

17

For the next few weeks, A levels hung over the house like the smoke from a battlefield. An unnatural quiet, punctuated by the occasional slammed door, hovered malodorously, even infecting Tom, who had just finished his SATs and didn't see why Nico should be so poisonous about a few exams. 'They're pipsqueak,' he said at breakfast one day. 'Easy-peasy lemon-squeezy.' He then proceeded to give a stirring rendition of 'I love my spag*hetti*, all covered in cheese, I lost my poor *meat*ball, when somebody sneezed.'

Nico slammed the cornflake packet down as a barrier between them, and Lucy tried to make 'don't' and 'sh' signals to Tom. He ignored them. Tom found exams, like life, very easy. Nico had always had to try harder.

'Rolled out to the *gar*den and under a bush, then my poor *meat*ball was nothing but mush,' roared Tom, in B flat.

Ned pushed the top of the cafetière down. It splintered, showering him in hot coffee and spraying shards of glass around the room. 'Shit!'

'For God's sake,' shouted Lucy, nerves on edge. 'Can't you be more careful?'

Tom looked scared, but stopped the meatball song.

Nico got up and strode through the coffee grounds and broken glass, and up the stairs as Ned ran cold water over his arm.

Lucy was ashamed of herself. If either of the boys had burned himself, she'd have jumped up with cries of sympathy. She seized the broom and began sweeping in penitence.

'I'll do that.' Ned patted the arm dry, and held it out for the broom.

'No, no, I can do it.' Her good-mother, good-wife credentials now hung on clearing up this mess. And she still couldn't quite suppress her irritation at his clumsiness.

'You'll be late.' He touched her arm lightly. 'You've got early surgery today.'

'I can manage,' she hissed.

Ned drew Tom towards him. 'Ready, boysey?' Tom nodded, still looking nervous. He hated arguments. 'I'll drop you off on the way to the hospital. Nico! Get a move on! I'll be late back, by the way.'

'Staying clear of the war zone, eh?' Lucy tried to make a joke, to mask her irrational sense of fury.

'For Christ's sake, woman, I am actually busy,' he lashed out. Lucy was shocked. Ned rarely lost his temper with her. It felt like a rejection.

'I was only joking.'

He looked at her incredulously.

'OK, so it wasn't very funny, but there's no need to snap,' she sulked.

'I don't know what's got into everyone in this

house.' He sorted and filled his briefcase, and checked the window to see if he needed a coat.

'What are you doing this evening?'

But Ned had picked up the post and was rifling through it. 'Boring. Boring. Boring. Oh, botheration.' He put the last letter, which was from the Inland Revenue, into his pocket. 'Sorry? Come *on*, boys.'

She turned away, kneeling on the floor partly to get the last splinters of glass up and partly to avoid his kiss. 'Nothing.'

'I'll see you around eleven, then.'

Lucy knew she'd been unfair. And there was no reason for any of it.

Perhaps a drink with Grace would sort it out. Lucy rang her on her mobile when she got the answering machine at the house.

'This evening? Oh, um . . . God, I think I'm doing something, hang on, yes, mm, it's just been confirmed.'

She didn't say what or suggest Lucy join her. 'Something nice?' Lucy asked, to prolong the conversation.

'No, not really, rather dull.' Grace clearly didn't want to say what she was up to. 'Look, I'm working tomorrow, got a mother and daughter planning wedding outfits, but come to lunch on Thursday instead. Even if it's just a quickie between surgeries.'

Feeling excluded by both Grace and Ned, Lucy resolved to do something worthwhile, like tidy the bathroom cupboard. It hardly seemed alluring. Lucy went into the kitchen and opened the fridge. She needed chocolate.

As the silky sweetness hit her brain with a comforting buzz, temporarily calming her, she thought. Grace and Ned. Both late. Neither wanted to say where they were.

What do you think? Grace wouldn't do that to me, she told herself, breaking off another square of chocolate. Her taste buds lit up. That's better.

Still, she knew things were flat between her and Ned, and she'd known it might become a problem. Just one more to cheer herself up, perhaps. Oops, it had broken off crookedly. Might as well neaten up the row. Still standing up, she considered the word 'relish'. She was relishing this. It was satisfying. It dulled the anxiety of not knowing exactly what either Ned or Grace – separately, of course – was up to.

She broke off the second to last row. Then she would definitely put the bar back.

But when's someone's as damaged as Grace is, they'll do anything.

There was no point in leaving just three glossy dark chunks, sitting in the fridge sending out waves of temptation. It would be like a radio-active substance, beaming out contamination until she gave in. Better just to get rid of it now. She stuffed the last three squares in, enjoying a brief high before guilt descended.

Five minutes later, her tongue was furry with remorse, and her head began to throb. Lucy thought it must be all the theo-whatsits. Those ingredients that give chocolate their high. Her stomach drooped, weighted down, and her skin felt silted up. She could feel the excess calories working their way industriously forward to layer fat onto her thighs, her hips and her cheeks almost as she dragged herself around the house.

Still, it had had a tranquillizing effect on her. There was no point in worrying about Grace and Ned. Ned had never, ever given her the slightest reason for concern, and Grace was her friend.

But Grace was desperate.

It was Owen, surprisingly enough, who calmed her down. This week she'd had to take time off during the day for his appointments, instead of the evening, but, for once, she didn't resent the drive. At least she was alone. The hedgerows were bursting with creamy cow parsley, elderflowers and hawthorn blossom, fringing the tarmac of the road with frothy white lace. It was all so green in the fields – a hopeful, vigorous shade of green, still bursting with potential, she thought, instead of the bleached certainties of high summer.

On the way to the hospital, he began to talk about the summers they'd known as a family, before Sarah died, and when Lucy had been a little girl. Every year they'd set up an old-fashioned tent in the same farmer's field and had cooked on an open fire, buying fresh eggs and milk straight from the farmer's wife.

'They don't let you do that now,' grumbled Owen. 'EC regulations about hygiene or some such nonsense.'

This was what she would miss. Soon there would be no one to say, 'Dad, do you remember . . .' to. The memories were stored like black-and-white snapshots. It had been a mile and a half, across fields and weather-worn stiles, to the beach, and they'd set off with sandwiches and swimsuits in their backpacks every day. The firm, ridged sand had been the colour of honey and the breakwaters, which Lucy always thought of as the remains of pre-historic temples, had stretched out to sea. In the rock pools tiny, transparent shrimps had darted almost invisibly between fronds of dark green seaweed. There had been a gentle clear tide that allowed Lucy to see her feet even when she was waist deep. She'd learned to swim under Owen's patient coaching, while Sarah had sat on the beach smiling, reading her magazine and buttering sand-wiches.

Sarah would have been a few years younger than Lucy was now. She had always seemed magical, serene and perfect. For the first time, Lucy wondered what had been behind the calm smiles. Had she ever sat there thinking about other men, or had Owen been everything to her always? Perhaps she had kissed someone else once, or even had an affair? It seemed most unlikely, but Lucy had only known her mother as an adult for such a brief time. Had Sarah wanted to travel or do something special once Lucy had grown up? Had she had ambitions or was she content to sit there, behind a brightly striped windbreaker, waiting for Owen and Lucy? If she had wanted more, Sarah had died too soon. Far too soon. Lucy still didn't quite believe it. A part of her still believed that there was a room somewhere, in their old house, where she could find Sarah ironing or sewing, and where Lucy could go to tell her about everything she'd done in the last few years. She'd wanted to find that room so badly when the boys had been born. She'd wanted Sarah to stroke their tiny, downy heads with wonder, and say, 'Oh, you were exactly like that at that age.' She'd wanted to hand the tiny, screaming bundles over to her mother and scuttle back to bed, with her head under the duvet. That's what mothers were for.

'I don't ever remember it raining,' she recalled the holidays again. 'And what did we do when it did? In a tent in the rain? Do you think everyone's childhood is bathed in an eternal memory of sun? I hope Nico's and Tom's is.' Grace's, she remembered, was not.

'Bathed in an eternal memory of computer games, I should think,' muttered Owen, but without rancour.

'What was she like? My mother. When she was my age?' Lucy suddenly wanted to know. As if it was a missing piece of a jigsaw puzzle.

'Sarah?' For a moment, she thought that Owen didn't want to talk about her, but he heaved a great sigh, and eventually spoke. 'She was lovely. She was the only person I ever wanted to come home to.'

'I think things were much easier then,' she mused.

'Oh, I don't know,' said Owen, surprising her. 'When she was around your age, you'd just gone to university, and the house seemed very empty. I think she was restless. Anyway she took up pottery, and suddenly we started to hear a lot about someone called Brian.'

Lucy was shocked. 'Brian?' She rummaged through her memory. There was no trace of a Brian in it.

'The pottery teacher.' Owen's wry smile acknowledged the cliché. 'We began to argue. About little things. She shortened her skirts and cut her hair into a fringe like Mary Quant . . .' His voice died away. 'Stopped looking like a wife and mother and started looking pretty fanciable. So I was sure something was up. I asked her. She denied it. We had a row. One of our worst.'

Lucy remembered the haircut, which had looked good. She remembered very few rows. Sarah, like Tom, had hated any kind of argument.

Owen turned his head away to look out of the window at the greenery flashing by. 'That was the day she died. I'll never forget that. She died before I could say sorry.'

'Dad.' She'd had no idea. All she could remember was his devastated face and the emptiness of the house, the huge hole that existed at the centre of every room. The nothingness of it all had frightened her.

'I even wondered if being so upset had caused her death,' he continued. 'But according to the

235

autopsy, she'd always had a faulty flap in her heart. She could have died as a child or gone on to live to old age. It was just fate that flipped it shut when it did.

'Anyway, this Brian came to her funeral.'

Lucy searched her memory for an unfamiliar face that day. It had been windy and grey, and she'd blanked the horror of it out of her mind. That hadn't been her mother in the coffin, swishing through the curtain to the flames. She'd cocooned herself inside an act. She pretended to be the competent, caring daughter down from university to support her father. Calm. Almost detached. Someone you could rely on. That way she'd been able to greet everyone with a sympathetic smile. There'd been hundreds of them, partly because her mother was loved, but also, she now realized, because she had been so young. Forty-eight had seemed cast in elderly dreariness to her in those days.

'At first I wanted to find out the truth, then punch his face,' continued Owen. 'But when he came up to me, and shook my hand, and said, "Brian Lacey. Sarah was a wonderful woman," I simply stared at him. He was just a boy. He couldn't have been more than twenty-five. He had long hair, and a Che Guevara moustache and an Afghan coat.'

Both Lucy and Owen sniggered at the memory of the large, ungainly, smelly sheepskins that had so typified an era.

'All I could think was, "What does it matter?" She was dead, and that's all I cared about. Maybe Brian did give her something I couldn't. If he loved her, in any way, I couldn't blame him. And if he made her happy, well . . . it was all probably just a harmless flirtation anyway. I didn't need to know any more. I had all my memories of her. I didn't want them spoilt. So I slapped him on the arm, grunted something I hoped was appropriate and never saw him again.'

Lucy tried to absorb what he was telling her. She wondered if he'd told this story now, because he saw more than she suspected.

'We never went camping after Mum died, did we?'

'You were too old. Into boys by then, not camping with your old dad.' Owen smiled at the thought of his mini-skirted daughter, with her false eyelashes and rust-red nails, risking a ladder in her stockings for something as potentially uncool as a tent.

She remembered that. The sharp, dark line between the sunny childhood and the storms of adulthood. The sense of loss that had permeated through the parties and dates. The sense of looking, sometimes desperately searching, for someone who could restore the balance to her life.

'I remember the first day you brought Ned back to meet me.' Owen seemed to have read her mind again. 'I knew he was the one for you. The others,' he made a noise that sounded like 'pah', 'they were just diversions.'

'Did you, Dad? Why?' That was what was so comforting about a parent. They could fill in the gaps for you in a way that no one else ever could.

237

'I could see that he knew what you were like. And loved you all the same.' Owen would usually rather discuss new treatments for greenfly than love.

Lucy was touched, then hurt. 'What I was like? Was I so very terrible?'

His face cracked in a smile. 'Of course not. But it's important that someone loves the bad bits as well as the good ones. We all have faults.'

'Me more than most, I suppose,' Lucy joked to cover up her surprise. Owen did notice things, after all.

'No.' Owen looked straight ahead, rigid with embarrassment. 'I'm proud of you.'

She couldn't quite acknowledge her pleasure to him, but her hands tightened on the steering wheel. For the first time, for a long time, she felt safe.

She would ring Ned as soon as there was time, and apologize for being such a bear.

She couldn't get hold of him when she got back at six. He wasn't answering the bleep, which was very unusual.

18

Grace phoned the following day to make sure she was coming to lunch.

'I have to talk to you. I've done something terrible.'

'Oh, no.' Lucy's heart executed a triple flip. Was this how people announced that they'd been to bed with your husband? It wasn't a situation she'd ever had to deal with before. Ned had come home very, very late, when she was asleep. There'd been the usual family chaos at breakfast so she hadn't been able to ask him, again, what he'd been up to. He'd muttered something about having left his bleep in the wrong jacket pocket, and having been at the hospital all along. Her throat tightened. Hold on, she told herself. Hold on. This is just a new thought that has flitted, completely irrationally, into your head. Nothing, absolutely nothing, justifies it.

'It's too awful,' said Grace.

'Surely not.' Lucy's voice sounded weak, even to her. 'What did you do?'

'I couldn't possibly say over the phone. It's almost the worst thing I've ever done. Promise you'll forgive me?'

'Er. I expect so.'

'Well, being me, I didn't even do it properly, of course.'

'Didn't do what?' Lucy could hardly bear to wait four hours to find out.

'I'm useless at all this. If this was the Middle Ages, I'd go into a convent.'

Oh, dear. Lucy tried not to feel too frightened. Whatever it was, she could deal with it. Sometimes, knowing Grace was like having a tornado for a best friend. You got sucked up into it.

'I paid for sex,' said Grace, as soon as they sat down. 'In the flat in London. When you phoned me on the mobile, that's where I was.'

'What?' In spite of her relief that Ned couldn't have been involved, Lucy was terrified for her friend.

'Oh, not with a man,' explained Grace, as if that made it better.

'What was it with?' asked Lucy, very slowly. Anything was possible.

'A woman. You see I read this article in *Cosmopolitan* . . .'

'I don't think you should be allowed to read magazines.'

Grace began to giggle, mainly out of embarrassment, Lucy suspected. 'Well, you know I'm always saying that I think I might fancy women? And it seems I'm not the only one. Bi-sexuality's everywhere now.' She leant forward as if trying to persuade Lucy to join a new religion or a political party. It was the kind of enthusiasm Lucy had enjoyed when Grace was espousing eyeliner. Lesbianism was a slightly more serious matter. Surely these were big life decisions? 'It's on the television,' she gushed. 'On the ads – what was that latest poster? Was it trainers? Or bras?'

Lucy shook her head. She hadn't seen it.

'Celebs – women – go to parties holding hands. All the popular programmes at least have the odd lesbian kiss. Even the cookery programmes.' Grace tossed out the names with confidence, although Lucy was sure she hadn't the first idea what she was talking about. 'It's the next big thing. Every woman has to have one. Lesbian experience, that is.'

'Not in Bramsea,' said Lucy. 'We've only just got fax machines up here, about fifteen years after everyone else. I think we might have to wait a few more decades for bi-sexuality.'

Grace was undeterred. 'And paying for sex is the ultimate shopping experience.' She really was spouting *Cosmopolitan* now, thought Lucy. Word for word.

Grace confirmed her suspicions. 'That's what *Cosmo* said, anyway. So there are now agencies – heaps of them – where women pay for women. Some actually specialize in first-timers – women who just want to see if they're really bi-sexual or whether it's just a fantasy. The great point is that if you engage someone from an agency, you don't have to go into a gay bar or pick up a stranger. Or hit on a friend. It's a business transaction. Like having a facial.'

Lucy wasn't quite sure about that.

Grace looked agonized. 'I knew you'd disapprove.'

'No, no. But I am worried about you.'

'Don't. I'm tough. Anyway, I called three agencies. It was all pretty embarrassing actually. The second agency said they had someone called Tracy, who sounded nice, and she phoned me.'

Lucy's heart went out to Grace. Sex like a trip to the hairdresser's.

'The first thing she told me was her bra size. On the phone! I didn't really want to know, to be honest. I mean, it made me feel so inadequate to start with.'

'Perhaps she usually sleeps with men, and that's the sort of thing they want to find out. You know how keen they are on measuring everything.'

'Mm. Well, very off-putting, I can tell you. Two cup sizes larger than me. Terrifying.'

Lucy thought that cup size was the least of the embarrassments Grace might expect in this situation, but kept quiet.

'She turned up at the London flat at eleven o'clock in the morning, which was the only time we could both do, and when I could be sure of Richard being out at work.' She giggled. 'It's not a very sexy time of day. It was a bit like having a plumber or an electrician round to fix something. But she looked very smart, with a pair of earrings I really, really liked. So we talked about those for a bit, and her shoes, which were fab, then she said, "Let's get business over first, shall we, so we can relax." So I paid her £350, for two hours of her time. It was really . . .' Grace screwed up her face, 'cringe-making. She actually flicked through the notes, licking her finger and counting them like a bank teller, and then stowed them away. After which she looked at me with a kind of fake simmer, unbuttoning her jacket. She was wearing a divine La Perla camisole underneath. So we talked a bit about the best lingerie shops, and she was surprisingly excited when she heard that I do make-overs. She said she'd always wanted one of those.'

Lucy wasn't sure how far into the two hours they'd got.

'So then I asked her whether she did . . . this . . . full time, and she said that she'd been a lap dancer, but the bi-sexual stuff offers better money, and a nicer class of customer, and she and her boyfriend were saving up to buy a dry-cleaner's.'

Lucy was surprised.

'The boyfriend works at the dry-cleaner's, and they want to buy the business with the flat above because they're both living with her mother, and that doesn't work, obviously, and –' Grace broke off. 'Anyway, by then she seemed like a real person, not some anonymous sexual experience, not that I could have had sex with a totally anonymous being, I don't think, but did I want to have sex with this perfectly nice future dry-cleaner? I mean, she was fine to talk to, but we ran out of conversation after we'd done the clothes bit. It seemed a bit bizarre to start kissing someone you wouldn't even particularly want to have lunch with.'

'I don't think prostitutes do kissing, do they?' asked Lucy, who thought she'd read this in some thriller.

Grace shrugged. 'I don't know. I don't know about any of it. I hadn't a clue what to do next. Do you just give orders? Or take your clothes off and expect them to take over? Should I have asked Tracy to undress me? Could I have possibly asked for oral sex as if it was a French manicure?'

Lucy shuddered. It was bad enough getting undressed in group changing cubicles in shops without asking a complete stranger to take one's clothes off. And wouldn't asking a virtual stranger for . . . her mind skidded over the words like Mrs Thing who'd come to see her at the surgery . . . be as embarrassing as going to the gynaecologist? Although not as painful, with any luck.

'I've never asked anyone for sex before. I've hinted, particularly with Richard, but I wouldn't know how to come out with it, and just say, "Hey, you there, I want it this way."'

Lucy worried that she was being too old-fashioned and judgemental about it all. Perhaps paying for a lesbian experience you didn't really want was perfectly normal, as the article had suggested. It just seemed so wrong for Grace.

'And anyway,' Grace continued, 'what would I be asking for? What do women do together? Would I reciprocate or just lie there? I feel completely useless with a man, let alone a woman I don't know. So

I tentatively mentioned a massage, because Tracy obviously wasn't going to suggest anything.

'She massaged my back – not very well, I might add – but didn't take any more of her own clothes off. And I didn't really want her to, because I thought my body might look terrible against hers. She was a bit stupid, but she was stunningly beautiful. I thought she'd find me revolting.'

Grace's body image again. Mind you, forty-five next to twenty-four wouldn't be great in daylight whatever you looked like. 'I don't suppose men think about whether prostitutes find them attractive or not, do they?' Lucy pointed out.

'Maybe not.' Grace shrugged. 'But I did. And I couldn't help wondering whether a man would have just got on with it, and that's why she didn't take any initiative with me. Then she asked me where I was going on holiday, and said that seemed very nice. And we discussed where she and the boyfriend were going, which was also very nice. But she wasn't a very good masseuse and I got downright irritated with the feel of her hands slithering up and down my back. If I want a massage, I know where to get a really good one. Eventually the two hours were up, and I put on my top and trousers, and we air-kissed, and that was it.'

'But Grace.' Lucy felt hopeless. The whole episode seemed extraordinary, considering that Grace kept talking about wanting an affair with a man. 'What on earth did you think you were you up to?'

Grace hunched her shoulders. 'I'm sorry. I know

it sounds stupid. But I thought – and I have realized that it's totally silly now, so you don't need to be bossy about it – that it could be the perfect solution. If I could go down to London once a fortnight for a woman, who I could just order and pay for, it wouldn't be like being unfaithful to Richard, and then everything would be fine. If sexual satisfaction could really be like having one's nails done, it would be so easy. That side of things would be sorted. Richard and I could then be perfectly happy together. There wouldn't be any involvement or anyone getting jealous or even much chance of getting found out because I'm always having treatments, and he wouldn't think twice if he walked in here and found me naked on a bed with a woman massaging me, and I wouldn't have to think about whether . . .' She trailed off.

'Whether . . . ?' Lucy hoped that Grace might finally have worked out what was really wrong, and be beginning to realize how much she needed to engage on the business of love with her mind, her heart and her soul rather than just her body. If it took an abortive episode with a lesbian prostitute to do it, perhaps it hadn't been such a waste of money after all.

'WhetherRichard'shavinganaffair.' The words came out in a rush, as if she didn't trust herself to get to the end of the sentence unless she ran all the words together. 'And that's why he doesn't want me.'

At last. Grace had faced up to the possibility. That was a step in the right direction. 'I think you must talk, properly and honestly, or you can't move forward,' she urged her friend.

'I just can't do it.' Grace began to cry. 'What if he leaves me?'

Lucy didn't have an answer. That was the problem. She understood it all too well.

19

For some reason, the niggle about Grace and Ned wouldn't quite go away. Was it Lucy's imagination or had Grace started inviting them both over, as a couple, in the evenings or, as a family, at weekends much more than she used to? And Ned, who used to protest that they shouldn't go out too much during the week, always accepted these invitations with obvious anticipation. Once there, round Grace's long, scrubbed kitchen table, or curled up in her capacious sofas, it no longer divided up into Grace with Lucy while Ned talked to Richard, but into a three-way conversation between Grace, Lucy and Ned. Lucy felt that her relationship with Grace had almost been invaded, while Richard remained the outsider, benevolently smiling and occasionally dominating the conversation without engaging properly with anyone. Even if he was away, Grace still invited them both. When he was around he always seemed pleased to see them, smiling at everyone's jokes and replying to any question asked of him. But when he volunteered a story or a reminiscence himself, the threesome – Lucy, Ned and Grace – would pause and listen politely, trying slightly too hard to respond or include him. There was rarely any contact between Richard and Grace, and sometimes

Lucy thought that the real reason why they were invited round so often was to prop up the illusion of a real marriage. She remembered Grace telling her that she thought that Richard tried to avoid being alone with her. Possibly it was really the other way round.

Grace flirted with Ned. She also flirted, to give her her due, with Nico, Nico's friends – he still moved in a group these days, like a migrating bird – and even, Lucy sometimes thought, with Tom, treating him, rather charmingly, as a grown-up. She reminded herself that Grace flirted with her builders and probably with the man who came to read the meter, the postman and every other 'safe' man she met. To Lucy's eye, there was something brittle and unsure about it, as if it was part of her defences, but she doubted that any of the men noticed or cared. She told herself, firmly, that the very fact that Grace was still flirting with him was proof that she and Ned were not having an affair.

One Sunday lunch, Lucy watched Grace lean towards Ned as if to confide a secret, touching him lightly on the arm, and looking directly into his eyes. Her top dipped, revealing the slight swelling of her breasts, and she saw Ned's gaze follow the curve. He leant back in towards her and teased her about something – Lucy couldn't quite hear what – and Grace tried to tap him playfully on the cheek.

'You beastly man.' But she was laughing. Ned caught her wrist to intercept the slap, and for a moment, their gaze locked. Grace caught Lucy's eye and dropped her hand.

She looked penitent, like a little girl.

For a moment Lucy felt angry. These weren't little girl's games. Then she caught sight of Ned, who was still laughing. He'd pushed his chair back and was running his hands through his hair. Age had given his jaw and cheeks definition. The lazy angel she'd married was getting hard and craggy, which suited him. Heavens, she thought. He is an attractive man.

Grace turned to Nico, on her other side. 'So are you going to bring someone out on holiday, or just veg out on a sun lounger with only boring old us to talk to?'

Lucy held her breath. Although the exams had risen to fever pitch, had passed in a mix of elation and despair, and were now just an apprehensive memory as they waited for results, she'd completely failed to get any decision out of Nico about who he wanted to bring to France.

Nico blushed. 'I'd like to bring Lawrence, if that's OK with you.'

Lawrence. Lucy struggled to distinguish Lawrence from the other gangling or strapping young men who crowded into her kitchen – always in groups of at least three – to raid the fridge for lager, making the room feel impossibly small. Ah, not a girl then. Lucy tried to deduce something from this, but it led to no particular conclusion.

Grace flashed him a brilliant smile. 'That's settled, then. We'll have such fun!'

Lucy tried to be interested in Richard's lengthy explanation of why buying very expensive cars as often as possible actually saved you money in the end – and thought about that flicker of attraction she'd suddenly felt for Ned.

'Have I told you?' Grace sparkled at Lucy now, to include her in the conversation. 'Phil Gray rang last night. He's going to come to France. For a week in the middle only, though.'

Lucy felt her cheeks colour. Phil in France. For a whole week. Suddenly she couldn't wait.

'Does that mean you're not going to consult him, though?' She lowered her voice so that Ned and Richard couldn't hear.

Grace touched her arm and gave a reassuring smile. 'Honestly, I feel so much better, I don't think I need to, and I think it might be a bit embarrassing vis-à-vis the holiday.' She saw lines of anxiety in Lucy's face. 'Things really are better round here, I promise,' she whispered.

Lucy looked at Richard. He was wearing a Panama hat and staring down towards the end of the garden. He hadn't exchanged a glance with Grace all day. She didn't believe that anything at all had changed.

Ned's gaze, on the other hand, rested from time to time on Grace with a look of affectionate amusement. That's the way he looks at me, thought Lucy, that's *my* look. From my husband.

Never mind, she told herself. Forget it. You're imagining things. Just enjoy the warmth of the sun and the sound of the birds.

They went on drinking all afternoon, in the June sun. There was a bed of old-fashioned rose bushes in the garden, planted in institutional rows forty years ago, and which the smart garden designer Grace had employed had longed to dig up. But Grace had insisted on keeping them, and their huge overblown cerise pinks and sunburst yellows overwhelmed the garden with the sweet boudoir scent of tea roses, the powdery florals reminiscent of a grand old lady's dressing table. Lucy's sense of well-being ebbed gradually to a mild, pleasant befuddlement, and when they got up to go, she was aware of having to make a special effort to talk a little more precisely, and she nearly stumbled at the steps. Ned, too, was far from sober, because Nico had now passed his driving test, and had been allocated the role of family driver.

She flung herself across the bed when they got home, after ushering Tom to bed.

Ned sat down beside her and began to stroke one breast, absent-mindedly, through the thin cotton of her T-shirt. The nipple, treacherously, hardened. She was irritated. She'd been feeling vaguely sexy, and wanted to fantasize about Phil, rather than deal with the flesh-and-blood demands of hands which felt all too familiar, yet didn't appear to make any connection with the yearnings she felt. Her head throbbed, and her throat was dry. She knew she was heading for a hangover, probably at about 1 a.m. She moved away, almost imperceptibly, removing his hand, conscious of being unfair to him. Guilt, however, is not an aphrodisiac.

For a moment, she thought she'd got away with it.

'How much longer are you going to go on treating me like an over-eager teenager who doesn't have the right to touch you?' He was angry, with that edge of paranoia that is fuelled by alcohol. 'Every time I put my hand on any part of your body, you flinch. Or brush me off.'

Christ. Lucy tried to sit up. 'That's not entirely fair. I don't.'

'Well, that's what it feels like. There's always some excuse why we can't make love, and when we do, it's as if you're doing me some huge favour.'

'I'm sorry I'm no good in bed.' She was aware of winding up the hurt, trying to wrong-foot him.

'I didn't say you were no good in bed.'

'That's what you implied, though.' She knew she was being unfair.

'Nonsense. You're twisting my words. What I actually said is that you behave as if you can't bear me to touch you.'

'That's not true. I love you.' She did. She wasn't lying.

'But?' He folded his arms and looked down at her.

'But I'm a bit tired, that's all.'

'You're always too tired. It can't just be that.'

'Can't it?' Lucy heard a dash of bitterness in her

voice. 'Perhaps you aren't tired enough to understand.'

'And what does that mean?' Ned was still standing, aggressively. 'I work very hard.'

'So do I.' She lay back again, feeling all the fight go out of her. 'And when I come back, I deal with what's happening here. You get what's left over. I'm sorry.'

Lucy felt as if she was going to cry. And she wondered if she was opening a Pandora's box that she might never be able to shut again. 'I'm sorry. It's not fair on you. I know that. I will try. I really will.'

'Great.' He sat down on the bed, with a resigned thump. 'That really makes me feel wanted. You'll *try* to sleep with me. That's very noble and loving of you. Not to mention sexy.'

Lucy stared at the duvet cover. She tried to focus, but anger tugged away beneath the alcohol. He didn't care. He just wanted to get his end away.

'Whatever I do,' she tried to keep her voice level, 'you criticize me. No wonder I can't feel sexy. I'm in the wrong if we don't make love, and if I say I'll try, then that doesn't mean anything to you. What else can I do?' She was aware that tears were threatening to choke the breath out of her and tried not to let her face distort with the effort of holding them back. What else could she do, except try? But if she did try, and it didn't work, what then? She struggled to catch her breath, and collapsed into the pillow, feeling as if her heart was being ripped out of her chest with the sobs that suddenly gushed uncontrollably. Stupid,

stupid tears. Why do we cry when we lose an argument?

There was a brief silence, and, for a moment, she thought he'd stalked out of the room in anger. She felt completely desolate. If Ned wasn't on her side, then who was? Who could she count on?

Phil.

But Phil was a fantasy. And a friend. There would never be anything more. Lucy felt more alone than she'd felt for a long time. Since before she met Ned.

She felt the weight of him dent the mattress, and he placed a hand, gently, on her shoulder.

'But I love you, sweetheart,' he repeated, in a completely different tone of voice, as if he really meant it.

Lucy couldn't answer.

He began to stroke her hair. 'I do, you know.'

She turned half over, so that her words wouldn't be muffled in the pillow. 'And I love you, too. I really do.' She avoided the bewilderment in his eyes. In her heart of hearts, she now realized that she didn't believe that he loved the real Lucy.

Over the years, she'd manufactured a Lucy that someone like Ned could love. A loyal wife, a loving mother, a good doctor. If he knew the real Lucy, he couldn't possibly love her. She tried to make internal contact with the Lucy she'd become, because surely she must be real by now. That Lucy would be worthy of love if only she could respond to it.

255

But she felt hollow and insubstantial. Unloved and unlovable.

'Tell me.'

Ned would never understand. He was a good guy, an ideal husband. 'Tell me,' he urged, again.

What could she say? I don't fancy you much any more? Hardly.

'It's not just tiredness, is it?' he asked. 'You never want it.' But there was no accusation in his tone.

Lucy suppressed the thought that she did want it, only not with him. With Phil.

'I didn't think you'd noticed,' she whispered. 'I didn't think you cared. As long as you got your end away.'

'Care?' He sounded surprised. 'Of course, I care.'

'I didn't want to say anything because I didn't want to upset you, and I thought perhaps it would go away . . .' She hid her head in her hands, curling up in a ball, and continued to cry.

'But it hasn't,' she eventually managed.

'Lucy.' He lay flat on the bed and took her in his arms. 'I don't want to lose you. And that's not just about sex for me.'

'You won't lose me.' She wondered if this was true. There seemed to be a terrible gap between them.

'I can't know things unless you tell me,' he said, softly, as if he was reading her mind.

She unlocked her limbs and began to open out and hug him back, feeling his familiar body warm and comforting, wrapped around her. Perhaps there was hope, after all. 'I'm being silly,' she muttered. She was still ready to backtrack on the whole conversation – perhaps pretend that it was some hormonal upset or that she was tired or worried about something else.

'What can we do about it?'

Lucy shook her head again. 'I don't know.' This, she knew, was cowardice. She'd read enough books to be able to make suggestions. 'There's sensate focusing,' she muttered tentatively, feeling rather a fool.

'What?'

'Well, you agree not to have full sex for a while, but do gentle stroking and massaging and telling each other what feels good. It takes the pressure off.'

Ned looked bewildered. 'Not off my willy, I wouldn't have thought. Do you mean that you're both lying there without any clothes on, touching each other and then not doing it?'

Lucy propped herself up on one elbow. 'You must have heard of it. It's a classic sex therapy.'

Ned raised his eyebrows. 'I've never heard of any sex therapies, classic or otherwise.' He caught sight of Lucy's expression. 'But if you want to try it, I'm happy to,' he added, amiably. She had the feeling that he was just humouring her, and that he'd initially been alarmed, but he was now merely trying to distract her. 'Shall we start now?'

'For a doctor, you are a bit dim sometimes.' But she pulled off her top, and considered asking for the lights off.

No. This was the beginning of a new time between them. She had to come to terms with her own body. If she couldn't, then how could Ned?

'Tell me what feels good.' Ned began stroking her breasts.

'That's nice,' she muttered, feeling that she had to appreciate it now that she'd made such a fuss. It was nice, anyway, surprisingly nice. Should she be doing something for Ned? The anxious thoughts chattered away in her head, like the monkeys on her shoulder, reproving her for being a rotten wife, bad in bed, and negligent about all the things she'd left undone downstairs.

She suppressed them. Sensate focusing, she told herself, was about enjoying the here and now. She concentrated on the soft tingling sensations that were waking up her body.

There was a knock on the door and she grabbed the duvet cover.

'Yes?' shouted Ned.

There was a muffled request from the other side.

'I can't hear you,' he shouted back.

'Why is the door locked?' This time the clear, high voice fluted through the keyhole, straight into the room as if by megaphone.

Lucy got up, flung on her dressing gown and opened it.

Tom was standing there, holding his teddy. 'I can't sleep. There are funny lights outside, and lots of banging noises. Can I come and sleep in your bed?'

'No,' said Lucy and Ned in unison.

'Just go back to bed.' She took him by the hand. 'It's probably fireworks. Someone's having a party. It never goes on very long. Fireworks are too expensive.'

Tom looked unconvinced. 'But why can't I come into your bed? Just until I get to sleep. It's much more comfortable than mine.'

'Because you can't.' She pulled Tom's bedclothes up to his chin, and kissed his beautiful soft cheek. 'Now, sleep.'

'But, Mummy?'

She paused at the door. 'Yes, poppet?'

'*Why* was your bedroom door locked?'

She was never sure how much they understood at that age. She'd overheard a conversation between Tom, Luke and another ten-year-old about the pop star Shaggy.

'What does shaggy mean?' Tom had asked.

'It's the name of the *Blue Peter* dog,' Luke had replied.

'Oh, no,' the third boy had said. 'It means sexing.' Then they'd spotted her and run off giggling. So presumably they did know that shagging wasn't about long-tufted carpets.

'Because sometimes I lock the door. To stop small boys from disturbing my sleep,' she concluded, hoping that he wasn't going to lie there traumatized at the thought of his parents shagging. Perhaps they didn't join up all the dots at that age. She locked the bedroom door again, as quietly as she could.

'Now, where were we?' Ned never seemed bothered by childish interruptions, but it always took Lucy a few minutes to re-create any feelings of sensuality she might have had, and sometimes the mood was broken permanently.

'Sensate focusing,' she reminded him. 'Not sex.'

'Not sex,' he agreed. 'Right. Just touching.'

'Are you laughing at me?' she demanded.

'Not at all,' he said, gravely. 'I'm deadly serious about this. So, where do we try next? Am I allowed to go south, or is that too advanced?'

'You could try.'

'I've got a massive hard-on,' said Ned, after a few moments of remarkably pleasurable stroking.

'Well, you have to just forget about it. We're not supposed to do anything more than stroking at this stage.'

He grimaced. 'But what do I do about it? I can't just leave it.'

They looked down at it, and Lucy restrained a giggle. 'I could always knock it on the head with a cold teaspoon.'

'It would be better to . . . you know.'

'Yes, but we're not *supposed* to.'

'I still don't see why not.'

'Because I'm supposed to be enjoying new sensations.'

'Can't you do it after enjoying the new sensations? I mean, you get new sensations and then I get sex?'

Ned sounded reasonable, as if they were discussing what to have for supper.

Lucy gave up. There didn't seem any great reason to hold out. The one-eyed trouser snake, she thought, just did not understand sensate focusing. And it was perfectly easy for her to give in. No skin off her nose, as it were.

As they slipped off to sleep afterwards, Ned spoke. 'I don't want to lose you. Ever.' It was the second time he'd said that.

'You won't lose me.' Lucy snuggled her back into the curve of his body. 'But can we try to sort this out?'

'Of course. Just tell me what you want me to do and I'll do it.' He made it sound so easy.

But I did, she thought, as she heard him start to snore. And you haven't.

That was not entirely fair. He had done what she wanted. For a bit. Then they'd done what he wanted. That was sharing.

20

When Olé Japan!, a new restaurant, opened up in late June, where the Laundromat had been on Bramsea High Street, Grace suggested that they try it out. 'Let's have a girls' night out. Each of us invite someone the other doesn't know.'

'And I deserve a post-A-levels celebration even more than Nico does,' said Lucy.

They compared notes while waiting for their friends to arrive, studying the menu, which, as the name promised, offered a choice of dishes that spanned the world from Japan to Mexico, while apparently missing out all the traditional restaurant dishes from Britain, Italy and France.

'It's enough to make you wistful for Sausage, Egg, Beans and Chips,' murmured Grace, frowning over Chilli Lamb in Chocolate Sauce and Sushi Tamales. 'Oh, well. Now, Serena's someone I worked with way back. She's something high up in a plastics company, and she's in the area for a few days because they're thinking of taking another company over.'

'Fiona and Rupert Forbes were next door to us, when we lived in our first little terraced cottage in Bramsea, and she had a daughter at the same time as I had Nico. Then her husband inherited a stack of money and they now live somewhere terribly grand.'

'What does she do?'

'She organizes her children beautifully. She dedicates her life to getting their homework properly supervised and makes sure they eat vitamins in balanced meals, visit museums, have nature-watching adventures or create papier-mâché sculptures.'

'She sounds terrifying.' Grace was unaware that Fiona was bound to say the same about her.

Women were like dogs, thought Lucy. So unalike in size and shape and style, that they could all be different breeds. Serena turned out to be an Irish wolfhound – big and rangy, striding through the restaurant like a confident cowgirl, flicking a silk shawl over her shoulders, her long slim legs in baggy jeans. Only her face, bony and deeply etched with smile lines, betrayed her age, probably her early fifties, thought Lucy. Fiona was one of the smaller breeds, tiny, pink-and-white and fragile, with hips the size of a child's, like a squeaky and blonde miniature poodle. Grace, of course, was a saluki or an Afghan hound. Lucy imagined herself as a labrador, stocky and friendly.

'You look terrific.' To other women, Grace was always so lavish with the praise that she denied herself.

Serena was matter-of-fact. 'I lost weight with the chemo, so I've tried to keep it off.'

'Chemo?' Grace paled.

'Breast cancer,' said Serena airily. 'The end of last year. All sorted now, though.'

Lucy watched her carefully, wondering if she wanted to brush it aside like that or whether she really wanted to talk, but Fiona leant forward with a question, and she lost the opportunity to say anything. 'I love your hair,' she squeaked. 'It really suits you. How's Ned?'

'Oh, fine. Fine.' Lucy searched her memory for anything that she could possibly say about him. She was still unable to get the niggle about Ned and Grace completely out of her head, even though she knew she was being silly. 'He's absolutely fine. And Rupert?'

'We split.' Fiona, too, sounded blithe about this upheaval in her life.

'Oh, no.' It was Lucy's turn to be appalled. Rupert and Fiona had been the archetypal happy young couple, apparently carrying on in the moulds that had been set by their parents and grandparents. Their meeting had been deemed entirely suitable by both families and had been solemnized by a white wedding at a smart cathedral. Their children had been conceived without any problems and spaced at neat, sensible intervals. Buying a glorious house in the deepest countryside had been the pinnacle of their dreams, and Lucy had expected them to repeat the entire process seamlessly with their own children and grandchildren.

'What happened?'

Fiona shrugged. 'We grew apart. That sort of thing.' Her voice hardened imperceptibly. 'He's living back in Bramsea again. With another woman. But it's all very civilized. I'm quite friendly with her, actually.'

Lucy tried to imagine being 'quite friendly' with a new girlfriend of Ned's, and her stomach contracted queasily. The thought of Ned not loving her was terrifying. Like seeing a great emptiness ahead.

'Well, I had a sort of on-off affair with a twenty-five-year-old Australian physiotherapist, so we'd both been playing away,' added Fiona, and Lucy wondered what had happened to the contented domesticity she'd emanated when they lived next door; those endless afternoons making papier-mâché pigs and calling to Chloe, Charlotte and Samantha as they trotted fat, cross ponies round a local field.

'Are you still with him?'

Fiona gave a wicked grin. 'No fear. He was a vegetarian.'

'How did that affect it?' Lucy felt stupid. Perhaps Fiona wanted meat-eating, caveman hunks.

'He always insisted on vegan condoms . . . you can get them in health food shops . . . anyway, we ran out, so I got some of the ordinary kind and he said he couldn't believe how little I respected him and his views. We had a humongous row, at the end of which I realized that I really didn't respect him, or his views. I only respected his todger, which was, I have to say, very respectable. But even so, not worth a lifetime of vegan condoms.'

Lucy tried not to look unfashionably shocked. 'So what are you up to now?'

'I've got to get a job. I need to be with people again.'

'What do you want to do?' Serena boomed across the table, as if she was interviewing a new recruit to the plastics company.

Fiona looked alarmed. 'I don't really know. I used to be a secretary, but I stopped work when Chloe was born. Eighteen years ago. Looking back, I now think it was part of the problem between me and Rupert.'

'Why?' Lucy remembered how much she'd envied Fiona being able to stay at home with her babies in those days, and how domestic and tranquil their house had seemed in comparison to her own untidy, chaotic life. Ned had once come back from a drink with Rupert, and told her that Fiona had been singing over the ironing. It had stuck in her head as the image of the perfect wife.

Fiona didn't seem to think so. 'I spent my life in tracksuit bottoms, never shaved my legs, cut my own hair with nail scissors and was generally a slob,' she admitted. 'And I totally lost my confidence. If I'd had to go out to work, I think I maybe wouldn't have lost sight of myself so completely, and perhaps I'd have had the courage to sort things out between us before it all went too far.'

They all looked at her. She wore a tight, lilac T-shirt showing a hint of cleavage, a short skirt revealing pretty, dainty, tanned legs and what could only be described as 'fuck me' shoes. There were blonde highlights in her boyish crop, and tiny earrings in each ear. Only the spider's-web lines around her eyes and a smattering of permanent freckles roughening the skin around her collarbones reminded Lucy that Fiona, who'd always seemed absurdly young to be a mother, was past forty.

'It's not all about the way you look,' said Lucy, thinking of herself and Ned. She hadn't given the eyebrow-tweezing, hair-cutting side of her life a moment's thought until Grace came along, and Ned hadn't seemed to mind. 'Bringing up children is a bit more important than having perfect nail varnish and cellulite-free thighs.'

Fiona shook her head. 'It wasn't about how I looked. It was about how I felt. I was repelled by myself. There was so much flesh everywhere – huge great lardy gobs of it in tyres round my waist, weighty saddlebags at my hips and the pain of all that gravity dragging my boobs down. Everything seemed to be oozing – I couldn't turn over in bed without milk going everywhere, but I felt so completely and utterly involved with this tiny being. And there wasn't any room for anyone else, not even Rupert, so I pushed him away. I think that if I'd had to go to work, I'd have had to make myself look reasonable, so I'd have felt better. And if I'd had to think about something other than the babies, I might have been able to communicate on some sort of a level with him.

'Then he had an affair. I felt horribly betrayed, but I sort of knew why he'd done it. And I knew that unless we started . . .' she looked surprisingly embarrassed suddenly, 'well, sex, again, I knew that was it. But, even after I smartened up and lost the weight, I didn't have the confidence to initiate anything, and he probably didn't either, not after the way I'd rejected him for years.'

'It couldn't just have been that,' soothed Lucy. 'Really. It's not as if any of us have confidence in that way.'

'Yes, I'm strictly a lights-off person,' asserted Serena, although there was a glint in her eye.

'I might have more if I'd done more of it in my life,' said Grace.

And I might have more if I'd done less, flashed up in Lucy's brain. She suppressed it.

'It's a pity you can't take lessons, really, and get a certificate,' observed Grace. 'Then you could hang it on the wall, and you'd know you had it.'

'It was bad enough failing my driving test four times,' said Lucy. 'I don't think I could face being the one who was last to get a sexual confidence certificate.'

Fiona's scarlet toe bobbed up and down again. 'I think that if I was still married, it would be different now . . .' She looked around.

The three married women gazed at their plates.

'Whatever you say, you're sexually confident, though, Serena,' observed Grace.

'Me?' She sounded astounded. 'With a scar across my chest where one of my breasts used to be?'

'But still,' persevered Grace.

'Well, we do have a really good sex life.' Serena tore

at a piece of bread, and smiled at it for a moment, temporarily lost in a secret world. 'I thought losing a breast would make a difference but it hasn't. Perhaps that's because my scar doesn't seem to worry Matt, which surprised me because he's quite squeamish, really. For example, he didn't want to be present at the birth of Joely.'

'Didn't want to be present at the birth?' Fiona sounded horrified. Lucy remembered that she'd held this as being one of the great sacred cows of fatherhood. A father not present at the birth was up there with the leading cads, fuckwits and adulterers of our time. You'd be more likely to be forgiven wife-beating or infidelity than a stint outside in the corridor in the hospital.

'I didn't want to make him,' said Serena. 'I knew how he felt, and I thought, well, there we are. Funnily enough, I think he regretted it in the end . . .'

'I think you were quite right.' Grace spoke softly. 'I knew Richard didn't want to be there when I had Luke, but I thought it would make us closer as a couple, and anyway, everyone said it was so important. But I hadn't even peed in front of him, and I'd never let him see me waxing my legs or flossing my teeth. So when I was splayed out, completely open and exposed, it was horrible. And things went wrong from the very beginning; by the end I was so attached to tubes and lines that I felt like a butterfly on a pin against the bed. He could hardly touch me. There was blood everywhere – all over the walls and the floors.

269

Even the door handle. I think he was traumatized.'

Serena changed the subject as Fiona opened her mouth to say something else about men in the delivery room. 'Well, I think it's amazing that we're still functioning at all after everything we've been through.'

Lucy slid another look at Grace, who was now fiddling with her fingernails. She still seemed to be the only one whose husband didn't want to make love to her. Even Fiona had admitted to pushing Rupert away in the first place.

'And what nobody ever told me . . .' Serena's voice carried effectively enough for a couple at the next table to turn their heads, 'was that middle-aged sex is one of the great secrets of life. There's only yourself – and him – to please, and you don't have to worry about all those issues of contraception and where it's all going. If only they'd told us when we were younger that the best was yet to come, we wouldn't have worried about it so much.'

Lucy felt scared. She'd hoped that everybody lost that kind of interest in their other halves after twenty years of marriage. She'd hoped that she and Ned were normal.

As Lucy lost track of the conversation buzzing around her, she thought of Phil. She hadn't seen him for three weeks because, in his quiet methodical way, he took a lot of holidays. He'd set up his life so that he could spend time on archaeological digs around the world. He'd come back, his skin like a battered leather suitcase and his stubble streaked with grey, and slip efficiently back into his slot, hardly mentioning what he'd done while he was away. Lucy often wanted to know more, but there never seemed to be time to ask him. He was always the one who asked the questions. She tried to imagine him being an ordinary, bad-tempered man with his wife, obsessing about tidiness in the bedroom or getting irritated by children's toys lying around, but she couldn't.

It had helped, him being away. She wasn't talking to him in her head quite so much, but she still couldn't focus on Ned.

'Another thing that no one ever talks about,' Serena hiccuped, penetrating Lucy's dream, 'is female mastur-bation. Waiter!' A waiter caught her eye and came over immediately, just as she was asking everyone how many of them masturbated secretly when their husbands were in bed beside them.

The waiter looked terrified.

'Four more glasses of house red, please. Actually, make that another bottle.' She looked round as he scuttled off. 'I mean, I do. But don't ever tell Matt, for Christ's sake, or I'll never get any sleep.'

The waiter, looking as if he'd swallowed a tennis ball, returned with another bottle and bolted. 'So everybody?' Serena sounded triumphant. 'As I thought. It's much quicker and more relaxing than revving up the old man, if all you want is a bit of relaxation and to drop off quickly afterwards.'

Lucy thought of her own secret, furtive spasms when Ned was sound asleep. It all seemed a bit of a waste.

Fiona, who'd been quiet for a while, suddenly piped up. 'I must say I was awfully cross when Rupert's father thought my vibrator was Rupert's electric razor and then threw it away because he said it was blunt.'

Before anyone could reply, she added, 'But I suppose it was time to get a more modern one really. The old ones are awfully noisy.' She turned to Lucy. 'Do you remember when we lived in Number 3, The Terrace? Next door actually complained to Rupert that they'd appreciate it if we didn't use our washing machine at three in the morning.'

She'd lost Lucy, along with the rest of the table.

She rolled her eyes prettily. 'It takes about as long as the spin cycle for me to come, so they thought I was doing the washing! It was so funny. Of course, Rupert hadn't a *clue* what they were talking about.'

Neither did Grace, Lucy nor Serena. Surely she couldn't have lain there enjoying herself with something that sounded like a Black & Decker drill and waking the neighbours without him noticing? Perhaps he'd been a bit deaf from shooting all that wildlife every weekend. You could never tell what people's private lives were really like, thought Lucy.

'There was a vibrator doing the rounds at my boarding school,' Grace said. 'I'd no idea what it was, but everyone kept saying how wonderfully relaxing and refreshing it was, so I asked to borrow it. The box said it could be used for all sorts of things, such as toning the neck. So I lay there on the bed, with this thing juddering away under my chin and couldn't understand what all the excitement was about.' She stared at her perfect fingernails.

'I went through a very off-sex phase when Joely was young,' said Serena. 'Discovering vibrators did help me to get out of it. It gave me such confidence to find out that I *could* come. And it's so quick.' She spoke as a woman on whom the demands of a board-level directorship, a small son, several charity commit-tees and a husband left little time for sensuality. 'If you've got thirty seconds to spare, you can have an orgasm. The other thing –' she leant forward '– and this is really a good tip . . . electric toothbrushes. The vibration exactly mimics the pulse of the female orgasm. You can't beat it.'

'Isn't that a bit unhygienic?' Grace sounded anxious.

Serena giggled. 'You take the brush off first, of course.'

'Most of the sex books do recommend vibrators.' Lucy thought of the books that Phil had passed on to her about another matter. 'A colleague . . .' She caught Grace's eye and could swear that she winked, so she started again. 'A colleague of mine suggested these books for this patient with sexual problems, so I bought them myself to check over their suitability for patients –'

'All in the interests of research . . .' shouted Serena. 'Of course!'

'Well, if I'm going to recommend a book to patients, I ought to know what it's like,' asserted Lucy. Everyone smiled. 'Anyway,' she continued, 'I discovered that there's nowhere safe at home to keep these things. I mean, you can't put them in bookcases, and even drawers aren't safe from Tom or Nico rifling through them to borrow a pair of socks or something. If I had a vibrator, I can't imagine where I'd keep it.'

'In the back of the cupboard where you keep the oven cleaner, bath de-scaler and stain remover,' said Fiona, with a tinge of bitterness. 'No one except you is ever going to go in there.'

'If he did more in the kitchen, would you do more in the bedroom?' bellowed Serena. 'I saw that as a headline in a magazine once, and couldn't imagine why there was a whole article written about it. One word would have been enough. Yes. Yes, yes, yes!'

She threw her head back in simulated ecstasy. 'Emptying the dishwasher! Yes, oh, more, more!'

The couples at the tables on either side stopped eating and looked worried.

Serena gave a fake-orgasmic gasp. 'Doing the laundry! Emptying the dishwasher! Hoovering! It certainly gives a whole new meaning to the phrase, "I want you to talk dirty to me".'

The waiter, obviously dying to get rid of them, offered to call a taxi.

As they all poured out of the restaurant, weaving

unsteadily past the video shop on the corner, they caught sight of a video being promoted in the window. *What Women Want* proclaimed the banner in front of the display.

'What women want!' boomed Serena. 'Ha! That's easy. Foreplay! That's what women want.'

An elderly couple walking a small terrier hurried past in the lamplit gloom, casting glances over their shoulders.

'Trouble is . . .' Fiona was slurring her words, but they came out clearly enough to send a couple of youths hanging around next to the bank opposite scurrying off. 'It's a message they absolutely don't want to hear. They're quite prepared to believe that there is such a thing as a clitoris, but when it gets down to it, they still think that what you really need is a jolly good shag.'

'Look, you have this taxi. I'll have the next one.'

Grace and Lucy slid in. 'Serena's not usually like that, by the way,' murmured Grace as the taxi pulled away. 'It's just that she has a very responsible job, and hardly ever drinks, so when she does, she lets herself go in a pretty major way.'

They both giggled briefly. Grace retreated into a corner, suddenly looking small and frail. 'It was all my fault, wasn't it?'

'What?'

Grace nodded at the taxi driver to indicate that she couldn't speak fully. 'You know . . . Richard. When Luke was born.'

Lucy suspected that she might be at least partly right, but she couldn't imagine a man who loved his wife allowing that to come between them so totally and for so many years.

'I don't think there's ever a simple answer to these things. It can never be entirely your fault.' She remembered what Grace had said at Sunday lunch. 'But didn't you say things were better?'

'Oh, yes,' said Grace hurriedly. 'Much better. Of course.'

Lucy worried about going to France for two weeks at the end of July, because it would mean leaving Owen alone.

He was impatient. 'I'll be perfectly all right. Don't be absurd. I'm not going to die in a fortnight. Nothing happens suddenly in this cancer business, you know.'

Recently, he'd seemed a great deal better. It was as if his decay had halted. Lucy began to believe that it had all been a bad dream, and that in the years to come, Owen would still be mending things and grumbling. They were weeding the strawberry beds. If he could keep the birds away, there would be a bumper crop this year. The tiny, tight green fruits were just about to burst into ripeness.

'Why don't you and I go somewhere first? With Tom, if he wants to come?' Lucy straightened up, wondering how Owen, at eighty-two, managed to garden for hours on end without finishing up completely bent double while she, at almost half his age, ached in every bone almost immediately.

'Don't you bother about me.' He continued jabbing away with the hoe, but she could see the effort it was for him.

'I think I could do with a break.' She was beginning

to learn how to handle him. They had got to know each other properly – perhaps for the first time as adults – now that their relationship had gone beyond monthly Sunday lunches and the obligatory few days at Easter and Christmas. 'Join me for a cup of tea so that I don't feel too guilty about it.'

Owen conceded that that wasn't a bad idea, but said he wanted to get to the end of the bed first.

After Lucy made the tea, she watched him walk wearily towards the house, but surely he was taking no longer than he had a few months ago. This was what he hated – the slow deterioration of his body. The visible crumbling of his strength. The way his body curved forwards with each step, trembling with the effort of inching forward.

'Seriously, though, Dad.' She took the tea tray out to the little terrace behind the back door, which was where he liked to sit. He lumbered through to the kitchen and counted out a series of pills. At the moment, he could administer his own medicines. Soon, he would have to be helped. Lucy still couldn't get him to talk about moving to their house or going to a hospice, although she was quietly beginning to gather up information herself. But, first, she wanted to take him away somewhere. 'If you could go back to one place in your life where would it be?'

For a moment, she thought he wasn't going to answer. They faced the garden, each of its beds planted in an orderly fashion – three rows of potatoes, then two each of carrots and onions, then the more exotic artichokes and squash, all boxed in tidily with railway sleepers around the edges. The herb bed was the nearest, and its fragrance gently blew over with a sudden summer breeze: frothy fronds of fennel and curry plant, broad green leaves of sage and sorrel and the woody, Mediterranean hardiness of the lavender and rosemary. For a moment, Lucy shivered, as the goosepimples rose on her arm. The breeze died and the warmth returned.

'I'd go back to London. To Number 10, Victoria Road. The first place we lived in.' He rubbed his face. 'Where you were born. When everything seemed so clear and bright, and we knew, like you know now, that we were going to be happy for ever.'

'We're a bit past that stage, Dad.'

His eyebrows bristled. 'I thought you might be.'

They sat in silence, and Lucy concentrated on the gnarled, twisted trunks of the apple trees her father had planted beyond the vegetable beds. They looked like Owen's hands – very, very old.

Eventually he hitched his trouser legs up to lean forwards more comfortably. 'Well?'

'Oh, we're fine. Absolutely fine. Really.'

'But . . .'

She hadn't confided in a parent for so long. It had been Sarah that she'd talked to, anyway, in those early days of boyfriends and clothes, and Owen had kept himself at one remove from it all. There'd been a sense of rightness about that. When it came to growing up, fathers might be loved, but they weren't always appropriate. They didn't want to think about their little girls as sexual beings. And by the time Sarah died, she'd moved away from home effectively, to university, then on to medical school in London.

No, it wouldn't be right to confide in Owen. He shouldn't be worried, not in his condition. She looked into the distance again. Beyond the tiny orchard, the fields stretched in swathes of brilliant green, meeting the horizon in a fringe of trees.

She didn't think she could possibly tell him about not fancying Ned any more.

'He's not playing around, is he?' This was a rhetorical question. Owen clearly did not think Ned was playing around.

Lucy shook her head.

'And you?'

She studied her fingernails. 'I'm tempted.' This was the first time she'd seriously admitted this to anyone. Her joking banter with Grace didn't count.

'Brian Lacey, eh? Or something more serious?'

She smiled. Owen could be very astute sometimes. 'Probably a Brian Lacey. But I do worry that if I'm not . . . nicer . . . to Ned, then he will find someone else.'

Owen nodded. 'It happens.'

'Did you? In the Brian Lacey period, I mean?'

He poured out another cup of tea. 'Yes. I did.'

Panic squeezed the air out of Lucy's lungs for a few seconds. She remembered the pain in her father's grey face when she'd let herself into the house after hearing about Sarah's death. He'd looked like a man whose life was over. Yet he'd been unfaithful. Did everyone have secrets? She tried to make her voice sound calm. 'What happened?'

'It was nothing really. Your mother'd been out late twice that week, because there was some dinner the pottery group were going to. Do you remember Angela? From the tennis club?'

Lucy screwed up her eyes to improve her memory. 'A bit bottle-blonde? Rather obvious?'

He winced. 'I loved your mother so much, that anyone trying to get my attention over her head would have had to be pretty obvious.'

Lucy was reassured.

'Anyway, this Angela turned up at the door with a bottle of sherry, and said that she'd bumped into the pottery group and knew I'd be alone, so she'd come to cheer me up.'

'Dad.' Lucy groaned. 'I take back the "obvious". "Predatory" is the word that comes to mind. And there was I at university thinking it was me having the wild time.' That first year, she remembered, she had been quite cautious. She'd met a few men she'd been interested in, but hadn't got involved. She hadn't even lost her virginity, which had been something of an achievement at the height of the Pill era, when men were put out if you didn't. Meanwhile, back in her tidy, suburban home, her parents, her staid, solid, middle-aged parents, had been frolicking with Brian and Angela. With Angela at least. She still didn't believe that Brian had been anything more than a flirtatious fantasy.

He smiled. 'Us men are simple creatures. We need obvious or predatory sometimes.'

'Did Mum find out?'

He took a final swig of tea and the cup rattled against the saucer as his hand shook. 'I never knew. She didn't mention it.'

That didn't mean anything. Her mother, thought Lucy, had been the type not to say. She wouldn't have wanted, in her words, to upset the apple cart.

The apple cart had clearly been teetering enough as it was.

'She was a great girl, that Angela,' mused Owen, with something approaching a glint in his eye. 'Matter of fact, I asked her to marry me after Hector – you know, her husband – died.'

Lucy was astonished. If Owen had ever married again, she'd have expected it to be to a perfect woman like Sarah. Neat and pretty, and always in the kitchen tinkering with something delicious for dinner. Someone who was always ready with a gentle, welcoming smile, always asking people how they were and drawing them out. Sarah had dedicated her life to making a house a home, not aggressively clean, just warm and comfortable and shining with happiness. She was nothing like brassy, obvious, predatory Angela.

'But she had several other offers,' sighed Owen. 'Angela was good at cheering people up.'

'Evidently.' Lucy swallowed her disapproval. 'So what do I do about Ned?'

'You do love him.' It was only half a question.

She nodded.

'Well, it's promising that you've said, "What do I do about Ned?" rather than "What do I do about this affair?" I don't know, of course, because we never got there, but I've always believed that our marriage would have survived Brian Lacey and Angela. I always thought it was just an interlude. Not serious. No woman was ever serious for me except for your mother. Although Angela came close.'

'I don't suppose Ned thinks of me like that. I mean, I wasn't his only serious woman.' Unlike Lucy, Ned had had several long-term girlfriends. He'd lived with one for almost ten years, and his first girlfriend was still in Bramsea. They'd gone out with each other between the ages of sixteen and twenty. Ned was Mr Nice Guy. Mr Steady Boyfriend. Mr Responsibility. Lucy sighed. Sometimes she thought she'd just come along at the right time, when the last long-term girlfriend had gone to York and he'd been looking round for someone to marry.

'I'm sure you are, you know.'

She shrugged. He would think that. She knew Owen's loyalty to his darling daughter was total.

'Spend some time with him,' advised Owen.

'We've got a holiday coming up. In France, with Grace and Richard. You met them at Christmas.'

Owen snorted. 'That's not what I meant. Spend some time together, just the two of you.'

'I'll try.' Lucy didn't want to say it, but she didn't have time. Not while Owen needed her. She was going to spend the next free weekend she had taking Owen back to London. It was something she could do for him. Soon there wouldn't be anything.

'I'll come away with you after France,' said Owen, reading her mind.

She put a hand on his arm. 'We can go before.' Suppose he deteriorated too much and they never managed to go?

He shook his head. 'No. My mind's made up. We'll make it a late-summer treat. I'm feeling better these days, you know. I'll still be around by then.'

'That friend of yours, Grace,' mused Owen, as Lucy cleared up the teacups. 'A bit of a minx.'

Lucy looked at him sharply. Did he know something she didn't?

'She's not really. Everybody distrusts her because she's so good-looking. She's actually very kind. And loyal.'

'Hmph. I'm not saying she isn't. But she doesn't know what she wants. And she'll be causing a lot of damage while she's finding out. That type always do.'

Perhaps Owen was right about Ned. They should spend some time together. He was usually home early on Thursdays. They could go out for a plate of pasta – just the two of them.

22

The following week Phil came back. It was high summer, and a low, dense heat hung over the town, broken only by intermittent showers. At night Lucy was too hot to sleep. She kicked the sheets into an uncomfortable ball, with vague fevered thoughts of Phil's hands and face. In the mornings, she felt swollen and tired, and when she saw Ned's dear, battered face, she flushed with guilt and snapped at him more often than usual.

On Tuesday, she tried on several different pairs of trousers. They were all tightish. She had been looking for answers inside chocolate wrappers rather more often than she might have liked recently.

But after washing the newly sharp bob and applying the eyeliner, she looked brighter and better. So did every other woman at the surgery. Mirrors were glanced into that morning, and hair was patted into shape a fraction more often than had been usual over the last four weeks. The receptionist, Polly, simpered at him. 'Lovely to see you back, Phil.' She fluttered her eyelashes at him over a pile of patients' notes. Lucy was irritated.

It was strange, seeing him again in the flesh. He had been in her head so often that, for one moment, she thought she might have created someone completely different.

But he had the same intense, observant eyes and bristly stubble. Brown, sinewy arms – hairier and more wiry than Ned's, but strong-looking – emerged from a short-sleeved checked linen shirt. He looked . . . she drifted off into a reverie, briefly . . . fit and lean, as if being outside so much had chased away the shadows. All that digging up shards of pottery and mummified remains, she supposed, feeling guilty about the chocolate again.

'Hi.' He kissed her on both cheeks. 'You look well. How's your dad?'

'Fine.' She racked her brains for something amusing or clever to say. 'Fine.'

'Good.' He smiled down at her, and she felt a treacherous warmth leap up inside her.

'Are you still driving out there regularly?'

She nodded. Surely she could think of something interesting to say? 'Yes.' She nodded again. 'Yes.' All the fantasizing had created a barrier between them in her mind. She hoped he hadn't noticed. It was funny how fantasies changed over the years. Before she got married, they were all about wedding dresses and babies, and the object of the fantasy professing undying love. Now she never gave wedding dresses a second thought, would have been thoroughly horrified by getting pregnant, and would have far preferred a declaration of passionate lust. Or just a snog would do. It was like going backwards into adolescence.

'Well, if you're going past Little Topping this Thursday and feel like a spot of supper, do drop in.'

Lucy tried to turn herself back into sensible, nice, middle-aged Dr Dickinson, the stalwart of the Bramsea Christmas Fayre. 'Oh, yes, absolutely. I mean, I just make his supper, er, sometimes, and, um, leave it, I can easily do that on Thursday, I'd already thought that would be the best . . . er . . .' Stop blathering, she told herself. If you can't say anything sensible, don't say anything at all.

'See you on Thursday, then? We can catch up on what's been happening round here. I've got a full list, so I'm going to work through lunch.'

'Yes.' She bobbed her head up and down again. Lust had completely deprived her of all intelligence. 'Yes. Er. See you then.'

Aargh. Eek. What was she doing? Cancelling Ned, for a start. She'd arranged to have a pasta night out with him this Thursday.

Owen would be disconcerted to discover that she was coming over but not staying to supper. She suppressed the guilt. She spent a lot of time with him. They were going to London together soon. She would arrange that now, this minute.

Ned agreed to babysit Tom on Thursday instead of coming out for a pasta with her. Lucy felt deeply guilty. 'I'm going to pop in to see Phil Gray on the way back, to discuss a few things we didn't have time to cover in surgery.' The first step in deception is to tell as much of the truth as possible. Was she embarking on deception? Last time she'd seen Phil she'd said that she wanted an affair, and now he'd invited her to his house. On the other hand, he'd always been friendly and it could so easily be nothing more than that.

Ned didn't seem to mind. 'I'll catch up on a few things.'

Well, he obviously wasn't worried.

Owen's rheumy eyes looked at her, bewildered, through his thick, greasy glasses, when she said she was eating at Phil's. 'But I'll sort your supper out first,' she added, trying to placate him.

'Don't worry about me. I can manage.'

She thought she might scream if he said that once more. He couldn't manage. And it was high time he accepted it. 'I'm seeing Phil Gray, one of my colleagues –' she turned away to the sink to hide her expression in the washing-up '– because we need to catch up with some urgent surgery business.'

When she turned round Owen was still looking at her. His sight wasn't good enough, she told herself, to pick up the guilt in her face.

'You can't get much past your old dad.' His voice was sad.

She pretended not to have heard. 'There's so much red tape now in the NHS – we don't have time to have meetings in the surgery.' There was, she thought, the faintest implication that this was a meeting of the whole practice.

He heaved himself to his feet. 'Well, I'm going to do some cutting back.' He felt his way, slowly and painfully, towards the back door. He was angry, she knew, but whether it was because she was lying to him or because he thought that she was cheating on Ned, she didn't know.

'You'll see better if I give those glasses a wash.' She held out her hand for them.

'I can see quite enough, thank you very much.' He tried to straighten up, and shuffled out of the door past her. She realized what he intended to do – to use some massive cutters to prune the hedge – and hurried out. This was definitely a sulk. They'd agreed that he'd no longer do the heavy stuff. She followed him out. At this early stage of summer the heat hadn't yet permeated inside the house, but walking across the garden was like moving through tepid soup.

'Dad. I'm sorry. You simply can't use those. They're too heavy, and it's too risky.' She picked up the shears. 'I can't let you.'

'It's not me who's taking risks.' His voice trembled.

'Dad. It's just a meeting. I promise. I won't do anything. Now, please. I'll bring Ned over on Sunday and he'll do all the cutting back. He's always happy to help. Please.'

Owen sagged in defeat. 'Very well. He's a good man.'

'I know. I know.' Too good for me, thought Lucy. That was the point of Ned. His goodness. He was so much better than she was.

But there went another chance to spend proper time with him. This Sunday the boys were both out playing matches all day, and she'd planned to have a leisurely lunch in the pub with him, followed by bed. It would be different if they had time, surely, especially if she wasn't as tired as she usually was at night. She might be able to explain sensate focusing a bit better.

At the moment, however, Owen needed them more.

'Be careful.' He placed an arm on her shoulder, as she left. They weren't a family for hugging and kissing.

'I promise.'

She hadn't said, 'There's nothing to be careful about.' She glanced in the mirror as she drove away, and he was still standing there, watching her go. She suddenly wanted to turn back, fling herself into his arms and cry. He was so very much her father.

Walking into Phil's almost-empty room again was a shock. It was very beautiful, but it would be so easy for him to pack up the one stunning picture and leave. It felt temporary. All that space was asking to be colonized, she thought. Women would want to put their stamp on it.

'Have you always been so stylish? In your home.' Lucy accepted a glass of wine, telling herself not to gabble. 'It's very fashionable.'

'Fashionable?' He looked surprised. 'I hadn't been thinking about fashion. My wife was good at all that.'

It was odd always hearing him use the words 'my

wife'. He hadn't said 'ex-wife'. He'd said 'wife', as if he still wanted her to belong to him.

'That picture.' He indicated the scarlet canvas with a tiny dot of orange in the corner. 'That's the only thing I brought away from my marriage.'

Lucy looked at it. 'It's brilliant,' she said, truthfully. 'Wasn't there anything else you wanted to keep?'

He took a sip of wine. 'There was, in fact. In the early days we used to go round antique shops together. Fenella's always had an eye for things like that, so we picked up one or two lovely pieces before the market got silly. But I didn't want the children to have any more holes in their life than they did. I don't suppose Jessie and Jonno missed me much, but they'd certainly have noticed bare patches on the walls where pictures used to be, or having three dining chairs instead of six. So we agreed to divvy up that side of things when they'd grown up.'

Lucy was going to interrupt and tell him that she was sure Jessie and Jonno had missed him, but decided to let him talk. He was usually so careful about what he said.

'Then, when Fenella married Simon, and they sold the house, she suggested that I come and take whatever I liked. It was always very civilized, our divorce. Much more civilized than our marriage.'

'But you didn't want anything.'

'I'd lived without it all for some time by then. So, no. It feels freer like this.'

'No attachments?'

'No attachments,' he echoed, with a rueful smile.

He opened the kitchen door. 'It's getting so warm.' A soft, warm breeze drifted through, like chiffon against her skin. Outside, the fading sun illuminated orderly rows of vegetables, as well as a vibrant border of flowers and a path leading past a weeping willow tree to a vista of curving fields beyond. There was more of a feeling of permanence outside. Of emotion, even. He had put real effort into creating life. 'They're like my father's,' she indicated the vegetable beds. 'You're a gardener.'

'I'm a control freak. I spend my life trying to get it all absolutely right. And then I go out into the garden, and it reminds me how anarchic life is. Something doesn't grow, even though you put it in exactly the right soil. Or it grows, but in the wrong direction and the snails or the birds eat it. Or it takes off and chokes everything else. It's humbling. Necessarily so, as far as I'm concerned.'

'You can't be any worse than anyone else.' Something somewhere had hurt him very badly, she thought. Fenella? For all her civilized behaviour? She wanted to kiss it all away. So did every other woman who came here, she suspected.

'How is your father?' He changed the subject. 'Salad OK for you?' He pulled some ready-prepared bags out of a tiny fridge, along with a couple of steaks and some garlic, which he chopped like a chef. She drank in all the details, using them as clues to the essential Phil. He cooked, he gardened, he had a lovely house. He was frighteningly self-sufficient.

He was a control freak, who'd been hurt.

It was strange, having food prepared for her by another man after all these years. It was quite unusual having food made for her at all. The weight of the endless meals she was responsible for slipped off her shoulders, and she sighed in relief. 'Lovely.' She leant back on the door frame. 'He's angry with me for coming here.'

'Oh?' His eyes were blue, she saw now, astonishingly blue for someone so dark.

'He doesn't think it's proper.' Suddenly she could talk to Phil normally again, and say what was on her mind. It was also, she knew, provocation. It gave him a chance to say what she was doing here.

'And is it?' He didn't give himself away easily. The oil sizzled in the pan, as he peppered the steaks.

Lucy took another sip of wine. 'What do you think?' They were dancing round each other.

He flipped the steaks into the pan, and took her glass away, placing it carefully on the table, lining it up so carefully and moving so neatly that she had no warning of what might happen next.

He placed both hands on her shoulders and kissed her on the lips.

It was like being struck by lightning. She surrendered her mouth to his. Hesitant, at first. Exploring with tiny, tentative butterfly touches, initiating a magical journey into unknown territory. Then more urgently. Wanting. Craving. His hands stroked tiny sparks of static along the back of her neck, as she drank drank in the new sensations. He was slimmer and more wiry than Ned. He smelt of the sea, of soap and newly ironed shirts. He tasted slightly salty and of good red wine. His short, short hair and stubbly face were coarse but silky, like glossy pony skin under her fingers, and she could feel the fine bones of his head beneath them, as the heat burned their bodies against each other. She wanted to explore the rest of him, to tease him, to make him laugh. To make him groan.

Her knees would give way if he didn't stop soon.

He stopped, his lips caressing hers briefly one last time, and turned back to the steaks, flipping them over. 'Exactly right.' He gave her a crooked smile.

Lucy was shaking. In her mind, she could see Ned, Nico and Tom. And Owen. She picked up the glass again, and sipped. 'I mustn't drink too much. I don't want to be breathalysed.'

'Don't worry. I won't let you.'

'Bossyboots.' She had promised Owen that she wouldn't do anything. It had been a real promise.

He tapped her mouth with a gentle finger and smiled. 'Lippy.'

These were terms of endearment. They were beginning to have their own language, and their shared jokes, the way lovers do.

It was frightening how quickly it could happen.

*

He set the meal down neatly on the bleached wood of an old pine table outside, and they ate in silence at first. Lucy could see alchemilla growing up through worn pavers, frilly and green against the grey, lichen-covered stones.

'Tell me about your mother,' said Phil, suddenly. 'When did she die?'

Her fork stopped halfway to her mouth. She would choke if she ate any more.

'When I was nineteen. At the beginning of my second year at university.'

'That must have been very hard for you.'

'Yes. Everybody was very young, so they didn't understand. They didn't know what to say to me, so quite often I'd see someone crossing the road to avoid me.' She still remembered how much that had hurt. She'd wanted to come back to the warmth of her friends after the funeral, to a feeling of belonging, but found herself treated by many as an emotional leper. Staying alive had become like tight-rope walking, with no one to catch her if she fell.

'And how did you deal with it?'

Lucy flashed her bright, shiny smile, the one she'd learned from those dark, rainy Seventies days when there always seemed to be a power cut or a strike. 'I partied. Lots and lots of parties. They were fun.' She didn't tell him what had usually happened after the parties, the way she'd looked for comfort and only occasionally found it. He wouldn't 'respect' her if she did. A stupid old out-dated term, but she'd got wary. That part of her life was over.

'Really?' He seemed to care.

'Yes.' All her defences came up. She needed them, anyway, because she'd promised Owen she wouldn't get involved.

'I missed her most when I had children of my own. She would have known how much they meant to me. She would have loved them as much as I did, and in the same way.'

'Surely Ned felt the same?'

Lucy thought about it. 'I think he felt as much. He'd certainly wanted children – that was why he married me. But no, I don't think he felt the same. I don't think men and women ever feel the same.'

'That was why he married you?' repeated Phil.

Lucy shrugged. 'I've sometimes thought I was the girl who came along at the right time. He loves children. He was tired of going to pubs.'

'You do give men a hard time sometimes. What went wrong?'

'Me?' Lucy was astonished. 'I like men. I'm sur-rounded by men. I look after men. I do not give men a hard time.'

Phil only smiled. 'More salad?'

'Anyway, what about you and women?'

'Me and women?' He laughed. 'A disaster area.'

'Come on, Phil, that's the easy answer. All the women round here adore you. You could have anyone.

You must know that. Why haven't you found some perfect woman and married again?'

'That's what I did the first time. It didn't work. Until I can live with imperfection – my own and someone else's – I had better stay alone. For everyone's sake.'

Lucy couldn't quite believe it.

'Anyway,' he gently pushed a strand of hair away from her face and tucked it behind her ear, and they were both silent for a second. 'What's gone wrong between you and Ned? If you don't mind my asking?'

It didn't seem right to be discussing her husband with the man who had just kissed her. And she didn't want to think about Ned, she wanted to make love with Phil. 'Well . . .'

'We don't have to talk about it,' said Phil. 'But I think you might need to.'

She told him. How she felt permanently guilty because Ned was a good man – he was her rock – and yet she didn't want him in bed. How sick she was of the endless cooking and organizing. How everybody wanted something of her, and she felt she had nothing left to give.

'Why do you say that Ned's a good man?'

She sketched out some vague, unsatisfactory answer. 'Compared to me, anyway,' she added.

'Compared to you,' Phil echoed. 'Why do you say that?'

Lucy stiffened. She didn't really want to answer

that. 'Oh, I don't know. I just feel . . . bad, I suppose.'

'Bad.' Therapists always repeat things back to you, she thought. 'In what way?'

'Because I'm not perfect. Not a perfect woman, like your wife. Or my mother.' If she went on in this self-pitying way, he'd stop fancying her. Or he'd realize she was a bit unstable and that would put him off. She did the shiny smile again. 'But then, who is?'

He ignored that. 'I'm just interested to know why you have this deep-seated belief that you're bad. You seem very lovely to me.'

She stared at her plate. If he really knew her, he wouldn't say that. Neither would Ned. All men had images of perfection – wife, mother, whore – and that hadn't changed in centuries, for all the burble that was spouted about women and power.

'All right,' said Phil. 'I accept that you don't want to talk about it. Yet.'

Her heart leapt at the 'yet'. It implied that they had something ahead of them.

'But I must ask you one thing. Do you think that having an affair with me will re-ignite your sexuality and help sort things out with Ned?'

'That sounds as if I'm using you. I'm not.'

'I know you're not.' He pressed her arm. 'That's not the problem. I'm just asking if you're looking for a temporary solution or a way out.'

'I don't want out with Ned.' Life without him was inconceivable. 'Perhaps I'm being cowardly,' she conceded. 'Maybe, years down the line, I'll realize I ought to be without him. But for hundreds and hundreds of reasons, I couldn't now.'

'OK.' He seemed satisfied by her answer. 'So an affair? Would that be therapeutic?'

She thought about the lies it would entail, the chance of discovery, the hurt on the faces of Ned, Nico and Tom. Of Owen's disappointment in her. Of knowing that she'd broken promises which she could never mend.

'No.' She whispered. The word was wrenched out of her. She wanted to call it back.

They looked at each other. Could they do it once? Under hermetically sealed promises of secrecy? Never to be repeated. Just to know, to really know what it would be like with Phil. Not to get involved. It would just be sex. Britain had the highest adultery rate in the Western world. Everybody must be doing it. Couldn't she just have one teeny-weeny affair to make herself feel better?

'I do terribly want to,' she admitted. She ached for him. 'But I don't know if that's enough to make it right.'

If only she could say it was.

But suppose it wasn't? Suppose it was the beginning of something they couldn't stop until irrevocable damage was done? Suppose just once turned into just twice? Then became a habit they couldn't give up? Like heroin.

A burbling noise vibrated out of her bag. Ned? Was

he checking up on her? She flushed with guilt as she rummaged in search of it.

'Yes?' Her hand was trembling so much she could hardly hear.

'Mummy?' Tom always sounded so much younger and more vulnerable on the phone. Her heart flipped. Something had gone terribly wrong.

'Darling, you should be in bed.'

'Mummy.' She could hear him struggling to get the words out. 'There's nobody here. Where are you?'

What had happened? Panic ignited in a familiar flame inside her. 'What do you mean?'

'Daddy's not here. And Nico isn't here.' She could hear him beginning to sob. He tried so hard not to cry these days. The boys at school teased 'cry-babies' mercilessly. 'I'm scared.' There was a wheeze in his voice, a legacy from the asthma that had dogged his earlier days. She'd thought that was all over. Be reassuring. Be calm. He's not likely to have a bad attack. Not after all these years. The doctor in her knew that a bad attack could easily come out of nowhere, but that it was rare.

'I'll come. Now. But it'll take me about three-quarters of an hour to get to you, so get into bed, and read a book and I won't be long. There's nothing to be frightened of. Nothing at all.' What on earth could have happened to Ned and Nico? Ned had never left either child irresponsibly. She had visions of him driving round the countryside to catch her in flagrante.

This is what happens if you try to have affairs, she realized.

She stuffed the phone back into the bag. 'I must go. Thank you for dinner.'

'Are you all right to drive? You look rather upset.'

And that was why she wanted an affair. She wanted someone who cared about her and only her. To whom Ned, Tom and Nico were two-dimensional. She pushed her hair away from her face. 'I'm fine. I must get back. Tom's on his own.'

He held her shoulders again in his firm grasp. 'I'm here if you need me. Just to talk.' The kisses this time were friendly ones, on the cheek, but she could feel his warm flesh against hers, lingering a fraction. She was briefly comforted.

He studied her face intently. 'Be careful. Please.'

She had to be off. Tom was on his own, wheezing and frightened.

'Thank you.' She turned her face away, so he couldn't see her expression, and almost ran towards her car. What could have gone wrong? Had Nico been hurt in some way? But then, surely, Ned would have called her. Tom was old enough to be on his own for a few hours, but not if he was frightened. She drove fast, scaring herself. It's not that serious, she told herself. There's been a mix-up. There'll be a perfectly simple explanation.

She was being punished. That was what it was. She must not do this again, or someone would get terribly hurt.

301

23

Lucy saw Ned as she hurried through the front door, in the kitchen at the back, making a cup of tea.

'How's Tom?'

He seemed surprised at the anxiety in her voice. 'Sound asleep. When I last looked.'

'Where've you been?'

He looked distracted. 'Here.'

She explained about the frightened phone call.

'Oh. Well, I did pop out for an hour or so, but Nico was in. I shouted up to him.'

'And did he shout back?'

Ned thought. 'To be honest, I'm not sure. But he never does. You know him. I saw him go upstairs only ten minutes earlier so I know he was there, and there wasn't any music so he'd definitely have heard me.'

Lucy was exasperated. Since the children had been toddlers they'd had a strict rule. Handovers have to be acknowledged.

'OK, OK, I know it was sloppy of me. I'm sorry. Let's see what he has to say.'

Still trembling from her drive, Lucy followed Ned up the stairs.

Nico's room was empty.

'Where could he be?' Lucy felt the panic rise again.

Ned steered her back downstairs to their bedroom, with an arm around her shoulders. 'He's eighteen. This is Bramsea. He'll be with his mates somewhere doing absolutely nothing, because there is nothing to do.'

He drew her into his arms for a hug. 'I'm sorry. I didn't mean to go out and leave Tom. And I'm sure Nico hasn't snuck off without telling for any sinister reason, either. He just forgot to tell us. In three months' time he could be in the drug dens of Amsterdam or Bangkok and we'll be none the wiser. Time to let go.'

'I know. I know.' Still furious about her panic-stricken journey, she wriggled out of his embrace, and opened Tom's door a notch. He was sleeping with his mouth open, his forehead damp in the heat, solidly and utterly asleep. She re-adjusted his bedclothes and kissed his soft cheek. In a few years' time, it would be bristly, like Nico's, and he'd be off to the drug dens of Amsterdam or whatever. She and Ned would have time to re-discover each other then.

Telling her body to forget its treachery, she sponged her make-up off. Sometimes when she looked in the mirror, she saw an old woman with flyaway hair and a gaunt expression. At others she saw someone quite different. Almost beautiful. They were fleeting impressions, and would immediately be replaced by her everyday face. This evening she saw a flash of beautiful, and the thought of Phil throbbed through every pulse in her being.

She didn't think she could sleep for wanting him. The night was close, and the air like dark velvet, soft and heavy against her skin. She would have to sleep naked, twisted in a sheet. That would make it worse. If she'd been able to cover her desire up with pyjamas and a duvet, she could almost have hidden it from herself.

But there was Ned, lying beside her, reading *Yachting Monthly*. If it was easing an itch she needed – the mechanical fulfilment of a penis inside her – then he was always ready to oblige. It could even be good. If only she didn't feel so cross with him for going out without checking that Tom was OK. So livid with him for being him, and not Phil. She lay back, looking down at her long, white body, noting the wobbly dome of her stomach and the snail-track lines of stretch marks on her breasts without remorse for the first time. Phil had wanted her. The dome seemed smaller as a result – a barely-there gentle curve rather than a mountain, and she could see some gracefulness in the shape of her breasts.

Ned looked at her over his reading glasses without seeming to notice her.

'Lights out? I've got an early list tomorrow.'

She didn't answer. She wriggled closer to him, psyching herself up. Anything to quench the terrible cravings.

He kissed her forehead and turned away, curled into a ball for sleep.

That was so unlike Ned. Fear fluttered inside her.

He'd never said why he'd gone out, or where he'd been.

But she couldn't forget how Phil had looked, the feel of his stubble against her face and the look in his eyes when he'd told her to be careful. As Ned's breathing evened out, she slipped her hand down between her legs and began to stroke herself, rhythmically, thinking of him. It felt impersonal and lifeless, and the eventual spasm left her sore and ashamed. She drifted off into a sleep punctuated by terrible phone calls from Tom, who seemed to be drowning in the grey-green sea off Bramsea beach, the ring of the phone and the roar of the sea all inexplicably mixed in an incomprehensible, menacing way. She swam all night in her dreams, desperately trying to reach him but every time she got close, a huge wave picked him up and swirled him away. She called and called for help, but Ned, on the beach with a pile of work, couldn't hear above the waves.

The following morning, her eyes rasping with tiredness and the sick, metallic taste of old wine in her mouth, she asked Nico where he had been.

He was whistling in the kitchen before she'd had time to get dressed. Thank God A levels were over anyway.

'Out.' He poured a huge bowl of cornflakes.

She explained about Tom.

He looked thoughtful. 'Oh. Sorry.'

'It's not that I'm trying to keep tabs on you, or

anything.' She was, of course. 'But it's helpful, when you live in a house, to let other people know what you're up to.'

He shrugged. 'Sure. No problem.'

A few months ago, there'd have been a few pithy, disdainful remarks about her small-mindedness or control complex.

It was progress of a kind.

She hoped to catch Grace when she dropped Luke off at school. She needed to talk.

'Looking for someone?' Josie Saunders, coming out of the main hall as she peered in, never missed much.

'Grace Morgan. Have you seen her?'

Josie's eyebrows rose sharply. 'Goodness, I'm surprised you've got anything left to say to her. I mean, you only saw her last night.'

Lucy was baffled. 'Last night?' For a minute she couldn't remember a thing about the evening. Her mind had gone completely blank in panic.

'I saw your car outside Grace's at about nine. Or was it your husband's car? I thought I saw him . . . I assumed you were there too.' Her teeth glittered in curiosity. 'Well I'm sure it was him, but I get so confused.'

Lucy realized she'd been deliberately targeted for Josie's malice. She'd probably purposely lingered around the school in order to collar her and let her know that Ned and his dark green Rover had been seen – alone – outside the Morgans' house.

'Oh.' She made herself sound as casual as possible. 'Of course. I'd forgotten. We're always in and out of each other's houses. Is that the time? I must dash.'

'It's wonderful to have such a good friend, isn't it? And she's *so* attractive.' Josie's honeyed tones followed her out of the school gates.

Ned, of course, could have been having a quick drink with Richard. Or dropping off or picking up something to do with the holiday (like what?). Don't panic. This was all just silly imagination on her part. Again. She had to call Grace.

Grace picked it up after the first ring. 'Yes?' She sounded happy and eager. 'Oh, Lucy.'

Was it her imagination or was that 'Oh, Lucy, what a disappointment'?

'Hi. How's things?'

'Good. Good. Very good, in fact.' Grace sounded as if she was in bed, replete and fulfilled. Or was Lucy's imagination inventing nuances that didn't exist?

It took Lucy a while to work around to what they'd done last night. The possible repercussions of it all reverberated like two mirrors opposite each other. If Grace was seeing Ned, she couldn't say anything about Phil, because it would get back to him.

If Grace knew – as she would have done, if Ned had been with her – about her seeing Phil later on, she didn't say anything. But then she couldn't, could she, or it would have revealed she'd been talking to Ned? Her head ached with it all.

Grace said that she'd had a lazy evening. 'Just hanging around. I made a chocolate cake and ate it.'

'Made a chocolate cake?' Anything less Grace-like – and less adulterous – could hardly be imagined, but it gave Lucy the opening she needed. 'On your own?'

'Richard's away. As usual. But Luke's had a bit. Choccy cake's not really his thing.'

So no clear answer. An implication that Luke might have been part of this chocolate-fest without actually saying that he was.

Grace didn't pig out on things like chocolate cake. She nibbled things like rice crackers or pieces of carrot. She always left half of anything on her plate. Chocolate cake was most unlikely, but on the other hand, that made it equally unbelievable that she'd made it all up.

They made an arrangement to meet, but Lucy thought there wasn't quite as much enthusiasm and warmth in Grace's voice as usual.

She put down the phone feeling isolated. If Ned was having an affair with Grace, did that give her *carte blanche* to go ahead with Phil?

No. It didn't. And she couldn't make assumptions. She must ask Ned again what he'd been doing when he'd left Tom alone.

She called him at work, feeling foolish. Ned sounded vague. 'I went to the pub. I told you.'

'But we've got beer and lager at home.'

'It's not the same. You women never understand.

I just felt like getting out. I'd been looking forward to a night out, and then it was cancelled.'

Your fault, in other words. 'Did you see anyone?'

He began to sound exasperated. 'Well, I chatted to Dave.'

The publican. That meant nothing. Dave would be non-committal if she tried to check up. He was, presumably, used to fending off husbands and wives alibi-hunting or alibi-breaking.

'But no one else?'

'What is this? The third degree?'

'I just wondered.'

He paused. 'Well, no one else comes to mind. I just pass the time of day with whoever happens to be in.'

She was fairly sure that Josie must have actually seen Ned, and not just the car, because the conversation had been so contrived. After all, if it had only been the Rover, she would have presumed that they were both there and not bothered to mention it. She had clearly enjoyed imparting the information.

Her first instinct was to call Phil. He was on her side, but it might change things between them. She didn't want to become needy, and she suspected that Phil, with his neat, tidy life, wouldn't want to become embroiled in a complex situation.

On the other hand, perhaps they could all be fantastically sophisticated and have affairs with each other, like Edwardians in country houses. Everyone would 'know' everything and say nothing.

In a small town with Josie Saunders around? Not to mention Luke, Tom and Nico, all of whom could be as deaf as a post if you asked them to tidy their rooms but whose ears flapped vigorously at the least sign of grown-up secrets.

Perhaps not.

And they were all going on holiday together in two weeks. At least this would give her a chance to find out what was really going on.

24

The holiday. It was becoming a reality. More than a wine-fuelled dream over a lazy Sunday lunch. It was time to buy the suntan lotion and mosquito repellant.

She already missed Grace as her friend. She'd lost someone she could talk to about anything at any time. It was like going back to school, when your 'best friend' went off with someone else. She felt lumpen and isolated, the butt of secret jokes that she would never hear.

Most important, though, was Ned. She thought of the way he laughed at Grace's jokes, and how he replied to her questions with tenderness in his voice. She had never heard him respond like that to anyone except herself.

Think, Lucy, she told herself. Think. Don't do anything in a hurry. Don't lose your temper. Don't cry. Don't sulk. No mindless, hurt retaliation until you're sure of the facts. Don't let anyone suspect anything. Think. And if you can't think of anything, carry on as normal. Watch and wait.

That's what cancer specialists often do with some malignant growths. They watch and wait, holding back on treatment until they can see signs of real damage.

She checked the time. Late for the surgery. At least

listening to other people's problems took your mind off your own.

Phil called at lunchtime. 'I wondered how you were. You seemed so worried when you left.'

Her heart warmed at his concern, at the same time as her knickers reminded her how very attractive she found him. 'It was just a misunderstanding. The sort of silly thing that happens in families.' She wanted to keep him on the line. 'Not at work?'

'I don't work on Fridays.'

She remembered that now. Phil, with the money he'd earned behind him, and no one else but himself to think about, had mapped out the perfect life. He worked, extremely hard and with dedication, from Monday to Thursday. The other three days were his. She wondered what he did with them.

'What are you doing this weekend?' She was fascinated by his life and who he spent it with.

'A gang of old friends are giving a fiftieth birthday party in Venice. I'm flying out this evening.'

There was something tremendously seductive about it all. Venice for the weekend. He'd already been to Amsterdam and Barcelona that year, as well as the archaeological dig. He had friends with houses in glorious places, and he could afford hotels. She tried to imagine being able to go off like that, without having to make sixty-five phone calls arranging everything for everyone else. Arriving on a water taxi and going to the hotel without counting out five or six pieces of luggage at every interchange. Watching the sun set over the domes of the Venetian palazzos without having to explain it all to someone, or reassure someone else that the food would be nice after all. The silence. The chance to do what you liked when you liked.

She became aware that there was a figure in the corner of this perfect dream, though. It was Ned. She'd want to share Venice with him. Perhaps that's what they ought to do – just take off together for a weekend. On the other hand, the boys ought to see it too, some time. She wouldn't want to go without them.

In a few seconds, her dreams had already equipped her with enough emotional baggage to turn it into another family holiday. She wrenched her thoughts away, and listened to Phil map out the drinks in St Mark's square, and a concert in a church that he particularly wanted to catch.

'Have a lovely time,' she told him. 'It sounds perfect.'

'I'll call you when I get back.' He rang off, leaving her wondering what he meant. Call her to make a date? Or call her as a friend? She put the phone down regretfully. If only.

Why couldn't she have a lovely, self-indulgent mini affair with Phil? To cheer herself up?

Because the first step was to re-ignite the intimacy between her and Ned. There was no doubt in her mind that this was where the problem lay. Their relationship was like that of flatmates. Or brother and sister. She had to learn to feel something. Phil's kiss – she briefly stopped thinking about Ned to dwell again on the glorious liquid sensation – had proved that she was capable of wanting, and if she loved Ned, which, of course, she did, then she ought to be able to want him.

And if she couldn't want Ned, perhaps her body was telling her something. She pushed that thought away.

Remembering *Becoming Orgasmic*, she decided to invest in a vibrator. For one thing, if she couldn't persuade him – and she had tried – that foreplay required a little more time and effort than tuning a radio correctly, he might get the message with a gadget. Men loved gadgets.

She tried to remember what they'd all said in Yo Latino! about where you got vibrators. Serena had recommended a website called Blissbox, she thought, and Sh! had one too. That evening she tapped away when everybody was out, ready to switch the PC off if someone miraculously crept into the room. Suppose Nico – or even Tom – started tracing what websites you'd called up? She'd heard there was no such thing as a deleted e-mail. Could the web pages she visited be followed by her husband or sons long after? She didn't know. Even taking an electrical lover seemed fraught with danger.

She found Blissbox without difficulty, along with

other, less female-friendly sites. There were vibrators with plastic veins and pubic hair around the base, modelled on the members of specific porn stars. There were jelly-feel models in candy pinks, with little revolving sweetie-like beads inside. There were the rabbits she'd seen in Sh! with their extraordinary protuberances to stimulate the clitoris and the anus (she winced. Only so much stimulation was required for the time being. She wanted a little foreplay, not to be skewered on triple prongs). She moved the mouse over the web pages to find less predictable, more 'discreet' versions in shapes that reminded her of powder compacts or mobile telephones. You could get yourself into real trouble there, she thought, whipping your vibrator instead of your mobile out of a handbag in a meeting at the sound of 'Scotland The Brave' or 'Ride of The Valkyries'.

Skimming through further, she found big vibrators like models of rocket launchers and little ones the size of a lipstick. She found pressed-jelly underwear that dissolved slowly on contact so that it could be licked off, fur-trimmed bondage kits and gels tasting of passion fruit or pina colada, along with flavour comments on various more conventional lubricants. There were 'designer' vibrators, to look good on coffee tables, presumably. There was a cylindrical thing with a mechanical tongue which mimicked oral sex and looked as if it had been bred too close to a nuclear reactor.

She eventually settled on a rabbit from Blissbox on

the grounds that the technology would fascinate Ned and it seemed the least frightening. She'd have to try it on her own first, though.

It arrived the following day, through the post.

'What's that?' Nico seized it. 'I'm expecting some CDs from Amazon.'

She grabbed it off him. 'That's hardly the shape of a box of CDs.'

'Just check, could you?' He hovered.

She bore it off, muttering excuses, and, when the boys had finally gone to their various tennis and cricket sessions, pulled it out of its wrapping. It was jelly-feel and a vibrant candy pink, with a wire attached leading to a separate control panel. There were two sliding control buttons for different levels of stimulation and a container for the batteries.

She hadn't considered the batteries.

C14 batteries. Not in stock at the supermarket.

She tried the electrical shop in the High Street.

'Oh, hello, Dr Dickinson.' The assistant was one of her patients.

'Oh, hi, Darren.' She was sure that any woman over thirty buying batteries must have an invisible banner over her head screaming 'For Her Vibrator'.

He was baffled by the demand for C14. 'I don't think we've got those. What's it for?'

'Oh. Er. My son's Gameboy,' she improvised, not

having the faintest clue about how batteries were sized.

'Gameboy uses double A. We've got *those*.' He put a packet confidently on the counter.

'He also wanted C14. For something else.' She stretched her face into an unconvincing smile. 'I don't understand all these electrical thingies.'

'Why don't you bring it in and we'll sort it out?' He was all helpfulness.

Her eyes watered at the thought of Darren with the jelly-feel protuberances and clitoral-stimulating rabbit ears. 'Mm. That's a good idea.' She began edging towards the door.

'Now what sort of an electrical item uses C14?' he persisted, his eyes screwed up in thought as he scoured the shelves. 'Linda? C14. Have we got any? What would they be used in? Dr Dickinson wants some.'

Linda, a bottle-blonde in her early fifties, had a look on her face that suggested to Lucy that she knew exactly what C14 batteries were used for. 'Ooh, Dr Dickinson . . . now let me see. Does it have a mains plug as well? Is it rechargeable?' Linda was clearly intent on torturing her.

'Honestly, it's no bother at all. Nothing urgent.' She'd have to go into Ipswich for batteries. Or down to London, if necessary.

'Ooh, look!' Linda, obviously having enjoyed watching her victim wriggle for long enough, let out a cry of victory. 'Here they are. Hidden behind the pop-up toasters. Well, I never! How many do you want?'

Lucy hoped, as she scuttled out of the shop with four batteries, banging the door shut behind her, that Darren and Linda weren't having a conversation – which would inevitably go round the whole of Bramsea – about Dr Dickinson using sex toys. There must be something apart from rabbit vibrators that used C14 batteries. Surely.

The next hurdle was getting to know her vibrator in private. It required almost as much planning as taking a lover, thought Lucy, wishing she'd chosen the little lipstick-sized version after all. The size and obvious-ness of something over ten inches long and made of vigorous pink jelly-plastic, plus attachments, made it essential to choose a time when everyone was out, especially as, bearing in mind Fiona's experience, she had no idea of how noisy it might be. She had to wait until the following Wednesday afternoon – her half-day at the surgery – which was a nuisance because it was usually the time she got on with the laundry and various other chores.

The chattering in her head was almost deafening. That patient needs more tests. Tom needs new cricket pads. Nico needs support (unspecified, mysterious). Ned needs supper. The garden needs weeding. The house needs tidying. Now another little voice was chipping in. You need to recover your sensuality. It's time to be sexy. Add it to the 'to do' list.

She closed the curtains. Not that anyone could see in – their house was opposite the common, so not overlooked – but the thought of using a vibrator in broad daylight made her feel uneasy.

Then she opened them again. This was all about feeling at one with her body. Losing her inhibitions. Finding her inner sex kitten. She'd rather be looking for a lost sock, frankly, and there'd be a lot more chance of success.

What do you wear for a vibrator session? Three o'clock in the afternoon was an odd time to be taking her clothes off. She locked the door (supposing someone came back unexpectedly?) and took off her jeans and knickers, feeling a complete fool. Putting the batteries into the vibrator was relatively straight-forward, and it didn't take her long to read the instructions, which, although fulsome in telling her what *not* to do, such as not using it in the bath or washing it under running water, had few suggestions on what she actually could do, apart from advising her to remove the batteries between sessions. Fat chance – they might get lost and she wasn't going to go through that C14 battery hunt again in a hurry.

Right. Moment of truth. She held it in front of her, and cautiously slid the control switch to 'on'. The jelly-feel penis waved and jiggled obscenely at her like some kind of water monster. So she was supposed to put that inside her? Hm. It was not an erotic thought.

She slid the control switch to the other two positions in turn. There were three levels of stimulation:

a steady tack-tack-tack, a faster, more dynamic whoosh – like a high-speed rail link, and a super-fast whirr like a dentist's drill. She turned it off, took a deep breath and slid it nervously in. Not too bad, really. Different, anyway. A nice change. She tentatively slid the control button up to 'on' and felt as if a small washing-machine drum was revolving inside her vagina. It was a perfectly pleasant sensation. Not exactly passionate, but then what do you expect from jelly-feel plastic? It's not as if she was planning to have its babies or take it home to meet her father. She experimented with moving the controls up and down in a stop-start fashion, like a learner driver trying to accelerate away from the kerb.

Without warning, the super-fast dentist's drill produced an orgasm in about twenty seconds, so quickly that she'd almost forgotten about it before she knew she'd had it. Hardly more than a sneeze, she thought. Well, that was sexual discovery for the day. It had all been rather sudden. Feeling tired, but not particularly sexually fulfilled, she decided to sort some washing.

Still, it was a start. The next stage was to see what Ned made of it.

That evening was her first with Grace since last Thursday. Would Grace look different? Act differently? Could Lucy seem normal with her, or would the tension on her face be an instant give-away?

She pressed the buzzer. Richard's smiling face answered the door. 'Lucy!' He always sounded so pleased to see her. It was difficult to reconcile what Grace said – or, rather, hinted – about Richard, with the hospitable man who was always happy to pour her a drink and ask after her patients. Lucy still hadn't really warmed to him, but she knew this was unfair. He might not be very exciting, but his heart seemed to be in the right place. She suspected that she'd never really shed her early prejudice about him. The holiday, she decided, would be a chance to get to know him properly.

'Grace! Darling! Lucy's here,' he shouted. 'Do come through.'

Grace came in, looking wary. How often had Lucy seen that look on her face? Or was it habitual and had Lucy only noticed it now? She couldn't decide.

'Lucy.' She kissed her on the cheek.

They stood, awkwardly, looking at each other.

'Well!' Richard often spoke in exclamation marks. 'You won't want me around. I'll be in my study, darling, if you need me.' And he bore his whisky out of the room.

'You . . .'

'Do . . .'

They both laughed. 'You first,' said Grace.

'I was just going to say you look terrific.' Apart from the slight air of tension – which Lucy might well be imagining – Grace did look better than ever. Her skin had the sheen that you saw on the very rich or very famous, as if she was lit from the inside.

Grace smiled. 'Thank you. And I was only going

to say do you want to come and see my amazing roses? It's a wonderful year for them, don't you think? All that rain, and now such lovely sunshine. I must say, I do think that so far, it's been the best summer I can remember in a long time.' She prattled on, as Lucy followed her out to the garden, and, once again, Lucy felt as if Grace was avoiding something. Running away in some way.

The best summer? It was sunny, but hardly spectacular. Perhaps Grace was thinking about something more than rain and roses? But all this could easily be Lucy's over-active imagination. She couldn't analyse everything Grace said and take it as an indication of guilt.

She was surprised to find Fiona sitting on one of the teak garden benches. Was Grace trying to avoid being alone with her? And how had Fiona and Grace suddenly become friends? Presumably they'd got in touch with each other after the girls' evening. Lucy had to stifle pangs of jealousy, and remind herself, firmly, that this was silly and childish.

'Samantha's upstairs with Luke, so I persuaded Fiona to stay for a salad,' said Grace.

Lucy smiled at Fiona, feeling ridiculous at being so cross.

'I can't wait for the holiday,' Grace added, putting her hand on her friend's arm. 'I'm dying to show you the farmhouse. It's authentic French rustic and so peaceful.'

Show me? Or show Ned? flashed into Lucy's mind,

but she merely replied that they were looking forward to seeing it. She was conscious of adding a tiny inflexion on the 'we'.

Fiona leant forwards. 'Oh, when are you going to be there? We're going to France this summer, too.'

Fortunately they discovered they would all be there at different times.

'Have you spoken to Phil recently?' Grace enquired.

Was this a trick question? Had Ned set her on to finding out what was really going on with Phil? Lucy was taken aback for a moment. This is what infidelity does to you, she thought. It distorts and deranges. There appeared to be no safe topic of conversation.

'He was in surgery yesterday, but we only had time for a brief chat.' This had been true. He'd touched her arm lightly and asked, 'Things OK?'

She'd nodded, wishing she could tell him everything. But just the act of telling would propel her into his arms. There was nothing quite so seductive as a man you could really talk to.

'He's looking forward to the holiday,' she said.

'Good.' Grace stretched her immaculately painted toes out and wiggled them. 'Bliss. So marvellous to have an attractive man around.'

My husband not good enough for you, then? Lucy almost snapped.

The evening stretched out ahead of them, misunderstanding and suspicion woven into the fabric of their conversation so intricately that Lucy felt her nerves begin to fray.

'I really need a holiday,' she said, truthful for the first time in hours.

'You look tired,' agreed Grace, sounding genuinely concerned.

'I've got the number of a very good acupuncturist,' added Fiona. 'You're probably run-down.'

She found the same with Ned. She couldn't help looking at him differently, as if her suspicions had drawn an invisible curtain between them. If he was vague, she wondered if he was being deliberately evasive; if he was definite about something, she thought he sounded too practised. If he asked her anything, she examined her answer minutely before speaking in case it gave something away about Phil, or any of her suspicions about Grace. There was almost no statement in the world that could not have two meanings, and no action so innocent that it might not be a cover for something illicit.

This meant that sex was the last thing she wanted when she got home from Grace's, a little earlier than usual. But it was no good waiting until all the violins were playing and the scene was set perfectly. That might not happen until they were sixty.

Ned was bemused at the suggestion that they should go upstairs and try out her new vibrator.

Lucy knew that she should have created a romantic atmosphere, lighting candles, dressing in delectable lingerie and introducing the idea gradually, but there was no chance of squeezing romance in amongst the sports gear, satchels, piles of washing and washing-up, and the paperwork that Ned would happily continue poring over until 1 a.m. unless stopped. If you wanted something round here, you had to say so, loudly and clearly.

'What *has* got into you recently?' he enquired. 'Is it the menopause?'

She nearly stomped off. There was nothing as irritating as men ascribing everything to hormones. 'Not yet,' she spoke firmly. 'All I was suggesting was that perhaps we should have an early night.'

'Fine by me.' Surely, six months ago he would have bounded up the stairs two at a time at the merest suggestion? Now he finished the last piece of paperwork, put it away methodically, closed down the computer, washed up his mug, and, eventually, when her nerves were screaming, mounted the stairs, first checking that Tom was OK and switching off his bedside light.

He got into bed nervously, as if he was expecting something in the bedclothes to leap out and bite him.

Lucy realized that going straight from 'hands off' to 'let's frolic with my new vibrator' was a bit sudden. She'd got it wrong, as usual.

They lay there, staring at each other.

'Well,' she said.

'Well?' he enquired. 'Where is it?'

'Here.' She produced it.

He goggled at the sight. 'Good grief. What do we do with it?'

She sighed. What did couples do with vibrators? The sex manuals had assured her that he would enjoy using it on her, apparently, while also enjoying the vibratory sensation on his own genitals. By the look on his face, Lucy didn't think he was going to let the pink monster anywhere near his own precious crown jewels.

'Did you spend money on this?' Ned sounded disapproving.

'Er. No,' she lied, not wanting an argument about wasting money to get in the way of possible passion. 'It, um, came from a medical company. They're always sending samples out to doctors.' She crossed her fingers. Ned was quite capable of realizing that vibrator companies did not send free samples of jelly-feel pink rabbits to GPs. Samples of vitamins, notepads and plastic pens engraved with the names of haemorrhoid cures were about her limit.

He was too fascinated to question her further, though, turning the vibrator over and over, and trying out the controls. 'Can I take it apart and see how it works?'

'No, you can't.' The sex manuals had assured her that the thought of a woman with a sex toy would have any man panting with excitement to the point of ecstasy, not heading to the toolbox for spanners and monkey wrenches. 'Careful of that,' she added, as he bore down on her with it turned on at top speed. 'I don't want an instant orgasm.'

He looked thoughtful. 'Is that what it does? It

ought to be issued to twenty-something boys for them to speed the girls up with.'

'You men have such a mechanistic view of sex. What about romance and passion?'

Ned studied the pink vibrator. 'You tell me. Well, here goes.' He switched it to its lowest level and moved it across her body and gently over her clitoris. If you forgot it was plastic, it was really quite pleasant.

As he smiled, his face crinkled into the corners of his eyes. Lying back, he looked quite good-looking, really. If you liked that sort of thing. She ran her hands over his stomach and down his thighs, hesitating to find out whether the rabbit was turning him off completely.

'Ha!'

'What?'

'You are interested.'

'Yes, my love, I am very interested. What did you expect?'

Lucy was beginning to feel quite interested herself. 'You could turn that off and we could . . .'

'No, no,' he said. 'I'm really intrigued now by how it works.' He accelerated the speed. 'Good heavens.' He began moving it in and out with an air of professional curiosity.

In spite of some delicious tingling sensations, Lucy felt as if her vagina had been hi-jacked for some kind of scientific experiment. 'That's my body you're playing with.'

'What? Oh. Mm. What does this do?' He turned it full on to the top, super-fast level.

'Listen.' She had to get this in quickly. 'Either we have full, proper sex now, or I will come with that thing inside me and promptly lose interest. Choose. Now. Before it's too late.'

'Oh. Right.' Ned didn't often get ordered to have sex. He turned it off, and moved on top of her as she came shuddering to a climax.

As they lay entwined five minutes later, they studied each other's faces. His dear old face, she thought. Getting a bit old, anyway. But nice. 'That was fun.' She kissed him.

'It was. For a change. But I like the way we do it usually.'

'Do you honestly?'

'Really. Truly.'

Am I as good as she is? Is it more exciting or more sensual, or simply deliciously different? Is it better with someone who can get turned on without the help of electrical appliances? The thoughts flashed briefly through her brain. No. Don't think like that. You don't know. It's all suspicion.

But it was enough to make her turn away. 'Good,' she mumbled, hoping it would get her out of any further discussion.

He stroked her back. 'What about you?'

'I'm fine. I'm absolutely fine.'

'Sure?' He kissed her shoulder. 'Thank you. For . . .' she heard him chuckle, 'something a bit unusual.'

25

Just as she was beginning to worry about leaving Owen for two weeks, he took a turn for the better. He sounded less quavery and more optimistic on the phone, and when she went over on Thursday evening, she found him digging in the garden with some of his old strength returned.

He straightened up and shaded his eyes. 'Come and have a pot of tea.' He set off towards the kitchen with an air of determination.

Cancer could be a funny thing, she thought. It could suddenly go into remission with no explanation, and, at his age, he could go on for years. She felt the weight of imminent tragedy lift off her shoulders and found she could breathe more easily.

'So. How's it all going?' He settled them in his favourite sunny spot outside the back door, on faded stripy deckchairs.

'Nico is on study leave now that his As are over, which means he lies in bed all morning, eats a loaf of bread, half a pound of butter and a pot of jam around midday and goes out until about 3 a.m., when he polishes off two or three pizzas, each of which allegedly serves four portions. I've no idea what he does, except that he seems in a fairly good mood about it on the odd occasion when our paths cross. I can't imagine what it's going to be like on holiday when he's under our noses half the time.'

'Hm. Is there a girl around, do you think?'

'Wouldn't he want to bring her on holiday if there was?'

Owen shook his head. 'Take her home to meet Mum? Let alone be saddled with her on holiday. You must be joking. I remember what you were like at that age. If we approved of someone you went right off them.' He chuckled. 'I had to pretend to disapprove of everyone. Not that that was always difficult. Do you remember that Nigel person?'

'Nigel?' Lucy was indignant. 'I never went out with someone called Nigel.'

'Looked like an overgrown King Charles spaniel? That long, woolly hair boys had in those days and great soppy eyes?'

'Oh, him.' Lucy cringed. 'Oh, God. Nigel. I'd completely forgotten about him. Oh no.'

Owen gazed at her with amusement. 'And what about Henry? The original Hooray?'

'No. I do not remember Henry. Absolutely not. No matter what you say, I refuse to remember Henry.'

Owen was enjoying himself. 'I saw Henry's mother at the Blakes' the other day. He's doing very well for himself. Chief Exec of the bank. Now there's a boy who's doing well for himself. The City's the place to be now, they tell me.'

She managed, with difficulty, not to haul Phil's

name into the conversation at this point. Owen would be on to it like a rat down a drain.

'And who was that chap with a straggly beard and holes in his jeans? He used to come round here after you.'

All those boys seemed so young and innocent and far away. They'd had the occasional snog and a certain amount of hand-to-hand combat under their clothes, but nothing more. Today, presumably girls knew, from reading magazines, the Ten Best Ways to Give A Blow Job and How To Suss Out His Sexpertise.

'OK, OK, point made. Whatever it was. Now you can stop tormenting me.' It was good to hear him joking again, though. He'd had a keen sense of humour when Sarah had been alive. She'd remembered coming back to the quiet, dark house after her death, and listening for the sound of laughter. It had always been so much a part of her childhood. She'd tried to fill the gap with her own jokes, but they'd often fallen into the silence, leaving her smiling alone.

'And how's my little Tommy?' Owen's voice carried the inflections of real love. She remembered how, eighteen years ago, the birth of Nico seemed to have restored his faith in life to him, and when Tom came along, he'd been as thrilled as Ned had been.

'He's had a Drugs Awareness talk at school, and was sent back with a wordsearch puzzle, devised, as far as I could see, by the police, based on all the different stimulants you can get.'

Owen's face wrinkled in puzzlement. Lucy had

been quite surprised herself to find Tom, tongue just sticking out of the corner of his mouth in concentration, carefully filling in the words 'speed' and 'ecstasy' in blue and red crayons.

'What's correction fluid?' he'd asked her.

'It's that white stuff you use to correct typing mistakes,' she'd said, wondering why he'd asked. 'Not much used these days.'

'Except for people sniffing it,' Nico had added, taking a packet of biscuits out of the cupboard and feeding them into his mouth at astonishing speed.

'Poppers,' Tom had muttered. 'C-R-A-C-K. W-O-O-D-G-L-U-E.' The tiny tip of pink tongue transferred itself to the other side of his mouth, as he selected a luminous green felt tip.

'Woodglue?' Nico had looked interested. 'I didn't know you could get high on that.' He'd leant over Tom's shoulder, so they could spell out the words together. 'There are good tips in here.'

Lucy had felt uneasy at the sight of her fresh-faced little boy spelling out the words 'heroin' and 'syringe', and filling them in with his primary-school crayons. 'What's this supposed to achieve?'

'It means . . .' Nico had paused to get the last three biscuits down at once, 'that when you leave a message for your dealer, you'll be able to spell the words correctly. The sign of a good education'.

She told Owen this story. 'What do you think? Are they over-informed about everything now? What good can an exercise like that do? Except give them the idea that solvents and heroin are about as harmful as coffee, tea and cola, which were also on the list.'

He thought about it. 'When you were that age, everyone was terrified that we were breeding a nation of addicts. So I think as many of them will survive as you lot did. In thirty years' time, they'll be worrying about school fees and bad backs, just like you and your friends.'

'I suppose you're right.' It was very comforting to have the perspective of the years. The twice-weekly visits to Owen's little cottage had become a part of the warp and weft of her life. Moving along with Owen in his tortoise-like time frame was teaching her to slow down and appreciate things like the sherbert-pink pom-pom roses tumbling down in great prickly sprays over his weathered garden wall. Grace had been right – this July was particularly beautiful. She sighed with satisfaction.

'Now, you're sure you're going to be all right when we're away? People are looking after you?'

'People are looking after me very well.' He patted her arm. 'Enjoy your holiday. Come back looking less tired.' It was funny, she thought, how someone who couldn't make out large things like road signs could still see the shadows under her eyes.

She didn't want to get up from the deckchair, so she let him make the salad for supper. It was comforting, too, to be looked after again.

'Yum, Dad, no one makes a salad like you do. It must be the mustard.'

'You can't beat a home-grown lettuce, that's what it is.'

Small, meaningless exchanges, but they soothed the edges of her fraying soul. Their conversation rambled over the past, bits and pieces of gossip from the village and Owen's advice on growing a jasmine-and-honeysuckle hedge.

'God, is that the time? I'd no idea it was so late.'

'It's still close to the longest day,' said Owen. 'My favourite time of the year.'

'Ah, well.' Lucy spoke with real regret. 'Back to my busy-busy life.'

'How's Ned?' Owen knew exactly what he was asking.

'Fine.' She hesitated. No point in upsetting Owen. Not when he was feeling a bit better. Elderly cancer patients could literally worry themselves into a relapse, she knew.

He nodded. 'I'm glad you've got someone like him.'

He came down the path with her, instead of waving from the front door.

'Thank you.' He looked straight ahead, but put a hand on her shoulder. 'Thank you for coming.'

She felt tears sting her eyes as she kissed his cheek. It felt like tissue paper, dry and fragile, and his bones under her hand were as frail and brittle as porcelain, but he was standing up straighter than she'd seen for months.

He took a lock of her wiry dark hair and gently pushed it behind her ear, stroking it back as it sprang out again. 'Have a good holiday. Look after yourself.' His voice trembled.

She had the feeling that he didn't want to let her go. As if pushing through an invisible barrier, she hugged him.

'Be off with you, now.' He pushed her away. 'I love you so very much, you know.' He spoke in an undertone. He hadn't said that since she was about ten. Tom's age.

Things do get better, she told herself, as she drove through the falling dusk, the headlights of the car picking out the poppies blooming in the banked-up hedges. Six months ago, this road was a duty. Now it's a pleasure.

Her sense of well-being lasted until the following morning, when she bumped into Fiona, shopping in Bramsea.

She looked embarrassed, as if she was going to pretend not to have seen her. Lucy decided to corner her. If she was getting pally with Grace, she might know something. The thought was irresistible.

'Hi. How are things?'

Fiona fidgeted with the shopping. 'Oh, well, OK. I suppose.' She paused. 'Actually, Rupert's getting married again.'

'Oh, no! But you didn't want to . . . ?' She put a hand on Fiona's shoulder.

'Absolutely not. But it's still upsetting. She's pregnant. I mind for the children, really. He keeps saying how much he's looking forward to being a father, and Chloe said, "But, Daddy, you are a father already." And he just said, "Oh yes, but this is different.""

'How awful.' Lucy was saddened. 'Oh, poor Chloe. And the others.'

'All set for your holiday with Grace and Richard?'

'Sort of.' Lucy knew it was unfair, but couldn't resist taking a risk. 'Has Grace talked about her affair at all?' Her heart went stone cold, frozen to the spot, while she waited for Fiona's reply.

Fiona flushed, and transferred the shopping bags from one hand to the other again. 'What do you mean?'

Lucy was ready to back off. 'Well, you know Grace. She's always talking about . . .'

'Oh, that. I'm really sorry, Lucy. I don't think I should be discussing it, especially not with you. Even if you do know. Look –' she put one bag of shopping down to touch Lucy's arm '– do bite my head off if I'm talking out of turn, but it obviously isn't serious, and it certainly won't go anywhere, so if you can bear to turn a blind eye, I think you'll find that it all blows over. I know it's easier said than done . . .'

Was Lucy the only person in the world to take fidelity seriously? Why on earth hadn't she had a fling with Phil? Apparently, it would have 'blown over'.

'I'm sorry,' said Fiona again. 'It's not my business. It was wrong of me to have said anything.'

'No, no.' Lucy tried to pretend that she, too, thought

affairs were minor irritations. 'I just wondered if it was public knowledge.'

'Oh.' Fiona looked relieved. 'Not public knowledge, I don't think. In fact, I'm sure not.'

'Oh, well that's something.' In the back of her head, Lucy registered that Grace and Fiona had, indeed, therefore got very close, and was surprised to notice that this was another painful blow. She wanted to cry. 'What about you?' she asked, trying to sound bright and breezy, and completely natural. 'Anyone around?'

Fiona shook her head. 'They're not exactly crawling out of the woodwork. It's not like being twenty-five. But there's someone in the background, although we're taking it very slowly. I don't want the girls to worry.'

'Much the best,' agreed Lucy, without realizing what she was saying. She was glad the holiday was so close. It was like a painful operation looming up – it was partly the waiting that was the strain. Once they were all together for two weeks, everything was bound to become clear.

26

Time compressed into a series of lists. Passports. Tickets. Insurance. Insurance? Ned punctuated these lists with suggestions of better ways of doing things, or queries as to whether she was doing it all properly.

'Haven't we already got insurance? Aren't we covered under some other policy?'

'What policy?' She hadn't got time to find out.

'We don't want two lots of insurance. It's a waste of money.'

'Oh, well. Sort it out yourself.'

'I'm operating up until eight in the evening the day before we go.'

'You're always operating.'

'Yes. I'm a surgeon.' This was usually as far as the exchange got before one or the other of them had to leave the room to do something else practical. Doors occasionally slammed, but it could have been the wind.

Tom's idea of packing was a Gameboy, a teddy bear, various board games, one pair of pants and a T-shirt.

'It's for two whole weeks, Tom. Seven pairs of pants, two pairs of shorts . . .' She listed everything on her fingers. 'Oh, and a *toothbrush*,' she screeched after his disappearing bottom as he scampered upstairs.

Nico was secretive but insisted on having one of the larger suitcases. For all the shampoos, deodorants, after-shave balms and other bottles he now considered essential, she presumed. He went shopping and came back with a considerable haul: black Gucci shirts, hooded tops and Diesel jeans with legs so wide that he could have concealed anything from a bag of ferrets to a group of friends inside each of them. At least he ironed them himself – so vigorously that they could practically stand up on their own, and he wore them so low slung on his hips that she was convinced they would descend to his ankles any moment. Under the fabric she caught a glimpse of 'trainers' that looked as if they belonged on a moon landing.

Lucy peered at them. 'What *are* they, exactly?' They seemed to have orange springs.

Nico muttered some inaudible brand name.

'Did they cost a lot?'

Nico shook his head as he took the kitchen scissors to two new T-shirts, slashing them in several places to achieve the right ripped look. 'I saved up my pub money,' he explained. There was always work for locals in the summer, fulfilling the extra demand in pubs and restaurants, or as lifeguards on the beach, or marshalling tourists in a myriad of other profitable ways. With the start of the season in July, Nico had got a couple of part-time jobs, which he'd return to after the stay in France. In fact, Lucy had been surprised that he'd still wanted to come, and had fully expected him to opt to stay in Bramsea, earning money for his gap year.

'Have you highlighted your hair?' He looked suspiciously sun-kissed.

Nico narrowed his eyes, judging the placing of the rip exactly. 'What? Oh. I don't know what you're talking about.'

The fact that he'd spoken in more than one syllable spoke of a guilty conscience. Oh, well. She highlighted her own hair – why shouldn't he? She just couldn't imagine Ned having done the same at his age. Thank God Owen wasn't here, harrumphing about 'pansies' and 'shirt-lifters'. The shock of having a grandson who dyed his hair would probably kill him.

Sunglasses. Sunglasses? Eek. Nico had firm ideas on which astronomically expensive designer pair he 'needed'. Last year's were not good enough. Tom had lost his. He would lose the next pair. Was it even worth buying him any?

The frenzied calls between her and Grace – Does the house have towels? Do we need to bring bedlinen? – restored some sense of normality to their relationship, but only while they were actually speaking. Otherwise, she felt like someone who had had tests for some killer disease, and was waiting for the results. There's no evidence, she'd tell herself. Nothing that can't be explained away easily. Nine out of ten lumps are benign. Nine out of ten pointers to adultery are red herrings. Be sensible. Be sane. Be calm.

And, for a few minutes, the pain in her heart would ease, and it would seem as if the sun had come out. Everything would be all right. When she knew, when she finally and incontrovertibly knew that these symptoms – even Fiona's extraordinary conversation – were phantoms, she would forget about this week completely. She'd occasionally be able to look back on it with a smile, and admit that she'd been a complete idiot about it all.

And then she'd remember that someone had to have the malignant tumour. Someone had to have the unfaithful husband or the betraying friend. Why not her? She might be the one out of ten. There was every indication that she was. Except that Ned, as far as she could see, was where he'd said he'd be for most of the time, although the accelerated pre-holiday pace of life meant that they rarely exchanged more than two sentences at a time. Almost everything he did, or didn't do, irritated her. How come he could simply swan in and pack a case while she whirled like a multi-armed dervish through three lots of packing?

'Cool it, Mum,' said Nico, passing the telephone as she put it down with a sigh. 'What does it matter if we don't have enough towels?'

'You won't be saying that if you've got sand up the crack of your bum and the only towels available are encrusted with it,' she replied, crossly.

'There isn't a beach where we're going.'

Aha. So he did take in information after all. She'd

sometimes wondered if she was living with a zombie from another planet. 'Take this upstairs, clever Dick. You've got room in your suitcase.'

'I have *not*.'

'Mum?' Tom appeared. 'I don't really want to go on this holiday.'

Lucy was exasperated. 'Why not? Luke's your best friend.'

'He's not. Max Stirling is my *best* friend.'

'Well, anyway, you like Luke.'

'I don't.' Tom stuck his bottom lip out. 'And I don't like his dad.'

Lucy froze. 'Why not?' She kept her voice light.

'He shouts.'

'Well, we all shout.' She shuddered to think what other children (Max Stirling, for example) might say about her household. 'When we're in a hurry. Is it just the shouting?' She studied Tom's face.

Tom shrugged, and wandered off, appearing to forget all about it.

That seemed OK. Back to the lists. Fake tan. The idea of her stocky marshmallow-white legs next to Grace's long, slender, honey-gold ones was alarming. But when did she have a couple of hours to stagger stark-naked round the bedroom with her arms and legs flapping out to the sides while the beastly gunge dried in orangey-yellow streaks?

Shampoos. Suntan lotion. Basic medicines.

'They do have chemists in France,' said Nico con-descendingly. 'I mean, if you don't remember the aspirins, you can just go out and buy some. I think they have soap as well.'

She glared at him. 'Just because you've been on a school trip to Boulogne, it doesn't mean you know everything.'

He grinned. He knew he was right.

The patients were also in a holiday mood, and queried her about inoculations and diarrhoea remedies. 'No, you don't need malaria protection for the Scilly Isles,' she heard herself snapping at one patient. 'No, it's not the water,' she explained in a ratty tone to another, 'but everywhere has its own bugs, and you're completely adjusted to the ones in Bramsea. When you go abroad, there are germs under the fingernails of people who prepare food, and they're different ones from the ones you're accustomed to . . .' The patient went pale green, and would obviously have preferred to have gone on thinking that no plumber south of Dover could manage an uncontaminated water supply.

Oh, why did going on holiday turn you into such a horrible person?

'Don't forget to cancel the milk and the papers. And get someone to feed the hamsters and guinea pigs,' said Ned, adjusting his tie two mornings before they left.

'Couldn't you do it?' She was harassed.

'I'm operating in an hour. I'm late as it is.'

'I don't mean now. I mean sometime. Why is it all down to me?'

'Because,' Ned gathered his last few things, 'you work part-time so that you can do that side of things. We discussed it. If it's not working, and it's too much for you, then let's get an au pair when we get back.'

He was half out of the door.

'An au pair couldn't do any of those things. And an au pair couldn't talk to Lawrence's parents about whether he's allowed alcohol, or if they impose a curfew, or should they be allowed on jet skis, and all that stuff. It's not just a question of packing, especially when you're taking someone else's child on holiday. Things have to be thought through. Anyway, that's not the point.'

'Well, what is the point?' He asked it quite kindly.

'The point is . . .' She struggled to articulate it. 'I wish we could do things together sometimes. As a team.'

'Well, we will be doing things together for two weeks soon.' He sounded bemused. 'And there's a limit to how much teamwork you need to cancel newspapers.'

'I suppose so.'

'By the way –' his head popped back in '– if there are any emergencies tomorrow, I might not get back till very late.'

'Do you have to operate on the last day before we go? Can't you be doing clinics or paperwork, or something more predictable?'

He looked at his watch, getting irritated. 'Well, I *could*, but it makes more sense to do it this way.'

The door closed behind him. 'More sense to you, perhaps.' She addressed the latch. 'But what about me?'

And what about the poor little babies with heart defects, her conscience reminded her.

Yes. Of course. She must be reasonable.

But she felt like making a scene about it. Throwing a tantrum. Asking him to choose between her and ill babies.

She could hardly believe her own thoughts. How mature was she being?

Trying to be mature, but simply feeling old, she continued the holiday preparations. The trouble was that there was no romance in their lives any more.

The mature side of her pointed out that there would be nothing romantic in Ned cancelling the milk instead of her.

The small, cross child screaming for attention inside her countered that she'd like to feel, just once, that her happiness was more important to him than anything else in the world, even sick children.

Oh, be practical. Get real. Get on with it.

If only she could talk to Grace about it all.

That was the most suspicious thing. Ever since she'd met Grace, they'd seen or spoken to each other almost every day. Suddenly their only communication was about practicalities on the telephone.

'I can't wait to see you all,' Grace would say, without suggesting anything sooner. 'It'll be such fun.'

Even the weather seemed uncertain of itself. Wind

whipped through the sunshine, sending litter scudding along the pavements. Lucy watched a supermarket carrier bag take flight like a bird, soaring up to the height of the church spire, then swooping, diving and curling in the eddies, before slowly sinking down to earth where it became just another piece of litter.

I know how that carrier bag feels, she thought. To believe that you can fly, just for a few precious moments, before you're cast back down to earth where you belong and realize it's all been an illusion.

That's why she wanted an affair with Phil. To fly again. To be excited. To soar gloriously over all this trivia and feel intensely alive again.

But the washing machine revolved, and the patients lined up in the surgery and the alarm clock wrenched her back out of sleep five minutes too early day after day.

27

By the time they left, Lucy was exhausted, like a tightly coiled spring on the point of unravelling completely. Their flight, although apparently smooth and punctual, seemed fraught with peril to her from the moment they left. As she double-locked the front door, she wondered if she would ever come back. It seemed oddly unlikely, while simultaneously being drearily inevitable.

The first hurdle was fitting nearly six foot of Lawrence, plus his backpack, into an already crammed car. He folded up his long body to occupy the least possible space, and it was clear from his entire demeanour that all he asked of the holiday was to be as inconspicuous as possible, and to be allowed to get on with mooching around with Nico with the minimum of adult interference. 'Don't worry about me' emanated almost visibly from the back seat. Lucy relaxed for a second.

The airport was a nightmare of endless corridors – no sooner had you rounded one corner than another apparently identical one stretched out ahead, and then another, as if they were all trapped in an eternal reflecting mirror. Gates 39–54 seemed as far apart as her house and Grace's were, and they were followed by Gates 55–61, and then 62–72 and onwards to eternity. Weighed down by books, hand luggage and coats, they trudged painfully on.

Once on board, settled in their seats, the Head Steward took obvious delight in pointing out extra things to worry about, as if the mere fact of defying gravity in an outsized metal pencil box wasn't already enough.

Her fingers tightened round her book as the voice informed them, with relish, that there was an extra, unaccounted-for, potentially lethal suitcase on board. 'We'll have to unload all the luggage and find it,' he said. 'We are responsible for your safety.'

Lucy swallowed at the thought of a suitcase with a bomb in it ticking away unclaimed beneath her seat.

'And if we can't find the suitcase in time,' the steward added, 'we may miss our slot. And then we'll be in the hands of Air Traffic Control before we can find another.'

His tone implied that the mercy of Air Traffic Control was only a marginal improvement on that of armed terrorists. Would they be left sitting in their seats, getting thromboses, for four hours before taking off? Lucy began rotating her ankles one by one, in the hope of staving this off.

Once in the air – after a surprisingly short delay, considering the fuss – they were asked to identify their nearest emergency exit. The two stewards pointed theatrically ahead and behind them, like matadors in a synchronized display. Lucy craned her neck but couldn't spot either the fore or the aft exit. Could she put her hand up and ask? And if she did know where it was, what then? In how many crashes has an emergency exit been of the slightest use?

They should never have agreed to this holiday. It was madness.

As the plane taxied efficiently down to Nice airport, she relaxed, determined not to worry any more. The holiday stretched out, in endless sunny days ahead, to be enjoyed.

Provided their luggage hadn't gone astray.

Although the empty carousel revolved endlessly, the luggage did finally arrive, in its entirety, and Grace, already looking brown and relaxed, was waiting for them on the other side. She kissed them all, even Tom and Nico, neither of whom actually flinched. It seemed they had acquired French manners already.

'Good flight?'

'Perfect.' Ned kissed her in turn. 'Absolutely no hitches.'

Lucy was too exhausted to say anything. The heat baked up from the buildings around, and her skirt stuck to her legs in an unflattering way.

Richard welcomed them all like the perfect host when they arrived.

'Wonderful to see you. Marvellous. Good flight? Good, good. Grace'll show you to your rooms. Join me at the pool when you've unpacked.' Beyond the double doors of a huge, cool dark room was a swimming pool, its ice-blue water sparkling in the sun-light.

Grace showed them to an airy white-washed room, with old open beams. Through a large window with big wooden shutters, Lucy could see fields of sunflowers stretching across the valleys outside. The room had a large comfortable bed, a big armoire and a single chair. As Lucy changed she could feel the broad, unpolished roughness of the stripped oak floor beneath her toes, like porridge. At last, after the cramped plane, the crowded roads in Britain, and the narrow, cobbled lanes of Bramsea, she felt her lungs open and spread into the space.

'I'm going shopping.' Grace hovered at the door. 'Just into the local village.'

Ned offered to lend a hand and Lucy tensed. Their first assignation?

But no.

'Nico and Lawrence have offered to come with me.' Grace giggled. 'They want to check out the action. I haven't the heart to say straight out that there isn't any. By the way, Lawrence appears to have brought two hundred cigarettes with him – do his parents let him smoke?'

Lucy had forgotten to ask them about smoking. The three of them exchanged looks of consternation. 'What if we forbid it, but don't police it very vigor-ously?' suggested Ned.

'Oh God, we should have brought someone else. I really don't want Nico to smoke,' said Lucy.

'He doesn't,' said Grace, adding, 'at least that's what he said when I saw Lawrence's fags.'

She closed the door behind her, saying, 'Luke and Tom are down at the pool with Richard, so you don't have to worry about anything.'

Ned and Lucy were left alone. They looked at each other like strangers, the vastness of the bed stretching between them.

'Better unpack,' mumbled Lucy, embarrassed.

Ned stretched himself out on the bed with a sigh, and Lucy arranged herself tensely beside him. After a few minutes of silence, she rolled into his arms for a cuddle.

He kissed the top of her head absent-mindedly before gently disentangling himself. 'It's a bit hot.'

He had never, ever before withdrawn his affection.

Lucy went to the window and stood there, wondering if she should try again, watching the shadow of an aeroplane, like a huge bird of prey, briefly blot out the sun overhead and sweep across the fields like a dark hand.

28

Lucy told herself, firmly, not to let one small gesture ruin her holiday mood, and went down to help Grace with lunch. In the kitchen, a cool, high-ceilinged room with an old-fashioned painted dresser, ancient blue-and-white tiles and a huge stone sink, Nico and Lawrence were carrying shopping in from the car. Nico even took things out of carrier bags and put them away. He looked much older, and very cool, with a smooth, bare, muscular chest, a pair of cut-off shorts and the leather thong around his neck. Lucy couldn't have been more surprised if she'd found him tight-rope walking or doing embroidery.

'Thanks.' Grace fluttered her eyelashes at the boys, as they strode out of the room with an easy masculine lope.

'Show me what goes where,' Lucy picked up a bottle of olive oil and a lettuce, 'and let me make a salad dressing or something.'

Lunch was outside, under the dappled shade of a pergola covered in vines, at a big rough-hewn table spread with colourful pottery and hunks of fresh country bread. Even bread and cheese tasted so much better outside, in France, on holiday. Patchwork fields of sunflowers and corn spread out around them, curving upwards to the horizon where a dotted line of houses and a church spire shimmered in a heat haze. A bird, so high that it was just a speck in the vivid blue, wheeled and swooped above.

Richard told them all, at perhaps slightly too much length, about the history of the house, the village and the surrounding area, and advised them on the chateaux and museums they 'simply had to see'. 'There's a Prune Museum, and a Sunflower Museum, and one dedicated to the art of bee-keeping,' he explained.

'I'm not much of a museums and chateaux person, myself.' Ned helped himself to a glossy salad of plump tomatoes, fragrant with basil, and tore off another chunk of crusty bread. 'I'm too knackered, to be honest. I don't plan on any trip longer than the one from the side of the pool to the table.' He obviously thought that sounded rude, and amended it. 'Although, of course, just let me know what you need done in the way of shopping or anything, and I'm your man.'

'Oh, you can't come all the way down here and not see anything. I simply won't allow it.' Richard was smiling, but Lucy had the nasty feeling that he wasn't joking.

Ned just laughed.

'I can't tell you how pleased I am to see you all here,' added Richard, and Lucy relaxed.

'When's Phil arriving?' Lucy darted a quick look at

Ned to see if there was any reaction, but Ned seemed oblivious.

'Not until the day after tomorrow.' Grace's eyes flickered round the table, checking that everyone had everything. 'Luke, darling, eat up.'

Luke stabbed his food viciously with a fork and ground it into his plate without eating any of it.

'No, really.' Richard placed a heavy hand on Lucy's knee, and squeezed it. 'I mean it. It'll be great to have someone else to talk to on my level. Two weeks of Grace's undiluted conversation . . .' He chortled. 'Well, I don't need to tell *you* . . .'

Lucy jumped up. 'I'm just going to get some water.'

Richard frowned. 'Grace! You're not looking after our guests. Why isn't there any water on the table?'

Grace didn't react. 'There's water at this end, Lucy. Or would you prefer sparkling? Luke, darling, you haven't eaten a thing. Shall I get you some yoghurt? Or I could make you some fruit salad.'

Luke got up and left the table without answering. 'Luke! Darling!' Grace wailed.

'He's spoilt,' growled Richard. 'Leave him. That's why he won't eat up his lunch like Tom does. Your mother doesn't spoil you, does she, Tom?'

Tom went scarlet. He hated being the focus of any kind of argument. 'Er . . .'

Why did Grace put up with all this? And why hadn't they noticed any of this at home? Luke had sometimes been a little difficult, but the boys had spent most of the time on the computer in another room, and Lucy had overlooked the occasional tantrum. And was Richard drunk? Lucy sat down again, inching her chair away from him surreptitiously.

At the end of the meal, Richard took a glass of wine, a pot of coffee and a pile of cups outside to the pool again while they all cleared away and washed up. Grace began making something else, peeling and chopping and marinading for dinner, she explained.

'Let me help.' Surely Grace wanted to talk? Had Richard and Grace been arguing? Or was this what they were normally like at home? Lucy tried to remember. He had occasionally said things that hadn't sounded quite right, but so intermittently that Lucy had always found an excuse for them. Perhaps the combination of sun and red wine was not a great influence on him.

'No, honestly, you've just arrived. You haven't even had time for a swim yet. Really. I've been here for ages, so I'm beginning to get bored. Go on, both of you. Richard needs company.' And Grace waved them out of the kitchen. 'He's a bit tired – he's been working so hard before he went away. So do excuse him if he seems a little . . . snappish.' There was a pleading note in her voice.

Snappish wasn't the word Lucy'd been thinking of. And she and Ned had been working very hard too before they got away. Particularly Ned.

Richard was reading an important biography, or, rather, propping it on his chest while he dozed. Lucy eyed him covertly, still wondering how such an insignificant-looking man had managed to capture a butterfly like Grace. He'd begun to go brown, but he was still outstandingly ordinary. A currant bun of a face rescued by a straight, thickish nose. Sandy hair, thinning a bit at the top. Bit of a pot, but not too much. Reasonable legs, if a touch on the spindly side, but then, what do you expect at our age, she thought. He was Mr Unremarkable. He could have been a major criminal, and he'd never have been identified in a line-up. He was the kind of man you pass on the street or talk to at a party without giving him a second thought.

But his personality, even asleep, cast a shadow over the glittering blue water of the pool.

Lucy decided to let the heat of the sun bake her bones into tranquillity. The sound of the cicadas and the low rustle of the breeze through the trees lulled her into a doze.

The boys, Luke and Tom, exploded into the water, showering the sleeping adults with an icy spray.

'Boys!' roared Richard.

Ned jerked up and looked around, bewildered.

Richard shouted at the boys. 'Bugger off!'

'It is their holiday,' suggested Lucy. 'They need to let off steam.'

Richard frowned but didn't answer. He got up, shook the water off the book and went inside.

Oh, dear. Now she'd made him angry. Lucy resolved to take no notice, but it was difficult to relax after that. Nico joined the others, diving gracefully in, and swimming rhythmically, like an otter, to the other end before Luke and Tom both attacked him simultaneously with water guns. They were joined by Lawrence. Lucy went back to her book. They could safely be left to frolic.

An hour or so later, Tom, shivering in spite of the heat, said he was cold. Luke was still in the water, floating on an inflatable armchair.

Lucy was surprised. 'It's baking hot.' She picked up a towel and began to dry him. He was shaking. 'I hope you're not getting sunstroke. How did you get so cold?'

'Mummy.' He sounded small and frightened.

She towelled his head vigorously. 'Yes?'

'Don't tell anyone. Promise?'

'I promise.'

'You really, really promise? Because I know what grown-ups are like.'

Lucy began to worry. 'I promise.'

'Luke held my head under the water. Until I couldn't breathe. Things began to go a bit black.'

'When? Just now?' Lucy couldn't believe that this could have happened under her nose. 'Where were Nico and Lawrence?'

'They went to play tennis. With Grace.'

'Did you do anything to Luke?'

Tom shook his head. 'I really didn't. We were just playing.'

Lucy opened her mouth to talk to Luke, but Tom nudged her. 'You're not to say anything.'

Tom must have been quite frightened to break the boys' prep-school code of *omertà*. She'd have to think of another way of tackling the problem.

'Luke's very rough sometimes,' whispered Tom. 'I don't like it.'

And Tom was no shrinking violet. If she could get Grace on her own, Lucy would have to say something, although Grace doted on Luke to such an extent that it would be an awkward conversation, to say the least. It was probably just horseplay that had got out of hand. She looked across the pool at Ned. Perhaps he'd have a solution. In the meantime, though, the boys would have to be watched more closely when they were in the pool. What a nuisance. Not having to watch them like hawks was part of the pleasure of their growing up.

Grace appeared from the tennis court and settled down on the lounger beside Lucy.

'Isn't this absolute heaven? I can't tell you how lovely it is to have you all here. Luke and Richard are just thrilled too.' She opened her magazine. 'And Luke and Tom are getting on so well.'

Lucy smiled uncertainly. Grace seemed so sincere that she couldn't bear to shatter her illusions. 'It's lovely to be here.'

29

There's a special quality to time on holiday. Lucy lay in bed on the first morning, and felt rich in the hours and days ahead. At this stage, she knew that they would be endless and that she would never have to return to the surgery. Lazily, she watched the sky turn slowly from pale forget-me-not blue to deepest cornflower. A few feathery clouds scudded past the open window, and she could hear the pock-pock-pock of early morning tennis players. A distant tractor worked its way across the fields, droning like a faraway insect. There was so much space here, compared to Bramsea's quaint little houses and picturesque cobbled streets. She stretched.

Ned had got up early. She put a hand out and felt the indentation in the bed. It wasn't even warm. She heard a cry outside, too indistinct to identify as 'well done' or 'out', but definitely Grace's, from the tennis court.

So Grace and Ned were playing tennis.

Lying in bed, with only the merest suggestion of a hangover (Why could you always drink so much more on holiday?), Lucy prayed that whatever had got into Richard was temporary. Everybody had their off days.

You should be understanding. Not judgemental. She was sure he'd back to his usual genial self once he'd relaxed.

Feeling happier about this, she got dressed and went downstairs. Grace was in the kitchen, making a shopping list.

'I thought you were playing tennis.'

'I was. Nico and Ned are out there now.'

'Need any help shopping?'

Grace smiled, and for one moment, Lucy saw the old warmth. Her heart leapt in response, but it also confirmed that she was right to think that something between them had changed at a very fundamental level. 'I don't need any,' said Grace. 'But if you'd like to see the shops, I'd love to have you along.'

They got into a small hot car and set out across the bumpy track.

Grace smiled as she drove, happiness fitting her neatly like a glove.

Could Lucy ask Grace directly? Did she really want everything brought to a head so early in the holiday? What would happen for the rest of the two weeks? She looked out of the window at the tiny stone village they were driving through. The cottages lining the road were shuttered and silent, with cracks and crumbling plasterwork, their blistered, peeling paint making her feel that history was just there, a few feet away, almost within her touch. The sun baked down on a war memorial.

'Can we stop?' Lucy found it hard to keep her voice steady.

'Of course.' Grace looked at her, worried.

'I wanted to see the war memorial and the church.' It was a way of buying time, of giving herself the chance to 'pull herself together'. She mustn't do anything stupid, or in a hurry.

She read the names of those killed in the 1914–18 war, engraved on the side of the stone obelisk. There were twenty-two of them. Twenty-two. From just a few streets of houses that made up this village and perhaps a couple of farms nearby. It must have been, literally, almost every young man of that generation. In one tiny village they had lost almost as many as had gone from the whole of Bramsea.

The same surname was repeated twice, then another three times, and another four. Brothers and cousins. She thought of Nico. They'd have been his age. It would have been as if Nico and Lawrence, and all their friends had been killed over a period of four years. The thought was impossible to comprehend.

An old woman in black trudged slowly into sight. With her bent body, and lined leathery face, she could have been in her eighties or nineties, but even she could probably hardly remember the faces of the Pierres, the Sebastiens and the Jean-Lucs that had marched off to war. She could probably remember the grief, though, of her mother, her aunts and her elder sisters.

Get it into proportion, Lucy told herself. If Grace

is having a fling with Ned, it's not going to be the end of life as you know it. You can survive it. She read the names one more time, and wished that she knew how to say a prayer for them. And for her and Ned, and for Owen, and for Nico and Tom, that they should grow up in a world where young men didn't have to die. She would talk to Owen when she got back, she decided.

Grace saw her serious face when she got back into the car. 'It's terrible, isn't it? I can't imagine what it must have been like. You get the feeling that these villages have been silent since then. That it's been nearly a hundred years since anyone heard the shouts of children playing in the road.'

'That's probably because they're all inside watching the television or playing on their Playstations,' joked Lucy.

Grace peered nervously at the crossroads. 'I think there's somewhere to park just outside the bakery.' She had to go forwards and back several times to get into the parking space. 'Fuck. Not used to any of this driving.'

She peered at the window, grinding the gears. 'Look, what beautiful apple tarts! Shall we buy one for tonight? The French do these things so much better than we do.'

However, Richard insisted on finding the 'best' restaurant in a nearby town, dragging them in and out of two others before finding one where the food, the wine and the table available met up to his requirements. He pontificated about wine to Lucy, Nico and Lawrence. 'You'll remember this, boys,' he said. 'It's part of your education.'

Nico smiled politely, but Lucy knew he preferred beer. It was at times like this that Richard, who was only about a decade older than the rest of them, seemed like a generation or two away. 'Wine's good for your health,' he told the boys. 'Better than lager.'

'Well, I suppose I must be proof of that.' Lucy was desperately trying to keep the conversation going. 'I drink masses of wine and never get ill.'

Richard looked at her. 'That's because you've got some meat on your bones.' He pinched her arm, rubbing her flesh painfully between his fingers.

Fat. Richard was calling her fat. Mortified, she flushed, suddenly feeling hideously unattractive.

At one point he focused on Grace and Ned, talking in low tones at the other end of the table, Grace tipping her head flirtatiously towards him.

'My wife's flirting with you, Ned.' He thumped his glass down just slightly too hard and a little slopped over the edges. 'She does this. She thinks it makes her seem more interesting than she really is.'

There was a brittle silence around the table, as a terrible British politeness gripped them all.

Grace smiled. 'Richard's very funny, aren't you, darling? It's a special kind of humour.' She added a low throaty laugh. 'You get used to it.'

The Dickinson family relaxed fractionally, and concentrated on filleting their fresh sardines.

'I wasn't joking,' Richard hissed to Lucy, squeezing her knee again. This new touchy-feely side to his nature appeared to be asexual, but it still made Lucy uneasy.

The two smaller boys bent their heads over mobile phones they'd borrowed from Grace and Lucy, sitting at the opposite ends of the table, texting each other. It wasn't exactly perfect manners, thought Lucy, tensing herself for a rebuke from Richard, but they had to do something in the endless waits between courses that important French restaurants imposed on their guests. She should have brought a book or some drawing paper.

Richard didn't object, however. It seemed that texting was an ideal way of keeping children seen but not heard.

Nico and Lawrence sprawled next to them, occasionally exchanging gnomic remarks in an undertone. Lucy was beginning to realize that two teenage boys together were significantly more self-effacing than one, and that all they required was to be allowed to play their music until three in the morning, sleep in and then loaf around the cafés in town. It was quite restful, really.

The evening ended amiably enough, as Richard reverted to his usual distant, benevolent manner, smoking a cigar, but when he ordered liqueurs all round, Nico refused his, on the grounds of drink-driving. Richard told him not to be so mealy-mouthed, but Nico shrugged it off.

'They drink a lot, the young these days,' said Ned. 'Much more than we did. But they never drink and drive, do you, Nico?' He patted his son's shoulder with pride.

Nico grinned at his father and ignored Richard.

Lucy could see Tom looking worried.

'What's up?' She whispered into his ear, because he'd never say in front of everyone.

He shook his head, and wriggled himself very close to her in the car.

She put out a hand. 'Mobile back. Before you lose it.'

His hands stayed in his pockets.

'Come on, old chap,' Ned urged him when they arrived back at the farmhouse. 'Fun's over. Bed.'

Tom stared at the ground and slipped his hand into Lucy's, but still refused to give back the mobile.

She waited until they were alone in her room, and finally extracted the admission that the texting had got out of hand. 'Luke's messages are bad. Really bad. And I don't know how to erase them.'

She managed to persuade Tom to get into bed, and, feeling weary, took the mobile to Nico.

'It's about time I learned. Show me.'

Nico whistled when he called up the messages. 'Christ. Not surprised Tom didn't want his mum seeing those. Tell him I erased them without reading them, and definitely without showing them to you.' He tapped away. 'That Luke's got problems.'

'First lesson in texting, now, please.' Lucy craned her head over Nico's shoulders to see how bad the messages were, but everything had been deleted. 'I ought to know.' She resolved not to be cut out of the loop in future. It had been sheer laziness that had prevented her from learning text messaging. All her friends were doing it.

She couldn't wait for Phil's arrival. The holiday already seemed divided into warring factions. She wouldn't mind his advice on dealing with the Luke–Tom problem. It was no good talking to Grace – she seemed to be on a completely different planet from the rest of them.

30

The following night, Lucy buffed and polished every part of her from her toenails to the tip of her head. She washed, rinsed and conditioned her hair attentively, applied the eyeliner as precisely as a micro-surgeon, outlined her lips exactly as Grace had taught her and filled them in with the lipstick that flattered her most before spending half an hour trying on sugar-candy pink and lime green cottons until she found exactly the right combination. Drinks by the pool before supper, Grace had said, while we're waiting for Phil. Lucy, usually so punctual, was the last to join them.

'Wow!' Grace, as always, was generous with her compliments. 'You look fabulous. I love that pink. It really lights up your skin.'

Ned met Lucy's eye and something passed between them. She wasn't quite sure what it meant. 'Yeah.' He poured himself a beer. 'Not bad at all.'

Richard raised his glass to her. 'Cheers. You're looking very pretty this evening.'

'Thank you,' mumbled Lucy. She didn't want compliments from that creep. She was suddenly so repelled by the insights into his character that had been revealed over the past forty-eight hours that she literally found him repulsive. She could hardly meet his eye.

They waited. Grace made light conversation.

There was a howl from upstairs and Luke appeared, wailing. It was an odd sound from a ten-year-old boy, not the high-pitched wail of the toddler but a deep-throated sobbing shout. Grace paled and jumped up. 'What's happened?' There was real fear in her voice.

As Luke gulped out some story – not very serious, as far as Lucy could tell – about having slipped and banged his head, Lucy's eyes searched out Tom. Had he retaliated for the pool episode? But Tom, rolling his eyes discreetly and shrugging his shoulders, appeared blameless. She drew him to her.

'He's a wimp,' whispered Tom.

Lucy moved away with him so she could talk. 'This afternoon you said he was a bully. Come on, be fair. He can't be both.'

'Yes, he can!' Tom was indignant. 'I hate him. Nobody likes him at school.'

'Nonsense. You've always liked him before.'

'I haven't. You like Grace. That's different.'

Lucy felt too guilty to reply. Had she allowed her friendship with Grace to dominate their lives?

Grace fussed over a lump on the back of Luke's head. 'Do you think we should take him to hospital?'

'Don't be absurd,' said Richard, re-filling his glass. 'Stop that idiotic noise, Luke. It's obviously high time you went to boarding school. That would sort you out.'

Grace shot him an agonized look, and Luke redoubled his howls.

'Let me have a look,' suggested Ned. 'With a GP and a paediatrician on the premises, I'm sure a hospital visit won't be necessary.' He felt around carefully and asked Luke a few questions. Lucy watched his hands, gentle but firm, work their way over the boy's head and neck.

'That'll be fine.' Ned sounded satisfied. 'A bit of a lump, but you won't even feel it by the morning.'

'I told you so,' said Richard. 'A lot of fuss about nothing.'

Grace took the boys off to the kitchen to calm them down with ice creams and biscuits. Richard looked at her departing back with obvious disgust. 'I've told her. That boy needs some discipline. She's spoiling him. Crying at the age of ten. For God's sake.' He turned to Ned, without thanking him. 'A top-up?'

Ned declined, and Lucy could see the lines around his mouth tighten. He looked expressionless, but Lucy knew him well enough to know that he was angry. Because he loved Grace? Or because Richard was such a bastard and Ned was too kind to tolerate that kind of behaviour from any man for long? Richard didn't seem to care about anyone, not even his own son. Although, admittedly, she did think Luke was making a bit too much of a fuss. Most boys of ten wouldn't have cried so loudly. They still did everything they could not to seem sissy. It could be heart-breaking at times.

Nico appeared briefly. 'Cool, Mum.' He shovelled in a huge handful of peanuts almost absent-mindedly as he passed the bowl, then scooped up another.

'What?' she jumped, guilty.

He waved a hand to indicate her outline. 'If you weren't my mum, I'd fancy you. We're off for a drink down in the village. See ya in about an hour.'

'Yes, that looks very nice, Lucy,' said Lawrence, which was almost the longest sentence she'd ever heard from him. Were those boys growing up or did they want something from her? She instinctively looked at her handbag, expecting Nico to plead for a hand-out, but they leapt into the tiny car and roared down the dirt track.

There was an uncomfortable silence. Lucy hoped Nico and Lawrence were all right. Not bored. Mind you, it must be lovely to be able to jump into a car, leave them all behind and go drinking in a new town, without any ties. Lucy could feel her dancing feet beginning to twitch. Ned seemed withdrawn, but then so he might be. If you're having an affair with your wife's best friend, you might well run out of things to say to her husband. Quite a conversation killer. Richard made up for it, telling them all his theory on how the Conservatives could win the next election. Underneath it all, though, everyone's ear was cocked for a car, and occasionally each of them would look at the ribbon of road just visible on the horizon, and screw up their eyes to see if there was a cloud of dust scudding along.

*

Just as they were beginning to talk about flight delays and the possibility of Phil getting lost, there was a low roar and a Harley Davidson bounced up the track and drew to a halt. Phil, in black leathers, dismounted and took off his helmet. His eyes crinkled up in a smile.

'Hope I'm not late for anything. Hi, Richard. Excuse all the dust.' He held out a hand for Richard to shake.

Richard was temporarily silenced, and just gazed at him, mouth hanging slightly open.

Lucy concealed a smile. 'I take it that you didn't fly-drive.' She was amazed, that with every detail about Phil etched into her brain, she'd hadn't realized that he was bringing the bike down.

He kissed her, smelling of leather and Eau Sauvage and a man who'd been travelling hard all day, as, with a quick, intense flash of his eyes, he assessed her. She knew what he was asking. Are you OK?

'Hi. I've got friends near St Malo and some more in La Rochelle, so I've been having a bit of a beach holiday on the way. Got some sailing in.' He was lean and brown. She felt the finest of touches graze her arm as he connected briefly with her.

Her heart lifted. She could talk to Phil. She would talk to Phil.

'Sailing?' Ned's eyes lit up, and soon they were nose to nose, talking about 36-footers and 38-footers, distances travelled and the measurements and dimensions of sail. No matter what you say, size does matter to men, thought Lucy crossly, they have to put a number on absolutely everything. She was left with Richard's interminable broadcast on the Conservative party, which she tried to edge away from so that she could help Grace with the food. But Phil's arrival had turned two families into a party. The atmosphere eased.

31

It was some time before she managed to talk to Phil on her own. On holiday, there is always someone else around – either by the pool, or on the shady terrace as the sun went down in the evening. The kitchen was Grace's, and attracted Nico, Lawrence and the two younger boys, who tore off huge hunks of French bread, plastering them with butter and Nutella, or grabbed ripe, juicy peaches and wolfed them down in a few seconds. Ned, too, lingered in there, with a beer or a glass of wine. Lucy avoided the room, in an almost deliberate determination to leave the possible lovers together. It might burn itself out. She mustn't seem jealous. Pretend nothing is happening. Perhaps nothing is happening, or even if it is, pretence can dull the pain and minimize the damage. She thought she must be going mad. There was no sign of an affair between them on a day-to-day basis. It could still be someone in Bramsea, or, more likely, London, whom Grace hadn't told her about. If you looked at it another way, there were hundreds of clues, from Ned's increasingly morose silences to seeing him take the sun lounger next to Grace's at the swimming pool.

For most of the time, however, the swimming

pool was Richard's. He lay on a sun lounger from breakfast till lunch, and then again, after his lunchtime siesta, until evening drinks. He never participated in any of the household chores, such as cooking, sorting the two younger boys, or shopping, and, as usual, seemed at one step removed from everyone else.

While he poured drinks, read books and newspapers, and pontificated at anyone within earshot, Grace cooked, cleaned and shopped. She swept the kitchen floor. It was as if she was making up for Richard's complete idleness by doing twice as much as the rest of them. If anyone seized the broom from her, she'd start shelling or peeling something to get ahead for the next meal, or wiping the kitchen table. But she was as serene as ever, and never seemed resentful. From time to time, Lucy worried that Grace was using all this domesticity as a way of avoiding intimacy with her. She frequently told Lucy how much she was enjoying the holiday and how wonderful it was to have them all there together. In the face of such apparent blithe conviction that all was well, Lucy felt it would be rude, or cruel, to imply otherwise. Used to her glittering, glamorous friend with her smart car and full wardrobe, she'd never really seen the price she'd had to pay for it all when Richard was around. Everyone does things slightly differently, and what couples work out between themselves is no one else's business. That's what Lucy told herself. She and Grace had both complained about their husband's inability to use a washing machine or to find the butter in the fridge when it was exactly in front of their noses.

But a man who literally didn't lift a finger on holiday de-stabilized everybody, regardless of how much his wife did to compensate. Ned and Phil – along with Nico and Lawrence – washed up, wrestled with the bulging black rubbish bags and drove into town for more beers or the day's bread, as Richard appropriated for himself the role of king, and treated everyone else as his courtiers. When Grace got up to clear the plates one evening, Ned leant back in his chair.

'It must be Richard's turn to do the washing-up tonight.'

Richard laughed. 'I have my wife a bit better trained than you do.'

Ned and Phil both got up to help Grace, and Lucy deliberately stayed in her seat.

'Oh, don't worry,' said Grace, taking their plates from them. 'There's hardly anything to do, really.' She pushed them back down again.

'Of course,' Richard sat back in a satisfied way, 'I suppose it's different if your wife does a proper job.'

'Grace works. She runs her own business,' said Lucy.

Richard's smile twisted in scorn. 'Showing a few women how to wear frocks. My dear, please don't ask me to take it too seriously. I do do the books for her, after all.'

But what could they do about it? Politeness still paralysed them all, because they were Richard's guests, and Grace was Richard's wife, and nobody wanted to spoil anyone else's holiday, particularly Grace's, by being aggressive.

Everyone's too nice, thought Lucy. She sighed. But what was the alternative? Being as horrible as Richard? No thank you.

There were smiles all round, though, on the day when Nico completely hammered Richard on the tennis court. Breathing hard, and running with sweat, Richard didn't say, 'Well done,' or shake his hand at the end of the game. In fact, he didn't even get to the end of the game, but threw down his racket and walked off the court before the last point was played and sat down heavily on the sun lounger, mopping his face.

'You really notice your age when playing with Nico,' said Ned, trying to sound sympathetic. 'I think I'm going to have to give up.'

'Nonsense,' gasped Richard. 'I was a bit off form because I haven't been playing much recently. Too busy, you know.'

That afternoon he suggested that they have a father–son tournament: Luke and Richard against Ned and Tom. 'Now that I've had a bit of a warm-up.'

Lucy suspected he was after revenge. Tom hardly knew how to play, and it was Ned's weakest sport. The Morgans had their own tennis court, and she knew that Luke had private coaching.

Ned later confirmed that it had been quite unlike any father–son match he'd played before. 'Usually, the fathers show a bit of mercy to the boys, but Richard deliberately targeted Tom. Tom was hopelessly out-classed anyway, but he aimed fast balls at him – a couple hit him and really hurt him. Every time Tommy made a mistake – and he made lots – he shouted out things like "Bad luck" or "You'll have to do a bit better than that." And when he did one or two good shots, he said nothing. Tom was more or less in tears by the end. Richard told him not to be such a bad loser.'

Lucy's heart burned with fury. Tom hated people to see him cry. It was the ultimate humiliation for him.

Phil offered to cook supper on the following day, and said that he'd prefer to shop for it himself rather than giving Grace a shopping list. Lucy suggested driving him, as the Harley Davidson was hardly a shopping vehicle. Everybody gave them something to buy, and Phil suggested that they might not be back for lunch. 'We might grab a bite in town.'

'Good idea.' Lucy felt a sense of release at the thought of time alone with Phil.

As soon as they got into the car, she was over-whelmed by the desire to gossip about everyone else. 'Have you noticed the tension between Richard and Grace?'

Phil grinned. 'The man's unbelievable.'

'Why do you suppose she allows herself to be treated like that?'

He shrugged. 'What do you think? You're her friend.'

'I don't know what to think,' admitted Lucy. 'I'd no idea that it was as bad as that. If you only see a couple together for a few hours at a time, on a social occasion when everyone's behaving their best, you don't realize. We'd never even taken much notice of Richard before. It's really Grace who's my . . . who's our . . . friend.'

'If he's been systematically undermining her like that since she was nineteen, I'm not surprised she hasn't got any confidence.'

'It's as if she doesn't even realize there's anything wrong about his behaviour.' Lucy was frustrated. She knew that she'd never have stayed five minutes in a relationship like that. She'd have told him to shape up or ship out. It seemed funny to think that outwardly it was Grace who had all the poise and confidence, whereas now Lucy realized that she was actually the stronger.

'He's like lots of bullies. They try to dominate because they're weak, not because they're strong,' commented Phil.

'I think you're right.' Lucy sighed. 'She doesn't even talk to me about it. We used to talk about everything, but she never mentioned anything about this.'

'There's quite an age gap between them, isn't there?'

'A bit more than ten years. Why?'

He nodded. 'You can imagine her at nineteen and him at twenty-eight. He must have seemed the height of sophistication and success compared to the teenage boys she'd have known. And the same again in her twenties and his thirties. He'd have had all the trappings of a successful businessman.'

'Mm. The gap would have been closing but he'd still have been ahead of her contemporaries.' Lucy could see where Phil's musings were going.

'Then, as she became a wife and a mother,' he continued, 'she grew up, started wanting to be treated as an equal. Became a woman instead of a little girl. He's a good businessman, obviously, as a straightforward deal-maker, but he's not as intelligent as she is, for starters. She's now obviously the one with the taste and character, and the ability to make friends. So in some ways, he started falling behind.'

'At which point, he got frightened.' Lucy was delighted at the way they were joining up the dots together.

'So, to keep her in her place, he started bullying her.'

'You hear about men outgrowing their wives,' mused Lucy. 'But in Grace's case, she's outgrown her husband.'

'Yes. Except that she hasn't realized it yet. And I think he has.'

'Are we being a bit psychological about all this?'

She paused at the junction, although there was no traffic around, and turned towards him. A look shot

379

between them, of complicity, and tenderness, and excitement at being in each other's company. Grace and her problems suddenly seemed very far away.

A van appeared from nowhere, behind them, and hooted. She jumped, grating the hire car's gears, and shot out into the road. 'Sorry.'

Phil smiled and leant back, touching her arm briefly, a spark of electric contact between them.

Even shopping has a magic about it on holiday, or perhaps it was the subtle thrill of being in a super-market with an attractive man who was interested in her. Everything seemed brighter and more colourful. A smiling, matronly woman manning a decorated wagon promoting local spicy sausages proffered them samples to try.

'Mm,' said Phil. 'Try one.' And he popped a spicy morsel into her mouth.

As they picked items off the shelves, they found out more about each other, probing like lovers.

'I love this nutty chocolate.' Lucy took her favourite brand off the shelf. 'It's better than anti-depressants.'

'My drug of choice is white chocolate.' Phil looked embarrassed, as if he hadn't meant to reveal so much about himself.

'What?' Lucy giggled. 'Not the manly bitter stuff?'

He nodded, sheepishly. 'But it's our secret.'

'You wuss.'

Lucy dreamed of days like this. She imagined them buying flowers from a pretty flower-seller in the market, and wandering up the side of the river to picnic with fresh crusty bread, cheese and a bottle of ice-cold wine. Or driving in an open-topped car, along a road that led to the horizon, the neat, Napoleonic rows of trees on either side marking their route like a guard of honour at a wedding. She and Phil could climb mountains without getting blisters or out of breath, and would be able to recognize the flowers and butterflies they saw on the way, or take a boat out on a lake, her hand trailing in the velvet water.

But the supermarket trolley, tugging her sideways and piled with everyday items, like bread and yoghurt, dragged her back to reality.

They wandered along the narrow streets, looking for somewhere to eat. Many of the old shopfronts were closed, as the heart of the town lost its business to the big out-of-town sheds on the perimeter, and Lucy wondered what would become of the gaily garlanded little square and the riverfront bandstand over the next few years. The decay was visible – the façade of a 1930s cinema sagged open to reveal a gaping hole behind, where people now parked their cars.

'There are only a few old people left in towns like this,' murmured Phil, narrowing his eyes against a tall, relatively intact building, a piece of gleaming restoration amongst the crumbling plasterwork. 'But, look, this is a hotel. With a restaurant overlooking the river.'

The hotel was exquisite, with air-conditioning, just a few tables and sweeping views of the river over an old wrought-iron balcony. The sudden chill of the air tingled like champagne against her cheek.

'So.' Phil's eyes met hers as waiters settled them into chairs at right angles to each other, waving napkins at them like matadors. 'Tell me. What's up?'

She couldn't bear it any longer, and told him everything else about Grace: about Richard's lack of sexual desire, Grace's own frustration, and the suspicions she had about Ned. Beautifully arranged plates of leaves arrived, and Lucy picked at the delicious, but unidentifiable mouthfuls, concealed amongst the fronds.

Phil was surprised. 'I must admit I hadn't picked up on any particular electricity between them. Grace is quite flirtatious with him, but she is with me, too. I don't feel that it's very directly sexy. It's just a manner that she has.'

'I know. But Grace is having an affair and she won't tell me who it's with. But unless she's been keeping secrets from me for much longer than I think she has, there's virtually no one else it could be anyway.'

'Hm.' Phil placed his hand on hers. It was finely shaped and brown, with the sinews of his arms conveying a sense of strength. There was a smattering of dark hair – just enough to contrast with her own paleness. Lucy felt something jump inside her, something that she'd lost sight of in the past few weeks. Desire.

Pure, unadulterated, liquid longing. She felt like someone who had been on a strict diet for months and was suddenly faced with a sumptuous, inviting box of chocolates. Dark, velvety sensations that she had forbidden herself for so, so long that she'd almost forgotten they existed tugged away at her. She knew, suddenly, the true meaning of the phrase 'swept away'. She could have been swept away by the smallest breeze.

It made it very hard to think straight.

'How serious do you think it is?'

'What?' Her mind was fogging up.

'Sorry.' He leant back but didn't remove his hand. 'Of course, it's serious. These things are never trivial unless you're a very different kind of person from you or me. I remember what it was like when I first suspected Fenella and Simon. Half the time I simply couldn't believe that such a thing could happen – I told myself I was going mad, and that it was all due to stress at work – and the rest of the time it seemed completely inevitable. I was literally paralysed with fear over it all.'

'You?' Phil always seemed so in control. She couldn't imagine him feeling frightened because his wife was unfaithful. She squeezed his hand in sympathy, and felt his warm fingers respond.

'Eventually I confronted her. Even then I expected her to deny everything. I couldn't believe it when she told me she was going. She packed her bags then and there.'

'That's why I don't dare bring it up with Ned. It's like asking him to make a decision.'

Phil edged his chair fractionally closer, and turned almost to face her. Lucy was aware that their legs were resting against each other's, almost interlocked in intimacy. 'I'm so sorry,' he murmured, stroking her cheek very gently with his hand.

Lucy knew that she stood on the edge of a precipice. Behind her stood the white-painted house in Bramsea, with its airy windows overlooking the sea, and Ned and the boys inside, secure and happy. And ahead was Phil, lies and furtiveness. But also, tantalizing and close, was the exquisite excitement of a fresh, newly minted love. The unique intoxication of the first time, with its sensual combination of intimacy and discovery and its promise to mix shame and passion.

All she could think of was how clean he smelt, like freshly laundered shirts, and how she wanted to feel the bones and muscles of his shoulder hard against her body. He felt strong. She could hardly breathe for longing. Surely Phil could hear. She struggled to control it.

A final fling couldn't hurt anybody, could it? It might be her last chance. She would be fifty soon, and nobody might ever fancy her again. And wasn't she entitled? With Grace and Ned?

She thought of affairs of the past, before she knew Ned, so lightly taken and so hastily discarded the following morning. If only you could bank some of that raw, irresponsible lust, and keep it for when you really knew how to enjoy it – as a milestone birthday treat, perhaps.

'There are rooms here.' Phil spoke in such a measured way that she wasn't sure whether she was on the receiving end of a nugget of tourist information or an invitation until he leant forwards and gently kissed her on the lips, a light, butterfly touch that she might almost have imagined. There was, for a moment, no one else in the restaurant. No one else in the town. Nobody else in the whole world. Just Phil. It was hard to find enough air in her lungs to speak.

Nice women don't have affairs, Lucy told herself. They don't have rough, passionate sex. If they did exactly what they liked, then who would look after everyone? Society cannot afford to lose its most trusted workers to the pleasures of the flesh.

The bleached, buttery stone on the opposite side of the river glimmered at her in the sunlight, but there was something about the way the river hurried past that reminded Lucy that there was more to this decision than just wanting.

Oh, but there isn't, she replied, discarding her conscience. She could bear it no longer, running a hand over the bones of his head and down the stubbly jaw to return his kiss with the same tantalizing, featherlight contact. The nearness of him suffocated her. She rose, her chair scraping against the wooden floor.

But.

But. But. But. Suddenly she knew what she had to say.

'We shouldn't be doing this.'

Phil pushed his chair back with a sigh and closed

his eyes. For a moment, Lucy thought he was angry with her. She sat back down, clutching the seat of the chair in both hands like a little girl.

But he ran his hands through his hair. 'It wouldn't be fair of me to try to persuade you. I'm free to do this. You're not.'

'No,' she agreed. 'At the risk of sounding clichéd, we could still be friends, though. Could we?'

His smile was wry. 'I'm a great deal better at friendship than I am at love. You'd have made the right decision.'

'Phil.' She touched his hand. 'It's not as if any of us are doing any better.' She was exhilarated, like someone who has escaped from a disaster. 'Shall we go back?'

Phil pulled her up, and she kissed his cheek. 'I have to sort out Ned. I don't know what will happen between us, but once you've been unfaithful, it's never the same.'

'He loves you,' said Phil.

'Ha. Not at the moment, he doesn't. We're like strangers.' Lucy spoke lightly, but something tight and coiled inside her began to unravel, and her breathing calmed at last. Unless Phil was just being nice. 'But, provided we both want to, I'm sure we can make it.'

'And if he doesn't,' said Phil, 'come back.'

'Thanks.' Lucy knew that you could never go back, but, even amongst the ache of having denied him, was pleased to have been asked.

32

The farmhouse was deserted, and the echoes of an unanswered telephone bounced between the flagstones and the rustic beams of the kitchen. Thinking of Owen, Lucy dropped the shopping and rushed to answer it.

It was Helen, Ned's secretary from the hospital. Couldn't they leave him alone just for two weeks? Lucy was exasperated. He worked so hard, he deserved at least to have his holiday in peace.

'Ned's not here. I don't know where everyone is.'

'Perhaps you could pass a message on? I know he'll want to hear it.' Helen was bright and breezy. 'Could you just say that the new appointment has come through and he's got it. Isn't that wonderful? He's worked so hard, for so long, and I don't think he's ever had the recognition he deserved. We'll all miss him, of course, but this'll be a real new start for you both.'

Lucy tried to collect her thoughts, paralysed with shock, while Helen burbled on.

'After all these years in Bramsea, you'll be sorry to leave it, I expect. But they do say a change is as good as a rest . . .'

'Yes.' Lucy tried to coordinate her brain and her

mouth to disgorge all the appropriate goodbyes, and stood there, knees beginning to shake, trying to work out a way in which this information could just be innocuous, a mistake, a joke, a dream. Anything but the potential end of their marriage. Anything but that Ned had been quietly arranging to leave and live in another town. They hadn't got that bad together, had they? And would he be going with Grace, or without? Reality tilted on its axis, and she knew she could no longer sort out supposition from fact.

'Bad news?' Phil stood outlined against the door, the brilliant sunshine of the courtyard at his back.

'I don't know.' Lucy tried to think. 'I just don't know. I must find Ned.' She raced out to the pool. Richard looked up. He must have heard the phone.

'Where's Ned?'

He shrugged. 'Out with Grace somewhere, I think. They said something about visiting the Sunflower Museum.'

Lucy began to feel even more frightened. If Ned and Grace were at the Sunflower Museum – which was too absurd to be true, anyway – where were the boys? Could Luke and Tom have gone off on their own? She didn't trust Luke not to get them into danger.

'Did they take the boys?'

Richard looked as if he was trying to focus on the tip of her nose. Lucy wondered if she had a mark on it until she realized. Oh, God. Drunk again.

He spoke carefully, enunciating every syllable. 'Not

sure.' He screwed up his eyes and added, 'You're a very good friend of Grace's. And Grace is a very good friend of yours.'

Now what? Where had this come from? She sat down beside him. He'd obviously got to that stage of tipsiness where information would have to be coaxed out of him. 'The boys? Are they with her?'

He shook his head, smiling beatifically. 'The boys are all together.'

Well, that was OK. Nico and Lawrence were both responsible enough. Although her heart was racing at the thought of Grace and Ned, almost definitely not at a Sunflower Museum.

Remember what you have just nearly done, she told herself. People who live in glasshouses . . . It didn't make her feel any better.

Richard gave her the intimate, sincere look that drunks give people at three in the morning. Except that this was three in the afternoon. 'And you're a very good friend of Phil's.' He waved towards the house, as if to indicate Phil, and Lucy worried about what he meant. 'And Grace is a very good friend of Ned's.' He looked at her with the sincerity of a ham actor simulating great passion, and she suspected that this was where the rambling, inconsequential statements (you could hardly call it a conversation) had been leading. 'Ned a very good friend of Grace's,' he repeated, slurring by now. 'I don't mind men being very good friends with my wife.'

Lucy wanted to scream. Was this the final evidence

she was looking for, or the ramblings of several bottles of rosé wine in the heat?

'Know why I don't mind?'

She forced herself to sound calm and sympathetic. This could be the key to it all. Richard might, at last, be about to confide in her about his sexuality. It was a last chance to reach him, help Grace, and free herself and Ned from the whole sorry tangle. To reclaim her marriage. 'Tell me.'

He laughed. 'Because I'm a friendly sort of chap.' He laughed again, slapping his thigh and pouring another drink. Lucy, screaming inwardly with frustration, wondered if she could suggest that he didn't. 'A very friendly sort of chap, myself. It's important to be tolerant these days, don't you think?'

This was getting them nowhere. Lucy leant towards him. 'Look, I know you probably think of me as Grace's friend' – oh no, this 'friend' refrain seemed to be catching '– but I am a doctor, and anything you say to me would be completely confidential.'

'Confidential,' he repeated. 'I like that. Confidential.' He nodded.

'Yes. Just you and me.' Lucy tried to think how she could phrase the next bit sensitively. 'Are there any . . . physical . . . problems between you and Grace? I do see everything in my surgery, and nothing could shock or surprise me. And I can probably help, you know.'

He attempted focusing again, less successfully this time, as it took her words a few minutes to sink in.

He gazed at her, incredulous, then, so suddenly that Lucy scarcely saw it happen, his hand swept out in anger across the table by his side. The almost empty bottle of rosé and the glass both slid across the tabletop and smashed on the poolside.

Lucy jumped.

'What?' he shouted. 'What has my bitch of a wife been telling you?'

Oh, no. Big mistake. Never challenge a drunk. 'Nothing. She hasn't been saying anything.'

'She must have. Or you wouldn't be offering this, what is it, *help*?' He emphasized the last word with a sneer. 'Or are you offering me your body, my dear? All this "just you and me" business? I'm afraid you're a little old for my taste.'

Lucy got up, trembling. 'No, I wasn't offering you my body.' She longed to add, 'And you're a little dull for *my* taste,' but the desire not to hurt anyone's feelings was too ingrained. 'I was offering help. Which you might need.' She took a deep breath, her politeness suddenly swept away by rage. 'And Grace needs love. From you. And I don't mean sex. I mean love. Not special techniques or super-stud marathons, or buttons pressed in the right order, or to achieve anything, like getting pregnant. Nothing clever or difficult at all. You just have to care enough to try.' She could hear her voice wobbling.

'Love?' Anger amplified Richard's voice, making it less slurred. Perhaps that's why drunks got so angry. It made them sound sober. A part of Lucy observed him dispassionately, as the pain of Grace and Ned alone together somewhere penetrated deeper and deeper, cutting off the circulation to her feelings.

'Love. Is that what you call it? You and . . .' He nodded back towards the house. 'Him. You needn't think I haven't noticed what's going on. And as for Grace, I'm afraid you're barking up the wrong tree. You've been deceived by my wife. She can be very convincing, you know.' He lit another cigarette. 'We . . . er . . . I think the vulgar term is "do it" quite regularly. And, although, of course, I believe in the sanctity of marriage, I have, on occasion, been tempted, and strayed. A man in my position, you know, is very attractive to women . . .' He smiled tightly. 'So I don't think any problem, as you refer to it, in our marriage, can possibly be due to me.'

Lucy's face burned as she made one last effort. 'There's nothing wrong with asking for help. There really isn't.' But inside she wondered if perhaps he was right. He was a pompous git, but perhaps Grace had been lying all along. How embarrassing. How cringe-makingly embarrassing.

'Quite,' replied Richard. 'And should I ever need it, I'll know where to look. Now, you've been very kind . . .' the distaste was back in his voice, 'but the holidays are the only time I get to relax, so if you'll excuse me . . .'

Lucy trailed back to her room, leaving the broken glass, worrying that the boys would cut their feet on it and wishing she could run away, back to Bramsea and Owen. The humiliation of staying on here, with Richard's embarrassment and distaste, facing Ned every day, looking Grace in the eye, not being able to have a showdown in case it spoilt everyone else's holiday, even feeling guilty about rejecting Phil . . . Oh, God. She sank down on her bed. Perhaps she should call Owen. She felt the tug of his love. She could talk to him. It would, perhaps, be better if she manufactured a reason why she had to go home early, to be with him, and leave everyone else to have a good time. And meanwhile, she could work out what she wanted to do. She went into the kitchen and picked up the phone.

It rang and rang. Out in the garden? At someone else's house? There were lots of perfectly good explanations, but suddenly Lucy didn't believe any of them. She told herself that her anxiety over Ned was making her imaginative. That cancer didn't advance suddenly, particularly not at Owen's age. She could ring in a couple of hours' time, when he would be preparing his dinner, and hear his hoarse, familiar voice with that tinny shake in it that betrayed his age.

She needed to speak to him before then. She wanted to know he was safe. Now. Lucy thumbed through her book to find the number of Mavis Fletcher, his nearest neighbour. Better to feel silly than sorry. Might as well just check.

'Oh, my dear,' fluttered Mavis. 'Oh, my dear. I'm so glad you called. I couldn't find your number anywhere, and I knew you were on holiday.'

Lucy's heart stopped, and the silence in the kitchen seemed very loud.

'You see, my dear, your father has had a heart attack. The day before yesterday. I found him in the garden. He's in the hospital now. And he hasn't been conscious while I've been there, so I didn't know where he'd put your number.'

'The day before yesterday?' Lucy was horrified to think that she had been swimming and eating and drinking, while Owen lay unconscious and alone. All that time and she'd never suspected anything.

'I'll come straight back.' She wrote down the details of the hospital on autopilot, her legs trembling to be off. 'I'm on my way. Please tell him.'

She pulled her suitcase out of the cupboard, then stopped. Tom. She couldn't leave Tom here, not when he was getting on so badly with Luke. On the other hand, he'd be furious at being dragged away from a swimming pool and a tennis court, and, anyway, it was almost half-past three. There was no time to go searching for him. He was probably downtown some-where with Nico and Lawrence. They'd been pestering the bigger boys for a pizza all week. Unless she went now, this moment, she'd miss the last flight back.

She put her head in her hands, and sat down on the bed, trying not to snivel with fear for Owen.

'Trouble?' Phil appeared in the doorway.

'I'll take you to the airport,' he said, after he'd heard. 'On the bike we can be there in under an hour. Shall I book you a ticket while you pack?'

She nodded, numbly. Ned could look after Tom, and Nico and Lawrence could look after themselves. This time Owen must come first.

Thank God you couldn't talk on a motorcycle, thought Lucy, as the wind stung the tears away from her cheeks and the road disappeared under her feet, from rough cart track into winding village road and then the long, straight highways, flanked by their tall green trees, and finally onto the harsh technological landscape of the motorway and the airport. All that mattered was to get back to England to hold Owen's hand and tell him she loved him. She'd never said that. In all the time she'd spent with him over the past few months, she'd never really said how much she loved him. She'd assumed he knew. She'd always thought there was still time.

Phil bought her an orange juice, then an English newspaper, and then a long, crunchy ham and cheese baguette, as she waited beneath the departures board, eyes screwed up for the first sight of its messages. 'They throw you a bun in a bag on planes now. You'll need something to keep you going.'

She nodded thanks, vaguely. Food seemed very unimportant. Everything in her life hinged on the electronic announcements as they rattled into place impossibly slowly. Nice to Barcelona had left on time. Nice to Istanbul was delayed. Nice to Paris was now boarding. Please, please, Nice to London Heathrow, please be on time. Be boarding soon.

'What shall I tell Ned?'

Lucy couldn't think straight. Her mouth was dry, almost metallic. 'Just say I've rushed home to see Dad.' She paused. 'I hope Richard doesn't take what I said out on him.'

'Richard's a coward,' said Phil. 'He won't dare attack Ned or me.'

'Don't let him near Tom or Nico, then. Or Lawrence. He's been trying to humiliate Tom all week.' Her heart wrenched for her cheerful little boy and the puzzlement in his normally happy face at the way Richard treated him. He was used to adults who were fair, and decent, and kind to small children. 'Oh, God. I should have taken Tom back with me.' She couldn't allow herself to think that she still might not get back in time. Owen would never go without her. There had to be a last goodbye. There had to be.

'I'll look after Tom,' Phil promised.

The departure board rattled into place. The plane to London Heathrow was now boarding.

'Phil?'

'Yes?'

'There's broken glass by the swimming pool. Someone might cut their feet.'

'Sh. I'll sort it.' He held her face in his hands. 'Forget about us. Everyone will be all right. Just go.' They hugged. The wiry strength of his body failed to stir up any of the powerful feelings of a few hours ago, but she felt the tears rise again in her throat. Now she really was alone. She hurried through security without looking back.

33

By the time she got on the train to Ipswich, it was ten o'clock at night. She placed her cheek against the grimy window of the railway carriage. She couldn't read. Or think clearly. She could only count the hours and the minutes and the miles, as she'd been doing for the last six hours, as she inched closer to Owen's bedside.

And further away from Ned. She'd known that Ned didn't have light-hearted affairs. He wasn't like her. But she couldn't believe that it had gone as far as applying for jobs in another city. It all meant that either the affair had been going on for much longer than she'd realized, or, for some other, more terminal, reason, Ned had begun applying for jobs secretly since before it started. All the time that she'd thought she was safe, that she'd believed he hadn't noticed the holes in their life – all that time, he'd been planning his escape.

The mobile burbled.

'Lucy.' Ned's voice was scratchy and far away. 'Thank God I've got hold of you.'

Her heart leapt briefly at the familiar, comforting sound of his voice. Once Ned was in charge, every-thing would be fine. Owen would be discharged, grumbling, into their care, and they could look after him properly at last.

Into her care. Ned would be in Bristol. A terrible emptiness swept over her.

'Why didn't you wait for me?'

Anger flashed. Was he accusing her? 'Because I didn't have time. Anyway, you were at the Sunflower Museum with Grace.'

'And all four boys,' he crackled, although she wasn't sure if this was an excuse or just Ned conveying information.

'What on earth did you take them to that for?' Lucy couldn't believe that anyone in their right minds – so Grace and Ned clearly hadn't been – could possibly take boys to a Sunflower Museum when there was a swimming pool and a tennis court to be enjoyed.

'They were getting on Richard's nerves. We had to get them out of the way, and the Sunflower Museum was nearest. Then I took the two younger boys into the village for tea, and Grace went into town with Nico and Lawrence to get something. They're not back yet. The sales are on, or something.'

'Oh.' Lucy was deflated. 'Richard didn't mention that.'

'He was too drunk to think when we left. You should have called me. I'd have come with you.'

Lucy couldn't bear to have a marriage-ending row on a train, on a mobile. 'The mobile doesn't work from the farmhouse.'

'I know.' Ned's voice disappeared in gaps. 'I'm

standing on a table in the attic, with my remote-control earpiece in, holding the mobile itself as high up towards the roof as possible.'

Lucy couldn't help a brief smile. 'Helen phoned, by the way. She said you got that job in Bristol.'

She wasn't quite sure if the fragile links between them had severed, or whether Ned simply didn't know what to say. There was a silence.

'Hello? Hello?' She was about to switch the phone off, when she heard his voice.

'I was going to talk to you about that.' His voice patched in and out, so that she could barely hear the words.

'Not on a mobile.'

'No. Not now.' He said something else, which she couldn't quite catch, as he started to sound like someone talking under water, then disappeared altogether.

Well. That was that. The cat well and truly out of the bag and roaming round the countryside killing all the wildlife. Lucy tried to imagine what her life would be like in Bramsea without him. And without Grace. Nico would be at university. The house, currently so full of noise and people, would be quiet. At least she'd be able to get Owen to move in, which might, if they were lucky, give them a couple of last years together. By then, everything would be different.

There was a single taxi waiting at the station, its driver dozing with his mouth open. Lucy managed to beat the only other passengers from the train to it. 'Sorry,' she gasped, virtually pushing them aside. 'Emergency.' She could hears murmurs of disapproval.

And as they swept through the wet, yellow-lit streets, she rehearsed what she was going to say to Owen. How she'd tell him she loved him. That they all loved him. That Tom, once he'd recovered from his humiliation at Richard's hands, had become determined to beat Richard and Luke one day, and had spent hour after hour out on the court practising. Tennis had been Owen's favourite sport, and he'd love to know that his grandson had what he would call 'backbone'. He'd be interested, too, to hear that Nico was almost a normal human being now, and could really be good company. He was sharp and witty, and made them all laugh. She racked her brains for more news of the holiday so that Owen wouldn't suspect that things had finally come to a head between her and Ned. She didn't want to upset him. They could talk about that when he got home.

She hurried through the twilight of the hospital corridors towards his ward. She'd come on a bike, a plane, a tube, a train, and a taxi but these last few hundred yards seemed the longest of all.

She was surprised to find him in intensive care. Somehow she hadn't reckoned on that.

The nurse was low-voiced and understanding. 'He hasn't regained consciousness since he was brought in. I don't think he's got very long now.'

Lucy was taken aback. Not conscious. She hadn't fully taken that in either.

Suddenly she was afraid of seeing him die, in a way that she hadn't been afraid of a death before. She couldn't bear to look at him, and she still couldn't accept that this wasn't all some hideous mistake. 'I'll just find a coffee,' she whispered to the nurse, trying to sound like sensible Dr Dickinson and not some frightened little girl. 'I've had a long journey.' The nurse nodded, and Lucy wasted fifteen precious minutes, finding a canteen that was open this late at night, and buying a filthy coffee that she didn't even want.

I should be with Dad, she told herself. After coming all this way to see him. These may be his last minutes on earth.

No, they won't be. They can't be. When I get back, the nurse will tell me that there's been some minor improvement. People do recover from heart attacks. She returned to the ward, almost with hope in her heart.

'You can go in now,' whispered the nurse. Perhaps she knew how scared Lucy was, because she ushered her to a place by the bed, and Lucy found herself sitting there, listening to the agonized rasping breathing that heralds death.

'Dad,' she whispered. 'Can you hear me, Dad?'

There was a painful rattle as he drew a breath in, and then a pause. Of around half a minute. His jaw hung slack and open on his chest, and his eyes were closed.

'Dad?' Could he hear her? 'I love you, Dad.'

She was about to call the nurse again, when he suddenly expelled the air in a loud, grating gasp. His chest fell.

She watched each hoarse intake of air, and the long pauses in between. As a doctor, she knew that Stokes-Cheyne breathing meant the end. As a daughter, she still expected a miracle.

She must have dozed off, because the next thing she knew was a nurse gently touching her. 'He's gone, now, love.'

She jerked awake. She hadn't even managed to be with him at the moment he died. She looked at him one last time. Yes, he had gone. Utterly and completely gone in a way that she could never have imagined. People sometimes talked about seeing their loved ones in a peaceful sleep, but this grey, gnarled corpse wasn't Owen, asleep or awake. This wasn't the man who'd flown kites with her, gone to her graduation, held her babies tenderly in his arms and made her cups of tea in his sunny garden.

She didn't know where that Owen had gone, but he was out of her reach now. She stumbled out into the corridor, and the nurse looked at her with sympathy. 'Is there anyone we can call to come and get you?'

She shook her head, missing Ned with a terrible,

bleak, hollow deadness. Missing Ned and missing Owen. She couldn't do this on her own.

But she could.

'Shall I call you a taxi?' The nurse pressed on. She had to get the body to the mortuary and the bed prepared quickly for someone else, Lucy realized. She nodded, still too numb and tired to cry.

And when the nurse asked where the taxi was to take her to, she gave Owen's address. She wanted to do something for him, something to show him how much she loved him. She would look after his plants.

It wasn't until she opened his front door, and kicked away a pile of circulars that had been delivered, and smelt the curious stale emptiness of an unoccupied house, that she realized, finally, that she would never be able to do anything for him again. There was nothing he needed or wanted from her.

As the taxi drove off and the door shut behind her in the breeze, she sank down onto the floor, amongst the newspapers and circulars, and began to cry in great, jerking sobs, each one of which almost broke her heart again.

When her crying storm had spent itself, her throat and nose were sore, and her eyes felt so swollen she could hardly see out of them, but she was so tired that she could hardly bring herself to care any more. She stumbled upstairs to the spare bed, the one she'd often stayed in over the last twenty years, and fell into its slightly itchy embrace. She'd always told him not to get polyester sheets. She must buy him some decent cotton ones. And, as if she hadn't told herself this a hundred times before, she fell asleep as the milk float creaked slowly past the window and a dog barked next door.

34

Lucy slept until about ten o'clock and woke up to the cries of children playing on the green in front of Owen's cottage. August. Holidays. No surgery.

She felt an initial lightness of spirit as she tried to work out where she was, and suddenly the horror of it all blotted out the sun. It was like hearing that Owen was dead for the first time all over again. She now realized that she'd never really believed he would die. In spite of his age, and his illness, it hadn't seemed possible.

A wave of sadness for her mother, dead now for thirty years, swept over her. While Owen had been alive, Sarah had never been completely lost to her. With Owen's death, Sarah had gone again, this time for ever. There was no one left now to share the memories with. All she wanted was twenty-four hours back again. Just twenty-four hours. That wasn't too much to ask, was it? Enough time to get to her father before he lost consciousness. It was such a tiny, narrow window, twenty-four hours. Surely time wasn't that inflexible? Couldn't she bargain for a little more, to take him to London as she'd promised?

But time, which had raced through her fingers like sand during the holiday, inched forward relentlessly, in painful seconds and minutes, each one harder to survive than the last. She lay curled up, until she could bear it no longer. There would be work to do. Forms to fill in. People to notify. Cupboards to be cleared. A funeral to be arranged.

She didn't want to arrange his funeral. It would be the final admission that he really was dead. It seemed wrong to put him away in a coffin, and see the coffin slide away. And if she had to do it, she'd do it alone. It would be private. Very private. She couldn't bear the idea of having to look after everyone else who'd be there. She heaved herself out of bed, feeling heavy, dirty and unkempt. Owen's shower, a thin trickle of water that never properly rinsed the soap out, left her sticky. She dried herself on a thin, worn peach towel. She'd never really noticed what an old man's house it was until now.

The rest of the day was spent in answering questions she didn't know the answers to, discovering how little she knew her own father.

'What were his favourite flowers?' asked the girl at the flower shop.

'He didn't really have any, I don't think,' said Lucy, trying to remember anything he'd ever said about flowers. 'He preferred vegetables.'

Their brows furrowed at the thought of a funeral wreath of cabbages and artichokes, which would have looked very stylish in Notting Hill Gate, but rather too eccentric for Bramsea.

'His favourite colour, then?' persevered the girl.

Lucy felt totally inadequate. Fancy not knowing your father's favourite colour. Come to think of it, she didn't know Ned's favourite colour, either. Or her own, even. She ought to decide really, and leave it written down somewhere, because Nico and Tom would never be able to cope with all this. She gave the floristry assistant a pleading look. 'Er, blue?'

'There's not much in the way of blue flowers at this time of year,' said the girl, looking anxiously round the shop. 'It would be better to die in the spring if you like blue, because then you could have hyacinths. Although I'm not sure that you can have them in a wreath . . . I'm only the Saturday assistant, you see,' she added. 'I'm not really trained.'

'No,' agreed Lucy. 'Oh, I don't know. What do most people have?'

The girl looked increasingly desperate. 'I'll put you down for a standard wreath, shall I? Or one with "Dad" in white chrysanths?'

'Will you be taking the ashes home?' asked the funeral director. 'Or shall we scatter them here?'

Lucy visualized herself carrying the jar home. Would she put it in the passenger seat, where Owen usually sat? Or relegate him to the boot with the shopping and the tyre-changing kit?

'You can decide later,' offered the small, round man in a dark suit, who had obviously seen the numb indecision before.

She bumped briefly into Fiona, who promised to

have them over soon, when 'everything calms down a bit' and asked Lucy to be sure to ring her if there was anything she could do. Neither of them mentioned Grace.

Lucy, wondering how 'calm' things ever would be again, tottered home to try to do more than scrape the surface of the death-related paraphernalia. What kind of coffin? What sort? Owen would have considered them all a terrible extravagance. Lucy knew that she really ought to do one of those brown rice and Birkenstock numbers, where family and friends heave a cardboard coffin downstairs and into a rental van themselves, burying the departed under some favourite tree. That would be the perfect ending for someone as keen on compost as Owen had been, but she didn't have the energy. Yet she couldn't help feeling guilty when she opted for the cheapest casket. Her dad deserved more than that. Yet he'd be the first to declare any frills a 'dreadful waste of money'. The only person who mattered in all this was him, and he wasn't there any more.

Bugger it all, she thought, kicking off her shoes. I'd better at least tell Mavis from next door about the funeral. With a sigh, she slipped the shoes on again.

There were two tears in the powdery cracks behind Mavis's thick glasses. Or perhaps her eyes were just watering.

'Thank you, my dear. I'll be there. Would you like me to tell everyone else locally, to save you the bother?'

Lucy opened her mouth to say that it would be

private, and then closed it again. People would be hurt. 'That'd be lovely.'

'I wondered if you'd spoken to Irene Fairfax yet?'

'Irene Fairfax?' Lucy had never heard of her.

Mavis dropped her voice respectfully. 'His, er, girl-friend.'

'What?' Lucy was too astonished to pretend. 'His what?'

Mavis looked apologetic. 'Well, it's a big step to introduce your girlfriend to your children, so I'm not surprised he hadn't quite got around to it . . .We're all a bit careful about that sort of thing, you know. Children do get so upset.'

Lucy contemplated pointing out that it was her fiftieth birthday in two months' time. 'I'd better go and see this Irene person myself, hadn't I?'

So adolescence was like honeymoons. In theory you only have one, but in practice you often get two or three of them, especially if you didn't get it right the first time.

Mavis nodded and placed a soft, reassuring paw on Lucy's arm. 'And I'll talk to everyone else, dear. Don't you worry.'

Irene ushered her into a tiny, neat bungalow with a swirly brown carpet, raised Anaglypta wallpaper and a host of tables and shelves covered in china orna-ments and photographs. She was dignified, but red-eyed, and her hands trembled. Lucy suspected that they always did. She made light, fragile conversation over a small plate of Bath Olivers, but it was clear that her mind was sharp and clear. Meanwhile Lucy was trying to decide what 'girlfriend' meant. Presumably it was a courtly-love friendship sort of thing. You couldn't imagine anyone actually 'doing it', as Richard had termed it, amongst the miniature baskets of china roses and tiny porcelain animals that littered every surface.

'It must have been a terrible shock for you. Your father dying.'

'Well, it was, a bit. For some stupid reason, I really didn't expect it. Not properly,' admitted Lucy, wondering how all these gentle old ladies managed genuinely to think of other people all the time.

'And I'm sorry you and I didn't meet before.' Irene poured out a second cup of tea into delicate bone china cups, very obviously the ones kept for 'best'. 'We were very fond of each other – I shall miss him terribly – but things were quite informal between us, you know. I have another ... er ... friend, and he saw quite a few ladies.' She twinkled. 'Widowers in particular can have a high old time, if they want, you know.'

It never stops, thought Lucy. Never mind fifty being the new thirty. Perhaps eighty is the new eighteen. With hip replacements instead of boob jobs. Worrying about Zimmer frames instead of zits. Victoria sponge cakes instead of packs of fags. The accoutrements had obviously changed, but the landscape was much the same.

Irene saw her to the door, moving slowly and carefully. 'Let me know if there's anything I can do. I shall miss him very much. He was very good, you know.'

Lucy couldn't quite shake off the feeling that Irene Fairfax had not been referring to morality when she called him 'good'. If she hadn't known better, she could have sworn she'd said 'good in bed'.

She shook her head. She was going mad.

As she walked back to Owen's house, she realized that, of course, eighty couldn't be the new eighteen. It wasn't the lack of smooth, firm flesh and shining abundant hair. It was the quiet acceptance of the complexity of love. At eighteen, anyone in such a tangle of relationships would have demanded exclusivity, and flounced out if they didn't get it. Owen and Irene, and her Other Friend, and his apparently long line of interested widows seemed to have woven each other into the tapestry of already intricate lives.

She remembered the song by Bachman Turner Overdrive, in the early 1970s, which had suggested that if you couldn't be with the one you loved, you ought to love the one you were with. She remembered the way they'd shouted the lines out, bouncing and contorting opposite unsuitable, and even unattractive, members of the opposite sex at medical school discos. It had encouraged any number of disastrous one-night stands.

Lucy found a tin of baked beans in Owen's kitchen

and heated it in one of his weather-beaten, half-blackened saucepans.

She would have to go home soon, but she couldn't bear to. Not just yet. It was all very well Owen and Irene and the rest of them coping with lack of exclusivity. They'd had an extra thirty years of practice. The thought of Grace and Ned together still made her feel sick.

Even though she'd wanted Phil, with every intention of going back to Ned with an almost clear conscience? Be fair, Lucy, be fair.

Ah, but I didn't. That's the difference. I didn't. And he – almost definitely – did. That is the critical difference. Isn't it? At least she would have to ask him, now, the next time they saw each other. It couldn't be deferred any longer.

The house creaked in the shadows. It's lucky I don't believe in ghosts, she thought. Although Dad's ghost would be lovely. She turned on all the lights, just in case. Nine o'clock. Too early for bed. There was nothing on television. And no one to telephone.

She missed Owen again, in a sudden dagger-thrust of pain so powerful that she could scarcely breathe. She would never be able to phone him now.

This time it hurt too much to cry, so Lucy pushed the half-eaten baked beans away and sat there, fists clenched, until the wave of pain receded slightly.

The doorbell rang. Mavis, presumably, with her news of who could and couldn't come and what people had offered in the way of help. Lucy was relieved. There was something comforting about talking to someone who'd known Owen, as if it kept him real for a tiny bit longer.

It was Ned and Tom. She was so surprised she almost screamed.

Tom looked pale and frightened. 'Is Granda's body here? On the table? Will I have to kiss it?' Lucy wondered what films he'd been watching. Some mafiosi gangstery thing where people paid their respects to dead bodies in their own living rooms, presumably. Granda had been his toddler name for him. It had been the full Grandad for years now.

She hugged him, and felt the chunky little body yield, then pull away. He was always torn between wanting the reassurance of cuddles and his need for independence. 'It's all right, darling. Grandad's been taken to the funeral place.'

Seeing the mortuary staff carry him away had been a shock. She'd nipped back because she'd left a carrier bag by his bed, only to see them roll his body into a blanket and lug it out of the door, as if he was just so much meat. They weren't rough, but they'd never have handled a living person that way. And yet she couldn't pinpoint the difference, not exactly. It was so subtle, the difference between the way you carry the dead and the living.

Remembering it, she couldn't resist pulling Tom to her again, to feel the softness and newness of his skin against hers, the warm, knobbly outlines of his shoulders, and to kiss the intricate beauty of the tip

413

of one ear, just to know that her Tom was still hers, and was here. He submitted to the embrace. She suspected that he was even glad of it, although he'd never have admitted it.

'Nico and Lawrence have stayed to finish the holiday. Grace said they'd be no trouble.' Ned didn't seem to have noticed that she hadn't kissed him.

'Time for bed,' she said, reluctantly. 'It's late.'

'I'm hungry.'

She risked looking at Ned, who'd been standing back with arms folded. 'Has he had any tea?'

'Burgers. Ice cream. Chocolate. Crisps.'

'Tom! You've had quite enough. There isn't any food here at Grandad's anyway. I haven't had time to buy any.' She took him by the hand, and went upstairs.

He could go in the other bed in the spare room with her. Ned could sleep in Owen's bed.

'That's OK, isn't it?' She shouted down the narrow staircase to Ned. 'I don't think Tom would want to be in Owen's room or by himself. A bit spooky for him.'

'Fine by me.' The good thing about Ned was that he took life at face value. He'd never read anything into these delicate, calculated manoeuvrings that any woman would instantly have spotted, dissected and wished to discuss.

On the other hand, she wouldn't mind him knowing that there was a tiny little problem between them. He was quite capable of simply not realizing that her flight hadn't been entirely about Owen.

*

414

For the first time for years, she stayed with Tom until he fell asleep.

'Don't leave me,' he said. 'I'm scared.'

I'm scared, too, thought Lucy. But she gently stroked his face. 'There's nothing to be frightened of. Grandpa's house is a friendly place.'

'Will his ghost come into the room?'

'There's no such thing as ghosts.' Lucy felt his loss all over again. She imagined the comforting presence of his spirit, wound round with a white sheet, still looking after her, still reassuring her that everything would turn out all right in the end. 'No,' she spoke sadly. 'There really aren't any ghosts.'

Downstairs she could hear Ned moving around. Helping himself to the whisky, she hoped. Or that coffee that tasted like iron filings. He must have been travelling all day. At some point, she'd have to face him.

Tom moved restlessly, and began to snore.

She went downstairs slowly, hoping that she could at least defer the Grace – and the Bristol – conversations until the following day. It was never a good idea to have an important discussion late at night after an exhausting day. She didn't think she had the strength to cope with any unpleasant revelations, but neither did she want to prance about pretending nothing was wrong. She'd better avoid him for the time being. From the sound of it, Ned was watching television, sprawled over the sofa. He'd probably be asleep by now. The way he'd done for almost twenty years. Irritated, she walked quietly past the living room and into the kitchen. The biscuit tin, a luridly coloured object with two kittens on the lid, had been pulled out and not put away. Typical Ned.

He opened the kitchen door. Lucy pretended she hadn't heard, and pushed her nose deeper into the larder.

'Lucy.' There was gentleness in his voice. 'Luce. Look at me.'

She wouldn't. 'Just tidying this out,' she muttered, most of her voice disappearing into a tiny packet of flour. If she could have faced him then, without accusation written all over her face, she would have done. She would have pretended everything was fine until the right moment to have the conversation. But she knew she couldn't carry it off.

It was a very small larder, and it was impossible to fiddle around with her face in it for long. She shifted a jar of Marmite from one side of the shelf to another. Ugh. It was sticky and he hadn't put the top on properly. There were a few old potatoes sprouting in the veg rack on the floor. She gathered them up. He'd dug them up less than a week ago. He'd been alive then. She held them in her hand.

Mistake. She was going to have to leave the cupboard to throw them away. Keeping her head ducked down, she moved quickly across the kitchen to open the bin. 'So messy in here,' she muttered.

Ned stood across the larder door, barring her return to its safe, dark, slightly rancid depths.

Lucy stared at the floor.

'Lucy.'

She looked up, steeling herself. She should wait till tomorrow to ask him, but she suddenly couldn't bear it any longer.

'I'm very sorry.' His voice was full of pity.

She flinched away. 'I'm fine.' Now, said her inner voice. Ask him what he's sorry *about*. No, wait, said the monkey on the other shoulder. Don't bring everything tumbling down now.

'No, you're not fine.' Ned seemed very in control. 'Talk to me, please.'

'About your job? About you going to live some-where else?' It was easier than talking about Grace. She wasn't ready to open the biggest Pandora's box yet (oh, but you must, reminded the inner voice).

'I won't go. If you don't want me to.'

'Just like that.' Lucy wondered how much anything mattered to him.

'Not exactly like that, no. But we can talk about it. Ultimately, it's up to you.'

'You don't really care, do you? It's all so easy for you, if you don't. You'll do anything for an easy life.' Lucy filled Owen's battered old kettle. It always seemed strange to have to put it on the stove, rather than plugging it in.

'I've said that I care enough for you to give up the

job I want.' She could hear anger beginning to fire up in his voice. Good. She was angry. He needed to know how it felt.

Lucy lit the gas, flinching at the soft oomph as it caught. 'Why didn't you discuss it with me before you applied then?' She turned away to pick up the kettle, her arm stretched across the top of the stove. 'If my opinion means so much to you?'

So fast that she never saw it happen, flames licked up the arm of her sweater as she screamed. She could see them near her face, in just a short second.

Ned grabbed her, beating at her arm, but as soon as he extinguished one flame another sprang up again. He picked up the bowl of water in the sink and threw it at her.

She gasped. The flames had gone. The sweater, surreally, seemed barely singed, but she could smell the acrid, chemical smell of burned hair.

It was a reflex. To run to his arms.

He pulled her in. 'You shouldn't have had to come home alone,' he whispered. 'I'm sorry.'

It was all so complicated. But irrelevant, beside the warmth of his body and the unconditional love she could hear in his voice. It was a tone that had been missing for so long that she had forgotten its timbre, but perhaps she had been too busy to hear it.

'Don't ever leave without me again,' he said. 'Just don't.'

'I won't.' She finally let go of the pain and loss into the scratchy wool of his sweater, sobbing with the wrenching gasps that seemed to turn her body inside out, leaving it open and vulnerable as his arms held her tight. The wool against her skin reminded her that it was in the heavy August heat that you often felt the first cruel pinch of next winter's cold, the season swooping from the sweltering, slippery heat of high summer to sharpness in a few moments.

'He's so utterly gone,' she managed to say, eventually. 'I can't feel him anywhere. And I thought you were going, too.'

Ned's voice soothed her, his hands stroking her face and wiping away the tears. 'I'm not going anywhere. Don't worry. I'm not going. Not unless you want me to.'

Ask him.

It's quite clear that he still loves you. So what does it matter if he also loved someone else for a little bit? For God's sake, just ask him.

Lucy took a deep breath and drew back. 'I thought you were having an affair with Grace.'

She studied his face, struggling to interpret the expression that crossed it. It wasn't surprise, or amazement, or indignation. There was hesitation, perhaps a certain amount of calculation, perhaps even regret. And something that could be called accusation, self-defence or even pain.

'I wasn't.' He took another breath. 'But I thought you were having an affair with Phil.'

This question was, of course, exactly why she had deferred talking about it all for so long. With that thud of realization, blood rushed to her face. She needed to think carefully. Confess all or keep some secrets? She hadn't betrayed him physically except with a couple of kisses, but those kisses would hurt. Telling him about them would inflict needless pain. She would tell Ned the truth – that she loved him, that she'd never stopped loving him and that she would be there with him for the rest of their lives.

She reached out to him, with hugs, and kisses, and reassurances, finally allowing herself to realize that no matter how far they might each have journeyed over the last few months, this was a real homecoming. But she had to suppress the thought that, at least on her side, the whole truth had not been told.

35

Lucy was so tired she could have slept on a bench. Ned took her upstairs.

'We can't leave Tom alone, he'll be frightened,' she remembered, mumbling.

'We won't.' Ned pulled her top off, then her jeans, and dressed her in her pyjamas, like a child.

Lucy thought she heard her own voice saying, Don't go.

'I won't.' And Ned guided her into the narrow bed beside Tom's, lying down on the edge of it beside her. She fell asleep against the warmth of his body.

At around six, she stirred and saw him asleep, sitting against the wall beside her, his head lolling close to hers.

'Ned!' she whispered. 'Go to bed. You'll be exhausted.'

He opened one eye. 'I can sleep anywhere. Close your eyes. I'm in charge.'

The thought of someone else being in charge was so heavenly that she dropped off to sleep again.

At half-past eight, she woke again, to see Ned with a cup of tea.

'Shall we go home?'

She sat up and nodded, feeling like an invalid about

to be discharged from hospital. She could still feel the pain of Owen's death, but the raw edges had begun to heal.

'And we've got almost a week of our holiday left,' he added. 'With nothing special to do with it.'

Bliss.

'We could spend the whole day in bed. As it's Sunday,' suggested Lucy, her brain fragmenting, as usual, into three. One part (hurray!) was unexpectedly telling her that Ned was looking crumpled and unshaven and craggy. Even, surprisingly, well, like a slightly older version of the Ned she'd fallen in love with so many years ago. Quite tasty, in fact. The other two sections of her brain were the chattering monkeys on each shoulder. Get up. There's so much to do. You can't sleep with him after he's had Grace. Suppose you caught something. Perhaps he's just being nice to you because your father died. Maybe he's too lazy to get divorced. And did you really say 'we'? Wasn't it just a slip of the tongue? Wouldn't you rather be in bed on your own, with a nice book?

Oh, shut up, monkeys.

The monkeys were offended into silence. You'll have to deal with the Grace business some time, they said, huffily. And funerals don't just arrange themselves. But we know when we're not wanted.

'I'll make some calls,' said Ned. 'Someone will take Tom for the day.'

Lucy started to get out of bed. 'Where's my bag? Fiona offered to help . . .'

'Don't worry,' said Ned. 'I'll do it.'

And Lucy lay back, sipping the tea and thinking that the words 'I'll do it' were almost more romantic than 'Will you marry me?'

It was the first time they'd been alone in their own home, without children, and with nothing to do since . . . well, probably since Nico was born, thought Lucy, as one of the monkeys peered over her shoulder and pointed out that they should get on with the holiday washing.

She ignored it, dumping the suitcase in the hallway. For some reason the house seemed emptier of Owen's presence than his own had been. Perhaps because this was her real life, and now she had to live it without him in the background. It seemed too sad to cry about.

Ned put an arm round her shoulders. 'It hurts, doesn't it?'

Lucy had thought she'd shed all her tears for Owen, but now she knew she never would. 'He's the only person who loved me for what I really was. With all my faults.'

Ned sounded surprised. 'I love you for what you really are. Of course.'

'No, you don't.' Grief made her angry at Ned, again, although she knew it was unfair. 'If you hadn't married me, you'd have married someone else.'

'Probably,' he agreed. 'And you'd have married that dreadful Tony Whatsisname I had to wrest you out of the arms of.'

'Never!'

'You would.'

'Well, that shows you. There's no such thing as true love. We just happened to come across each other at the right time.'

'Is that what you think? There wasn't any "happened" about it as far as I was concerned. I knew I wanted to marry you when I first saw you, but you were embroiled with someone else. And not the ghastly Mark, either. Some other creep. I was beginning to think I'd never manage to catch you between boyfriends.'

'Ned! I thought you were asleep when we first met.'

'Oh, no.' He stroked her hair, gently and rhythmically. 'I knew all about you by then. I thought you were wild. A bit too wild, perhaps, and you needed someone to calm you down. And I knew that I was calm, a bit too calm, perhaps.'

'Oh.' She'd never realized how well Ned did know her after all. She didn't have to hide anything from him. Except Phil, of course, and that was quite a minor misdemeanour, like concealing a new dress in a credit card spend, and claiming that it was all car insurance. 'So you knew about . . .' The floodgates of talk, stoppered by years of trying, fruitlessly, to be the perfect wife, mother and doctor, opened. She told Ned everything – except Phil – and he talked about how he'd begun to conceal his hopes and fears, because he'd thought he was disappointing her by not getting promotion.

'Honestly not. I was only disappointed when you were, probably *because* you were,' explained Lucy. 'But I knew that you weren't an automatic promotion person. You love what you do. That's the important thing. Not being able to buy wide-screen TVs before Richard Morgan does.'

They decided to spend the day in bed, which initially triggered off a stab of alarm in Lucy. She suppressed it. She could manage sex. No problem.

'Bed food.' Ned had popped round the corner for supplies. Chocolate, fruit. 'Nothing that needs preparation. Nothing with crumbs. We can order a takeaway if we want something more substantial. Wine. Water. Newspapers.'

Lucy tensed as he got into bed beside her. Perhaps they should get the sex over and done with. Then they could enjoy the day.

Ned picked up one of the newspapers, broke off a square of chocolate and propped himself up. 'Colour supp? Or News Review? You choose.'

Lucy buried her nose in the colour supplement, sliding her leg comfortably over Ned's. He smiled, absent-mindedly, stroked her leg, and picked up the sports pages.

Perhaps he didn't want sex. Lucy turned the idea over in her mind.

No, Ned always wanted sex.

Perhaps he was being nice to her. Giving her a bit of space while still being supportive.

Too subtle for a man.

Perhaps he didn't want her. The feelings of insecurity came flooding back. The spectre of Grace, with her perfect body and her flirtatious ways, hovered over her shoulder, beckoning the chattering monkeys back.

She could always make the first move.

But that would be . . . she gazed unseeingly at an article about soup . . . it would be, well, a bit tarty. She flinched at the word. For a wife. Wives hinted delicately. One-night stands made direct approaches. She'd put all that behind her. She was now a wife. Look what happened to Grace when she'd asked Richard for sex. He'd despised her.

Forget Richard. And Grace.

Ned had known what she was like even before they married. A sexual advance wouldn't turn her into a complete harlot in his mind.

Lucy involved herself more intricately in the soup article, which promised to solve all her problems, but became aware of a sensation that, if she hadn't almost completely forgotten what it was like when Ned was around, might just possibly be described as lust.

Love the man you're with. She should try it.

She placed a hand, tentatively, on his chest.

He picked it up, still reading, and kissed it, then replaced it slightly lower down.

That probably hadn't been intentional. Had it?

She'd been more confident than this once, hadn't she? She'd felt secure in the knowledge that her thighs

426

had had sheen and hollows, where they now resembled pink marshmallows.

But it wasn't so much about the bulges and hollows, as about the space in her head that had been occupied by the monkeys for so long. She felt it open out, yielding and wanting at the same time.

She began to unbuckle Ned's belt. The sports pages wavered slightly but stayed in place. She hesitated . . . suppose . . .

She had been married to him for nearly twenty years. She had to trust him. And herself. She ran her fingers down the zip and released his trousers.

The thick, hard column strained against the waistband of his boxer shorts. 'Ned!' She was almost angry that he'd made her work so hard. She tore away the sports pages. 'You . . . you . . .'

He grinned and pulled her to him. 'I was waiting for you. To come back to me.' His hands, broad and sensitive, ran over her body, leaving a surprising trail of sparks where they touched. 'Why are you still wearing clothes?'

'Because –' she bent over him, feeling the roughness of his cheek against hers, his hand under her clothes pinching her nipple gently, and wondering how someone so familiar could feel so new at the same time '– I haven't taken them off yet.'

Most of their married sex had taken place when they were already undressed. Wearing sensible, buttoned-up pyjamas that slipped off easily, or long, shapeless nighties that were no challenge. Now she had to struggle to kick her jeans and pants off, and couldn't be bothered with the rest.

Ned seemed different. Perhaps that was because the connection between them had been broken for so long. She wanted him too much to think about that now, moving her body against his fingers, and slipping down over his cock with a shudder of pleasure. With each stroke, she felt herself open out to him completely, as if there could be no more to strive for, and yet there was always more, higher and deeper every time, until she heard herself cry out and his groan in reply, and she sank, satisfied and delighted, against his chest.

'Wow,' said Ned.

'Wow,' agreed Lucy.

'And all without vibrators,' teased Ned.

Lucy was embarrassed. 'OK. I know that's not what it's all about. All that mechanical stuff is pretty irrelevant. Sorry.'

'You don't have to be. I think it was good for us to look at each other differently for a bit. Learn new things.'

As Lucy snuggled down against him, she suppressed a faint internal alarm bell. Ned certainly had learned new things. She stroked his chest, and propped herself up again.

'Fiona Forbes thought you were having an affair with Grace, too.'

Ned's eyebrows went up. 'Really?' He looked at the ceiling for a few moments. 'I suppose she must have seen us together or something. There was that time we all went to the cinema and you got delayed at the surgery and didn't join us till halfway through. And when Grace lost her car keys on the beach and I had to give her a lift home for the spare pair, then back to the car again . . .'

Lucy giggled. Of course. There were so many times that could have been misinterpreted by other people, particularly in a little town like Bramsea where everybody talks.

'Oh, God. We didn't use anything else either.' Ned, curling his fingers through her slightly damp hair, changed the subject.

'We never use anything.' The pleasures of getting older. No bits of slightly smelly rubber that pinged out of your hand at just the wrong moment.

'Mm. But that was a real baby-maker.'

She sat up. 'Oh, no. Not that.' But something stirred inside her, a kind of romantic nostalgia for the perfect happy ending.

He laughed. 'Would it be such a bad thing?'

A drench of cold reality washed over her. There was so much she wanted to do with Ned. It seemed years since they'd had time just to be together, just to enjoy each other's company without responsibilities. She'd forgotten how good it felt. 'Absolutely. We've only just got our lives back. I've only just got you back. I don't want to share you again.' She curled back into the crook of his shoulder. 'Anyway, I'm too old.'

'Probably. But it's not absolutely impossible, is it?'

She sighed. 'Pretty much. Chances of about 50,000 to one, or something.'

'Good.' He tightened his arm around her. 'For a moment, I got quite carried away.'

'Yeah.' She thought for a second. 'Me too. But that bit of our lives is over.'

'Do you mind? Is that what the last few months have been about?' His voice wasn't as casual as she suspected he'd like it to be.

She turned to look at him. 'You noticed.'

He rolled his eyes.

'I wasn't sure that you did.'

'I knew something was wrong. I thought it was me.'

They were still too fragile to talk about everything that had happened in the last few months, thought Lucy. It seemed pointless to puff more suspicion into the air. 'Tell me about this job, then. Were you trying to escape?'

He kissed her affectionately. 'It was never meant to be a secret. That was an accident.'

'Was it?'

He lay back and looked at the ceiling. 'You know I've been up for promotion before.'

She nodded. He'd never got them. He wouldn't play the game. People who made appointments thought he was a maverick. Didn't like the way he neglected paperwork, or covered it in coffee. And forgot to ring them back. It was generally agreed that he was a talented doctor, and that patients loved him, but they didn't want to trust him with any more responsibility.

That was the gist of it, according to hospital gossip. Lucy had got used to people almost feeling sorry for her being married to him.

'I haven't told you about the last few. Because I really didn't think I'd ever get them. It wasn't serious. It was like a game. I just wanted to see if I could do it.'

No wonder they thought he was frivolous.

'And now that you've got it?'

He shrugged. 'You've got a life here. Tom's still at school. We belong here.'

'And if we didn't?'

He turned to look at her. 'If we didn't, I'd love to do it.'

'So let's go.'

'Go? Just like that?'

'Exactly like that.' Her heart lifted at the thought of change. Finding a new school. Thinking differently about her own work.

'But what about you?'

She snuggled into him. 'I love what I do. I always have. But I've been doing exactly the same stuff for fifteen years. I'd like to find a new challenge, too. Bristol. It's a city. Maybe some inner-city work would be good. Working with real deprivation for a change rather than middle-class sniffles. I don't know. I haven't even thought about it properly. But I'm on for anything. We could rent out the house. Come back to it in a few years' time. And Tom's due to change schools anyway.' It was amazing to be able to say that. On for anything.

'Do you promise you're not just saying that? Not just trying to keep me happy?'

She kissed him. The first proper, real searching kiss that she'd given him since the sight of Nico's perfect little fingernails all those years before had made her realize how vulnerable and precious life was, and had made her almost afraid of living it. 'I promise.'

'If I get you another cup of tea first,' he murmured, 'can we begin again where we left off?'

Lucy laughed. 'You've finally realized. Being given a cup of tea is every woman's idea of perfect foreplay.'

He tweaked her nose. 'I know. But you're usually so busy getting one for yourself and everybody else that you don't often give me the chance.' He traced the line of her jaw. 'What about a deal? I'll help more, if you actually let me, and let me do it in my own way and my own time. You don't have to do everything yourself here, but you can't expect us to do everything exactly the way you do.'

Lucy was amazed. 'I'm not that much of a perfectionist, am I?'

'No.' Ned thought for a few seconds. 'Just in a tearing hurry most of the time.'

'Mm.' Perhaps there was something in what he said. Lucy felt the monkeys loosen their grip on her shoulder, and troop out of the room. 'We'll be back,' they warned her.

'Not if we have anything to do with it,' she muttered mentally, snuggling further down into the softness of the bed.

Ned reappeared ten minutes later with two fragrant cups of tea. 'So.' He settled himself in, drawing her to him, the weather-beaten creases of his face suddenly so close and so loved. 'What shall we plan for your fiftieth birthday?'

She sat up, suddenly filled with childish expectation. 'A party. A great, big, thundering, drinking and dancing and behaving extremely badly party. Inviting all the people who seem to have shed their husbands and wives in the past five years and seeing who gets off with whom.'

She would even invite Grace.

'As long as you save the last dance for me,' said Ned.

36

There are so many people here, thought Lucy, standing
by the door of a crowded, roaring room, welcoming
people to her party. And a few, painfully, who weren't.
Owen and Sarah. Her parents. There were gaps in the
fabric of the evening, where they should have been.
Owen's death had left a hole, like a bomb crater, in
her life, and she hadn't yet walked right round it to
see how big it really was. One day she would leave the
cavity behind, and only look back at it occasionally,
but she hadn't quite reached that stage yet.

And Grace wasn't here. She hadn't even heard from
her. She'd had a polite, sympathetic, but almost formal
letter from her, expressing sorrow at Owen's death
and offering any help if Lucy needed it, but she hadn't
called, and Lucy hadn't called her. She hadn't replied
to the invitation either, which had hurt Lucy, although
she knew that was silly. She knew, deep down – she
didn't know how – that Grace felt guilty about her,
but she didn't want to challenge Ned again. Perhaps
he and Grace had done what she and Phil had done.
Gone to the brink. She could hardly blame them, but
she didn't want to hear about it. Or perhaps Ned was
still lying to her.

She refused to believe that. But if she needed any

final proof that something had definitely happened between them, this distancing was it, yet she still missed her. The friendship with Grace had been like an affair: exciting, stimulating, intense, and even passionate, and it hurt to know it was over. Grace was suddenly like the man who never called you. Lucy felt rebuffed. As if she'd been stood up.

But all their other friends were there. Fiona had cropped her hair spikily short and dyed the tips scarlet. She looked like a sexy pixie. Phil, lanky and cool in a black cashmere polo neck and his black leather jacket, inclined towards her to hear what she was saying. Fiona's former husband, Rupert, who'd been so golden and privileged as a youth, was now as stout and bald as an egg, and came with his new wife, who looked exhausted in a severe suit and a single string of pearls. Fiftieth-birthday parties were so strange, thought Lucy. At first glance, you'd think there were people of all different ages there, but if you looked closer you saw that most people – except for a couple of second husbands and wives – were about fifty, too. It was just that some still looked thirty-five, while others, in floral skirts with elastic waistbands and baggy sweaters or formal suits straining at the buttons, looked about sixty. The secretary from the surgery, who Lucy'd always suspected of having designs on Phil, came with her new husband, a widower, who was amazingly nice and amazingly in love with her. The 'children' – Nico and his friends, who were circling with wine and nibbles – looked like pale, unformed versions of these faces, while, darting between everyone at shoulder level, but looking almost grown-up for the first time, were Tom and his new best friend, Si.

And there, suddenly, laughing down at her mobile phone as her fingers flashed over the buttons, leaning against the front gate in a seductive black tube of a dress, was Grace. Lucy watched her, as the tip of her tongue licked her top lip, like a cat. With a last, secret smile, she switched the mobile off, walked into the house and put it down absent-mindedly on the hall table, as she looked around to say hello.

Lucy stepped forward. 'Grace.' They air-kissed.

'You look fabulous.' Grace assessed her. 'I told you that eyeliner would solve all your problems.'

'It's certainly changed my life.' Lucy kept her voice light.

They hesitated.

'Where's Richard?' Lucy hadn't seriously expected him to come.

'I've left him. I finally got the courage.'

'I don't believe it! How? When? Tell me, tell me.' For a moment it was how it used to be between them. 'Seriously. How is it?'

'Scary. To be honest. But now I know there was no other option. The how – I just found a solicitor. Richard's moved down to the London flat. For the time being, I'm here in Bramsea.'

No wonder she hadn't heard anything on the grape-vine. Richard not being around would hardly be news.

'And the when was as soon as we got back from holiday.'

'Good.'

'It is good, isn't it?' Grace looked serious. 'You're leaving, I gather.'

Lucy nodded. 'Promotion. For Ned.'

'I'm so glad.' Grace seemed to mean it. 'But I'll miss you.'

Why stop calling me, then, was what Lucy longed to ask, but restrained herself. 'Me, too. Now, find yourself a drink. Nico's in there somewhere, alternately making phone calls to his friends and dispensing bottles so efficiently that one senior consultant has already been dragged out and is being sick in the flower beds.'

Grace gave a little, embarrassed smile, and edged towards the crowded room. 'Is that Fiona? Doesn't she look great? I must – ' And she gesticulated towards Fiona's shifting hips. Lucy thought she could see Phil's hand move across her vision, but someone else, carrying two glasses and singing, moved between them. Grace vanished.

Lucy picked up the mobile phone. She could read the last text message by pressing a few digits. It would be inexcusably nosy. She had no business to do it. She could see who Grace had been texting, with that intimate smile, only five minutes ago.

Did she want to? She and Ned were moving to another city. Did she really want to bring everything toppling down?

With a few quick taps, Lucy took a deep breath, and pressed the buttons of the phone.

Grace reappeared, and held her hand out for its return.

But Lucy had seen the number. It was hers. And the message. *Need to cuddle you lots. Can't wait to see your face. N.*

So it had been Ned all along.

'I'm sorry,' said Grace. 'I never wanted you to be hurt.' The clichés, thought Lucy, stunned. The clichés.

Grace turned, and pulled someone towards her. 'Nico. Nico . . . She knows.'

Nico stepped forward, and put his arm round Grace. 'I'm sorry, Mum. It's just one of those things. Don't blame Grace.'

Grace began gibbering. 'It's not serious, Lucy, I'm not going to ruin his life . . . he's going to university next week . . . there'll be lots of girls his own age . . . it was just that I was so lonely with Richard, and he made me feel . . .'

Nico grinned, looking like Ned. 'You can ruin my life any time you like, Grace. Come on. Let Mum get over the shock.' And he took Grace's hand, and led her away.

'It was Nico.' Lucy turned to Ned. 'It was Nico all along.' That was why he'd grown up so much this summer. The gawky boy had turned into a confident young man. It was just hard to get her head around it. Now that she knew it was Nico who'd taken the car to Grace's that evening she'd spent with Phil, she knew that Ned would have walked out to the pub, to sit silently over a pint and bottle up his feelings, because that's what he did. He'd turned away from her because he'd thought she was having the affair, not the other way around. She should have asked him about Grace, when she first suspected.

Or not. She might not have believed him. Sometimes just having the conversation can make events spiral off in a different, even more dangerous direction. You could go mad, wondering if you'd done the right thing. Lucy looked at the walls of her home, at the painting of the sea by a local artist, which they'd bought together, to the darkened room full of friends, to the garden-door curtain whose fringe had been gnawed by a pet rabbit (long dead), to the wonky lampshade in the middle of the hall and all the piles of old invitations and reminders that built up and made a house a home. She'd come very close to losing it all.

'Did you know about Grace and Nico?'

'No. At least, I once thought something might be going on,' said Ned. 'Then I thought I was imagining things. It didn't seem worth mentioning. It would just have caused trouble, and, if there was something, I thought it would burn itself out. After all, it's hardly the first time a teenage boy has had an affair with one of his mother's friends. I remember being completely obsessed with my mother's bridge partner, Pauline . . .'

'And . . .?'

'She was very educational. In more ways than one.

Many more ways than one, in fact.' Smiling wickedly, he dropped a quick kiss on her lips. 'Now. Dance. You and me.'

'Ned,' she protested, as he propelled her towards the dark room, 'I always thought you were faithful to that first girlfriend of yours.'

'Ah, well . . .'

37

The following morning Lucy's head felt as if it was being squeezed in a vice, and she couldn't decide whether a cup of tea would make her feel better or horribly sick. Perhaps a glass of Tom's Ribena would be safer. They say it's good for hangovers. She sank carefully down on a kitchen chair and surveyed the last remains of the party. The caterers had taken most of the mess away, and Ned had promised that he and the two boys would help her clear up the rest later.

Six months ago she would have sighed and done it herself before they got back, because she wouldn't have wanted the day to spin out of control.

Now she was content to wait for them all to return from football. It would be quicker and easier with four pairs of hands. Outside the window, the trees glimmered and rustled in the cold, clear sunshine, their leaves turning the colour of new pennies. Images of the party drifted pleasurably through her head as she pushed a few empty wine bottles out of her immediate field of vision. Phil with Fiona. That was a definite possibility. They were both such perfection-ists, and they'd both had the edges of their ideals blunted. Don't matchmake, she told herself. Not every relationship has to have a happy ending. It might not have to have an ending at all. Perhaps Phil could help Fiona re-discover her sense of her own self-worth, and Fiona might manage to establish a tiny, if temporary, colony on the isolated island that was his emotional world. Maybe that's all they needed for the time being.

Beneath it all, however, throbbed the ache of Grace's betrayal. OK, it wasn't as bad as taking her husband. Nico was free. He was an adult. He could make his own choices. But he was also her beloved son, and Grace had been her friend. She felt cut out. She felt uneasy. She didn't quite know what she felt, except that she didn't like it. Was that jealousy, or was it something more fundamental and protective than that? Grace, at the very least, had not been totally honest, and that cut to the heart of the friendship.

The doorbell beeped so hesitantly that Lucy wondered if she'd misheard. Not the milkman wanting to be paid, please, she thought. She didn't think she could focus on writing a cheque. Perhaps she shouldn't answer it.

Habit forced her to her feet, and towards the door, so slowly that by the time she opened it, Grace was halfway down the path again, as if running away.

'Oh!' She turned, apologetic. Her face looked ravaged in the low-slung, sharp autumn sun, deeply craggy, with huge shadows under the dark eyes and all the lustre leached from her skin. She looked almost yellow and very thin. If Lucy didn't know better, she might have thought Grace had not taken her make-up off the night before. But Grace had once told her that she couldn't sleep unless she'd cleansed, toned and moisturized. She'd never fallen asleep with her make-up on, she'd said.

'I brought you a birthday present.' Grace indicated a prettily wrapped parcel on the step.

Lucy was embarrassed. 'Oh. You shouldn't have.' The words were mechanical, but she meant them. She didn't want anything from Grace.

Grace looked at the path. 'And I wanted to say sorry.'

Lucy was still fascinated by the way Grace moved, and by her deep husky voice. A part of her wanted to say that it didn't matter, of course it didn't matter, and if Lucy couldn't understand Grace's need and vulnerability, then who could?

Another part of her said that what had gone between her and Grace had died, and could never be resurrected.

'Could I come in?'

Lucy silently opened the door and Grace sloped in with her long, loose stride. Lucy followed her into the back.

'Sorry about the mess.'

Grace looked around her as if the wine bottles, half-empty glasses and scattered possessions were invisible.

'I . . .'

'I . . .'

'You first,' said Lucy, waiting, wondering if Grace

443

was going to produce a charming, heart-rending and beguiling explanation.

'I told you I was a bad person,' said Grace, when Lucy had made her a cup of coffee.

'You can't use that as an excuse. Anyway, I don't think you're bad. I just don't think you cared enough.' Lucy meant cared enough about 'me' or 'us', but also 'cared enough about Nico'.

'I tried not to do it. When he first . . . I mean when we first . . . well, I went to a wine bar in Bramsea on my own one evening, not long after that stupid episode . . .' she blushed, 'with the bi-sexual prosti-tute. It made me realize that whether you're into men or women, and however much of an itch there is to scratch, there's a whole mental, emotional and physical spectrum of compatibility into which sex is inextric-ably bound, along with everything else. You can't isolate it. Or I can't. Maybe some people can.'

Lucy shook her head. 'Not me.'

'And I'd started to try to find out, discreetly, if Richard had anyone else.'

Lucy raised her eyebrows in a question.

'Not a whisper. If he has another woman, she's barely visible to the naked eye.'

'Or the naked Richard, probably.'

They both giggled, then Grace looked sad for a mo-ment. 'I just had to get away from the house, and you were out somewhere. Nico was with a group of friends, and he left them to join me. I couldn't believe he found me attractive, but he was very straightforward . . .'

Lucy raised a hand, as if to fend off detail, and Grace blushed.

'I have to explain something. I suddenly thought, "Wow. Someone finds me attractive." Then I thought of all the times you've told me I was, and the other compliments I get sometimes, and it occurred to me that perhaps some of them might be true. Perhaps I do have a right to feel attractive.'

'You do. And I don't need to know all the hows and whys.' Her voice sounded tinny and false to her, but Grace didn't seem to notice.

'But I didn't feel it would be right to . . . go ahead. So I sat down with Richard the following evening and told him that I needed our relationship to have a physical side. That I completely understood if he was tired, or stressed, but that I'd like us at least to try.'

'What did he say?'

'He said, "I can't believe you've said that. I need a breath of fresh air." And he walked out.'

'Did he come back?'

Grace nodded. 'And went on as if we'd never had the conversation.'

'Did you try again?'

'Yes. I waited until we were in bed – I had to wait for ages, because he did everything he could to delay it. Then I told him I'd meant what I said, but that all I asked of him tonight was for him to talk about it.'

'And?'

Grace swallowed. 'He looked at me as if I repelled him, and said, "It's sad when women of your age want

445

sex. Pathetic, really. I mean, what man is honestly going to want to sleep with a woman of forty-five?"' Her voice was shaking. 'It was as if he hated me for asking.'

'But didn't you say, actually I've just had a very good offer and if you feel like that, I shall take it up?'

Grace shook her head. 'Of course, what he said made me completely doubt everything. I just lay there and looked at the ceiling all night. I just couldn't face being told that it was all some sort of adolescent joke. And even if it wasn't, I still knew it would be wrong to have an affair with him, anyway.' She looked at Lucy. 'I did try very hard not to have it happen.'

Lucy felt uneasy. 'Did you ever find out what had gone wrong between you and Richard?'

Grace shrugged. 'I know this sounds silly, but I've now realized that he doesn't really like women. Not flesh and blood ones. He used to tell me I was perfect, that I was his doll. It was obviously his biggest compliment. All those years ago, when I thought our sex life was normal, he used to shower before we made love. Then again afterwards. He'd jump up immediately. And then he'd still have his normal bath in the morning or the evening. It was as if he had to scrub away any trace of femaleness and sex. That even when he did find me,' she wiggled her fingers in the air to indicate quote marks, '"attractive", he was still repelled by the real me underneath it all.

'Then the fertility treatment put that side of our

446

life under a great deal of strain, and I became less and less perfect. Pregnancy and that terrible birth were the final straw. The doll was broken. Children go off toys when they're damaged.'

Lucy believed Grace. It fitted. She hadn't been straight with her over Nico, but Lucy had never known Grace to actually lie, while Richard had been bombastic and boastful at every turn. He'd never have admitted a sexual problem to her, and wouldn't have thought twice about pretending a sexual vigour he didn't have in order to divert her suspicions.

'So what happened next?'

'I bumped into . . . well, Nico . . . again, and he asked me what my decision was, and why I hadn't called him. So I told him the whole story. He was amazingly mature about it, you'd never have thought –'

'Did Richard suspect anything?' Lucy wanted to change the subject away from Nico. And to know if Richard was normally so vile on holiday.

Grace shook her head. 'I've been very careful. He certainly hasn't said anything. If he was even remotely suspicious . . .' she shivered, 'I can't imagine what he'd do. Let's just say it wouldn't be very pleasant.' She rubbed a finger nervously against a tiny, invisible stain on her suede trousers. 'I know I should just have left him, and not got Nico involved. But Nico's got no preconceptions, you see. No baggage. He doesn't expect anything of me, and I don't expect anything of him. For the first time, I can be the person I was

447

always going to become.' She looked at Lucy. 'I'm probably not making much sense.'

'I'm not sure that I really want to talk about it.' Lucy was uneasy.

Grace smiled. 'How ironic. You've always said that talking would help. And talking to you, over all these months, did help. You gave me the confidence to see that Richard is . . .' She looked around the room, as if a definition of Richard might be written on the walls or the ceiling. It wasn't. ' . . . a selfish git,' she concluded.

They both burst out laughing.

'He is, rather, I'm afraid,' said Lucy. 'Why ever didn't you notice it before?'

'Oh, I don't know. I would say that it's because I'm stupid, or useless or incapable of surviving on my own, but I've decided to stop thinking like that about myself.'

'Did you ever talk to Richard? Sensibly. About what had gone wrong between you?'

'Sort of,' admitted Grace. 'The trouble is that the sex thing is such a no-go area with him, and it's hard to talk about the relationship without mentioning it. But, anyway, I now know that I got too obsessed with thinking that it was the main problem in our marriage, and that if only I could fix that one element, everything else would be sorted.'

Grace sounded much saner these days. Her long fingers warmed themselves around a blue-and-white mug bought as a joke years ago. It was inscribed, 'You have to kiss a lot of frogs before you find your prince.'

448

Lucy hoped that Grace didn't think that Nico was her prince.

'I don't know why Richard didn't trade me in for a younger woman, except that he's never rated sex very high on his list of priorities, and a divorce is so expensive. Perhaps he just couldn't be bothered.' There was still such pain in Grace's voice. The hurt had gone very deep over all those years, thought Lucy.

'What do you think he'll do now?'

Grace looked resigned. 'Marry someone else – she'll have to be quite young and easily impressed by the flash car and the smart restaurants – as soon as possible. Poor girl.'

Lucy knew she had to be fair to Grace. 'You taught me a lot, too. Eyeliner and things like that. And enjoying myself. I found the person I always used to be.'

Grace grimaced. 'Trust me to get the superficial stuff right.'

'Don't knock it. Life without fun is grim.' Lucy was embarrassed at being so honest and changed the subject again. 'And he still doesn't have any suspicions about Nico?'

Grace shook her head. 'He finds me so unattractive that he literally can't imagine any other man wanting me. In spite of all that stuff he said on holiday. That was mainly alcohol talking.' She winced. 'It's not as if he's an alcoholic, because he goes for months with just a couple of glasses each evening. But beyond that, about halfway down the bottle, a different Richard emerges, and it's pretty horrible. I'm sorry about that, by the way, I could see what a shock it was for you. I kind of thought you knew, and you could handle it.' She gave a small, bitter laugh. 'Funnily enough, we never seem to go on holiday twice with the same people.'

Lucy remembered how keen Richard had been for them and Phil, whom he'd only just met, to join them. 'I should have noticed.'

'Anyway.' Grace smiled. 'Never again. I won't let anyone treat me – or my friends – like that in the future. I don't think things are going to be easy, but I'm determined that they'll be better. I'm going to sort out Luke, for example. It's been difficult for him growing up in a house full of tension, but I've also poured all my love and expectation into him, and that's too much for one small boy to take. I've had to admit that he's turning into a miniature version of Richard under my eyes, and I'm going to try to do something about it. He needs boundaries and so do I.'

'I should get professional advice on that, if I were you,' suggested Lucy.

'I will. Anyway, what about you? Are things with Ned . . . ?'

But Lucy no longer trusted Grace enough to share details with her. She stuck to the safe topics. 'Ned's great. I'm excited by my new job – it'll be much tougher, because it's a real inner-city practice with AIDS, drugs, crime and just about every other problem you could think of, but now that I'm not dragged down by babies and toddlers, I think I'll enjoy the challenge. And Tom's going to a much more academic school, which he needs, to be honest. He's been coasting for most of his life, and I think he'll lose interest soon unless he gets his teeth into something.'

'So, all round, a brilliant future for the Dickinsons.'

Lucy had carefully not mentioned Nico.

Grace fiddled with her coffee mug. 'You see, I'm not looking for anything any more. If I find something, or someone, that'll be a bonus. I'm just going to get on with being me, and bringing up Luke as well as I can. I won't see Nico when you move and he goes to university . . .'

Lucy didn't want to think about whether they were going to see each other again in the weeks leading up to that time.

'And I'm moving back to London again, with Luke. So I'm going to learn to survive on my own. I'm going to work, more seriously. And I'm going to date – probably less seriously, if anyone will have me –'

'They will,' interjected Lucy.

'And make new friends.'

They looked at each other.

'But I'll never forget this year,' said Grace softly.

'No,' agreed Lucy. 'Neither will I.'

'Do you suppose we could have lunch together sometime, when we've both settled in our new lives?'

Lucy knew that if ever she did count Grace as a friend again, it would be a very different Grace. She believed her, about it all, but the friendship had been damaged. She didn't know whether it could be repaired. She would miss the old Grace, though, with her vulnerable laugh, her almost desperate warmth and her frivolity. She put an arm out to touch Grace's bony shoulders. 'It would be nice. Let's see.'

Grace got up to go. 'As a fellow mother, I know what that means.' As she reached the front door, she turned. 'I hope it goes well. Everything.'

Lucy nodded. 'And you.' On an impulse, she hugged her, feeling how soft and fragile and delicately scented she was after Ned's stocky masculinity. Grace clung to her for a moment, as if she didn't want to let go, and then stood back, brushing her eyes with a hand. 'Goodbye, then.'

'Goodbye.' Lucy watched Grace walk to the long, low black car and get in without looking back.

Acknowledgements

A big thank you to everyone at Penguin, especially Louise Moore and Harrie Evans, and also to Anthony Goff and the team at David Higham Associates.

Thank you too to: Claire Gerada, Graham Campbell, Jane Campbell, Rita Carter, Charlotte Churchill, Sonya Churchill, Gillian de Bono, Emma Duncan, Jacqui Eggar, Victoria Elliston, Amanda Fitzalan-Howard, Sebastian Faulks, Cassandra Jardine, Jackie Jones-Parry, Sarah Kilby, Petra Leseberg, Kate Mann, Clare Parkinson, Anita Robinson, Sarah Stacey, Corinne Sweet, Hilary Talbot, Jane Wroe-Wright and, of course, Rosalind and Freddie Iron and Margaret Campbell.